T0244533

THE STARS ARE DYING

CHLOE C. PEÑARANDA

BRAMBLE

TOR PUBLISHING GROUP

NEW YORK

This is a work of fiction. All of the characters, organizations, and events portrayed in this novel are either products of the author's imagination or are used fictitiously.

A Bramble Book
Published by Tom Doherty Associates / Tor Publishing Group
120 Broadway
New York, NY 10271

www.torpublishinggroup.com

Bramble™ is a trademark of Macmillan Publishing Group, LLC.

The Library of Congress Cataloging-in-Publication Data is available upon request.

ISBN 978-1-250-35566-9 (hardcover)
ISBN 978-1-250-35567-6 (ebook)

Our books may be purchased in bulk for promotional, educational, or business use. Please contact your local bookseller or the Macmillan Corporate and Premium Sales Department at 1-800-221-7945, extension 5442, or by email at MacmillanSpecialMarkets@macmillan.com.

First Bramble Hardcover Edition: 2024

Printed in China

0 9 8 7 6 5 4 3 2 1

Dedicated to you.

The smallest voice can make the biggest change.

You are the brightest star.

AUTHOR'S NOTE

Please read with care. While not core themes, this book touches on subject matter as follows: domestic violence situations, emotional manipulation, grief and loss, explicit sexual scenes, fantasy violence and gore, suicidal ideation, overcoming addiction.

THE REAL

ARANIA

FESARIS

MISTVEIL

LAKE OF
NEITH

VESTIL

PYXTIA

ALISUS

CONSTANTS   BA

VOLANTIS

PROLOGUE

He'd learned that dying, no matter how slow and painful the seconds before a final breath, was nothing compared to living infinite more days without the one he loved.

No—love was too mundane a word for the split in his soul she cleaved in her wake.

For two hundred years he'd watched the same constellation as though it were the only one in existence. Now it had begun to fade. A fraction every week that no other would notice. To him it became a countdown.

He faintly adjusted the magnification of the telescope so as not to miss a flicker, his sight mapping the twelve points. Always the same order. He didn't even know he'd adopted the pattern.

Even in the fading light she was magnificent.

Yet he didn't plan to be here when the earth quaked for her return. Years, perhaps decades, still from now. He didn't plan to remain the reason those cracks continued when she came back.

Knowing this was the last time, he lingered a little longer. Then he sighed, stored the final sight, and pulled away.

Sitting on the low ledge of the open archway window, he lifted the glass of liquor he held, clinking it against the metal telescope. "I tried to find a way. It's been as hopeless as it was back then," he said. Over the years he'd become so detached that no emotion plagued him now. "But I'm also glad you won't get to see all that I've become. Your disappointment might just be the thing to break me."

The alcohol burned down his throat as he tipped back the contents of the glass. His tight grip shattered it, but he didn't feel the slices through his palm. There was nothing that could hurt him anymore.

"I never got the chance to ask you what you saw." A fist tightened in his chest, but the agony was all he had to remember how real she was since time tried to blur the images. "How you saw past it all and for a fleeting moment made me believe there was something *good* in me. I'm sorry you were wrong."

Standing, he slung on his black cloak, steps crunching through glass shards as if they were all that was left of his old existence.

"At least I won't be able to hurt you anymore."

They all cowered at the hooded shadow that passed them. Shrinking back, bowing their heads, avoiding his stare as he swept through the castle halls.

The black glittering marble of the floors, broken only by white pillars and the occasional sculpture, appeared sinister with the figure who occupied the space now. Before, there was beauty in these halls. But what was once the darkness of dreams and a clear night sky was now a kind of death.

The people he swept by whispered a name—one that had attached itself to him not by choice, but by the sin he represented. The god he was all but a mortal form of.

In the throne room, the ruler had been expecting him.

He saw the leathery, taloned wings of the guard the king was in conversation with before he was dismissed. A nightcrawler. Perhaps the worst of the three vampire curses, nightcrawlers couldn't touch the daylight.

The hooded male spoke his intent. "We agreed one century. I have given two. Now I have come for what you owe me." His voice was as cold as ice and as dark as night.

The king wore a crown, but it was as good as a child's costume. An image with hollow authority. At least without *him*. But he'd given far more time in service than they'd bargained for.

"If what they prophesize is true, we must find her first. The celestials are already being sighted on this side of the veil, testing our defenses. Magick will weaken again, and we can stop the return of this war before it has a chance—"

"No," the hooded male growled. It rattled through him. Rage so sharp and lethal It shifted midnight to black and leaked cold shadows through the room.

The king observed them cautiously.

"If you want to keep that throne against them, and keep the vampires believing in your reign, you'll have to do it yourself."

He didn't enjoy the idea of leaving now. In fact, that was too light for the feeling that tore him to his very core at the image of her facing it all without him. Until he remembered he was the cause of everything that had shattered his world—*hers*—many centuries ago. To be without him was the only way she stood a chance.

The king spoke. "What will you do . . . if you manage to make it back at all? It is a world you do not know. One that may cast you out permanently before you can discover a thing."

He didn't care. None of that frightened him. He didn't care if instead he became trapped in a void of nothing. It was better than being the reason they would not win the war about to rise again.

"You have become legendary. You would give it all up?"

"Tell me where to go," he said through gritted teeth. His mind was made up. It had been two centuries ago. He would turn on the whole damn world before he gave another year.

Choking filled the room as he slipped into the minds of every guard, cutting off their ability to breathe.

"If you keep me here, I swear I will kill you. I never wanted that crown, but I will take it."

"Very well," the king said, eyes of disappointment and resentment locking with his.

He had long since hardened to the beads of rejection.

"If this is to be farewell, I would like to show you the way." The king turned, and the hooded male let go of the guards, who gasped for their stolen air. "Follow me."

1

I didn't think I'd be so reluctant to greet death as the man I watched die. From above, I was a mere spectator to his pleas for his children, his wife, and the job he wished to spend the rest of his years working for the one who stood to claim his life.

He didn't know I was there.

Every time I watched a man on his knees, I couldn't help my need to observe from the high rafters, wondering if I'd relate to his pleas if my own breaths were numbered. With my fragmented memories only spanning five years, I had little to attach my purpose to.

It was as if Hektor Goldfell heard no cries as he gave a nod to the brute of a man pinning the victim down with a single large hand on his shoulder. He wouldn't spill blood—not in this room. He wouldn't disturb the bustling nighttime entertainment in the main room of his establishment with this man's death.

I pinched my lips at the sickening twist of his neck, fortunately not hearing the crack over the chatter and low music before his body slumped. It churned my stomach all the same.

As though he'd exerted himself, Hektor slumped into the nearest booth, flicking his chin so the few locks of red hair weren't touching his eyes anymore. When two beautiful women slipped in either side of him, I averted my eyes, lying down on the wooden beam only a little wider than my spine. My glittering silver hair spilled over the sides, along with the sheer material of my skirt, which floated in the air. But I didn't fear anyone finding me here. They never looked up.

My fingers brushed the ornate black hilt of my dagger idly. I wasn't permitted to dance or entertain like the women below, but I still enjoyed the lightweight elegance of their movements.

Skillfully, I got back to my feet, perhaps childishly copying one of the ladies who was trying out the art of theft among the newest group of esteemed card players. Distraction came in her fluid movements. I crossed over the wooden rafters, light on my toes, twirling like she did, and studied her movements, pretending it was I who attracted the men's lusty eyes, their gazes preoccupied enough to miss her hand purposely placed on one's shoulder to divert his attention from her other hand dipping into his pocket.

I couldn't see what she stole, but her blue irises gleamed triumph.

She twisted and perched on the edge of the table, arching her back as she lay so as not to disturb their game. I reclined backward until my hands felt the wood, legs rotating in the air, and my next blink canceled out the dizzy sweep as I straightened again. Then I leaned back against the vertical support with a sigh, casting my gaze away from the busy candlelit room to the gloom of my vantage point. Cloaked in shadow, I felt no more than an insect caught in a spider's web. It was hard to believe we were in the same room.

Sometimes I wished the guests would see me just once, even if I disappeared in their next blink since I was a prize only to be known by one man.

My eyes found Hektor, who hadn't moved at all, though the women were now spilling themselves over him. His deep green irises were the one set I'd never want to be found by up here.

Within these grand walls he kept me safe from the horrors outside. The *vampires*. Different species of them who consumed blood or souls and kept the humans afraid.

But they, like us, were under the control of the king.

The main room was bustling with talk of the Libertatem, a centennial trial hosted by the wicked ruler in the Central Kingdom of Vesitire. Five humans, the Selected, from the surrounding kingdoms would be sent off in the coming days to compete for one hundred years of safety from vampire attacks. When our world upended into chaos three hundred years ago, following the king's conquest in the war he announced henceforth that the humans would fight for peace, and the vampires would be kept under control by his enforcement of the Libertatem trials. I suppose it gave the people something to look forward to. If their kingdom won, they'd have freedom to leave their homes without terror for themselves and their children for a generation. If they lost, at least it was a break of pageantry in their bleak lives.

I think everyone knew deep down but didn't want to acknowledge that their beacon of hope was a lie of oppression. I couldn't relate to the excitement that buzzed through people's talk of it, but I understood.

Spirits were fragile. Hope kept them from breaking.

As I remained confined within these four elaborate walls with rarely any opportunity to venture beyond them, I didn't know as much of the outside world as I yearned to. All I could do was pluck kernels of insight from my frequent eavesdropping during these envious nights of beauty, gambling, and seduction.

I spent hours here listening in to the discussions of guests more eagerly than usual but my interest rooted more personally.

Four more days until the Libertatem send-off.

A clock ticked each minute in my mind as if it was an opportunity slipping through my fingers like sand and a grip on my heart squeezed tight at the thought of my longest friend leaving as our Selected from the southernmost Kingdom of Alisus.

My memory went back far enough to remember Hektor's hold on me, but not what had chased me into his comparatively safe arms. He'd brought me here and told everyone the story of how I wouldn't be alive if it weren't for him. Now, five years later, from what I'd been told, I was around the age of twenty-three, and I knew he'd never let me forget that debt.

My hand hovered over the two long scars that ran from under my jaw to the hollow of my neck. Though I couldn't recall the face, nor the moment it had happened, phantom jolts of searing pain erupted whenever I thought of it. Like when I fixated too long on the raised skin in the mirror, trying to find the memory. Another mystery perhaps owed to what I'd fled from.

What remained a despair I could never voice was that I would never know who I was before Hektor.

"You're safe now, Astraea," he had said.

Those first words I would always remember. Hektor hadn't just found me, but also my name, which once heard I knew was mine.

In that respect, he possessed both my lives.

I didn't know why, of all the company surrounding him now, he took favor in me. I surely wasn't the only one to bring comfort to his nights. I'd watched women of all beauty give him their convincing affection. Those from fair skin to dark skin, of natural hair color or hair enhanced with Starlight Matter—magick that spoke to their wealth. Right now, a woman with glowing brown skin slipped a hand over his chest, in under the material he always wore with the first few buttons undone. Her long, dark hair appeared dipped in fluorescent rose paint. Another with a porcelain complexion and catlike yellow eyes hooked a slender leg over his lap.

I looked away. No matter how often I watched his nightly affairs, it never erased the question: Why did I choose to stay?

The answer came easily: I had nowhere else to go. And while he indulged himself in others, he came to me with an affection I consumed greedily and craved deeply.

Love was a drug laced with its own cure.

A new figure entered the room, wavy dark blond hair falling loose from his half-tie to frame his face. While he ordered a drink and leaned casually at the bar, he cast his sight up by habit. I didn't shrink away from being caught by Zathrian's ocean-blue eyes. I thought I'd face punishment from Hektor the first time Zath noticed me up here so long ago, but he'd never spoken of my frequent eavesdropping.

I matched his subtle smirk as he lifted a glass to his lips. Hektor rarely trusted anyone, but Zath had quickly climbed the ranks to become one of his closest men over the past year. I'd watched many come and go, mostly leaving his service by death, and Zath was the only one to have ever paid me notice. I considered him a friend.

Zathrian's head jerked, a subtle signal, as Hektor removed the woman's leg and shuffled out of the booth. My breath hitched, and just as he was intercepted by some men in fine wears, I began to make my way back to my rooms in case they became his destination.

The manor boasted far more of them than necessary. Hektor's establishment was a well-known venue for the elite. Men and women with enough coin to kill their problems rather than face them. He didn't host just one thing; Hektor Goldfell directed the most discreet but deadly network of spies and assassins in all of Alisus. Some of them I envied more than the dancers. Seeing their leather wears and glinting weapons never failed to intrigue me.

The dagger I owned, another secret, Hektor would never suspect I knew how to wield to some life-saving capacity. If he were to find out who I met with when he was not in town, I knew the consequence would come in the form of an ornate iron key sealing me inside tighter walls until our trust could be mended again.

The rough cadence of his voice caused the hairs on my nape to rise as I glided through the main halls like a ghost. *When did my room become so far away?* These winding halls were mocking me.

Swiping up a sheer blue face covering, I tied it over my mouth and nose. The ladies wore them sometimes, a beautiful accessory to add mystery and intrigue to their performances. The masks didn't conceal much, but it wasn't for Hektor I added the extra measure; I did so for the small chance my stealth might falter and I'd run into any of the guests.

His voice kept advancing, and he would know me from any angle should he turn the next corner. My pulse raced with my steps. I wouldn't make it to the end before then. I did something I'd never done before, but it would cause no harm.

The doors that lined each side of the halls were marked with a star. Purple for occupied, white for vacant. These rooms were for private entertainment, strictly for dancing, though for any further desires patrons could rent a different room to follow.

Spying the first white star, I had no other option. I slipped inside, swiftly closing the door and leaning my forehead against it. My chest rose and fell hard as I strained to listen for Hektor's voice to pass, but everything beyond the door was canceled out and all that filled my hearing was gentle notes. A soft song in the large, low-lit room. But I couldn't find the source when I turned.

My next breath caught, and I kept deathly still as though my presence could be denied.

I wasn't alone.

Yet I'd been certain of the white star that couldn't be mistaken while under enchantment.

I saw him then. Or at least part of him. A form near blended into the darkness he sat cloaked in. He didn't look at me, and I could hardly see a face from the shadow casting over his eyes. His cup of wine bore all his attention, lazy fingers swirling around the rim as if he'd yet to notice my intrusion at all.

Or had been expecting it.

No—not me. But *someone*.

I took careful steps into the space, and with one deep inhale I headed over to the side of the room, mind racing with what to do. Though I dare not glance his way, my skin ignited with scattered pinpricks of attention that made me believe he'd finally sought me out.

He had to be watching me.

My pulse beat hard in my chest as I felt a featherlight caress across my shoulders that drew forth a gasp. When I looked, no one was there. The man remained exactly where he was, and I was wrong to have thought he cared about my being here.

In my irritation I picked up the decanter. The slosh of water filling my cup was all that disturbed the music. Still, I couldn't find the players of the song that felt like an embrace, something about it familiar and soothing. Personal even.

I took a long drink, hoping the water would stay and not dry out my throat again as soon as I placed the cup back down.

Is he waiting for me to begin?

The steps I could take I played out subconsciously, tempting my body to enact them as I'd done to no audience but shadow. That was all this man was. I could pretend to be dancing along the precarious rafters as a silly imitation to those gifted in the skill. The worst to come of it would be no payment if I didn't meet his expectation. I didn't need that.

Nerves turned to thrill as a surge of electricity touched the tip of my spine when the song changed. As if it had been picked to ignite the pleasures of my body alone and guide a dance I would craft myself.

One night. How often had I dreamed of having one night to release that kind of expression?

I thought his eyes were upon me with the vibrating awareness. I wondered what color they were. It shouldn't have mattered, but I skipped through green, blue, brown . . . None felt right for the shallow fire that rippled over me.

The song became elevated, an acoustic rhythm running straight through me. The pitch changed direction as if I were standing in the middle of an orchestra with instruments taking their turn around me. My feet glided toward the center of the room, only responding as the music coaxed.

I had nothing to lose and a moment of carefree performance to gain. Not only for him, but myself.

So I danced.

My movements pushed and pulled, with gravity flowing the light materials of my skirts and what was draped around my shoulders, attached to my wrists. The air cooled my skin, wrapping around the few inches of bare midriff that heated when I stepped light and twirled slow. I felt myself dancing through the darkness between stars. Each time they touched me I erupted with exhilaration, not ever wanting to stop.

I looked up and found the starry sky blinking back at me through the glass roof. Something about the night always awakened me more than the daytime.

When my gaze fell back down, I remembered the stars weren't my only spectators.

His fingers stopped circling his wine, and though I still couldn't see his face, the music gave me a surge of confidence to edge closer to him. Until I forgot his presence once more.

My leg eased up sideways, my body curved, and my hand curled around my ankle, testing my flexibility, as the song grew to a climax. Then the notes flared, coming down like a flurry, and I let go, my leg hooking to spin my body in time.

I felt alive. Free. This kind of exhilaration topped my untold proclivity for fighting, though both gave similar thrills.

I didn't know when I'd come closer to the stranger, but in my high of adrenaline intrigue seized me, and before I knew it, I was right before him. But he didn't look up.

My hand reached for his chin . . .

So fast I couldn't make a sound, a grip lashed around my wrist, disorienting me for a second before I blinked back to clarity as I was spun around. The new impression against my back snapped my awareness to my newly compromised position.

His hold pinning my wrist to my shoulder loosened.

My heart thrummed wildly, unknowing of what to do. To my error I'd overstepped. I couldn't call out like any of the other women in danger—if Hektor were to find me here . . .

"You are not what I expected."

I took a moment to breathe against the silvery gravel of his voice. His fingers shot sparks across my skin as they trailed down the length of my arm, occasionally slowing as though he were taking in every one of my silver markings.

"Oh?" It was all I could muster as fear of an oddly spirited kind tightened my throat.

"You move as if you make the music that calls to you."

I wasn't sure if it was a compliment, nor why I hadn't expected the commentary on my performance, but it heated my cheeks. "I hope it was to your satisfaction."

My breath stuttered when his fingers combed through my hair, tipping the wavy silk tresses to expose my shoulder.

"Very much so," he said, and I shivered with the brush of his fingers that began on my scar. Like a phantom touch. "But more importantly, I hope it was to yours. It seems freedom becomes you when you dance, and I have to wonder what it is that makes you feel caged."

I couldn't understand his words though they stoked something within me. I stiffened at where his attention was fixed—on the long, unruly imperfection Hektor claimed ruined me. He said he loved me with it though most would not.

"Who did this to you?" His tone grated with bitter-cold notes.

I thought I saw tendrils of black smoke snaking around the edges of my vision, but I couldn't move, unsure of where the anger rippling through me had come from. "I don't know." My reply snapped me back to our situation. Sense had become blanketed by the enchantment of his skin on mine, but reservation prevailed. He had no right—should have no care—to know any of my history.

His other hand found the cut of my skirt, and while it tingled, his roaming faltered. By the time he found the small sheath empty I whirled.

He was too fast. Once again, my action was trapped by his quick intervention. He fixed his eyes on the lethal point he'd intercepted from being lodged through his ribs and then trailed down the wavy purple length, over the cross guard crafted into beautiful black wings.

Only when his eyes lifted to mine did my firm stance slacken. I stared into irises alive like molten ore, glittering a golden amber that reminded me new dawns were a beautiful thing. Everything I'd seen, from coin to jewels, was now an impersonation of what treasure should look like, and more importantly, the value it held.

"A stormstone dagger," he observed with approval.

My mouth turned paper-dry with my galloping heart, all too aware of our proximity and the way he towered over me. I tried to pull my arm, but he held me still. I locked those golden eyes with challenge, unsure of where my bravery had come from but seizing it nonetheless.

"Let me go, or I'll scream and flood the room with guards."

His mouth grew in a slow curl, dimpling one cheek. When his other hand reached up, I jerked again until my muscles locked still. The tie of the sheer material covering the lower half of my face came undone, drifting to the floor as one less barrier between us.

"I don't think you'll do that."

My lips parted, but no words came. How could he know? My gaze traveled along his defined cheekbones until . . .

I gasped, yanking away with enough of an electric shock that he released me, and I stumbled a few steps back. "You're . . ." I couldn't speak it, blinking again as though I would be wrong, but it didn't change.

The delicate points of his ears.

"Does that frighten you?"

The only beings I'd known to have such an attribute were the vampires. This manor had become my shield from the viciousness of *his kind*. Hektor didn't allow them within his establishment, and I had never known how he kept them out when they were creatures that took what they wanted without morals.

"Are you going to hurt me?"

"You think I want your soul or your blood. I'll admit, one is highly tempting to hold, the other to taste. But what if I told you I'm not what you think I am?"

"I would ask what it is about me that makes you take me for a fool."

"Your lack of perception."

"Excuse me?"

He stalked toward me, slipping one hand into his pocket and drawing my attention to his attire. He wore an impeccably tailored lapel jacket, all black with fine gold embroidery to complement his eyes. Pressed pants tucked into expensive boots. Everything about him was dipped in shadows, giving the illusion they moved for him. As I trailed my eyes back up, gold markings on his neck caught my attention through his open top, inspiring an urge to get closer and discover what it was.

I hadn't realized I'd been trying to keep some distance between us until I met a stone pillar.

"I can feel your soul. And I can show it to you if you'd like."

I didn't get the chance to respond as he reached for me. I gave a shallow cry when his palm pressed between my shoulder blades, drawing me tightly to him, but I was helpless to move when my back curved at the tug of something he pulled from my chest. The world became bright and wondrous as I stared into a pulsing sphere of silver and twinkling stars. It whispered, though not with words; it radiated with an inviting warmth my fingers reached for, a prickling starting in the tips to beat through every inch of me.

"Consuming it, that is not my existence."

As though his hand had surged into the depths of me, I gasped when that sphere of otherworldly energy pummeled back, winking out the hypnotic light. I took a second to blink, breathing hard until the lingering pressure reminded me he had yet to release me. I couldn't describe how those few seconds felt. What he'd done to me could have been a masterful trick of allurement, and I'd become ensnared by it.

"You just—" I could hardly breathe, hardly think.

His hand remained on my chest, lifting only to trace the points of my markings. I remained flush in his hold like prey finding twisted beauty in its capture. But I didn't feel the hard pressure of him as I expected.

"You didn't take any of it?" I dared to ask. I didn't feel any different. No— that was a lie, though the fluttering in my stomach and my racing pulse I considered preferable to having years of my life stolen.

"No."

"Did you want to?"

When those amber eyes flicked to me, they almost rivaled the rush of adrenaline from his trick. "I have no use for your soul outside your body, Starlight. A few fractions further and you would be dead, not knowing how to guard it."

I couldn't believe my own inquisition under the circumstances. "Humans can protect themselves?"

His palm slipped across my cheek, and instead of balking like I should, the tenderness made me weightless. His touch gave no warmth, but it was not cold either. "I said *you*."

This wasn't right. His closeness, the intensity with which he watched me, as though I would blink and see someone other than the monster I'd been told I should perceive him as.

"Should I be afraid?"

The moment his hands dropped from me I swallowed the protest, at mental war with myself for the naïve cloud that had overtaken my sense of self-preservation.

"No one can tell you how to feel. You observe, you draw on your knowledge, and you handle the responses your judgment makes."

I thought on his words. Maybe I even admired them, but I fell short in one aspect that didn't seem fair: knowledge.

"I know nothing about you."

"Then what does your instinct tell you?"

Impulsive things, I thought. Everything but what I knew to be logical: getting far away from him. Instead, I asked, "Will you tell me your name?"

His silence was an assessment of me. Eyes of gold flickering with stars.

"Nyte."

"That is not your name."

The curve of his mouth grew. "Why ask my name, only to deny my ownership of it?"

I could admit I found the name fitting, if hard to believe. Though I didn't have to, as my traitorous eyes took my argument and silenced it with wonder. His hair couldn't conform to simply being black; it was midnight, the kind of color that could shift tone from a depthless obsidian to strands of a deep navy in the light. The disheveled tresses falling over his dark brows were an entrancing contrast to the gold of his eyes. Sometimes I thought they changed—that they'd glow or dull or flicker. For my own sanity, I chose to believe it was nothing more than the influence of candlelight, even though I knew he hadn't moved and no wind had disturbed the flames.

Then there was his neck. The obscure tattoos there stole my attention. A constellation, perhaps. The rush of desire to pull back the material of his jacket doused me with incredulity. *What an inappropriate thought.*

He remained still, watching me with intrigue while I shamelessly assessed him.

I swallowed hard. "Nyte," I echoed, the word like a comet—fleeting, but a flare of dangerous brilliance wrapped in beauty. "Like what surrounds us right now."

As I said it, we both looked up. The domed roof encased us in our own globe of soothing darkness and constellations. It shimmered like peace, but I often wondered if it was simply my own confusion that thought the stars were dying, slowly stretching farther apart, and that turned my admiration to sadness.

"Exactly like that, Starlight."

Our eyes fell back down to meet.

"You have called me that twice now."

"And you have not corrected me, so what am I to do?"

My pulse surged up my throat with the step he took that left only a slither of space between our bodies. I breathed in light notes of mint and something woody.

"What am I to do with *you?*" The last word tapered off as a caress, traveling from his tongue to race down my spine.

Impulses roared to ignore reason and find out how his warmth would embrace me. How different he might feel compared to Hektor, who was always so cold even when lust should smother it.

His hand raised, and still I did not stop him. I was held by him. Not by any physical means; what pulsed between us drew forth a current of electricity I wanted to keep building. Grazing under my chin with his fingers, he tilted my head back. Those irises dazzled against the moonlight, flooding his features to highlight high cheekbones and the sharp angle of his jaw. His lips formed a perfect bow, and realizing where my attention had dropped lashed me back to reality so fast a gasp escaped me.

"Nothing," I offered. "I'm not of any interest to you."

A brief darkening of amber shivered over me.

"What would you know of my interests?"

"It's not hard to guess from where we are," I breathed, willing my throat to find full words, but it dried out and I licked my lips.

It was the wrong thing to do. His fiery gaze flashed to them with a flickering glow. I had never allowed another to get this close to me before. I had never *wanted* it out of all the handsome men I'd watched in Hektor's main room. Even now my mind battled with itself over why I stood rooted despite the rationality to gain distance. There was nothing good to be gained in those ethereal eyes, nothing more than a dangerous allurement, and I was allowing myself to become pitifully trapped like so many others who had come before me.

My body shook when his fingers combed through my hair. I watched him examine the tresses as they spilled over his palm. Curiosity danced across his features.

"Do you use an enchantment?"

Many had believed so before—that the strands of hair that shone iridescent were not of birth, but the result of something I'd consumed. My denial was often wasted breath. Only I knew it was humorous for one to believe I could afford the magick that could give the same result.

"No," I answered, not caring if he took it as the truth.

His gaze slipped back to me, twinkling with mischief. "Like Starlight."

My face fell at his poor attempt at flattery.

His mouth quirked. "And these?"

I sucked in a breath when his featherlight touch trailed over the curve of my shoulder, resisting the fluttering of my lids when tingles shot through me. I shook my head, remembering myself. "No," I whispered. "Are yours . . . an enchantment?" I tried not to look at the exposed skin of his chest, though locking his stare flushed me with far more heat.

"No."

That caught my intrigue. I wanted to know how, mystified I had this one thing in common with him. What were the odds that someone with such a similar attribute could have found me?

His proximity became too much. I feared the snare he could become. I dipped away from the marble pillar, my hair slipping like shimmering silver silk from his fingers, and stiffened against the embrace of the cold.

"Your dance," he said, his voice seductive but creeping like shadow. "It was most exquisite."

"And it is finished," I said, ignoring the inkling of disappointment that came with my dismissal.

I didn't know why he was here or how he'd infiltrated Hektor's defenses. I wasn't sure that knowledge would be safe. I needed to leave and forget the beautiful stranger. Though I knew the moment I did, I'd never see him again, and that fact stole my will to leave.

Maybe it was foolish to find desire in danger, but only when both were presented did I realize just how long I'd lived without touching either. Now both had come to form in front of me, they tempted me like the remedy to an ailment I never knew I had.

"Not for me," he said.

Those low, rumbling words were nearly lost when the door creaking open made me leap back in horror. Before I saw the intruder, something floated down in my vision—the blue face covering—and I snatched it, securing it clumsily as the man entered fully.

"My apologies, ma'am." He rushed out upon seeing me, averting his gaze as though I had been caught naked. "I was directed here. I'll have to speak to Hektor—"

"No," I called a little too quickly. "I was just leaving. Do not concern yourself with Hektor—I am on my way to him now. You will not be disturbed when your lady comes, I assure you."

The older man dipped his bearded chin respectfully.

Before I made my way to the door, I remembered my company. I scanned the room. Twice. My mind reeled when I found nothing, for the only exit required passing the gray-haired man still lingering by it.

Yet the only semblance of night was in the sky that watched over me as I cast one last look up and left.

2

I hadn't fully exhaled my breath of relief when I slipped into my rooms and froze still against the door. Hektor eased out from the darkness of the washroom.

"Darling," he said, the tone he used raising the hairs on my arms. "Where have you been?"

No answer would be justifiable when his rule was that I remain in these three interconnected rooms at night.

"The roof terrace," I answered—the one place out-of-bounds to his clients. "I needed a moment for air."

With his shoulder-length red hair tucked behind his ear, he approached with the green eyes of a predator debating whether to strike or give mercy. I noticed the glass of water he carried, and my body reacted with a flush of need at what it meant.

In front of me, his smooth hand reached for my jaw. I suppressed a flinch. When his hold came soft I relaxed, gazing at him with a submission I often despised. I'd done nothing wrong, only stolen a kernel of freedom within the walls of confinement.

"Open for me."

My lips parted, and his thumb pressed down before the capsule landed on my tongue. Then his mouth came down on mine—a single deep kiss that tasted of spice and alcohol. He pulled back, stroking his knuckles over my cheek while extending the water out to me.

I accepted it eagerly, my throat still dry from my encounter with the stranger just a moment ago. Hektor's touch, I couldn't help but let the thought pass, did not awaken anything in me, and I wondered if it was merely that I expected it, or that when he held me he showed his affection the way I'd seen him admire his prized collections.

The capsule eased down my throat like it did every week, though it wouldn't always stop me from falling ill. Hektor had sought many healers, spared no expense, but even magick wasn't enough to cure me. They deemed my blood unable to sustain me like it should, and that shortage left me weak often without the medication.

His hand snaked around my waist, drawing me tightly to him. Too tight, and I felt the warning. "Don't leave again without my knowledge, Astraea. We have talked about this."

I nodded, running my hands up his chest, and he eased off with my caress. "I'm sorry."

He kissed me again, and I tried to answer to it, but my lips were numb.

"Don't you have guests to attend to?" I said, pulling back.

The shake of his head sank my stomach. "I'm yours for the night." Taking my hand, he led me over to the bed. "I will be gone tomorrow, and I will miss you."

I knew this from the information I'd eavesdropped upon days ago, thrilled his departure would give me one last opportunity to see a friend before she left for the Central City as this year's Selected. There were very few people who knew of my existence thanks to Hektor's tight rules, but Cassia Vernhalla I liked to believe would still have been my closest friend even if that weren't true.

Hektor's fingers brushed the loose strands of my hair behind my ear as he pulled me down to straddle his lap. I had never questioned the effects of his touch until now. How I craved the humming vibrations of the stranger in place of the vacancy when Hektor's hand ran up my thigh. Before he could discover my dagger, I pushed his chest until he lay and undid the buttons of his jacket with a slow seduction. I knew he loved to watch my ice-blue eyes dedicated to him.

I'd managed to slip my dagger off and conceal it beneath the mattress by the time he positioned himself over me under the silk sheets, and then our skin moved against each other's. I wanted to feel something. I wanted the electricity I'd experienced with the stranger. Never before had I known what it was like to crave dancing in the rain until I was touched by a night storm. Hektor's breath blew into my hair as he thrust into me at a steady pace, but I couldn't stop my mind from drifting elsewhere.

My head turned, and the night watched me as it always did, but this time the thought sparked a new pleasure I couldn't feel with Hektor's efforts alone. The stars turned to eyes of glittering amber, and though I wanted to cast them away, all I embraced was how they made my slicked skin tingle with heat. I imagined how the tall, powerful form of something so wrong to desire as a vampire—if that was what the stranger was—might feel when waging war between the sheets. Before I knew what I was doing, my head tipped back, my eyes slipped closed, and I could think of nothing else but him.

Reaching down my body, I circled the sensitive bud between my legs, but it was *his* hand driving that pleasure, *his* body against mine, and I didn't care for the sinful conjuring of someone else inside me.

Hektor enjoyed my sounds, my movements that began to answer him, but it wasn't enough. His scent still clogged my senses while I longed for the coolness of mint and sandalwood. I didn't usually take control, but frustration drove my action, and I flipped us until my palms were braced on his chest to keep him down so I could breathe clearly, fantasize about what I wanted. And I came so close.

One last glance at the night beyond the tall glass balcony doors and I unraveled. Every piece of me was wrapped in floating bliss, every nerve trembling, and as my lids clamped shut there was only one face there—a face with golden eyes that gleamed and a mouth that gave a wicked smile at what I'd done.

Hektor followed my climax, but I couldn't look at him in my shame, slipping off to lie beside him while we both caught our breath.

"You are remarkable," he said, praising me. "It fills me with pride to know you'll miss me too, darling."

I wouldn't. I never did, and that always struck me with disappointment. He gave me everything, yet I couldn't give it back no matter how much I tried. When he was gone I could breathe lighter. I could move around the halls without glancing over my shoulder. And my most forbidden secret: I could slip away from this manor and see my one companion, whom he'd known nothing of in the entire four years.

I'd learned Hektor's protection came at the price of having to harbor so much from him. I didn't enjoy it, but I feared what would become of me if I succumbed to the suffocation of his rules. For so long I'd fooled myself into believing he meant well, that love could be cruel and twisted but he cared for me nonetheless. But sometimes I wished his love would bind my chest instead of my wrists.

"How long will you be gone?" I asked.

"A few days."

I should have known he wouldn't be exact. He wouldn't give me a time to be right back where he expected me, which meant cutting my leisure time short to be safe. I found humor in the concept of safety in my mind. Maybe there was something wrong with me for enjoying the taste of danger each time I snuck away from the measures Hektor put in place.

"Can I come with you?" I blurted. I didn't look at him when the sheets moved and his lips pressed to my shoulder.

"Not this time."

Not any time, I thought. When I asked, the answer always came the same. I rolled onto my side, tucking my hands under my cheek, and watched the twinkling of midnight until Hektor's breathing deepened behind me. Though my body felt lonely, I was glad he never held me.

I lay awake for some time, until the music from earlier played quietly in my mind and I slid my lids closed. What eventually pulled me into darkness was the low vibration of a silvery voice I didn't want to forget.

I drifted in and out of consciousness. A sharp pain in my arm jolted me awake, but my vision was blurred, and I moaned sleepily.

"Shh. Sleep, darling."

With the hand that smoothed my forehead, I couldn't fight the gentle caress luring me back to a depthless void.

3

Heaviness weighed on me when I awoke. My eyes stung against the bright light spilling into the room, triggering the throb of my head. I forced myself up on my hands, taking a few seconds against the dizziness that threatened to sink me back down.

Not today, I thought. *Please, not today.*

I groaned through a hoarse throat at the sickness that had crept over me during the night. I twisted to Hektor, but my body turned cold when I saw that his side was empty. I blinked, pulling back the sheets and swinging my legs out of bed, shivering violently when my bare feet pressed to the freezing marble floor. As I reached for a long cotton robe, I found out why the day shone so bright, as beyond the glass lay a blanket of sparkling white snow that stole my breath.

Despite my poor state I smiled. The snow was a beauty I looked forward to every year, and it never failed to spark the child in me.

The child I couldn't remember.

I scanned the ostentatious room, lingering on the nightstands, but there was no note. No indication of how long Hektor had been gone. I had to find out if I'd slept a whole day away as I'd done before in illness.

Dressing quickly, I opted for a thick blue gown and swung a navy cloak over my shoulders. High stockings for the cold and black boots for the snow. I checked the clock on the mantel that told me midday was approaching. Pushing aside the fog in my mind, I decided I could ask the kitchen staff how long Hektor had been gone.

I pulled on the door handle, my body stiffening when it didn't open. My heart rammed against my chest as I tried again and again and again, until tears filled my eyes and stung my nose. But I didn't stop rattling the door as if it would somehow unlock with the sheer will of my desperation.

"Milady?" The soft feminine voice that broke through my sobbing belonged to Sira, a woman who tended to me sometimes, but the handmaidens never stayed long in Hektor's employment. I rested my forehead on the wood.

"Please let me out."

"It's just a few days, Stray."

I whimpered at the other voice and the soft nickname he used. "Zath, please."

"I don't have a key, or you know I would."

My nails sank deep crescent moons into my palms. "How long has he been gone?" I tried.

His pause almost slammed my fist to the wood until Sira mumbled quietly, "Two days."

I cried harder but kept silent, biting my lip until I tasted blood. *Why?* I had done nothing but sneak out for a moment, and this punishment seemed unjust even for him.

Phantom hands began to crush my throat, and I gasped for breath, backing away from the solid wood and stumbling to the glass doors. I rattled the handles over and over, but they wouldn't budge, and I crumpled to the floor, dizzy with sickness and heartache and the shock of my solitary confinement.

I hated him. Though even that emotion brought pain when I didn't want to think that of him. I wanted out. *Needed* out.

Permanently.

The thought rushed to me with such clarity I stunned myself. Maybe because I knew the window of opportunity was crawling closer, and maybe because there had always been a part of me waiting for this push. Hektor wouldn't know he was the one to topple me over the edge when he'd been my only reason to stay. Not through any sadness to leave him, but the fear he'd chase me to the ends of the world before he'd let me go.

As the Selected of Alisus, Cassia would be leaving within the week. Once she did, that window of opportunity would slam shut then disappear. Not only would I have sealed my fate here, but I'd never see Cassia again.

My hands tightened in my braids with my turmoil. I tunneled away in the darkness behind closed lids. A bubble grew inside me so violently it nearly screamed free.

A *click* smothered the barrel of grief in my chest. I looked up, scared to test what I thought it was, but desperation got me clumsily to my feet. When the handle of the glass balcony door pushed all the way down and the frozen air hit my face, I released a noise of joy. I scanned inside and out, but no one was there. With my first step out onto the pure crystal snow I didn't care anymore.

"And how do you plan to get down?"

I gasped at the voice. A silvery echo that rang through my mind. I slipped as I twisted and whirled to find the form that never revealed itself. Breathing hard, I debated trying to answer back, but the absurdity of that sealed away my thoughts.

At the snow-covered stone railing, I peered out. The height would most certainly cause a bad injury, perhaps death. "I can climb," I said aloud, comforting myself at the thought of his voice being my own internal coaxing to get past this hurdle.

The snow added laughter to my reckless decision, but I had no other choice. It had been months—too many—since I'd had a chance to venture beyond the manor, and this was my last opportunity to see her.

"You should be inside, Starlight. You are not well."

I huffed, swiping a gloved hand over the edge to reveal the flat stone I'd hoisted myself onto. It wobbled immediately, but I didn't dare look down. "I won't get another chance."

In full health I wouldn't have doubted myself as much as I did now. I'd spent many years testing my balance and did not fear heights, but my weakness, paired with the weather I loved, had become my nemeses. I wasn't confident I could complete the journey down unharmed.

"There's a ledge covered in snow, but your grip will hold."

I saw it, listening to the guidance in my mind. My body turned taut. All that kept me from the fatal drop was my toes straining along a window ledge and my fingers curled painfully above me. I shuffled along without letting myself rethink this decision.

"Stop."

I did, awaiting his next instruction as I glanced down the wall.

"There are four sunken holes, very small, but you can do it."

The words of confidence didn't correlate with my body's response to lock tight. I took a deep breath and slipped one foot off then crouched, wedging it into the gap. My lack of flexibility added to my weak muscle made the lunge down painful. I didn't overthink until I was down another floor of the manor, my cheek near grazing the frosty stone wall I clung to awkwardly.

"Very good."

"I don't need your praise."

A low chuckle vibrated through me, so real I had to pause, if only to enjoy the last notes of it. I shook my head, looking around for my next move down since the jump was still too high.

My head pounded, and I thought if I tried to look for my next aid I'd lose my grip. I lunged down and shuffled across another window, praying no one would see me before I could clear it. Panting, I thought I was low enough to attempt a jump, but I couldn't check with the strain it took to hold my position. I began to succumb to panic.

"I can't do it," I breathed.

"You don't really have another choice."

I wanted to curse at that deep voice of faint amusement. Frustration pricked my eyes as I thought of Hektor and how desperate he'd made me to resort to this.

"Along to your right there's another ledge. It's wider."

That direction came with a calming caress on my senses I absorbed gratefully, finally finding the will to focus and eyeing the next point. I yanked my foot out of the hole, reaching over . . .

I didn't know what slipped first, only that my hold to the wall gave completely, and I was falling too fast to do anything but brace and hope the snow had gathered thickly enough to ease the impact. My eyes squeezed shut.

My fall was broken faster than I anticipated. Not by the cold embrace of snow, but something that infused the air with notes of mint. Arms that held tight, and I wanted to keep floating in them.

The ground firmed under my feet as my eyes snapped open. A gust of wind blew loose strands of silver hair across my vision. Dizziness swept in, and my hand reached out to the wall while my head whirled around.

I was alone.

"Where are you?" I dared to ask, feeling silly when silence answered. I couldn't be certain the haze of my sickness wasn't conjuring it all. I huffed a laugh in remembrance. "It's daytime. I suppose you belong to the night."

"I never would have told you my name if you were going to get witty with it."

"It's not your real name," I accused. "But I like it." Too much. Which only added to my growing wonder if he'd been my own delirium all along. Even last night, when all I'd wanted was for someone to *see* me. Had I really become so pitiful in my loneliness?

My chest contracted with the minor exertion of getting down. The voice was right: I should be inside and was in no state to endure the day. I didn't care. Shaking off the ripples of company that didn't exist, I lifted my skirts to begin the trudge through inches of snow.

I smiled. I grinned. And though my body ached and protested, I skipped into the woodland with my eyes watery from the cold or my thrill at running free.

Leaning against a tree, I paused to gather breath. I hated these woods for the eerie darkness that was cast over them even in the brightest of summers. They felt like another realm where nothing cheerful lived and creatures of sin could thrive.

Being surrounded by clusters of thick timber bodies flashed horrors as far back as my living memory went. Had I been running from the soulless, the shadowless, or some other dark creature? Fear creeped over me that one could emerge at any moment. Until Nyte's voice reminded me of the fool I was. Already caught in the sights of one—*him*—I chose to be content.

"You have to keep moving."

I knew this, yet my lungs protested.

A cracked branch under my boot triggered a burst of wings, followed by an awful caw from a bird. My muscles went taut, but I began to stumble toward the town.

"Keep silent."

My dry lips parted to ask why, but I thought better of it. I couldn't stop surveying my surroundings, my skin crawling with a sense of foreboding that made every instinct inside of me scream at me to go back.

I relaxed a fraction when I spied a couple. The man held the woman tightly while she arched into him, and I nearly looked away from their intimate kiss until I saw the first thing to turn my body ice-cold.

His pointed ears.

There were three types of vampires I knew to exist. Those who fed on souls: the soulless, who could be identified when their form cast no reflection. Those who fed on blood: the shadowless, told apart as their form cast no shadow. And creatures that were the reason people kept doors and windows locked tight after nightfall: the nightcrawlers, winged vampires who could not walk during the daytime.

The first rule of survival was to never give a soul vampire your true name. It was how they drained the soul attached to it. Days, months, or years of a human's life.

The second rule was to never willingly give a nightcrawler a taste, for once you did, you became their obsession, sometimes a lifelong toy whom they would visit after dark—and perhaps it was consensual, but if not, you couldn't escape their infatuation unless you killed them. Or more likely, they killed you.

I watched the scene before me with horror, trying to back away soundlessly as the vampire detached himself from the woman. I couldn't bite back my shuddering breath of terror at seeing her body dangling limp in his arms.

He'd taken it all . . . every decade, year, hour, *minute,* of that woman's life.

The soulless locked eyes with me instantly. His skin was partially gray over his neck and along half his face, with eyes of obsidian that could consume the sun. He seemed to be indulging on the life-form he took, breathing as if the air were a drug he couldn't get enough of, and I watched in both twisted fascination and complete stilling fright as the grayness of his skin faded to match the pale complexion of the rest of him.

I tripped back as he let the woman's body go without care, and my hand lashed over my mouth too late. He took his first step toward me as my ankle caught on something and dread tensed my fall. In my haste, my palm cut on a branch, but before my cry could escape at the sting, a form crouching over me turned it into a gasp.

His eyes weren't black anymore. A mossy green hue began to flood his irises. Locking onto them stole my fight, and instead I felt the whisperings of my desire to stay conflicting with the repeating nudge to run. He was beautiful. The kind that shouldn't be natural, further cracking the illusion I was being sucked into.

"Oh, little lamb," he cooed, and even his voice pulled me into a trance. "Didn't anyone teach you not to go wandering alone?"

I remained still as his attention fell to my bleeding palm, and he grabbed it. My vocals were silenced in sheer terror, and I watched as he pulled it closer to his face and took a deep, savoring inhale. The air breezed across the wet blood there, and to my complete shock, his tongue lapped over it with slow delight. My stomach heaved and I tried to yank my arm free, but he had an iron grip.

Those ethereal green eyes pinned me, wildly captivated. "I've not come across the likes of you in a very long time."

I tried to reach for my dagger at my thigh, but my layers of clothing made it too difficult. The soulless fixed his hungry gaze on my neck. Was it possible for one vampire to crave both blood and souls? I didn't think it was beyond reason, but certainly a new horror to discover at the wrong time.

"I was going to entice a name out of you, but you are made of something far more delectable than a soul. It looks like someone has tasted you before," he said, leaning in closer, and my adrenaline raged fast and hot. "I wonder how they had the restraint to let you live."

He became transfixed, letting go of my wrist to cup his hand to my neck. His vile body pressed into me harder against the damp ground, and his breath blew hot across my chilled ear.

"Don't—" I whimpered.

It was hopeless to plead with a merciless creature. All I could do was slip my eyes closed and brace for the pain.

It never came.

Before his teeth could puncture my flesh, he let out a shrill cry that sent a sharp wince through me. Then he was pulled away, and I scrambled to push myself up. Propping myself up on my hands, I faltered at the sight of the soulless on his knees and the sword protruding from his chest.

My sight trailed up to my savior, and the light splitting through the heavy canopy made him appear ethereal. Lengths of dark hair were braided tightly and held back from his face. Though he fixed a lethal look on the vampire, his features were beautifully soft against dark skin.

"Get up," he barked.

That shook some sense into me. Covered in leaves, and with twigs catching on my clothing, I tried to brush myself off as he removed his blade. The soulless fell limp to the ground. My heart was a wild creature threatening to break its cage.

"Thank you," I said breathily, trying to subdue the nausea rolling through my stomach.

The vampire's blood added a sheen to the dirt and wilted the winter leaves, so stark I thought it to be black. I watched the man who'd saved me lean down and clean his blade. Only then did my breath catch at the familiarity. The deep purple steel I had only seen the like of once before. My hand subconsciously skimmed my thigh, feeling the bulk under my clothing that confirmed my stormstone dagger was still there.

"You mortals run around as if death is a fable," he grumbled, sheathing his blade and finally straightening to land his full attention on me. When it did, something changed in his expression. It relaxed, turning to an assessment as he trailed deep brown eyes over every inch of my face, and I shifted under his keen interest. "What is your name?" he asked carefully, as if there was one he hoped—or expected—to hear.

I shook my head, mouth floundering, because I didn't feel comfortable offering that piece of myself so readily to a stranger, soulless or not. His attire consisted of leather wears beneath a deep purple cloak that was clasped at one shoulder. It was somewhat different to what I'd seen around Alisus on my short ventures, with its scaly black texture and the craft of the materials.

"Thank you for saving me," I said quickly, trying to backstep a few paces when he advanced slowly. "I-I have somewhere to be."

"I asked you a question."

The warning in his tone rang through me. I thought to take off running, but within me cried the hopelessness of that decision as I was sure to be caught.

"Please . . . I just need to get to the town."

He lunged for me when he was close enough, and all I could do was stand fast as feeble prey in his grip. The man searched my eyes wildly, as though his answer were written all over me, and the harsh lines of his face smoothed out. Then his eyes widened, stunned. I tried to struggle when he slipped a hand into my cloak to take my wrist. Tears gathered in my eyes as he pushed up my sleeve.

His hold slackened when he observed the markings there. I took the opportunity to yank my hand free, bracing to fight him off, but he didn't reach for me again.

"Forgive me," he said. His unnerving stare made me feel like a ghost he'd stumbled upon. Then he *bowed* his head.

I didn't know how to react to his quick switch of emotion.

"By the stars, Auster will be disappointed he didn't come with us this time."

It all made sense then, and I almost relaxed. This man believed I was someone else.

"You're mistaken. I'm not who you think I am."

The man looked me over from head to toe. Then he smiled. Warm, and like he'd found some long-lost treasure. I couldn't reciprocate.

"You have to come with me," he said, reaching for my arm, but I jerked away. His frown turned to confusion. "You're not safe out here. Come."

As he reached for me again, a low voice eased out like the calling of death.

"I don't think she wants to go with you."

We both turned, and the man swore, retrieving his stormstone sword. He angled it toward the two soulless who stalked over to us. I couldn't believe more of them had found us so soon when I'd passed through these woods so many times without seeing a single one.

"You need to run," the man said under his breath. "I'll hold them back. Don't falter no matter what you hear."

I'd wanted to get away from him, but now the thought of leaving him wreaked havoc within me. I didn't think I'd be of much use, but I retrieved my dagger, prepared to stay with him. Regardless of his motives with me, he didn't deserve to die like this.

"Listen to him."

I shook my head at Nyte's voice interfering in my mind, sparing a quick look around, but he was nowhere to be seen.

The man's gaze skimmed the weapon I held, then he hooked a brow as if it added further merit to his observations. I couldn't focus on that when the cruel smile of the first soulless edged closer.

"I can handle this. You must get to safety. We will find you again," the man said.

I didn't want to be found by a stranger again, one who'd decided to stake a claim on me, and my arm faltered holding my dagger. My mind rushed through the many heinous reasons he could want me, making running seem like the best option.

"Bold of you to venture on this side," the soulless drawled. "You could advance many in our army. Both of you."

"Run—now!"

I didn't contemplate this time. As the man lunged toward the vampires with impossible speed, I ran. My feet stumbled, and I cursed desperately when the snow slipped my footing, branches catching on my ankles and clothing. Every step felt too slow, but I didn't stop.

A loud cry I recognized as my savior's rang in the distance, and I whimpered. Guilt swam in my stomach, exertion torched my chest, and I thought they would catch me at any second to kill me the next. I hadn't even learned his name, and if he'd given his life for me, I would forever be plagued by this cowardly retreat.

"You're almost there. Keep going."

Nyte's voice came soft this time, a gentle comfort. Tears streamed over my cheeks, and then I wanted that man to find me as he'd promised, if only to confirm he'd triumphed against the soulless. But it was two against one, and my mind replayed that final cry as his downfall.

I broke through the tree line, immediately doubling over on my knees. I heaved and spluttered, but there was nothing to bring up, and it only stabbed through me.

"You must keep moving. Where are you going?"

Nyte's question gave me some ground to stand on. I couldn't waste the precious time I had and risk the soulless catching up to me.

"The Keep," I answered, glancing skyward to estimate the time as I'd been taught by my friend. But time was becoming a mystery of its own with the nights growing longer each year.

I pulled up my hood as I edged toward the town. The clamor always jostled me, and I stilled. Sounds like wheels and hooves clamoring over stone, the bustling traffic of bodies I could wedge myself between. Every time I came here, months apart, I remembered all over again another reason I resented Hektor's tight leash and why I'd always asked to accompany him on his trips away. I didn't want my heart to race at the mere thought of being here. I hated the cowardice that rose in me, overwhelmed by the confrontation of civilization. Crowds I feared being trampled by, getting lost in, or which would prevent me from breathing.

I almost eased back a step until I gasped at the force that formed to stop me. "You're not real," I muttered.

I didn't turn around. I didn't want to be right.

Hands trailed up my arms over my cloak, fingers squeezed lightly, and I wanted to melt in the assurance no matter who it came from.

"I am whatever you want me to be." Nyte spoke aloud, his gravelly tone racing over my skin. "And right now, you do not want to turn back."

I nodded. More than anything I wanted to push *forward*. His cloak of safety allowed a surge of defiance to break over me. The darkness, the night. It followed me even now, and I grasped confidence from the stars.

Sheathing my blade back at my thigh, I forced myself onto the streets that had become a dangerous mix of slush and ice with the footfall. I trod carefully, but I didn't anticipate how busy the town would be at this hour. Blurs of color, flashes of fabric and coin and faces, made my head spin. I bumped into people twice my height then half of it, apologizing but receiving nothing except disgruntled looks in return. I breathed through the growing hysteria of being smothered by bodies, touched by strangers.

"Take the next left."

I curved into the quieter alley, not slowing, but breathing greedily the air no longer tainted with odor and heat. At the end of the alley, I could see the large building crafted of the most pristine white stone and glass.

Alisus Keep.

This was where the reigning lord lived with his wife, five children, and many noble houses of the kingdom. The eldest of the ruler's daughters, like me, harbored a soul for wandering. Sometime four years ago began the warm notion we were bonded somehow. How else would we have crossed unlikely paths the first time curiosity made me leave the manor?

I tentatively stepped back onto the open streets, glad I was out of the bustling chaos of the trading port. My skin was slick though I shivered with the cold. The contrasting temperatures advanced my exhaustion. Each step added a new phantom pebble to the weight in my boots, and I didn't know if I would make it.

When I saw the large black iron gates, I stopped in an underpass to plan, pressing my back to the stone and slipping my eyes shut in an attempt to subdue the fainting spell that peppered my vision. Not here. Not where I was completely vulnerable and alone.

"What is your plan now?"

I couldn't open my eyes to see if Nyte would be there in real form. Instead those piercing golden irises found me in the confines of my mind.

"I could think if you would leave," I muttered breathily.

"You can hardly stand."

My body turned rigid with alarm, lids snapping open, when his voice echoed down the tunnel rather than in my thoughts. I couldn't see him—not fully. He kept to a shadowy dip and blended in seamlessly as if he hadn't spoken.

"Is any of this real?" I asked, though I became afraid of the answer.

"What would make this real? A sound?" He spoke so slowly, smooth like icy smoke. "A touch?" Then a lick of wind blew behind my ear and down my spine, its caress heading in a deliberate direction. "A scent?" Notes of mint filled my nostrils in my next deep breath. "A taste?" I thought I felt a tingling pressure on my lips, and I gasped.

I stepped away with the flush of my body.

"You made your point," I said, breathless as I didn't truly believe it, but I needed a distraction from him. "I'm going to ask to see the reigning lord."

"I'm sure they'll send out a carriage for you to save the long walk on foot."

"If you're not going to be helpful, you can damn well leave me alone."

"I can't," he answered with a soft gravel. His deep inhale devoured my scent, his mouth so close to my ear I should have been fearful. Logic screamed I shouldn't be this comfortable with his closeness, but I was so confused and caved to being a lamb in the clutches of a predator if that was what this was. Something about him was addictive, though not in the way of the soulless who'd tried to trap me as his willing victim. I couldn't explain the difference. I only knew my will right now remained mine, and falling for Nyte's allurement was entirely my own cloud of foolishness.

My breath whooshed from me when, contrary to his words, his faint impression disappeared completely on the next gust of winter wind. I turned and my chest rattled when a man and woman with linked arms stepped into the underpass. I blinked my surprise away to study the people's wears. Fine furs and impeccably groomed hair on both heads. Paired with their poise, I concluded our destinations to be the same.

"Are you heading into the Keep?" I blurted before they stepped into the daylight.

They startled, eyes roaming over me as though trying to determine if I was worth a response at all. Their scrutiny made me shift my weight, and I refrained from examining myself through their eyes. Hektor had a taste for the finest things; I had nothing to be concerned about there.

"Indeed, we are," the man said at last.

"Might I join you?"

The woman's eyes narrowed a fraction. My shoulders didn't relax until she eased a small smile.

"Has your escort abandoned you, dear?"

I didn't get to answer before her hand stretched out, releasing her partner to link arms with me.

"I understand you must feel embarrassed to be seen walking in alone."

That was *not* my concern. Though it seemed good enough for her, so I nodded, plastering on a sad smile. Unexpectedly, her palm touched my cheek, and I flinched. Her arm retracted as if my reaction had frightened her.

We stared at each other, and I couldn't fully decipher what crinkled her brow and had her scanning my face then my body again, but my stomach churned, and suddenly I wanted to abandon this plan. Her mournful expression stirred within me a desire to protest and deny whatever it was that looked like pity in her eyes.

"Come, dear," she said softly.

When our steps moved, I remembered to stay focused. This woman meant nothing to me, and I would never see her again once I made it inside with an excuse to part.

The guards outside the Keep didn't question them after inspecting the man. I didn't know who I'd linked arms with, but they had to be of a high family name to be granted such unfaltering acceptance. I'd always had to be in Cassia's company to make it this far. The eldest daughter of the reigning lord, she despised these surroundings as much as I did mine, and the familiar jittering nerves of confinement threatened to surface. It was why we preferred to spend time away from both, high up on the hills overlooking the main city.

"Halt."

I froze and the woman guiding me jumped with fright when a strong voice intercepted us halfway down the entrance hall.

"What can I do for you, guard?" The man stepped forward, defensive.

My eyes landed on the guard, my blood racing at his tall form and hard expression around pine-green eyes. They studied me, calculating. He was very handsome with his brown locks combed back neatly, though a thick strand rebelled to curve over one temple.

"Name?" he asked me directly.

I swallowed hard. "Dallia Omarté."

His chin lifted faintly in approval. "You are far from your quarters of the Keep. Might I escort you there?"

I relaxed, giving the woman who'd helped me past the gates an assuring squeeze to let me go. "Thank you," I whispered to her.

She gave a smile, though I could see the confusion on her face, and sweat began to form under my layers. I looked to the guard, giving a nod for us to leave before the echo at my back raised the hairs on my nape.

"I thought their daughter had left for Helvisar in the fall . . ."

The hand on my back jolted me to keep pressing forward despite my nerves.

"She did," the guard muttered, leaning close to my ear. "And you're lucky no one is going to listen to her rambles, Astraea."

4

Down an open stone hall lined with archways that led out onto a small courtyard, a hook on my arm pulled me from my wonder and awe at the Keep.

"What are you doing here?"

I snapped my attention to Calix. "I had to see her. It might be my last chance." My nerves spiked. That wasn't my only reason. Not anymore.

"Shit, Astraea, you look like hell. You shouldn't be wandering around in this weather."

"Thanks for your concern, but I'm here now. Can you take me to Cassia?"

Calix surveyed the quiet area. A few humans walked along the opposite path. The Keep was far more tranquil than I thought I'd find it at this hour.

"What if you were found?"

"I was." I tried a smile, which earned a scowl from him. "By you."

Calix grumbled as he steered me to continue walking. "I would not have been able to get you out of detainment had someone else discovered your brazen infiltration."

"Reihan would have come."

"You can't refer to the reigning lord without title around here," he scolded. "Cassia's the most important person in the kingdom right now. You'd do best to remember that."

I winced at that. As Cassia's personal guard, Calix was highly protective of her. He tolerated me for her sake, helping her sneak out to meet me, which she was only permitted to do once a month or less given how scarcely Hektor left his manor. While Calix's presence wasn't nearly as bright and yearned-for as the reigning lord's daughter's, I considered him a reluctant friend.

"You really know how to bring down the mood—" My steps stumbled at the squeal from across the new open courtyard. I knew that voice in any pitch, any tone.

Every negative aura dissipated when I saw Cassia. Her black hair was tied in a braid, the loose strands around her face indicating she'd been training with the bow she held for some time.

I tried to advance, but Calix's arm extended in front of me. Cassia gave a quick scan around to the person I assumed was her swordplay mentor, then to their surroundings, before deeming it safe to come over. I relaxed my scowl at her guard.

"I wasn't expecting you," she said, throwing her arms around my neck. "Stars, I worried you wouldn't visit before I left."

My arms tightened. "I would never have let you go without a last good-bye," I said.

When we pulled apart, the words I wanted to blurt became lodged in my throat. My mouth floundered, and Cassia seemed to notice, maybe even reading what I wanted to say by the hopeful widening of her eyes. She waited patiently, but I couldn't speak with the lingering presence around us. There would be no taking it back, and I knew once I'd planted the notion in Cassia's mind she would do everything she could to seal it as she had tried to over so many months.

"We need another bow," Cassia said to Calix behind me.

"I'll get Fenson to retrieve—"

"You'll be far faster. And a quiver of new arrows, please."

I couldn't see them, but I imagined the soft plea she used was accompanied by the widening of her blue doe eyes. Unlike the silver-blue of mine, Cassia's were a deep sapphire shade that could entrance a person.

The soft crunching of grass signaled he'd obliged.

"I'll continue on my own," she said to her mentor, Fenson.

"Your father insisted—"

"One more hour isn't going to change me now," she interjected.

After the reluctant dismissal, Fenson left too. Cassia took my arm, leading me into the center of the small courtyard. I gleaned the five targets that had been set out over the far side. Some hung over the stone arches, others were propped on the ground, and people could pass under the walkway behind them, but it remained deserted.

"Did something happen?" Cassia asked as we sat on a bench. Her gloved hands took mine, hope and attentiveness clear in her shining irises.

Five years ago, before we met, Cassia had won the kingdom trials that decided the best candidate to be put forth for the Libertatem. For the prize of immortality and the honor of bestowing safety from the vampires upon the kingdom.

"I—" Once again my words were choked as if my mind were taunting me that this course of action was ludicrous to take. The world had always called to be ventured, and I remained too afraid to answer it. With a squeeze of assurance from Cassia's hands, I said quietly, "I don't want this to be the last goodbye."

Cassia's smile stretched wide as if she'd been waiting so long for me to come to this decision and had lost all hope that I would. "You want to come with me?" she clarified.

I nodded, and she gave an excitable squeal.

"Oh, Astraea, I'm so relieved! I knew you would come to your senses. This is an opportunity of a lifetime!"

My smile faltered. I was unable to match her thrill since the reality wasn't an adventure between two friends getting to leave their humble kingdom, the one chance in a hundred years. Cassia would be competing in a set of trials for which there would be only one victor.

"This year will be different." Cassia spoke to my turmoil. "I can feel it. The vampire attacks have been growing more than ever. Something's not right. I think he's slipping."

"The king?"

Cassia nodded. "The great King of the Gods isn't so powerful anymore," she drawled with brazen mockery.

I glanced around, a dark stroke of foreboding coiling my spine as if I would find him watching. "How does he gain such a name?"

"For his victory in the Faelestial War. They say he united the fae and vampires to fight the unfair hierarchy and dominance of the celestials. Haven't you heard this before?"

I hadn't, and until Cassia's fate had become tied to the Central Kingdom, my sheltered existence in the manor had left me clueless and naïve.

"Do you want to know what I think could beat the King of the Gods?" Her deep blue eyes sparkled.

My brow curved in question.

"The Queen of the Kings."

I smiled at her childish enthusiasm as if it were a fairy tale, but our world was far from that. "Whatever book you've been reading, I want to borrow it."

"I came up with that on my own! Maybe I should write one." She nudged my side as she stood, retrieving her bow and extending it to me. "It came to me in a dream, actually."

"After a night of drinking?"

Her mouth curved a wicked grin. "Maybe. Since I'm about to leave this place, I had to give my father a few lasting antics to remember me by."

She sang the words as though her life that was about to change didn't hurt her, but I saw the truth. The faint wince around her eyes, and how her brow would lift for just a second to prevent the threatening fall of sorrow.

"What if he makes you one of them—a nightcrawler?" I said, suddenly overcome with the dread that had trickled through me when I'd first heard of the victor's personal prize alongside the safety that would be granted to their kingdom. "The immortality—"

Cassia shook her head. "His four Golden Guards have been seen plenty in daylight."

"Four?"

"Three Libertatem winners, and I suppose the first was a test."

"That's not reassuring."

"It's the only chance I have."

My mouth opened to speak to her nerves, but she studied me from head to toe with new assessment.

"You look unwell."

"Not enough to stop me from coming. I'm fine," I insisted, reaching for an arrow before she could fuss.

I preferred to throw small daggers, but archery was a close second pastime of mine thanks to Cassia. She was masterful with the weapon. She accepted a new bow from Calix when he returned, and I fixed an arrow in place while she leaned in close to ask him for something else.

"We'll be leaving in three days," Cassia chirped, coming up beside me and raising her aim. I admired her perfect form and laser focus before she let her shot fly with the release of a breath. It hit dead center of the farthest target. "I thought your overprotective husband was against it."

I shot her a dead look before letting my own arrow soar. While not as perfect as Cassia's aim, it hit close to hers. "Hektor is *not* my husband."

"Does he know that?"

I rolled my eyes, swiping another arrow. "I'll deal with him."

Evading Hektor wasn't something I'd factored into my reckless decision to leave with Cassia for the Central. I'd thought of it many times, and most plans I'd calculated required the stars to align and grant me the timing to slip out for long enough that I'd be too far along the road for him to track us by the time he realized.

My doubt surfaced all at once. The danger I'd be placing Cassia in inspired more fear than anything that could come for me. If Hektor found me before we reached the Central . . .

"What do you need?" Cassia's gloved hand went over mine.

Pulling my gaze up from the arrow, I pointed to the icy grass, lost in thought. I took a deep breath. I couldn't lose my nerve now. "The exact timing that you'll be past the city gates. I'll have to meet you out there."

"Done. Don't bring anything that might slow you down. I'll take care of it."

I couldn't believe that in just a few days I could be venturing free, bursting from the cage I'd known, and I was exhilarated above my fear to discover what lay beyond.

"We're really doing this," I said.

Cassia beamed brightly. "Yes, you are."

I'd never spoken much about Hektor, but somehow I didn't need to. What I treasured about Cassia was her ability to know what a person needed without prying. She was fierce and brave, and I envied her for it often.

"Your mother would be so proud," I said quietly, unable to stop the slipped thought.

Cassia smiled, sad but grateful. "She should still be alive. Yet that soul-sucking vampire tested the one law of protection we have. She died aged only thirty-one, before I could even walk. I don't want to have children if that's the life they could face, losing a mother far too soon—or worse, losing their own years."

I nodded in understanding, but as always, Cassia seemed to read my expression before I could change the topic.

"You'll find out where you came from," she said softly.

It was something I had no leads on, but Cassia had always been hopeful in sparking fresh ideas for where to start looking for my parents—if they were even still alive.

"Perhaps we'll have more luck in the Central."

"Or it could take me further from the answer," I muttered, kicking at the grass.

I didn't hold much hope that anything could be found in the Central. With all borders locked, I had to have come from Alisus. The price of leaving with Cassia might be to accept that my past would be forever lost. As I thought about it in that moment, I knew my choice wouldn't change.

Maybe it was time for me to stop hunting for the past, or I would never be prepared for a hopeful future.

"Don't be so negative. Regardless, I'm so glad you changed your mind to come."

I smiled, still wary, knowing the chains that held me to Hektor's manor could be shortened with my attempt to flee. "What will Calix say?"

Cassia waved her hand. "Let me worry about him."

I simply watched in admiration as she continued to fire arrows with such precision and focus as if she were one with the weapon.

"Do they tell you anything about the Libertatem—what you could face?" I asked to fill the silence.

Cassia blew frosted breaths in her exertion. "Not really. We face the king's trials but there's little knowledge on what they'll entail. One Selected is victorious and will live the honor of serving him."

I couldn't agree with her term: *honor.*

"The other Selected . . . do they get to go home?"

Cassia's grim look dropped the silent answer I anticipated, but it filled me with terror for my friend regardless.

I asked instead, "You're not afraid?"

She smiled sadly. "I've known my fate for many years."

It was like she'd already anticipated her downfall in the Libertatem, but I could never accept that. Cassia *had* to win.

The Selected who won their games over the last three centuries had been sworn in as the king's Golden Guard. Not only had they won a century of safety for their kingdom, banishing any vampire from the land, but the human victors had been gifted immortality.

While I shuddered at the thought of the sacrifice for such a prize, I couldn't deny Cassia would dominate with a position in the guard. And she wanted it more than anything.

"When you live forever, don't forget about me," I mused. It was intended to be a lighthearted comment, but it weighed the air heavy.

"Maybe I can pledge for both of us." She nudged me as she passed.

I thought of having years beyond my mortality. Who I was now wouldn't wish for that. No bird in a cage would want to live that way forever. But as I pictured the possibility of a door through which to fly free, suddenly the world felt too vast to be seen only in human years. Only then might I envy those who had centuries of youth to explore.

Calix returned, along with a servant girl who beamed brightly at Cassia. I accepted a steaming cup of tea, biting back my moan when I removed my gloves to feel the warmth shooting up my arms from my palms.

"How did you get here?" Calix asked, relaxing his stiff posture now he was off duty to lean against the wall.

"It's not far," I said.

"Are you going to tell me what's up with you now?" Cassia shot me a pointed look.

My muscles were still tender and my body couldn't decide what temperature it wanted to stay at. I imagined my impromptu venture had ruffled my appearance more, and I subconsciously ran my fingers through my hair.

"Just a bit of fever. I don't think it's contagious though."

I was sure it wasn't, but Cassia knew nothing of my illness, and I wanted to keep it that way. She was strong and brave and incredibly skilled, and I guess a part of me longed to prove myself to be even a fraction of those things.

"I hope not. I won't be off to a great start if we arrive at the Central unwell," she mused.

I tried to match her smile, but my stomach hollowed out with every mention of the games. And my looming escape to watch her in them.

"We?" Calix interrupted, looking between us.

"Astraea is coming with us, and you only have this one chance to complain. Use it wisely," Cassia said, firm but with a playful smirk Calix rolled his eyes at.

"That is *not* a good idea."

Cassia huffed. "That's all you have to say? You're coming with me—what's one more mentor?"

"A mentor of what?"

"Delightful company."

"You're saying mine isn't?"

"Exactly."

I sipped at my tea as I watched their exchange, unsure if the flush of my cheeks was from that or the tension humming electric between them.

"They release the profiles of the Selected for the Libertatem tomorrow." Cassia sighed, taking up a seat on the bench. I joined her. "The kingdoms will be unsettled. Thirty days—only thirty days in the next one hundred years—they open the borders for all to choose if they want to move. Then, when they're locked again, thirty more days will decide if they put their faith in the right victor to earn their safety from the vampires."

"It's not right," I said. Pitiful words to describe our barbaric reality.

"No, it's not," Cassia agreed. Her sights were fixed on the targets, distant as though she were thinking deeply on the matter and it wasn't nearly the first time it had consumed her thoughts.

"I did not know we were expecting company." The deep voice of Lord Reihan, Reigning Lord of Alisus and Cassia's father, traveled over to us.

"Neither did I," Cassia chirped, always so bright in his company.

My heart yearned to see it. I adored their relationship. It reminded me this was something I'd never had, or at least couldn't remember having—but that sometimes felt worse to believe.

"It's good to see you, Astraea."

When Reihan spoke to me it was like being touched with the warmth of a father. His presence I had come to treasure over the years.

"You know, when my girl leaves, you are welcome here anytime. To stay, should you wish."

The offer burst in my chest. I set my teacup down on the bench. "Thank you, but I—"

"Astraea is coming with me."

I whipped my head to Cassia, not surprised she would blurt it out so eagerly, but I hadn't had the chance to warn her against it. The more people who knew, the higher the chance of Hektor finding out before I was long gone.

Surprise lifted the reigning lord's dark brows. Then his mouth broke into a wide, fatherly smile. "I am glad. My Cass hasn't stopped whining about your decline for months." He pulled his daughter into him with one large fur-clad arm. She giggled when he went to tousle her hair, trying to shove him away.

Every time I witnessed their carefree relationship, I wondered if I would ever recover the memories of my own father that were lost to me.

His palm encased her cheek, his face still a smiling mask, but his true emotions spoke through his eyes. He was mournful. They were mere days from being parted and had to prepare for the possibility that it could be forever.

"Councilman Tarran awaits you, my lord," a messenger called across the courtyard.

The reigning lord's brows drew together in reluctance, but his duty was something he never took lightly. Reihan turned to me, and the moment his arms opened I stepped into them. It was more than just an embrace; it was a thank-you and a farewell. Both squeezed so tightly in my throat I didn't think I could speak. His warmth I savored, stored in the most precious parts of my mind. It was the closest thing to a father's love I might ever remember.

"Stay safe, my child."

When we broke apart I only nodded, not trusting my voice wouldn't betray the brave smile I wore for him.

When Reihan left, Cassia's arm looped around mine. "It's so damn freezing I can hardly feel my nose. Let's get warm."

5

As Cassia tossed her bedding haphazardly onto the floor, I caught flying cushions and got hit by others, which drew out fluttering chuckles from us. Removing my dagger and cloak, I placed them by the fireplace as Calix started a fire.

"Can you stay tonight?" Cassia asked.

I wanted that more than anything, but I couldn't be certain Hektor wouldn't have returned by morning since sickness had taken two of my days away already. I studied my fingers as I shook my head. "I should return before nightfall."

"Why does he demand you so tightly by his side?" Her tone of frustration left me riddled with guilt.

"It's complicated."

Cassia sighed. "Stay for rest and supper."

I chuckled at the nudge to my side.

"*Oomph.*" Cassia dropped down on the furs and cushions beside me. "What do we pass our time with now?"

I nestled down with her. The warmth of the fire waved over us, and Calix stood, going around us to perch on the bare bed.

Content to be in her company and with the setting soothing my muscles, I lay back. "Nothing," I whispered. "Nothing at all."

My eyelids fluttered to the gentle notes of Cassia's voice, sometimes Calix's, as we talked for hours, and I clung to every second. We filled up on small sandwiches and chocolates and, after much persuasion, two cups of wine.

I was starting to regret the indulgences now. They coaxed me to rest, though I was trying desperately to stay awake.

"You can sleep," Cassia muttered. "I'll deal with your overprotective husband if he comes looking."

Awareness snapped me awake with the realization I'd been drifting. Shaking my head, I propped myself up, plastering on a smile. "*Not* my husband," I grumbled.

Calix leaned up on his hands on the bed, so casual and off-duty I could pretend he was a friend.

"Do you want him to be?" Cassia shifted with giddy attention, then she huffed, sinking back down with an overdramatic sigh. "What if I miss your wedding! Losing wasn't an option before, but now—"

"I don't think that will happen," I said quickly.

What sparked within me came unexpectedly. Denial. A rush of something that stirred yet more reluctance to go back to the manor tonight.

"The Selected for the Libertatem," I said to divert the subject and calm my racing heart. "Are they all women?"

"They could be, but that's very doubtful." Cassia gave a long breath of relaxation. "When falls Night, the world will drown in Starlight," she recited.

The words tugged on something in my mind, familiar but without context. "What is that from?"

"A fable," Calix chimed in.

"Hope."

Calix eased a crooked smile at Cassia's frown of disapproval.

"A prophesy that is the only way to be free of the king's reign of terror," she went on.

That caught my intrigue. "What does it mean?"

"I think if we knew, someone would be working to achieve it. All we can do is hope the gods still remember us and set the path for those to right what went wrong five hundred years ago." Cassia shuffled down, her fair skin glowing with the signal of twilight, and my gut sank with the reminder I had to leave soon before nightfall.

"Have you ever heard of the celestials?" Cassia asked.

"Fairy tales?" Calix mused.

She threw him a glare over her shoulder, and I chuckled, sinking fully back into the marvelously soft cushions with her. We lay, heads near touching, and stared at her ceiling, which was painted with constellations. I envied the room and how she'd brought our shared love of the stars into it.

"They were the most powerful beings to have lived, but something went wrong. Something that saw them overpowered by the vampires all that time ago, and they could no longer protect us when their own people were targets. The souls and blood of humans sustain them, but they say celestial blood makes them a near unstoppable force."

"Then three hundred years ago the Faelestial War wiped them out," Calix concluded.

"I don't believe that. Many don't."

Drowsiness lapped at me as I listened to them talk of the tale. Over the painted roof I imagined wings. Mighty black wings with feathers that gave off a midnight-blue hue, so beautiful I wanted them to be real with an ache in my chest. Then feathers of a different set—still dark, but with catches of deep purple against the moonlight they both glided through.

"Where would they be now?" I asked quietly, allowing my lids to slip closed so I could fantasize the image in my mind. How it would feel to soar through the air and race to touch the stars.

"They're protected beyond the Celestial Veil," Cassia said with wonder.

"No one knows if that exists," Calix countered.

"Because you would have to be in the Central to see it, and we will be."

My lips could hardly break a smile, wanting to give in to the weight of sleep. The more Cassia talked, the giddier I became, so anxious for the countdown to leaving for the Central that my excitement was drowned out by fear.

"During the time of the celestials, the Golden Age, we were at peace. Then, with the rise of the vampires, the age of man deteriorated and the celestial leader either left or died, and no one knew what to do."

"So they left us at the mercy of the vampires, who established their reign over the six kingdoms." Calix joined in with a note of boredom that told he didn't believe in any of it.

"And Althenia remains independent beyond the veil no man, fae, or vampire can pass through without their invitation."

"Are they trapped there?" I asked.

"Possibly. It would make it easier to forgive them for leaving us here."

"What happens to those who pass through?"

"No one has ever returned for us to really know what lies beyond. My guess is immediate death from whatever was cast to create it."

I thought of what it would look like. Thick, rolling darkness without any shine. Nothing like the kind I craved of the darkest nights. Though I shuddered with ominous notions, I wanted to see it.

"I want you to have this," Cassia said, sitting up and reaching behind her neck.

I knew what she was moving to unlatch and straightened too. "No. You can't give me that."

"Oh, hush," she scolded. Once the pendant dangled between her fingers, she stared at me with expectance. "It is my Seal of Alisus and I can give it to whomever I like."

My protest remained. I felt unworthy of the gift, but I knew Cass wouldn't take no for an answer. I turned as she beamed, scooting closer, and the metal was warm from her skin as she secured it around my neck.

"Just for safekeeping, until you win," I said quietly.

I knew it was a promise she couldn't make, and my brow pinched as I twisted back to her.

"Exactly," she said, cupping a hand to my cheek.

I weighed the pendant in my palm. The familiar crest of Alisus beveled the metal: a constellation behind an ornate design like a blade or a key without teeth.

As we lay back down, Cassia's fingers lacing through mine made me sigh with contentment.

"Let's make a promise," she said.

I nodded though she couldn't see it.

"If we're lost or apart, we'll look up and know we're mapping the same stars. And should death part us, we'll know the other made it to the skies when the star that shines the brightest gives three blinks."

Nothing had ever wrapped me so wholly in peace but inspired such despair. I gave her hand a squeeze, allowing my eyes to close for just a moment.

"Three blinks," I promised.

6

I jolted awake, the urgency of knowing I was not where I was supposed to be surging through my mind. I scanned the view through the tall balcony doors. It was dark, but the first signs of day would break within the hour.

"Shit," I said, scrambling to my feet.

"Can't we sleep in for once?" Cassia groaned, rolling over from where we'd fallen asleep by the dwindling fire.

"Why did you let me fall asleep?" I threw my cloak over my shoulders, fingers fumbling with the clasp in my hurry.

"You needed it. Look at you—there's more color in your cheeks already."

"I told you I needed to be back." I couldn't stop the panic from slipping into my voice.

As I hooked my cloak shut, warm hands took my trembling ones.

"What are you so afraid of?" Cassia forced my eyes to hers, but I couldn't voice what truly stormed in my mind. The fear of Hektor arriving at the manor before me.

"I just promised Hektor I would be home before nightfall. He'll think something happened to me."

"Damn, I'm sorry. I thought he would have had enough sense to guess you'd stayed. That you're safe here."

I gave my best convincing smile. If Hektor knew I came here . . . If he found out the *reigning lord* knew who I was . . . I didn't want to think of what he would do.

"Two more days," she said, pulling me into an embrace. "I'll send instruction, and I'll see you in two days."

The reminder that the world was about to burst before me in such a short time shot a wild thrill through my stomach. "Yes," was all I could say, but my smile lifted to a genuine grin.

"Okay, now go, before your overprotective—"

"If you call him my husband again . . ."

Cassia giggled as she shoved me toward the door. "Let me get Calix to escort you back."

"I made it here fine by myself. I know the route."

A silvery voice floated in my mind, paired with golden irises that reminded me I wasn't entirely alone. Shadow or not, I had some comfort in his company.

"Day is only breaking. Be careful."

I raced out of town, dangerously slipping on ice, but I had to make it back before him. The woods made my skin crawl with unease, sparking an irrational fear that there could be soulless—or worse, nightcrawlers—lurking. The fading colors of night made this journey more challenging than the last.

I thought I heard wings; mistook the charcoal barren branches as them too when the wind animated them. Or perhaps some wild animal would launch out of one of the many hiding places to devour me instead. I couldn't decide what terrified me more: losing part of my soul, my blood, or having my flesh torn.

I shook my head to dispel the panic gathering from nothing more than tales that had been told to scare me. Tales that made me so compliant in Hektor's bonds I may as well have tied them myself.

Something lunged out into my path, and I shrieked, colliding with it. Strong hands gripped me, and my eyes trailed up from a leather-clad chest to the blue eyes of Zath.

"Fuck, Astraea, you have no idea how concerned I've been. What were you thinking?"

My heart skipped a beat and fright choked my throat. "I was thinking I couldn't spend the last night I had to see Cassia locked away like a prisoner." I shrugged out of his hold, my frustration dissolving into dread. "Will you tell him?"

"Of course not," he said quickly. His expression was exasperated as he drove a hand through his unbound dirty-blond waves. "Anything could have happened to you out here. But we don't have time to argue—Hektor will be back any moment. Come." He took my gloved hand, ushering me along until the glowing windows of the manor drew out a whoosh of relief that I was back safely. It conflicted with my slump of disappointment at seeing the elaborate cage.

We used the main door this time, knowing there was nothing the staff could do. They wouldn't tell Hektor since every one of them would face punishment for my leaving and being at risk. My protection, I had witnessed, he took as seriously and made as personal as any job.

"Milady!" Sira's shout startled me. She skipped over, hooking my arm with a frantic look around, but mercifully the early hour revealed no one else.

"Get her upstairs," Zathrian ordered firmly.

The maid nodded, but before we reached the top of the first flight of stairs, the clamor of hooves at the main entrance shot through me like electricity. Sira and I exchanged a split-second look of horror before we took off running. My rooms were on the top floor of the three-story manor.

Sira took my cloak as I removed it, and my hands grappled with the ties and buttons of my dress as Hektor's voice echoed distantly. Inside, she finished helping me strip out of the dress, and I slipped into a silver nightgown then got into bed just as she stuffed my outdoor clothing haphazardly into the closet. Footsteps grew louder, closing in on the door, and my heart beat hard as I forced my eyes closed, feigning sleep as it opened.

"What are you doing in here?" Hektor asked Sira with a quiet warning.

"Checking her fever."

My teeth clenched at the quiver in her tone, ready to damn the ruse and stand up for her if he thought to punish her.

"And she is well?"

The gentleness he switched to I didn't expect. I focused on keeping my breath steady and my body from turning rigid as I listened to the floorboards creak toward me.

"I believe so."

"Leave us."

The bed dipped and his soft fingers brushed my temple as the click signaled Sira's exit. I chose then to inhale deeply, fluttering my lids as though he'd awoken me. I swallowed through my dry throat, scratchy from the run here. I hadn't gotten a moment to relieve it. My small smile turned to a round of coughing, and Hektor reacted immediately, heading into the washroom and running the water.

I propped myself up against the headboard when he returned, and he sat by me again as he handed me the glass. His tenderness now, I couldn't deny, inspired hopeful notions, like a fleeting glimpse of what care and happiness should be between two lovers.

"How are you feeling?" he asked, running a hand over my leg under the sheets.

"Better," I admitted. "I wasn't so when you left. It came on so suddenly I haven't managed far from bed these past few days."

He smiled knowingly, and I wondered if he'd felt my fever the morning before, and if so, why he'd still locked the door. Remembering the confinement, my endearment soured to anger, my grip tightening painfully around the glass. He detected nothing, but the mask of compassion he wore cracked, and I wanted to hate him. I wanted to shout and demand why, but that would only bring out a more frightening wrath I couldn't contend with.

I was feeble and weak and nothing like Cassia, but I longed to be, if only so I could be the breaker of my own chains.

"As you are becoming well, perhaps some air away from the manor would lift your spirits," he said, taking the glass from me. He leaned in, planting his lips to mine, and in my shock at his words I pulled out of the kiss. He smiled—the kind that eased the hard lines of his face and gave off a soft handsomeness. "The send-off in a few days, I think you will enjoy the spectacle they plan to make of it."

Why would he offer this now?

Never had I hoped more for Hektor's tight protection to hold firm. He'd refused for me to attend Cassia's send-off weeks ago; now I rose with anxiety knowing I needed him to be otherwise occupied that day so I could slip away. Long enough to gain a lead and hope he wouldn't suspect my relationship with the reigning lord's eldest daughter.

"I would love that," I said quickly.

"Good. There is nothing more valuable to me than your happiness."

I believed him. Only, Hektor's view of my happiness was an illusion of his own making. He thought this protection he offered, the wears and the jewelry, his affection . . . that it was enough. Life would be easier if I could convince myself it was, but no matter what he showered me with, I couldn't fill the void inside of me that yearned for something coin couldn't buy. Or perhaps a fantasy that didn't exist at all.

Hektor stood. "I have some things to see to, but I will be back tonight. You should rest to be as well as you can for it."

I nodded, grateful for the alone time when I had to figure out how the hell I was going to orchestrate an escape plan in mere days.

When he left, I sank back down as the sun kept rising. I couldn't sleep. I couldn't do anything but reel at the thought of what was to come.

7

I didn't venture out of my rooms the following night. Instead I hugged the blanket around my shoulders tighter as I stared up at the midnight sky, leaning against the balcony doors that allowed a chill to seep in for my last night here. I wouldn't risk being caught. No—I had to be as obedient as he believed I had always been to have any chance of eluding him tomorrow.

My mind taunted and laughed that no matter what I tried, even if I made it a day, a week, away from him, he would always find me so long as he lived.

And so came a dark thought, one that had stroked my mind before in the heat of Hektor's worst moments: I had to kill him.

Every time I truly thought of the idea, I expelled it with horror. No matter what, I couldn't forget everything Hektor had done for me. He'd found me, sheltered me, given me fine things most could only dream of. Just never a *life*.

This wasn't living.

To distract myself, I looked again at the small binding that had arrived by post yesterday. Flipping it open to the name that clenched a tight fist in my chest, I saw Cassia's profile as the Selected of Alisus. There was no drawing, only a list of her strengths and weaknesses. I flipped through the others, but each time, my blood turned hot and my pulse raced as I imagined her having to face them, knowing they'd have to die for Cassia to win.

Two women, three men, and only one victor.

I closed the booklet, refraining from scrunching it up in my palms in my rage. This wasn't right. Humans needing to prove themselves worthy to *live*. That was all the Libertatem was.

The last to win was Arania. Right now, they were the only one out of the five kingdoms to be living in peace with the vampires prohibited from their land. I only knew this, along with other vague but interesting knowledge like Arania being the westernmost kingdom, from stories I'd overheard spying inconspicuously from rafters of Hekor's main room. Or when I would sneak out with Cassia to the humble town establishments where we'd listen to travelers' tales passed on from ancestors. There was only one time when humans could pass beyond their kingdom borders and choose a new life to share their knowledge: now. Once every hundred years with the centennial cycle of the king's game of control.

My door creaked open without a knock, and I whirled in fright.

"Just me," Zath said with a smirk of amusement.

"You shouldn't be in here," I said, glancing behind him as if Hektor would appear any minute.

Zath waved off my concern, stalking over to the seat near the blazing fire. "He's busy with a bunch of crooks just back from his latest kill order."

The flickers of amber highlighted what he carried, and my eyes lit up to follow him. As he placed the two books on the table, I sat, eagerly examining their titles and promptly flicking through one.

"I don't know if they're any good," he said.

"They're perfect," I answered, not even caring what was written in them as I was sure to gain *something*, however small, from the scriptures.

Books were rare in Alisus, even in the Keep. We all had our suspicions it was to keep us from learning anything that could teach us how to overthrow the High Ruler of Solanis. Knowledge could turn into the most dangerous weapon.

I flicked my eyes up from the words to utter my gratitude to Zathrian. He smiled, broad and as excited as I was, even though he had no interest in books.

I'd once read a story about two lovers and their struggle with a family conflict that wouldn't allow for them to be together, but neither of the lovers had struck me as the true hero of the tale. The real hero was her brother. He reminded me of Zath.

When I first met Zath, it wasn't an instant connection. No one ever showed me any interest, and initially he was no different in his primary role of pleasing Hektor. Then he saw me. He wanted to *know* me, and slowly I gathered the same feeling I remembered from immersing myself in that story for a while. Zathrian was a living semblance of the bond I'd felt through those pages.

"I'm leaving tonight," he said, dulling my good mood at receiving the books. "Hektor wants me to oversee a trade in the North Port."

Zathrian was an excellent spy. It wasn't often I heard Hektor speak of any of his men, but Zath had quickly become an invaluable asset to him.

Then I realized, as the first real protest to my joining Cassia . . . I would also be leaving Zath behind.

"What's wrong?" he asked at seeing my ghostly stare.

My mouth opened but snapped shut. I could trust him, I knew that. Yet . . . this was my only chance. And if there was even a slight chance he would tell Hektor, I couldn't risk it. Heat rushed behind my eyes, so I flipped through more pages as a distraction. "Nothing. I'm just going to miss you."

Zath reached over to tousle my hair, and the chuckle it pulled from me as I fended him off brightened the room. "I hope to be back for the last of the send-off celebrations. Save me one of the little round sponge things with the chocolate filling."

My lips pinched. I couldn't bear to look at him with my lies. "I'll save you two if you're prompt."

Zath leaned in, his hand cupping my neck as he planted a soft kiss to my forehead, and I sighed knowing the contentment of safety—*real* safety—was about to slip away from me. "All the more reason to hurry the crooks along," he mumbled.

He reached the door, and my racing pulse surged me to my feet.

"Zath," I called.

He paused to throw me a look back.

"Thank you—for everything."

His dark blond brows knitted. I hadn't meant for it to sound like a good-bye. Then his expression eased with a warm smile, and he nodded. My heart broke with the click of the door.

I wasn't used to expending so much emotion, and I was growing so tired. I spent the next hour flipping through the pages of a book so worn some of them came loose.

The next one to crack free from the binding took my breath away. I stood slowly, discarding the rest as I stared and stared down at the wondrous image. I vacantly wandered over to the fireplace to catch more light that would reveal the finer details.

It was a map. Entranced, I marveled at how the pinpoint I stood on at this very second was smaller than a speck of sand on this parchment. I couldn't believe a realm so vast could be displayed on a single sheet. I'd never seen a map before, and the visual of Solanis was nothing like what I could have imagined.

It was breathtaking.

The Central earned its name literally. Vesitire proudly occupied the middle of the landmass, the other five kingdoms surrounding it. Those were divided from each other by the king's guard border control, and these kingdoms would compete against each other. Then, on Vesitire's right . . .

My fingers traced with wonder where the veil cut off access to the magnificent realm of Althenia. There was an island, streams breaking off to make it appear as if the land made a six-point star. My imagination exploded with imagery, but I knew I could never visualize what beauty truly lay there. In the realm of the celestials.

A soft knock drew my attention, and Sira slipped into the room with a warm smile. "He's called for you, milady. I was sent to make sure you are appropriate for his guests."

Immediately, my palms clammed up. "What guests?" Hektor never invited me out of this room when the establishment was full for the night.

Sira helped me into a new white gown. I despised the pale material he favored me in, turning nauseous at the sight. Over it, a long-sleeve cropped coat with a high button neck. No markings on show. Which only twisted my gut tighter with the dread that I would be seen by people.

She styled my hair with some elaborate braids, adding crystals that complemented the glittering strands through my silver locks. In the mirror the candlelight reflected off every jewel I wore from head to toe.

A spectacle.

Walking the halls so openly at this hour, I didn't know how to carry myself. Usually, I'd be seeking the next shadow to become one with, straining my hearing to detect every nearby voice. But most of all, I'd be keeping track of exactly where Hektor was. I stood tall, clasping my hands behind my back, but that felt too stiff. I folded them in front of me but quickly dropped my arms to let them sway loose.

Sira nodded her head for me to go in through the open doors.

Hektor's study.

My throat burned dry. There was not a single memory I harbored from there that had ended well. Sira tried to appear encouraging, yet I could always see the cracks in a person's mask. Her concern, mixed with my own, drummed hard in my chest. I took a deep breath and headed through the doors.

The low chatter of voices raised every hair on my body. I counted first. Six men, some standing and others sitting on the ornate brown leather couches. Smoke filtered through the air, but not enough to choke me. I found the source as the first one to notice me. A middle-aged man with shaggy but well-kept brown hair finished the drag of his pipe before his shadow-lined jaw eased into a predatory smile. I stiffened with the overwhelming urge to retreat when, one by one, every new set of eyes turned more of me to stone. I feared I wouldn't be able to move.

Then I found him.

Hektor seemed to be the last one to cast a lazy gaze my way from his single tall chair facing the others. "My darling, come here."

At the command I took a second to breathe, watching the flex of skin around his eyes, his subtle irritation that I wasn't by his side before he'd finished speaking. The click of the door jolted me from my stupor. A quiet rumbling of chuckles grated over my skin, and I wondered if it was my fear they found amusing. Heat crept over my cheeks though I had nothing to feel embarrassed about. I walked the few paces to Hektor, sliding my trembling palm into his awaiting one.

"You look absolutely stunning," Hektor said, his gaze admiring as it moved over me slowly. I wanted to shrink away. "Doesn't she?" He gave the invitation for the other six men to observe me, feast on me, and all I could think of was *hunger* as they took me in. I stood as prey in a circle of vultures, and my mind was racing with the thought of what I could be here for. Never had Hektor summoned me to be among any of his guests.

"May I?" a low voice asked. One of the men stood slowly from the opposite couch, and my feet grew roots to prevent me from doing something that would enrage Hektor. This man was studying me. A short blond lock tipped over his eyebrow as he tilted his head.

"You can look, but touch and you'll lose that hand."

I was glad of Hektor's protection, but as he cast an adoring gaze at me with a nod to step forward, my eyes pricked with tears. Humiliated, I stood as a spectacle to these men. An object to observe, a prize to weigh, a sum to consider.

The blond man came closer, and as his hand rose to my chin I almost flinched—until another shuffle of movement had him shifting playful brown eyes to the side.

One of Hektor's assassins eased out from shadow, the glint of his blade catching on the firelight. I wanted to be any lost place in the world but right here.

Don't let him see your fear.

"Don't test me, Fennik," Hektor drawled with all the power of the room.

Fennik's mouth grew in a slow curl as he returned his eyes to me. "How can we be certain she is what you say?"

That sparked my interest, though not with anything good. I listened to Hektor stand, ripples of his presence encasing me as he closed in. When his fingers brushed over my neck I drew a shallow gasp, stepping back, which only pressed me tighter to him.

"You don't have to be afraid," he whispered over my ear.

Afraid was not the reaction bubbling inside me. It was embarrassment, vulnerability, and I hated every note of it. My teeth clenched as he undid the buttons of my overcoat. His hands slipped into the material, peeling it from my shoulders with purposeful attention like the grand unveiling of a statue. And the eyes of the men widened to gawk at me as such.

I couldn't hear through the pounding in my ears. My gown was sleeveless with a low, curving neckline, and instinct made me hug my arms as though I were naked at the attention of the strangers raking over me. I bit back my whimper when Hektor took my wrists, gently guiding my arms to my sides.

"She is the most unique thing," he said with an air of wonder, trailing slow fingers over my silver markings while the other men studied me.

Not out of affection, but to show his claim over me.

"If she is as valuable as you say, surely not even an island is enough of a trade."

"Volantis isn't just any island, as you are well aware. Many have coveted the volcanic isle, many have gone to your Overlord with high prices indeed, and never has he been tempted to sign away his claim to it."

"And you think she is the price that will make him finally break?"

"Vermont would not have sent you in response to my letter if not."

My corset became too tight, the air far too thick. I couldn't be hearing this right. Hektor couldn't be talking about me as no more than a currency to trade.

"I'm not for sale," I whispered. Every inch of me was vibrating, but I had to react.

Spinning, I didn't even make it one step before Hektor caught me. His hands on my arms were tight, but I couldn't feel it with the cold embracing me. My eyes stung more. I couldn't stand the thought of them seeing my tears and I wished for Hektor's pain to keep them from falling.

"Don't cause a scene," Hektor warned, a low breath across my ear as he stroked my hair.

"Please don't do this," I said.

"It is for us, darling, trust me."

I never had, and I never would, trust the manipulative Hektor Goldfell.

"We have yet to see if she is capable of anything you say," Fennik said. "Vermont will want to see her."

That wouldn't happen. I would sooner run from this manor and not stop until the fire in my lungs killed me. I would sooner kill all of them. The thought was as soul-tarnishing as it was liberating.

I couldn't make sense of what they wanted with me—what lies Hektor might have told in this grand scheme to win an *island* by fooling a pirate overlord.

"Then he should have come here himself," Hektor replied. His hand stroked along my arms, and I couldn't shrug out of it, not wanting to turn and face those men who feasted on me.

"You know he wouldn't risk crossing the sea and leaving Volantis open to threat," Fennik said.

"Then I wonder how he has not gone mad ruling without a counsel he can trust to operate in his stead."

"Volantis produces the highest value minerals. It makes up a great deal of trade across the entire continent. I'm sure you can see why the temptation of greed might have made even those he trusts the most willing to risk a civil war to claim a vacant throne."

"What I can see"—Hektor turned me slowly in his grip, and I dropped my eyes pitifully as I faced them again—"is that Vermont wants this trade to sever his ties to an island that has become a great burden, but he does not want to let go of the wealth associated with his position. This gives him exactly what he has wanted for a very long time. A new lifetime of security."

Fennik looked me over again, and while I wanted to avert my gaze out of repulsion, I studied him back. All of them, not wanting to miss a thing.

"That is how you keep the vampires away?" he asked skeptically.

"We have an arrangement. One that will continue in my absence."

Fennik drilled his eyes into me as if I were the answer to that protection. "Why don't they just take her?"

Hektor chuckled with smooth arrogance. "That secret will remain solely between Vermont and me."

I didn't listen to the rest of their exchange in the next few minutes, remaining numb instead. My mind had never scrambled so desperately to make sense of how my small existence could be shaken and bartered. *One more day,* I repeated to calm myself. He wouldn't get to trade me as I would disappear tomorrow.

Only when we stood alone in his main study did I start to climb out of my reeling thoughts. "How could you?" I breathed. I didn't want to feel the hurt that cleaved me at his betrayal. It shouldn't have come as a surprise, but I realized, after all he'd done, I still believed that in his own twisted way he *cared* for me.

Hektor sighed like he'd been anticipating my outrage and believed it would be something else he could brush off. I watched him with building resentment, balling my fists as he wandered over to the liquor cart and poured two tumblers of whiskey. He brought one over to me, extending his hand, but I didn't reach for it.

"I knew you would have met me with reluctance if I'd told you of this before, but you know nothing, Astraea. This manor has kept us thriving, but there is more out there for us. I plan to give you a throne like you deserve."

"There is no *us,*" I spat. It wasn't often I lost my composure around Hektor. He was a snake whose rattle was always shaking, one wrong move away from striking.

I didn't care this time.

One more day.

Hektor's expression tightened, so close to breaking. He inched the glass a little closer. A test.

As much as I wanted to shatter it, I needed answers before I made my choice.

"What have you told them of me?" I asked, taking the whiskey only to get him talking.

As I took my first sip his shoulders relaxed a fraction. He drove a hand through his messy auburn locks before sliding it into his pocket and pacing away. "I convinced them you have celestial blood," he said so casually I spluttered.

"You said you couldn't find anything on what my markings mean."

"They mean nothing, darling. Likely a product of your mother consuming too much Starlight Matter." He braced a hand on the mantel as he stared into the firepit, downing the last of his drink.

"Why do they believe it means something?"

Hektor's mocking laugh made my cheeks flush with embarrassment. "What matters is that I have no intention of giving you up. I'll admit I am a bit wounded you believed otherwise. We'll make the trade, and I'll have all of them killed to get you back. I think it is time for a change, to grow our kingdom into an empire." He turned, the fire blazing a frightening, hungry power across his face. "I have given you everything I possibly could here. Now I want to make you a queen."

I shook my head, and the darkness that began to shift in him made me tremble. His hand tightened around his glass, and I saw the second he snapped. Ringing filled my ears when the shattering sound split the room. His glass rained down from the wall it hit as he crossed the distance, advancing for me, and my own glass slipped from my fingers.

"I have given you *everything*," he said with a lethal calm. "I can take it all away. Every memory you have is because of me. Do you think I wanted to shelter some runaway whore? You *begged* to stay with me then."

"I didn't—"

His hand didn't choke me, but I gasped all the same. He backed me up until I felt the desk and then he leaned further into me.

One more day.

This flare of determination I'd felt before, but never so strongly. I was going to fucking escape him before he could ever dream of using me again. It had to end, and now the frost was clearing to show Hektor would never change. This was who he was.

"You're right," I said. My hand flattened on his chest. "I'm sorry."

That calmed him enough that he began to bunch up my skirts, and my stomach twisted with nausea. "Why do you test me, Astraea?" he sighed, continuing his climb up my bare leg. I pushed back my repulsion.

"Not here," I tried.

He didn't listen, and the clink of his belt made my eyes slip closed. *One more day.*

I would run. I would run and run even if it killed me.

A voice rumbled through the door before Hektor could fully undo his buckle. I could have whimpered with relief, but a coat of shame was also cast over me at hearing Zathrian on the other side.

"There's trouble in the main room," Zath said. I was glad when he didn't enter to find us in this position.

Hektor growled low in annoyance. He took my face, planting one long kiss against my lips, and I wanted to turn to dust and escape. "We're not done here," he said, holding me with feral green eyes. "I'll have him escort you back to your rooms. Do not leave them until I return."

Hektor righted his clothing, and the moment he left . . . I crumbled.

Something that had been straining for far too long finally broke, and I fell to a pitiful state on the ground. I tried to release it fast enough that I could rally some composure before Zath came back. *If* he came back. I couldn't stop crying and thinking.

"There is no sight more tragic than this."

Nyte's voice stopped my sobs. It eased out like it was made of the darkness clinging to the corners of the room.

"Broken potential."

"How did you get in here?" I sniffed. His commentary stung, though I was too exhausted and hollow to show it.

Featherlight fingers coaxed my chin up. I sat as a pitiful heap, my dress fanned out around me, and I could only imagine my hideous tear-stained face from his slow, disturbed assessment.

"What are you?" I tried. Perhaps he would save me from the failure of trying to escape. Perhaps he would prevent my vacant existence from wasting more breath in this world.

"It matters not what I am, but why I have come," he said. "You want to escape, and I can help you."

I contemplated, drowning in his flickering amber irises that began to entrance me. "Are you . . . death?"

That teased out a wicked amusement, and he dropped to a crouch. "To many. But that is not what I offer you."

"I don't want your help. I won't trade one owner for another."

"Starlight," he drawled, his head tilting curiously, "there are two kinds of belonging. Possession . . . and alliance. One of single ownership, and one of mutual desire." He looked over the sorry sight of me with a sigh.

"What could I do for you?" I whispered. Nyte had come to me at my most vulnerable, desperate point. As though he'd been there waiting all this time, longer than perhaps I knew, to present me this offering.

"That time will come."

I shook my head. It was too much of a risk to owe something when I couldn't be certain what he desired.

"Then stay to find out that right now your cage has a door, and once it seals, this time it will not lock. It will simply cease to exist at all."

He went to stand, but my impulse was to lash out. My hand curling around his wrist felt almost like holding a ghost that had been given only enough of a form to be present for a moment.

"I don't want to remain here," I whispered. My heart beat furiously.

"Is that your acceptance?"

One beat. Two. Three.

"What do you need me to do?"

His mouth grew in a slow curl, but it was his irises that flashed a liquid gold, wild and thrilled. Nyte's palm slipped over my cheek, and before I knew what he was doing, his lips were pressed firmly to mine. The stars awoke behind my eyes as they slipped shut. One by one they expanded into flares, shooting across the sky we were suspended in for those few seconds.

"Think of me, and I will answer," he spoke to my mind. Then he pulled away, lingering against my mouth to say aloud, "Long for me, and I am right here with you."

The door burst open, and in a blink I drew back with fright . . .

Nyte was gone.

"What the fuck did he do to you?" The threat in Zathrian's tone was unexpected, and I dragged my ghostly, bewildered look to him. He was shuffling out of his jacket, and my lip wobbled at the tender gesture when he kneeled beside me and its warmth embraced me.

This was safe. Zath was safe. And real.

Nyte . . . I couldn't be certain if he was my own tormenting conscience.

"I don't know who I am," I croaked.

His pinched brow eased from harsh lines to a soft understanding. He looked briefly at the markings on my chest. Even the first time he saw them he hadn't seemed to find them odd. Not like the other men had earlier. They meant nothing.

Yet still they were a mystery that stacked to my growing frustration.

"What do you want to do, Astraea?" Zath asked softly, carefully.

I met his blue eyes, and they were so filled with determination my heart skipped a beat. "I'm going to leave," I confessed in a fearful whisper lest Hektor be listening. "With Cassia, tomorrow."

Zathrian shook his head, and my pulse spiked, gripping his arm in a plea. "It has to happen tonight."

My back straightened at his declaration. "He'll follow me," I breathed— not with reluctance, but I hoped his firm face wouldn't change with my worries. "He'll kill you if he finds out you knew."

Still his determination did not change. "Come. You need to pack what you can. Discreetly, so he won't suspect a thing."

Zathrian helped me to stand. I couldn't believe what he was saying. I wanted to do this. *Gods,* nothing awoke with such a thrill and purpose than to take this dare for myself.

"I thought you were supposed to be gone."

"I was. But then I saw those men and heard your name mentioned. He's never spoken of you to anyone before, and I got worried. I stalled for a while until I saw Sira leading you here. Then I heard—" Zath paused, and my sickness arose along with the understanding he'd been eavesdropping enough that he'd caused the distraction deliberately.

"Thank you," I said, though it was not enough.

He smiled sadly. "Come on."

As he led me out to the deserted halls, my nose crinkled. Never had I truly realized how much Zath cared for me. He was willing to risk his job, his life, to help me escape, and I didn't know what I'd done to deserve it.

In my rooms, my mind tried to lock into action. Finding a satchel, I began to think of the essentials I could need.

"Pack what you can and keep it hidden. We're getting you out tonight, even if it puts us on the road ahead of Cassia."

I nodded hearing the words, but my blood was roaring. I was really going to do this. I smiled, huffing a laugh as I swiped at my tears, blinking them back furiously to see the articles of clothing I was choosing. Then I headed into the bathroom for my pills.

"I'll have to leave for a few hours to convince him I'm gone for his task. But I'll be back before he usually retires for the night. Be ready."

I cast my gaze to him as he lingered by the door and nodded, wearing a bright face and trying to appear brave. Zath forced a smile too, seeming reluctant to leave me. But I could handle a few hours.

"I'll be waiting," I said.

He nodded, and the moment the door clicked shut my heart leaped up my throat. I gathered a couple more things and paced the room, jumping at every slight sound and praying Hektor wouldn't return early. Then I stood by the balcony and watched the stars as the only thing that could offer me a wave of calm while I waited to escape, to be free and able to not look back for the first time in my life.

8

With the soft knock at the door, I folded the map I'd been studying for hours since Zath had left me. I was equal parts terrified and exhilarated to discover the person behind it.

It was neither Zath nor Hektor.

Sira lingered timidly without entering, and her ghostly expression sent a chill deeper than the winter's touch down my spine. "He sent for you," she said with enough regret that I began to tremble. Had the men returned, and he'd thought to progress things faster with his plan?

My breathing picked up. "What for?"

"Another guest, milady." Sira spoke apology in her eyes, and I couldn't bear it.

Desperate to find a place to hide, I even spared a glance over at the balcony with the ludicrous notion I could attempt to escape that way again. I rolled my shoulders, taking a deep breath to compose myself before I even knew what guest it could be. Then, with a nod, I followed her out.

The whole way to Hektor's study I fidgeted with my skirts, combed my fingers through my hair, and focused on inhaling regular breaths when my lungs threatened to stop taking in air. The door to his study was slightly ajar, and I heard him before I saw him. The other voice . . .

Time slowed when I entered and matched it to the face.

I blinked several times, hoping it wasn't true, that perhaps I'd fallen asleep waiting for Zath. Still nothing changed. Cassia's expression lit up at finding me.

"Ah, there she is," Hektor drawled.

My skin crawled. His tone was cheerful, but I heard the fury underneath. I dared to look and found that all too familiar mask he wore. His smile was pleasant, but those green eyes blazed.

"What are you doing here?" I asked Cassia. It came out as barely more than a whisper past the hands gripping my throat, and I nearly raised my own to be sure they weren't real.

"Returning this to you," Hektor answered before the words could slip from her parted mouth.

When I beheld the purple metal of the dagger he offered out, the room tilted, my situation turning worse. I shifted a step, floundering for how to respond since nothing would open the ground and save me from this confrontation.

"Thank you," I said, sliding a look to Cassia, whose bright face started to fall. I tried to wipe away my horror, forcing a smile to erase the concern that pinched her brow as she studied Hektor and me. Even Calix shifted his weight, his hand resting on his sword with careful observation.

The tension in the room could be cut with a knife.

"I'll give you a moment to say goodbye to our esteemed *Selected*." Hektor made to leave, stopping by my shoulder. His gaze, though unmet, turned me to ice. He slipped from the room, and still I couldn't relax when the three of us stood alone. The click behind us jolted the first movement through me.

"Why did you come here?" I asked vacantly, staring as if I could still deny it.

"To bring your dagger and give you the plans for tomorrow. I was around the town anyway and thought to come myself—"

"You could have given it to me tomorrow," I said, blank with fading hope. It was over. "Just one more day."

Cassia took steps toward me, and I tried not to break as she didn't know what she'd done. All she'd exposed. "Astraea." Her eyes scanned me, and only then did I relax, realizing I had to stop her observations from running wild—that I was something *weak*, something to be *saved*, when I didn't want to be either.

"Sorry," I muttered, reaching out to hold her arms as she did mine. "I'm just surprised to see you."

With her slow nod she didn't seem fully convinced. I pulled her in for an embrace. Calix kept his expression firm, though I didn't believe it was fully out of concern for me. As he watched our interaction his focus remained on Cassia.

"Now I've seen the profiles, I don't know, Cass. The woman from Pyxtia might give you at least a worthy match," I said lightheartedly.

Pulling away, Cassia chuckled, and I started to relax into the knowledge that at least in these moments with her I could find a gift no matter what came next.

"I think so too."

"We should be getting back," Calix interrupted.

A wave of grief washed over me, but I would not cry. Would not give her that last image before she left.

"The send-off will be full of commotion. We'll pick you up on the road outside the city," she said. "Tomorrow afternoon."

How could I tell her it was over? There would be no escaping Hektor's leash, which would be reduced to nothing once they left for this.

"If I'm not there—"

"You will be."

My teeth ground at her damn persistence. Her brow began to knit. Cassia would storm off to Hektor himself right now if she suspected anything, and I couldn't risk that. So I put on a smile and embraced her again, meeting eyes with Calix and hoping he understood my pleading look: that if I didn't arrive, he *had* to force her to go without me.

For the first time, he looked back at me with something like sadness and understanding, giving one single nod. It was all I needed.

Cassia and Calix left, and I remained looking over Hektor's desk.

Don't let him see you weak.

I didn't turn when I felt him enter with a gust of cold that seeped to my bones.

"The reigning lord's daughter," he said with mocking disbelief. "You can imagine my surprise." He entered my peripheral, his movements slow like a snake primed to strike.

Breathe. Breathe.

He laid the dagger on the desk in front of him. "Where did you get this?"

I didn't answer. There was no point when nothing would soften the strike to his pride that I'd defied him. *Eluded* him.

By now I knew his impulsive triggers by a shift of energy. I braced.

His hand wrapped around my nape, pushing me forward, and my lips tightened against a cry as my palms met the wood to stop the force. His mouth met my ear as he said, "You know what your silence does to me when I expect answers."

"I found it."

It wasn't a lie. I'd always figured it had been left by one of Hektor's men, or perhaps a guest, when I'd come across it while wandering surreptitiously one night three years ago after spying on an inspiring training session below the manor, but I'd never seen the likes of the purple metal on them since. I'd stolen the dagger brazenly and spent the weeks following on a razor's edge of anticipation that I'd be caught when it was declared missing.

"What displeases me more are your lies." His grip tightened a fraction, and I prepared for what he might do . . .

A knock made the air shudder out of me. Hektor paused with a deep breath of anger, releasing me, but I whimpered at the fist he slammed that rattled everything on the desk before he called for the person to enter.

I didn't know who it was, but, catching words but not whole phrases, I concluded it required his attention and he would unleash his wrath toward me on everyone else until he got the chance to come back.

As they continued to talk, I despised my cowardly submission and reflected on the hand still imprinted around the back of my neck. I wanted to tear it off. I wanted to hurt him back, to make him *fear,* and my dark thoughts . . . I didn't feel shame for them.

My eyes were pulled by compulsion to the wavy purple steel, the image of driving it straight to its beautiful black wings into Hektor's chest filling my mind. Could I really do it? My fingers subconsciously reached for the hilt, my grip already firm as I calculated the steps I would take to plunge it to where I wanted before he could stop me.

Hektor's hand lashed around my raised wrist, and I yelped. "Does it make you feel brave, darling?" he cooed.

I despised him. I *despised* him.

"I might let you keep it if you tell me everything. How long you have been sneaking away from this manor without my knowledge? It must be some time, and I am *fascinated* to know how."

His mockery slammed my teeth together. Hektor spun me around. An arm around my waist brought our bodies flush, and I wanted to *kill* him.

"I want to know everyone you met. Everyone who knows your name and about me. Everything you've told them." He took my jaw in a painful grip that caused my eyes to sting. His green eyes burned through me as I prepared for something to finally *snap.*

Like the flip of a switch, his face relaxed all at once. I had to blink at the contrast. He stroked my cheek with false love, and I feared this more than his true wrath.

"Come with me."

He took my hand, and I had no choice but to follow. A creeping unease settled, and my breathing quickened at the thought of where he would lead me to. It put a strain on our joined fingers. His grip tightened with the warning glare he shot me over his shoulder.

"Hektor, please," I tried, but I didn't stop walking. "You don't have to do this. I'll stay locked in my rooms."

"Now I know you've found a cunning way out, I cannot trust you'll stay in there until I have the balcony doors looked at."

My eyes scrunched shut. *I will not cry. I will not break.*

We came to the door, and everything in me dropped at the sight of the thick iron bars from wall to wall at the end of the room. I choked a dry sob as he continued to lead me to the cell, straining against his hold again, but with his groan of frustration all I could do was brace. My back hit the wall and my head followed with the hand that wrapped around my throat. Pain shot through my skull, but I pressed my lips tight together. His frightening expression was made even more monstrous by the light pooling in from the entrance. Hektor seethed in silence, and I held still.

"Look what you did," he said as though he cared. His hand uncurled from my neck, smoothing down the back of my hair where it throbbed. "You moved too fast and hit your head."

I nodded vacantly. Hektor sighed deeply, planting a kiss on my cheek.

"You don't have to do this," I whispered.

There were no windows in this room, and when the door was sealed, the darkness that would devour was not of wonder and beauty. It taunted abandonment.

He didn't listen. The high pitch of the cell door opening rattled every bone in my body, and I stopped before it.

"If you loved me, you wouldn't do this."

Hektor turned me to him, his hand grazing my cheek. "It is because I love you that I do this, Astraea. Trust I take no pleasure in it."

I could have fallen to my knees. There was no changing his mind. If I fought, I would lose. If I tried to run, I would be caught. In this helpless existence I was trapped.

He coaxed me inside, and my drifting steps passed the bars. I tunneled far to keep from breaking in a frantic plea that would only feed his superiority; fuel the control he had over me. I stayed silent when the cell door echoed a groan and shut. A stiff tremor shook me to my core with the resonating click of the lock. I made it to the feeble cot, but I couldn't feel my body as I sat, curling my knees up to my chest.

This place welcomed me with the cruel embrace of satisfaction at seeing me again after so long when I'd promised it never would. I'd managed to stay away from Hektor's worst punishment for a year. I would have taken anything physical over this, but I knew his mind was made up, and to disobey would only follow one with the other.

So, I didn't look to him again when I knew he lingered there. I wondered if there was a shred of regret in his heart that made him doubt his choice, but ultimately one thing would never change about Hektor Goldfell. Come right or wrong, he never took back a decision.

Only when true darkness fell and lonely taunts replaced his presence did my cheeks turn wet with tears and my chest echo with the sound of my sobs. Only when I had no one did I truly break.

9

I tried to count the minutes. Then, when seconds skipped and slowed, the hours. My fingernails split trying to tally them on the wall I was curled against. Twelve, though I would never know if I was right.

In this feeble state as the frightened pet in a cage, I couldn't convince myself I harbored a shred of bravery. I had walked in here. There remained only a small inkling of spirit as I recalled the one time I'd stood up for myself. When Hektor first caught me wandering his establishment among the guests three years ago, I fought him for weeks, resisting his touch, fighting the hands he laid upon me. I apologized to the part of me I'd locked away that Hektor had succeeded in silencing me only when I had nowhere else to go.

Now I didn't care. Even running into a soulless would at least be my choice, but this . . . this *cell,* was not.

What I desired the most was not food, though my stomach ached. Not a blanket, though my body tensed against the cold . . .

I wanted my dagger desperately. The feel of it had become tangible, and I practiced various maneuvers in the air that Cassia and Calix had taught me. My eyes could have been closed, so thick was the darkness while my head rested against the icy stone.

I reached out, tracing the wings of my dagger, until a flicker of light stopped me. Small twinkles of stars formed in front of me, and in my delirium I reached for for them. Touching them, I drew a shallow gasp at the low vibration, the enticing pull to reach further into the small expanse that widened. The thump against my ribs was all I could hear, and my hand met something solid, my fingers curled around it, and I couldn't believe it to be what my mind concluded.

I pulled it toward me, and the small galaxy reflected off the metal that appeared black before the light winked out completely.

I didn't immediately move. My fist clutched tighter, expecting reality to wipe my imagination clean with laughter when my chipped nails bit my palm.

They didn't.

My fist remained clamped around the hilt, and I was no longer certain I was awake. I couldn't see it, but my fingers reached over the cross guard, feeling every ridge of the carving of feathers I knew without question. Then they felt along the unmistakable wave of the blade.

My breathing came short with adrenaline, needing to confirm it further, and so I grabbed the sharp end in my palm. I cried out immediately as it sliced through skin, but the pain was numbed in my euphoria.

It was *real*.

I stood from the bed. The stormstone dagger trembled in my extended grip, but I released a sob of elation at the impossibility and fear that this was a trick and it could be stolen from me at any moment.

"I would kill him, but that vengeance has the chance to be yours."

I spun at the silvery voice, unable to make out a thing in the pitch-dark, but his presence rippled close. I angled my blade in the direction I thought him to be.

"Very good," he said, sending gravel over my skin at the proximity, and when I turned again, I would have struck true were it not for the hand that caught my wrist. "When you go to use your beautiful darkness, make sure you aim for his heart."

"You're not really here."

Yet he guided my hand higher, until the tip of the blade rested against something I could drive it through.

"You're not real."

"Try it," he tempted.

"You want me to stab you?"

"If it helps ease your mind, yes."

"Now I know you can't be real."

His chuckle turned my mind in contradiction to the delightful shiver that ran through my body.

"Nyte." I said his name, enjoying the sound of it.

"Starlight."

I had to touch him. My hand holding the dagger fell only for my other to rise. He inhaled deeply when I came so close to grazing his cheek before he caught my wrist again.

"You're bleeding."

I'd forgotten about the wound that didn't hurt.

"It's nothing."

I thought his breath blew across my palm, but there was no warmth. My fingers met soft skin—lips—and I was too stunned by the electricity coursing through me to move.

"What are you doing?" I asked.

I wished I could see him. I wanted to feel *more* of him, and the dark gave me brazen confidence. It offered his company, though I didn't know how it was possible.

I stepped closer as he guided my hand away from his mouth, letting it go, but when he cupped my cheek, something sparked to life in my chest and chased out every desolate thought of my surroundings, my situation, just for this fleeting moment.

"I have to go," he said.

"Please don't."

Mint and sandalwood drifted over me until a tingling on my lips caught my breath. "Do not beg," he whispered. "Certainly not for me."

The flame burning within me snuffed out, and the smoke that remained threatened to choke me.

He was gone.

The echo of his touch lingered on my face, but his phantom presence was snatched cruelly by cold emptiness. I stood alone once again, bewildered by what I'd conjured.

"I'm not going insane," I said to myself, beginning a short pace. "I'm not losing myself." I bit at the raw tips of my fingers, but I couldn't feel anything.

I had lost myself long ago. My strings had been tied the moment I accepted salvation from the first thing to offer it, and I'd been naïve to never question his love as control. His gifts were control. His *protection* was fucking control. And I wanted to give it all back and keep running barefoot through that forest no matter what other arms might catch me instead.

I slapped my palms against the brittle stone with a cry.

Then I heard voices beyond the door. In my terror that Hektor might take the weapon from me again, I hastily stuffed it under the pillow. My pulse clawed up my throat when the commotion grew louder. There was shuffling, a few thumps that made my body jerk, and I braced myself for Hektor to barge in with an unhinged anger.

The door didn't burst open. Whispers sounded as it was carefully unlocked, and when it opened, my eyes stung, and I winced against the light.

"Shit."

I couldn't see him, but the muttering of his rage filled my eyes, and I whimpered. "Zath?"

"That bastard," he growled, storming over to the cell.

I cried. With twinges of shame at where he'd found me, and in world-caving relief as the jingle of keys became the melody of freedom.

"We're getting you the hell out of here."

The moment the cell door swung open my arms wrapped around him, needing desperately that solid reassurance he was real and warm. I couldn't stop shivering from the cold. "He'll kill you," I sobbed, suddenly over-whelmed by what Zath's intervention meant.

"Not if I kill him first."

I unhooked my arms, shaking my head with the horror that filled me. I took a step back into the cage, but Zathrian's arm hooked around me to prevent it.

"Never again," he growled.

Zath tried to pull me, but I was riddled with a fear so true, haunted by my many memories of Hektor taking the lives of those who had displeased him. For what Zath had done . . . my stomach cramped at the thought of the display Hektor would make of him.

"You have to go," I pleaded.

"Listen to me," he said firmly.

My hand curled around the iron bar at his shift toward me. Impatience twitched his jaw, but I could suffer his disappointment so long as he was safe.

"You must trust me. We've already wasted too much time, and there is not a fucking chance I'm leaving you alone here for another second. So you either use those legs, or I'm seconds away from hauling you over my shoulder."

Zathrian spoke like a commander, how I imagined one would speak to a soldier out of their wits with fear in battle. I'd read a short tale once, one of history, that lingered with me still for the heart-wrenching notion of what it took to fight for what you believed in.

My hand slowly uncurled from the bar.

Zath's hard frown eased a little in relief. "We need to go," he said, softer now, extending a palm.

I looked at it, trying to silence the thought that to accept was to seal his end.

"What the hell is taking so long?"

I gasped at the feminine voice that hissed through the darkness. "Cassia?" I whispered, afraid I was mistaken about the silhouette in the doorway.

She ignored me to say, "We have less than five minutes before someone notices the bodies." Her tone was one I'd never heard before, so focused and demanding.

"How?" I choked out.

"Not now," she said then dipped out of view again.

Zathrian grabbed my hand, but before he dragged me out I reached back, smiling in triumph as I felt the dagger and thanking the stars for their mercy. I willed them to keep watch over us as we jogged out to the hall.

"Where are we—?"

A hand clamped over my mouth before I could finish, strangling my scream. I tore my hand from Zath's as he drew a long dagger, aiming his blade, but my worst fear was coming to pass. How could I have believed we'd make it out when my chain to Hektor would always return me here, into his arms?

Cassia lifted her bow, nocking an arrow with expert attention on her target.

"You're staying right here, of course," Hektor said in a chilling calm. His arm encircled my waist, and I turned nauseous at the vile stroke of possession. His palm eased away from my mouth, only to brush my hair over my shoulder.

"She's not staying with you for another fucking minute."

I'd never heard such venom from Zath.

"What a disappointment you have turned out to be," Hektor said darkly. "Though I'll admit I never saw this coming, and for that you have my respect. A fine spy indeed. But I cannot wait to make an excellent show of your death—"

"No," I said. The word clawed through my throat like sandpaper. "I'll stay. It was my fault, and I'm sorry. Just let them go."

As Hektor's warm breath blew across my ear, I turned so painfully stiff. *Pull yourself together.* Zath shifted, fury lining his threatening face, but I pleaded with my eyes for him to let me go.

"I like to hear you owning your mistakes."

Hektor stroked down my neck, over my shoulder, and I trembled at his touch, which felt shameful with our audience. I dropped my eyes in cowardly submission, unable to stand my only two friends seeing me like this. Vulnerable. When I'd spent so much time with words convincing them I was not.

The string of Cassia's bow snatched our attention. "My father could have this place shut down and you executed for this."

"For what?" Hektor challenged with cool arrogance. "You are trespassing on *my* land, Cassia Vernhalla. I think you'll find I have a rather upstanding but private agreement with the reigning lord. I will give you this one chance to leave alone. Forget this and your father will not hear of it."

Her chuckle was so dark and dry. "You'll have to make a better offer before this spears your throat."

"I'd expect nothing less from our esteemed Selected."

"Please just go," I said, barely a whisper, the only pathetic soul in this confrontation. I was unworthy of the deadly conflict that was only because of *me.*

"I have this place surrounded," Hektor drawled as if boredom became him. "You wouldn't get within five feet of the door without my signal stopping you at every turn."

"You'd have to be alive to make that signal."

I shuddered at the sudden intrusion of Calix's voice from behind. Hektor hissed in my ear, and I tried to turn just enough to see him.

Instead I met eyes with Zath, whose gaze flashed down only for a second, and mine widened in remembrance. My fingers flexed around the handle of the black dagger I'd almost forgotten about in my numb, frightened state.

I could use it. I could do this.

Until my pulse raced and my fingers clutched tighter because I was too late. *Foolishly, cowardly* too late.

Hektor's hand trailed the length of my arm, over my clenched fist, and he raised our hands until the dagger was pointed at Zath. "How did you get this? My study is across the manor," he mused.

"The only way out of this . . . is you."

I tensed at Nyte's echo in my mind.

Hektor's touch went to unfurl my fingers.

"Be your own savior."

I blinked against a wave of adrenaline at what I was about to do.

My hold released and the dagger fell, only to be caught in my other hand. Without drawing another breath, I twisted my wrist, and the stomach-churning resistance of my blade submerging through flesh only lasted for a second before Hektor's cry snapped me to my senses. I whirled, and the sight of the crimson dripping from my blade only struck me with horror for a moment before Hektor fell to his knees. His green eyes shot up and he reached to grab me, but my blade struck again.

With two hands my vision came true, both wrapped around the blade I'd plunged into his chest.

We locked wide-eyed, bewildered stares.

He would have come after me.

Worse, he would have killed Zath and Calix, possibly Cassia, for what I had done.

Hektor had to die, though his dark grip on my soul didn't relent at this knowledge.

Rage turned to agony as I stumbled back, still clutching the blade, not knowing what else was happening.

What have I done?

"We need to go." Cassia's voice jerked my stiff body, barely a drowned whisper, while ringing filled my ears at Hektor's strained chokes of pain as his life faltered.

"You have no idea what you're doing," he rasped. "I kept you safe. They will kill you as soon as they know."

I couldn't feel the hands gripping my shoulders, but they forced me to turn away from the man I'd thought I loved. The man who had given me shelter and safety, whose life I had taken in return. Calix motioned to Cassia down the hall. Zath guided me, but I felt no more than a ghost on a leash. Their lips moved, but I couldn't make out words.

Then I looked for him—Nyte—certain I had heard his voice, but no eyes of dawn were revealed.

I didn't get time to dwell on my storm of confusion as I gave over to the force driving me.

"Astraea!" Cassia's urgency sliced through me, and only then did sensation return to my skin. "You're in shock, but I *need* you to hold it together until we get out of here."

"There will be an alert soon," Zathrian said. "I'm going to stop as many of them as I can. Take her with you."

That command registered dully, along with Zath's first steps away. "Don't leave," I said—a pathetic ask after all he'd risked for me, but he couldn't put himself in danger again.

"You're free now, Astraea," he said softly.

Zath strode away, and my first step after him was stopped by a hook around my elbow. Snapping my head around, my argument didn't escape when I beheld the fierce urgency on Cassia's face. She took my hand, and I was about to let her lead me out of the manor when I stopped suddenly.

"I need something. I'll be quick. Please, Cassia. I'll meet you in the woods in five minutes."

"It surely can't be worth the risk. This whole manor will be coming for you in less than that."

"We've risked ourselves enough," Calix argued, shooting me a look of agitation I couldn't react to. "Let's go, Cassia. She'll meet us, and if not, we've done enough."

Though it stung to hear, I was grateful for Calix's harshness this time. Cassia's jaw worked with reluctance, but I turned and sprinted with all the stealth I'd mastered through these halls.

Bursting into my rooms, I rushed into the closet where I'd stashed the satchel. I couldn't leave without my medication, especially not knowing exactly what it was yet to find more. I stuffed myself into boots, knowing my outfit was too elaborate for an escape, but that I had no time to change. I slung on a thick navy cloak.

My steps out of the room stumbled when I heard the shouting. Then the pounding of footsteps that grew louder before wild faces came into view, and I gasped, whirling back as they called my name.

I slammed the doors shut, frantically searching for *anything*.

The dresser chair.

I dragged it, jamming it under the handles.

The brutes outside battered into it, and I leaped back, heart lodging in my throat.

To my mercy, the balcony doors remained unlocked. The bitter air nipped at my cheeks, the snow already melted, and come nightfall I imagined the wet stone would be ice with the temperature.

Hastily, I climbed onto the stone railing, recalling the few maneuvers I'd used the first time, but like the last, I panicked, clutching the same ledge.

"Jump," Nyte said, his voice fluttering in my chest like a reprieve I had no right to with the mystery he remained.

A loud bang of splintering wood left me no choice to even check if he was real or not. I closed my eyes as I let go, cutting through the air for mere seconds before I met the ground, surprisingly on my feet. My hands clutched Nyte regardless.

He didn't release me. My lids snapped opened as I was pulled lightly, but my protest was smothered by his hand. My mind scattered to the other one that had slipped under my cloak, brushing over my abdomen while my back was pressed to his front.

Nyte uncovered my mouth, and I was close to choking on my pulse at the voices on the balcony we stood under.

"What a thrilling evening," he remarked.

"Why are you helping me?" I breathed, bewildered by his reappearance.

"We still have a deal to bind—I can't have you dying now."

So that was real. I tried to process what he'd said. "You didn't bind it?"

I should have felt his chuckle, but I only heard the low amusement. "No. I need something else from you for that. But I wanted to be sure of your willingness before I helped you any further."

I turned, but he kept me flush to him. His finger pressed to my lips while his gold eyes flicked up. I had the urge to bite, but as if sensing it, his hand dropped while his mouth curled.

"I could cross you."

"I could make you regret that."

What am I thinking?

"Are you a vampire?"

That made his smile falter. It smoothed to dark indifference. "You already know more about me than you should."

"You're the one who keeps showing up, yet you did not harm me when you could have done."

"You seem to have a habit of finding yourself in difficult situations."

"I didn't ask for your help."

We stared off, the growing intensity sparking my realization of how intimately close we were. I pushed off him.

"Is this what your kind does—stalk their prey?"

"Until you shed your sheep's clothing, it would seem so."

"If you're not going to take my soul, this gains you nothing."

"I am highly entertained. The most I have been in *many* years."

"My life is not an *amusement*," I hissed.

The pause between us made me contemplate my brazenness when he could end me any second. He stood tall and powerful, and I had to remember my dangerous magnet of attraction to him was a trap.

"No, not to anyone again." His voice softened with his cooling eyes. "It is your own now, as it should have always been."

"You don't know anything."

He studied the sky for a brief second with a long sigh.

My attention roved over him. "So you aren't immune to the cold." It wasn't much of a gain to figuring him out, but I observed his winter cloak nonetheless.

The corner of Nyte's mouth tugged. "I crave your warmth as much as you do mine."

My cheeks flamed. "I don't want anything from you."

He gave a barely-there nod as if he approved. "I don't need to take your soul, Starlight." He took one step forward, and I couldn't be sure what it was about him that didn't trigger my instincts as it should. His fingers hummed across my temple, and I became entranced by the beauty of him searching me. Tucking the wild strand of silver hair behind my ear, his voice dropped to a gravelly whisper. "And no matter what happens, or what you feel, you should never give it to me."

I took a breath. A blink. A *hesitation*. "We won't have to worry about that," I breathed.

"Astraea."

The hiss of my name made me whirl away from his touch. Cassia waved at me frantically while keeping cover behind the trees in the distance with Calix. I knew from the loneliness that had begun to embrace me that Nyte was gone. I didn't even look to confirm it as I jogged toward them and broke through the tree line.

I couldn't decide why I yearned to remain a while longer in his presence, nor why my mind settled, but I was sure it would not be the last time.

10

We didn't stop for anything, racing through the forest then slowing when we merged into a town to avoid being seen.

Pressed against an alley wall, Cassia turned to me with a deadly focus. "I need to be back at the Keep for the send-off. Stay with Calix. I'll meet you down the road out of the city soon." She forced a smile, and I could only imagine the frightened child I must look to her.

I nodded, trying to pull myself together with even a shred of the confidence Cassia radiated.

Exchanging one look with the guard, Cassia nodded to him in a silent language I would never understand.

"Let's go," Calix grumbled to me, hooking my arm as Cassia took off.

I shrugged out of his hold but said nothing, following his command until we came to a wide road crammed with bodies. The people's excitement filled my senses. My breathing became labored at the thought of squeezing between them. Some looked to Calix, offering respect upon seeing his uniform and moving out of his path where there was space to do so. He didn't keep track of me, and I rushed to keep up before any gap could form between us.

Compelled to look back, my horror spiked.

"Keep up," Calix said, low to my ear, and his annoyance was clear.

"It's Hektor's men," I mumbled, watching the brute forces charging through the masses.

Women with blonde hair or those with hoods up were spun around as they searched for me with no degree of respect. Calix swore, and this time I allowed him to pull me along, tripping over myself, but he added a speed I had no choice but to match. My heart raced, bringing on dizzy spells, and I couldn't catch my breath. I couldn't go back there. I *wouldn't* go back there.

Hektor was dead, and I could only imagine with a churning in my stomach the revenge his lethal followers would take on me.

"Hood up, Astraea," Calix reprimanded.

I shook myself for being so flustered and not thinking straight. As we came to the end of the tightest cluster, I stuffed all my silver hair into my hood. Bodies tapered off, and we headed away from the direction the majority of the town skipped toward.

An arm hooked around my middle, its owner so tall and built he took me off my feet, and I cried out.

"Did you think you could get away, girl?" he snarled.

Calix drew his sword but didn't brace to fight. I locked eyes with him in terror, but his own were conflicted. His eyes scanned at least three men from the pattern of his observation. And he stayed silent.

"There is nothing Hektor prized more than you. I think it's about time you tell us why," another said, leaning in so close I felt his breath on my ear.

I was a frightened deer too spooked to move, and I was without the dagger Cassia had taken from me. "I don't know why," I whispered, but they would not believe me.

The one who held me took one step back, clutching me tight, and all I could do was silently plead to Calix—though I had no right to ask for his help against three men. His fist flexed around his sword; his jaw worked. Calculating . . . or *debating*.

It was over.

The sound of choking filled my ears as his hold on me relaxed enough that I could seize my chance. I reached deep within myself to drag forth the desire to survive. To fight for the life and freedom I deserved. My hand wrapped around a dagger in his belt, and as I whirled away I turned and pinned him with the point.

I didn't need to as the three men fell to their knees. The sight of the bloodied arrow tip through each of their chests churned my stomach. Silence pierced me as I looked around for my savior, but all I found were lingering humans with mouths wide as though they were screaming, but I could not hear them.

Nyte didn't reveal himself, and maybe I would never know if it was him who'd saved me. I wanted him to speak to my mind, but it was silent. Even as I glanced again at the bodies and felt nothing at the sight of death.

I turned to Calix, and we stared off for a long moment. He looked at me as if *I* had killed them, eyes wide with confusion and maybe an inkling of fear. I didn't know what to say to him when all that flashed within me was the moment I would never forget—a second where I hadn't been certain he wouldn't let them take me.

"Let's go," I said, surprised by my own calm and how my feet obeyed.

I didn't look back.

Calix hung back from me for some time. I didn't care, powering ahead and only waiting for the moment he would tell me to stop or where to go. The incident with Hektor's men wouldn't stop replaying in my mind, though not for the reasons I expected.

I wanted to know if Nyte had been there, and occasionally my sight strayed as if I would catch something that might give him away. A stroke of darkness through the trees or a note of mint on the wind.

"I'm sorry I wasn't quicker to react." Calix broke the silence at last.

I almost huffed a laugh. "No need to apologize. It would have saved you my intolerable company for however long we are to venture for."

"It wasn't because of that. I just . . . There were a lot of them."

I didn't point out I'd seen him emerge triumphant in combat against four men. Though he seemed to know his own words were bullshit.

"You're nothing but a danger to her."

I did laugh then, lacking any humor. "You're right," I said, and I stopped walking to face him. "But you are also wrong, Calix. Cassia is my friend, and I am hers, though it seems you've never understood what that means. I would lay down my life for her—perhaps faster than you."

I knew the remark would earn the glare of defense that hardened his features. "What did you do back there?" His tone turned accusatory.

"You were watching me the whole time."

"Someone killed those men."

"What are you implying?"

"Who are you, Astraea? All this time since you barged into Cassia's life she might have been content with your secrets, but I am not."

"I don't have secrets," I hissed.

"Hektor?"

"She knew about him."

"But not his treatment of you."

"Because look what happened!" My chest heaved and my eyes pricked with shame. "I knew my life with him wasn't conventional. I loved him. I *thought* I loved him. Yet I also thought his cruelty was kindness. He kept me safe."

"From what?"

"Everything. I—I don't know."

Calix shook his head, and my cheeks heated in embarrassment.

"Think what you want of me. I don't need your approval."

Finally, his features began to soften. My fists clamped tight, fingernails digging into my palms, because I would not show that my trembling insecurity had been provoked by him.

"I wish I could be sorry," he admitted. "But I will always put Cassia's safety above anything, no matter what it makes me seem to you or anyone else."

My shoulders relaxed with the common ground we stood on. I couldn't take his distaste for me personally when I resonated with him on that despite everything.

The rattle of wheels across stone alerted us both, and I turned to spy the carriage in the distance. We watched it approach, but just before it could stop Calix crept up close to me.

"You have only ever been a danger to her."

I couldn't swallow past the marble growing in my throat, but I smiled at the carriage when the door was flung open and Cassia's bright grin greeted us through it. With the echoes of Calix's words, accepting her hand inspired a twinge of selfishness. I wouldn't let him drive us apart.

"How was the send-off?" I asked, settling in close by her side when Calix sat opposite her. I refused to let his face dampen my rising mood.

Cassia groaned, and I chuckled. "Wildly over-the-top. As though it doesn't only add pressure to the situation."

I squeezed her arm but had no words of comfort for where we were heading.

"How are you holding up?" she asked, twisting on the bench to give me her full attention.

I mirrored her. Her question threatened to bring too much to the surface at once. Things I didn't want to confront right now. "Can we talk about something else?"

Cassia gave a knowing smile with her nod. She drew back her cloak, working on a buckle before extending the sheathed dagger to me.

My eyes lit up at the sight of the black wings.

"You haven't given it a name," Cassia mused as I took it.

Fixing the holster to my thigh, I hummed. "I didn't know it needed one."

"All great blades have a name. Right, Calix?"

Maybe it was childish of me to refuse to look at him and busy myself with a buckle instead, but his last words to me were still branded deep, and I knew I'd see them on repeat in his eyes.

"For warriors, yes."

I ground my teeth.

"Then Astraea's should have one," Cassia chirped.

I flashed her a look of surprise and blushed. "I'm hardly that," I muttered.

"Not in that clothing," Cassia observed.

I fixed my cloak to cover my ruined white gown again. "There was hardly the time to consider better options."

"We'll get you something more fitting in the first town."

I nodded gratefully, and though her voice always soothed me with the only safety and comfort I knew . . . I wanted silence. For time to still for a moment so I could face what I had done. All that I had run from.

Looking out the small window, I eased over to it, leaning my head against the velvet side and watching the glow of twilight spill across the passing trees. I stared through them, but flashes of the soulless I'd encountered skipped my pulse, so instead I watched the rolling clouds as exhaustion crept up to me. But I wanted to witness the stars awakening.

"I'm glad you're here, Astraea," Cassia said softly.

My brow pinched. "I'm glad you came."

I didn't know how much time had passed when I gave over to a moment of rest. The carriage jostled steadily, but it was dark—I could tell from the fluttering of my heavy lids.

"She could have gotten you killed," Calix said quietly.

"You're afraid of the Libertatem. Don't take that out on her, please. I need you both."

"Cass . . ." He breathed her name with a soft yearning I'd never heard before.

I peeked again and found them sitting intimately close. Cassia's palm met his cheek, and at the same time they leaned for each other. I clamped my eyes shut when they kissed. My body grew hot, my presence an intrusion on their intimacy, and I tried to tune them out.

My chest clenched for them. I wished for them to be happy, yet despite them having the freedom to give in to each other out here, we all knew the clock was ticking. Moments together were to be treasured, and I was glad they were making them count at least.

I wanted to look outside, to glance up at the night and find my own peace, but I kept still and silent, feigning sleep. Instead I found my mind slowly flooding with midnight swirls and starlit pools. I nestled contentedly into the corner of the carriage as a slow, familiar song joined the tango of constellations, and soon I was dancing with them.

11

The town we had stopped in came alive by midday. I tried to follow a craving triggered by a sweet cinnamon scent, only to be distracted by earthy florals that attracted me to a different stall. In my exhilaration I could hardly decide where I wanted to go in the market labyrinth.

"I knew you couldn't come to the Keep often, but I didn't realize just how locked up Hektor kept you," Cassia commented. Our arms were looped together, but often my excitement strained our connection, and we giggled as we walked through the stalls.

"He wanted to keep me safe. I was well provided for."

Cassia arched a brow. "You don't need to defend that piece of shit anymore."

My mouth opened, only to close with the realization that was what I'd been doing, and that I'd come close to repeating myself in different words. Was I really defending Hektor? I couldn't be sure when all I wanted was to wipe the pity from Cassia's eyes. It doused me with the shame that I'd spent so long in denial when I could've been breaking free from him.

"His asshole personality suited his looks," she said, pulling me along the road. "You can do better, and you deserve so much more."

I had to wonder what Cassia saw in me to say such things. More so, I wanted to agree but couldn't find what it was within myself that smothered my confidence with cowardice.

I finally spotted the source of the cinnamon scent as it grew stronger. It was rare to come by the spice traded from the northern kingdom of Astrinus. I delighted at the pastry stall until I remembered I had no coin. I could just look, but as I took my first step forward Cassia's grip steered me the opposite way.

"After," she said, her voice kicking up with excitement. I followed her line of sight to what had caught her attention: a small shop selling fabrics. "We need to get you something proper to wear."

"I have no money," I admitted.

She didn't answer me, only pausing to throw Calix an instruction over her shoulder to wait for us outside. He grumbled his reluctance, and I cringed at their quick back-and-forth, feeling in the middle until the overprotective guard agreed.

The bell chimed above our heads, and the interior of the shop expanded farther than I expected. So many colors exploded before me, different fabrics and styles, and I was so swept away by the wonder of it all I didn't feel Cassia slipping away from me. My fingers brushed over lace and silk, some formed into various garments and others long strips just waiting for a creative mind to craft them into something beautiful.

Toward the back of the shop I was drawn not to anything of vibrancy; the stark blacks and leather materials inspired a thrill. Some were matte, some textured with scales, some with hints of color, and my fingers skimmed over a leather corset with deep purple embroidery I thought to be alluringly dangerous.

"Great choice," Cassia sang behind me.

I stepped away from the combat wears. "I was just looking."

"You would suit it. I've never seen you in fighting attire."

"I have no need for it."

"You think I didn't pick up on how often you would ask about mine back at the Keep?" she teased, twisting around me and picking up the corset I'd been admiring. "I love a pretty dress, but it's comfortable and empowering to wear leathers every now and then."

"We're heading to the Central. I should be in something more presentable." I hadn't failed to notice the expensive elegance of Cassia's gown. The gold and blue radiated against her skin, and her hair was styled in elaborate braids that made her appear nothing less than royalty.

Cassia huffed her agreement and dragged me back over to the dresses, where an eager seamstress stood waiting with a measuring tape.

At least an hour passed, and I didn't know the last time I'd laughed so much, but Cassia drew it out effortlessly as I tried on multiple gowns.

"We're going to the Central, not to a funeral."

I admired the black gown embellished with silver I'd picked. "I like it."

"How about something brighter?" The seamstress came over with bundles in her arms.

"Not white," I said a bit too quickly.

"The black is perfect," said Cassia, snapping me back to my present surroundings. Her hand ran over my bare arm, turning curious as she examined my silver tattoos. "If we can't find out who your parents are, perhaps there will be more answers to what these could mean."

"They mean nothing," I mumbled with a note of bitterness I took from Hektor.

The seamstress maneuvered around me with various dark silks to fashion removable sleeves for the cold.

"Did you ever ask him?"

"Yes," I said in a huff of frustration. "Hektor said he couldn't find anything about where I'd come from after he found me. He told me he'd exhausted many resources trying."

"And you believed him?"

"How could I not?" I realized immediately my response was not for Cassia but myself. I swallowed, knowing my excuse was pitiful. "I should have fought harder for myself," I reflected quietly.

"You're the most resilient person I know, Astraea. Don't discredit yourself, or his manipulation still holds you."

I gave her a smile when I couldn't agree. My skin itched as if Hektor's hold remained there as something physical, and I forced down the bout of fear that no matter how far I ran it would never let me go.

Cassia said, "I think he knew more about you than he let on."

"It doesn't matter now." *He's dead.* They were the words I couldn't speak.

Not wanting to talk of it, I picked out a new black-and-silver cloak and gloves.

"We're not giving up looking for answers for you," Cassia said carefully, heading to the payment desk. "How can you expect to grow a future if you don't know the steps you've already taken?"

Memory stole me from the shop with chilling clarity. How fast I had run, how the cold air had wrapped around me, and the terror in my chest that had never fully left. "If there's one thing I do remember, it's that the only way to outrun a monster is to never look back."

Her eyes spoke of agreement. As I watched her hand over coin for everything new I owned, I didn't know how I could ever repay such a sum. I had nothing, not even while living in the manor draped in fine wears.

"You and Calix," I said, needing the distraction from myself. The color that flushed Cassia's cheeks made me bite my lip to suppress a squeal. "Had you kissed before?"

Her blush rose with her wide eyes as she hooked my arm. "Yes."

I gasped. "You didn't tell me!"

"Shh."

We burst into quiet giggles in the corner of the store, knowing the guard was right outside.

"It was only a week before you last arrived at the Keep, and then he was with us the whole time. I didn't have the chance."

"Have you slept with him?"

"No. But I can't deny I want to. I think I love him, Astraea. I think I have for some time, but with the future so uncertain . . ."

There was that word. Love. So obscure to me I wanted to know how she was certain of its touch. I took her hands. "You should enjoy every second." Though I didn't have a great friendship with Calix and was quite sure he'd rather I were gone no matter what became of me, I was thrilled for my friend.

Cassia nodded, grateful.

As we headed out I could hardly suppress my grin. Meanwhile, Cassia adopted a rare shyness, barely able to look at Calix.

Only when the stars started to come out did we realize we'd spent the whole day perusing stalls.

"You won't make a great impression on the king if we arrive late," Calix enlightened us.

I was riding a freedom high, on no countdown to return to the manor, with no lingering fear that I'd be discovered, and trying not to think of Hektor at all as I despised the guilt still settling within. We hadn't intended for this stop to last so long, but we couldn't help stretching out our carefree hours.

"We'll pick up pace to compensate. It will be fine," Cassia said to him, leaning into his side, and I unhooked my arm from hers to give her some space.

As they admired a stall of small weaponry, I found my sights drifting away and decided to give them a moment alone while I wandered over to another merchant. I looked over the small boxes, each one beautifully crafted with burned designs, and was immediately drawn to one that looked familiar. I had to refrain from lifting my sleeve; the waxing moon phases on the black box were exact to those marked in silver on my forearm. Then, above them, the same phases waning.

Unlatching the hook, I found inside a small barrel with scattered metal studs. My fingers skimmed over a lever on its side, and I turned it. My eyes lit up as notes floated from the tiny invention, unable to understand the mechanics, but it was then I understood magick could be created. People could give stars a sound, and each one raised gooseflesh on my skin, the pitch like pinpricks. The speed of the melody depended on my turns, and I became wondrously entranced by the song.

"Do you enjoy music, Starlight?"

The box jerked in my hands, but I clutched it tight to keep it from slipping. "Why must you do that?" I hissed without looking.

The man behind the counter finally turned, eyeing me and my surroundings suspiciously.

"Do what?"

"Show up so unexpectedly."

Featherlight fingers grazed my chin, flickers of shadow crossed my vision, and my head turned at his phantom guide. "How might you like me to announce myself?"

Those golden eyes had started to become a beacon of attraction.

"You have an intrusive habit of touching me."

"You have an inquisitive will to allow it." He dropped his hand slowly. "Maybe you even desire it."

Nyte had so far never failed to fluster me, but I was learning to suppress my reactions. His mouth twitched as though he knew.

"The shadows," I said. "Do you command them?"

"Some things are far more thrilling to be felt rather than told."

My lips parted. I could have sworn a touch eased around my nape, and I had to place my own hand there to be sure.

"I must say, darkness suits you so." He trailed his gaze over my attire, and I stifled a shiver.

"Why are you here?"

"Can I help you, ma'am?" The man behind the counter came closer, eyeing the space beside me warily. He didn't react with the terror I expected, and I wondered if vampires walked more casually around the humans than I thought.

Remembering the box I held, I said, "This song is beautiful."

When he saw what had grabbed my interest his furrowed brow eased to a bright eagerness. "Ah, she's one of my best compositions. I call her 'Ballad of the Soul Gods,' inspired by the Faelestial War."

"Soul gods?"

"You do not know the tales, child?"

I had the urge to correct him, but my lack of knowledge of our history shrank me to the young and inexperienced persona despite my twenty-three years.

"A tragically poetic story," Nyte mused.

The man didn't react at all.

I asked, "The celestials are real?"

"Of course."

The more people who confirmed this to me, the more my mind soared free to picture them.

"Ask him what happened to the *soul gods*."

I flashed Nyte a look as his tone dropped darkly. "Why don't you ask?"

He only gave an amused half-smile.

I scowled. "What happened at the end of the war?"

"The gods battled, and they say they nearly destroyed each other and the world in their wake. Unfortunately for us, the vampires won, and the celestials hid themselves to avoid annihilation beyond the veil."

"The king . . . he is a god?"

The man's shrug revealed his next words would be guesswork. "Perhaps not him, but the one the people feared for a long time until he turned silent. The king lacks influence without the one they called *Nightsdeath,* and if you ask me, it is why the vampires are getting out of control without their fear of him."

I wasn't sure why I slid Nyte a look; all it did was drop the temperature further when I noticed his expression of wrath and sin. This man's tale aligned with Cassia's, and something about Nyte's reaction told me it was important.

"Darkness is growing," the man continued. He glanced skyward, to the stars, and I was compelled to follow. My pulse skipped. "And people seem to forget the hope that comes to see it again."

"You believe the stars are dying . . ." I trailed off, speaking more to myself as I tracked the growing expanse. It was something I had thought of before, so to have someone else see it was the first flicker of confirmation that I was right.

"I do. And it is a terrifying thing, what must come for our salvation if the star-maiden has indeed returned."

I'd never had my interest seized so wholly. No—it didn't feel as simple as that. What unsettled me made my hands tremble and nudged at something in my mind that only grew frustrated to be rattled and not opened. Potentially a memory. I needed to hear more.

"When falls Night, the world will drown in Starlight," Nyte said so quietly I had to look to be sure he'd spoken.

"What do you know of it?" I asked him.

When our eyes met, something pulled within me. The firmness of his face was broken only by the note of sorrow that turned his irises a shining amber.

"My dear, who are you speaking to?" The man snapped my attention back.

Brow furrowed, I was about to state the obvious when Cassia became the second person to startle me, near knocking the beautiful box from my grip again. As much as I wanted to hold onto it, Cassia had already spent far more coin than I could ever repay. Before she could offer to purchase the box, I set it down, letting my longing gaze linger on the twin moon phases.

"We'll have to get rest in the carriage to keep to schedule," Cassia said. Her arm looped through mine, and I whirled to Nyte. He was gone, of course. But as I smiled at the stallkeeper, I couldn't rest my confusion at his last words.

"We should be able to stop tomorrow night for a proper bed," Calix said as we made our way back to the road.

I squeezed Cassia's arm. "A proper bed, huh?"

She caught onto my meaning immediately, eyes widening at me while she suppressed her smile and led us a few quickened paces ahead of the guard. "Astraea," she drawled. "I didn't expect teasing from you about bedroom affairs."

"And why not?"

"You never spoke of yours." She looked to me as if she'd made an error, but I shrugged, finding the confidence to speak openly now that I would never go back. I didn't need to convince myself of the opposite of what I was about to confess.

"Things with Hektor were fine at first. We weren't intimate until around a year after we met. Then soon it became routine, but I wasn't the only one he took pleasure from."

Cassia gave a disgruntled sound. "I wish he were still alive so I could take a stab at him myself."

I couldn't respond to that. My fist flexed with the muscle memory of pushing my dagger through his chest. "Was it monstrous . . . ?" I feared to ask. "How easily I took his life?"

"It's not easy when it haunts you still," Cassia said. "But he should have known a leash has two ends and it was only a matter of time before you strangled him with it."

I huffed a laugh, but there was no humor to it. It was only an attempt to let her words sink my rising uncertainty about myself.

"But no, it was incredibly brave what you did, Astraea. If it makes me monstrous to think that, I'm glad there's two of us."

12

We suffered through a night in our awkward sleeping arrangement, jostled by the carriage's movements until we stopped at an inn in the next town. I said nothing about the unfairness of Cassia having Calix to lean against for comfort. They shared a room two floors down from mine, the only remaining vacancies the establishment had.

I paced restlessly around my own room. It wasn't anything other than the night that kept me awake, but I glanced out the small box window often to track the stars by habit. I was considering leaving the room, having not changed out of my gown or even taken off my boots, when a soft knock made me jump.

The door creaked open, but I relaxed as soon as I saw the familiar head of sleek black hair. Cassia beamed at me upon finding me awake. She didn't enter fully; instead she thrust out her hand, and though it was concealed in a rag, the sloshing when she wiggled it told me she held what had to be some kind of alcohol.

"I can't sleep either. Come on," she whispered loudly.

Her grin made my giddiness break through. I didn't care where she planned to go as I slung on my cloak and followed her out. We slipped through a door that startled my nerves to pass, the words STAFF ONLY: DO NOT ENTER written on it, which Cassia seemed oblivious to. Then we walked up a narrow staircase until we exited onto a flat stretch of the roof that glittered with a coat of frost.

"Is this really a good idea?" I asked, hugging my cloak tighter while my breath blew out in clouds.

Cassia giggled, wedging something into the door to keep it from locking us out. "Probably not, but I don't really care."

I couldn't help but join her in her soft amusement.

Cassia slipped, catching her balance, and my own footing skidded as I jerked toward her. We laughed at how clumsy the ice made our steps, and began to slide on purpose, until the air speared our lungs and the night was alive with the sounds of our joy.

We slumped down, catching our breath from our childish antics. Cassia had fortunately managed to keep her stolen liquor safe. I wasn't thrilled with the whiskey that had always been Hektor's preferred drink, but I longed for the effects it could bring to pass the night and take the cold away.

Cassia took the first long drink, and I winced with her before she held it out to me.

"How did you slip out from Calix?" I asked. The liquid burned every second it was in my throat, but I swallowed several gulps.

"He sleeps like the dead, thankfully."

"Did you two . . . ?" I tried to be subtle, but I couldn't help my grin.

Cassia flushed, pushing me sideward and swiping the bottle. She took another drink before answering. "Not all the way, but we did . . . things." She set the bottle down, burying her face in her gloved hands like she didn't know how to talk of it. "With his hands, and his *mouth*. Stars above, I didn't know people could *do* things like that."

I bit my lip, thrilled by her excitement. "I can't believe you went this long without giving in to him. He's been pining after you for years."

Something fell in her expression, and I wanted to retract what I'd said, but she was quick to brush it away. "I want it to be right. And an inn on the way to the Central isn't exactly *romantic*. Maybe it's silly after all this time, but I want it to be perfect."

My hand reached for hers. "It's not silly at all." Sighing, I pulled my hood up to lie against the slanted side of the roof. "None of it matters if the feelings aren't there. You've had that to treasure with him for far longer than sex."

Cassia joined me in lying back. "You didn't . . . ?" she asked carefully.

"I don't know what I had with Hektor. I knew that it was safe and that I had a lot of figuring out to do before I could face the world without his help. He told me he loved me often; I said it back, and sometimes I truly believed it. I wanted life with him to work after all he'd done for me, but he would always be cruel. Now I don't think I'll ever say that word again. Love. Because I'm scared to think of him with it."

"I should have seen it sooner," Cassia said.

I shook my head, mapping the stars with no hard feelings. "It wasn't your job to see it, and I didn't want you to. I was planning to leave him eventually. I just needed more time, and that's why I didn't agree to go with you. I didn't want you implicated in that escape plan when I knew he would come after me."

Cassia sat up abruptly, swiping the bottle and taking several swigs before holding it out to me. "To the death of that bastard. And to your bravery for breaking free."

I didn't think I deserved her praise, but I accepted the offering. The burn of alcohol began to numb, and I wasn't certain how much more I drank before I set it down panting.

"Now, if only I could get my damn memories back," I said. My balance swayed a little as I got to my feet. "Maybe if I'd had a better lover in the past I could even exchange scandalous bedroom affairs with you now."

Cassia planted her hands on her hips, slipping as she got to her feet, and I giggled. "He didn't even satisfy in the bedroom? Stars, I hate him!" she yelled skyward.

"Shh . . ." I slipped and skated over to her, the air becoming an infusion of our laughter and alcohol. "We can't hate on the dead—they might come back to haunt us," I said.

Cassia huffed, reaching into her cloak and fiddling with something for longer than necessary with the effects of the whiskey. She unclipped the belt of six small daggers, taking three before holding the others out to me.

"Precarious heights and very sharp implements don't pair well with whiskey," I commented, but I took the remaining knives anyway.

"I figured we could both use a release," she said. Finding a discarded wine crate, she sloppily set it up across the roof.

"Sounds like you got plenty of that tonight already."

Cassia gaped at me, and it was too easy not to enjoy the teasing. It drifted all our burdens afar. "Fair point," she said, composing herself and taking an expert stance.

Knife throwing was a particular favorite sport. I'd tried swords, but they never felt right compared to the lightweight precision of daggers. Despite her impairment from the liquor, Cassia's first knife lodged into the wine crate with perfect accuracy.

"If there's one thing you're not allowed to give up on, it's love, Astraea. That's a demand."

I threw my own blade, and it hit close to hers. "I didn't say I'd given up. I love you, don't I?"

"I don't just mean platonic love," she amended.

I groaned, rolling my eyes. "What's it good for anyway? Lust can be satisfied without such things that only serve to trick or make one vulnerable."

"Just promise me you won't stop believing it's out there for you." She turned to me after letting go of her second blade.

My brow arched at her seriousness, and I used my next throw to distract myself from the unease that threatened my growing buzz. "I'm sure you won't let that happen," I mused.

"I'm not always going to be here."

My arm dropped at her sudden change of tone. I couldn't look at her, barely able to keep my lip from wobbling.

The crack of a whip against stone made us both whirl around. It came from over the edge.

"Hurry up!" a man hissed.

I copied Cassia's stealth to crouch and observe the commotion. Finding a large cage on wheels, I nearly gasped at the forms being forced inside. It looked to be something crafted for animals, but these were people, albeit like none I had seen before.

"They're fae," Cassia said with an air of wonder.

The term pricked my interest, faint knowledge trickling in, but it was overshadowed by the sorry sight of them. I couldn't understand why they were being *herded*. Some had dark skin, others pale, plus some beautiful shades in between, and they could've almost passed for human if it weren't for their pointed ears. Except some had particularly mesmerizing traits. A tall, slim male wrapped a tail around his lower leg to prevent it from being stepped on. Another petite female had small horns peeking out of short black hair. They all kept their heads bowed, submitting to the voice of authority that threatened punishment if they didn't enter the iron wagon.

"I wasn't sure if it was true," Cassia said quietly. Her brow firmed with calculated anger as she watched them. "People see the fae so rarely that many believed they were extinct with the celestials."

I had certainly never seen them, only in fairy tales—or those I had thought to be. "Where are they taking them?" I dreaded to ask.

The man with the whip cast his eyes up, and we ducked lower on instinct.

"To the Central," Cassia said. "I guess it's true. They used to say the king enlisted all fae to join his army after the Faelestial War and they were to re-side in the Central. They have earthbound abilities. From the Mother Deity. They weren't weakened by the quake centuries ago—that only affected the solar magick the celestials depend on."

"They're being forced," I said, though it was an obvious observation.

"Not all of them. But the fae were great allies with the celestials. There were those who believed in the King of the Gods and joined him. Others resisted, and they were said to be hunted, given one last chance at *mercy,* and if they didn't bend to him they were killed."

"Stop, please!" a woman wailed.

My pulse spiked as we lifted ourselves enough to look over the edge again. I wanted to tell her to stop as I watched her run straight toward the vampire holding the whip, but it wasn't he who halted her. A hand went over my mouth before I could gasp, and Cassia held me. Wings swooped down, near blending into the night, but the moon revealed a leathery texture as they landed.

Nightcrawlers.

"I'll be okay!" a younger female fae cried, sobbing as she was pushed into the carriage. Her hair was the tone of honey, a beautiful mix of brown and blonde in a high braided ponytail against a fair complexion.

I strained against Cassia. *Stars,* I wouldn't be much help, and it was a fool's impulse, but watching them felt so damn helpless it was tearing me up inside.

Cassia removed the hand from my mouth.

"Please," the woman tried again. She was human, and I wondered if that was her daughter as something felt so heart-wrenchingly maternal about her plea.

"This is all the more reason to win the Libertatem," Cassia said with a low, lethal edge. "Not just win but destroy it. They would be safe from this barbaric round-up too if there weren't vampires here to carry it out."

Cassia had never seen her position as a burden. The bravery in her desire to become the people's savior would never fail to strike me with powerful pride.

"She will serve the true king, or she will die," the soulless leader sang cruelly.

"No—!"

I lurched back in horror at witnessing the nightcrawler lunge for her, head angled for her neck, but it wasn't her scream that pierced the night. It was the younger fae's. My blood turned to ice with it and my heart cracked. The fae tried to exit the wagon, but the iron bars slammed closed sharply.

"We have to do something," I breathed.

Helpless. I was so useless and helpless to them.

Cassia knew it. "We'd only get ourselves killed and lose our only real chance if we don't make it to the Central."

The fae girl clung to the bars as she cried. I wanted to hold her, comfort her, and tear her eyes away from the gruesome sight she was locked onto. The soulless cracked the whip against the iron, making me wince, and the carriage jolted forward.

The nightcrawler let go with a guttural moan and my stomach heaved.

We slumped out of view against the slanted part of the roof, and my breaths blew clouds against the bitter temperature as I tried to calm myself. This was real, this world of monsters I'd ventured out into as someone vulnerable and out of her depth. Cassia took my hand, and I squeezed back. She was all that was keeping me safe and grounded when I didn't know how the hell I'd ever survive the lurking terrors on my own.

She swiped the bottle of whiskey and took a long drink until she panted, extending it out to me. I took it eagerly, needing to erase the cries that echoed in my ears even after the rolling wheels of the carriage were long gone.

Standing, I flipped my final knife then threw it.

Cassia eased a smile. "At least I've made my mark on you," she commented, watching the blade soar to hit the center of the box.

"I'm glad you pestered me into it."

"It wasn't like you took much coaxing. You're practically a natural with the blades and a bow. You picked up the same skill level in three years as I did my whole life."

I shrugged. "I wouldn't say the *same* level."

Cassia's final dagger hit a little off to the left. She huffed. "You're right. Sometimes better."

I waved her off. "You've had more to drink."

As I said it, Cass swiped the bottle again, holding it up to me with a devilish smirk before she brought it to her lips. Then she squinted at the bottle, tipping it upside down to be sure it was empty.

"We probably shouldn't have drunk it all—" A hiccup escaped me, and we broke into quiet giggles that made the grim event we'd witnessed easier to deal with.

My face fell as I glanced one last time over the side of the building. All was still. Yet the speck on the ground that could have been mistaken for a crate reminded me a life had been taken and discarded as no more than that.

Cassia's backtracking snapped me out of my tunneling sorrow. "Seriously, sometimes it's like you have this whole trove of skills somehow locked away."

"Hardly," I said.

"Except for swordplay."

"Swords are heavy."

"We all have our weaknesses."

"And yours are . . . ?"

Cassia pretended to think long and hard, and I nudged her playfully. "It's cold as shit," she said through chattering teeth. "Come on."

I followed her inside, where clumsily we made it to the main room that hosted nighttime gambling and drinking. It was still thriving.

Cassia was already at the bar ordering a drink while I scanned the establishment carefully. It wasn't as esteemed as Hektor's. The air was heavy with notes of cheap ale and unwashed bodies. The furniture was all wooden and aged. My vision was lagging and sometimes doubling. It had been so long since I'd even come close to being drunk, but I was riding an unexplainable high tonight and could conquer anything.

At a rowdy burst of laughter and jeering, I found a man standing from his seat in frustration and defeat while those around him jostled him playfully. Another seated man rearranged something on the table.

"My prize still stands, lads. Two gold coins if you figure it out."

A tankard was thrust in front of me, and I took it but didn't look away from them.

"What do you think it is?" I asked Cassia.

She squinted over at them. "A game, perhaps."

"A puzzle," a low voice corrected.

I turned to find a tall man with dark brown hair and gleaming brown eyes. My intuition told me not to trust him, and I shuffled closer to Cass, studying what I could of his attire and finding some element of it to be familiar—such as the texture of the leather, almost like layered scales. The form was fitted, and an elegant cloak was clasped at one shoulder.

"You're great at those!" Cassia's cheer stole my observations.

"No, I'm not," I insisted as she tried to drag me away.

"Sure, you are! Remember that time . . ."

Cassia reeled off every memory of us playing cards, games, and figuring out the smallest riddle while she pulled me over to the table. By the time we stood before the men, all attention was on us.

I looked down to see what it was. Matchsticks had been arranged in the shape of a boxy house, and my brow furrowed, my mind already trying to figure it out without hearing the object of the game.

"You ladies want a try?" the older man coaxed.

I surveyed them again, wanting nothing more than to leave at the crawling sensation I'd been here before. But my sights on the puzzle kept me in place.

"She does!" Cassia exclaimed, pulling out the chair and pushing me down onto it.

I could figure it out quickly. Then we would sleep.

The man gave a hearty chuckle that relaxed my nerves around the others. "No one has solved it tonight, girl. Have your try. Move two matches to make five squares. Once you move them, your try is up."

I barely heard the final sentence. The room drifted away as I rearranged the matchsticks over and over in my mind. The noise of the inn faded, and the only thing that took me a few beats longer than necessary was my drunken state.

Picking my two chosen matchsticks off the roof, I crossed them vertically and horizontally, placing them inside the body of the four-matchstick house. I grinned, but when my senses returned it wasn't as rowdy as I remembered. When I looked up, the men were blinking at the table, stunned, though I couldn't understand why. Cassia's squeal beside me jerked my body.

Finally, the man parallel to me began to rumble with laugher, leaning back in his seat. "Drinks for the ladies! They've earned it," he called across the room.

I became rigid with alarm. "Let's go," I said to Cassia.

"Aw, but this is so fun! There must be another one!"

When two small glasses were placed in front of us, my gaze trailed up to the hand that had left them. The brown-haired man fixed eyes of intrigue on me. Then flashes of gold hit the table.

I shook my head. "I don't want your money."

"Something wrong with it?" he challenged.

It seemed to attract the attention of the others, whose eyes roved over me. I realized my error in making them think I was wealthy enough to deny such a prize.

"No. Thank you." I swiped the coin.

Standing, I pulled Cassia up, but before I could guide her away she held the prize drink out to me.

"Cheers!" She clinked her glass against mine, and I couldn't help but search for the brown-haired man. He was nowhere to be seen.

Tipping the burning contents down my throat, I took Cassia's hand, and we left the main room. Once we were out from among the commotion, exhaustion hit hard and fast. The steps felt like a mountain, and I knew we'd overdone it tonight. Our suffering tomorrow would be our punishment.

Cassia didn't go back to Calix. She continued to follow me up the stairs as I cursed the top-floor position. "Did you see their faces?" she laughed into the wall, and watching her roused my own bubble of giggles.

We crawled pathetically upstairs, tumbling into each other and earning various hisses to be quiet from other guests peeking out at the commotion through their doors. I locked mine once we were inside the room. Then we threw ourselves onto the bed, unable to change or even take off our boots. The room tilted nauseatingly.

"You should go back to your overprotective *boyfriend*," I slurred.

"He's not my boyfriend," Cassia said, just as drunk and tired as me. I smiled, getting to tease her back about it now. "And he's certainly not my keeper. I want to stay right here." She patted the bed, and I smiled as my lids slipped shut.

I should take off my shoes. Stars, it had been so long since I'd consumed this much alcohol. The last and only time that surfaced in my memory was when I'd slipped into Hektor's study while he was away. One glass had led to two until I'd consumed the whole bottle and he'd come back to find my sorry state sprawled across his desk. My punishment was to be locked in my room for three days. Now I grinned, darkly joyous at his death since he couldn't ever reprimand me for this again.

"I want to see the world," Cassia said through our peaceful silence. "All five kingdoms competing in the Libertatem. Then Constants Bay, Volantis, the Central, even Althenia."

It was a wonderful thought, to see the whole continent in our lifetime. Maybe Cassia could if she won immortality and joined the Golden Guard.

"Do you think we can cross the veil?" I asked, enjoying the fantasy.

"I think we could convince the celestials to let us through."

"You can be very persuasive."

"Do you remember that time we snuck out to the winter show? We convinced the set coordinator we were sisters of the pianist."

"Yes, though I'm still certain you could have gotten us special tickets by asking your father."

"That would have been no fun!"

While we laughed, notes of sorrow started to weigh on me. I missed those days.

"I like to dance," I said, unsure why I felt like sharing the unimportant secret. I rolled onto my side to get comfortable. "I don't think I've ever told you. Hektor's establishment had many who were gifted at it. They were beautiful to watch."

Cassia faced me, and my lids fluttered open onto her thoughtful expression. "You're beautiful too, Astraea. I can't wait to see you dance. On a stage someday."

13

I couldn't remember the sound I'd drifted off to, nor for how long I'd slept. A creak by the door awoke me. Thinking Cassia had decided to leave for Calix, I rolled onto my side, cursing at the realization I'd fallen asleep fully clothed. I should have at least taken off my boots.

Groaning, I pushed myself up. Rubbing my eyes, I could barely make out the figure by the far end of the bed. Until a choked sound raised every hair on my body and I discovered not one person, but two.

"Cassia." I could barely whisper her name. I tried to lunge up toward her, but I swayed, and something caught me.

Someone.

"Impressive how fast you figured out that riddle."

The hairs on my nape stood. I knew the voice, the locks of brown hair and hazel eyes I would see if I turned, but I only focused on one thing. Cassia.

Crying out, I strained, but his grip was like iron. A heat crept over every inch of me, taking me away from that room—from myself. Desperation took over. I'd never seen Cassia so still, not fighting back.

"It will be over in a moment. Then I'll collect my reward," the man cooed in my ear.

When a cold lick of metal came to rest along my neck . . .

I would never know where my delirious instinct came from.

Reaching in front of me, my hand felt the familiar hilt, not even remembering where I'd last left it in my desperation, only that I'd done this before. My stormstone dagger emerged in my grip from a void of dark starlight, flipping as I drove it through his ribs behind me.

I met my mark.

The man's loud cry rattled my senses, and my adrenaline coursed fast. He fell to his knees, and as I spun, the slick glide of my blade stunned me too late. Blood pooled over his hand where he clutched his neck, and I stumbled back in horror, dropping my dagger. The clamor of it didn't register, only the man's chokes. I couldn't believe the precision of such an attack.

"Cass," I breathed. That all-consuming fear seized me again, making me forget the gruesome way my victim coughed on his own blood in the final seconds of his life. When I turned, I didn't advance, but the dagger I'd swiped soared.

This man let out a shrill sound as I lodged the blade in his back. He let Cassia go, and only then did I see his pointed ears as he released my dearest friend from what I would forever remember as death's kiss. Yet how had he known her name to take part of her soul?

Feral brown eyes turned toward me, and I watched Cassia's body fall to the ground in utter shock and panic, my fight instinct draining away. He managed to reach and pull the dagger free. When he held it, outrage hardened his expression.

"I can't say I'm disappointed I get to kill you instead," he said, tossing my dagger away.

Then he lunged for me.

I cried out at his vise grip on my arms. His eyes snapped to my neck, and panic made me immobile. Sinful fingers traced over the unruly scar, and the soulless . . . he *licked his lips.*

He smiled, revealing two pointed teeth, and I believed I would die today. "Just a taste," he breathed, as if something had overcome him. Vacant eyes wouldn't let go of the claim he'd made on my throat. His lips pulled back, head leaning in . . .

"I said aim for the heart."

I stumbled back as the soulless gave a piercing wail, releasing me. I watched him fall to his knees, body jerking, and as his face hit the ground I found my dagger protruding from his back—on the opposite side from my first strike. A high-pitched ringing filled my ears, and I searched frantically for Nyte, whose voice held such rage and malice I trembled at its echo.

He wasn't here.

Real time crawled back to me, settling the worst dread of my existence. I stayed rooted to the spot, unable to turn around. Until I heard her voice croak.

"Astraea . . ."

My eyes filled when I saw her. My steps were weightless until I gave in to gravity and fell by Cassia's side, the elation of hearing her snuffed out cruelly when I beheld the weak sight. I had never seen her so *scared.* "You'll be all right," I said, trying to be the brave one, but that had never been me. It was always Cassia who made the monsters seem small. Her skin was too pale, her breathing labored in short, wheezing gasps.

"I don't—I—I don't feel good."

Cradling her to my chest, I tucked her hair away with trembling fingers. "You're just in shock, but he let you go. You're going to survive it."

There would be no telling how much time the soulless had stolen from her, but my mind reeled that it was too much. Far too much.

"It doesn't hurt," she said, her voice barely a croak as if it had aged a century. "I'm just tired."

"You can't sleep," I begged.

"I-I'm so glad you came . . ." Cassia's gaze became glassy, staring skyward. Her hand went over mine, and I clutched it tight, though it created another crack in my heart. "I didn't want you to feel alone again."

The splinter deepened, and I bled sorrow and anguish and terrible dread, drowning in my own despair. *This can't be happening.* Her eyes fluttered closed, but I rocked her awake.

"You've never left me alone. Please—you can't leave me now." I broke. I couldn't stop the helpless flood from filling my lungs as I *begged.* "You're all I have."

"I didn't get to tell him . . ." she said.

I blinked furiously to keep every image of her clear.

"He told me he loved me tonight, and I . . . I should have said it back, but I didn't. Can you tell him for me?"

"You're going to tell him yourself, Cass."

"Promise me you'll tell him I love him." Her hand shook as she tried to raise it to my cheek, and I held it there, not feeling the stream of my tears until she brushed them slowly.

"I promise," I whimpered. *No, no, no. Cassia has to live.*

"We need to win, Astraea."

"I need you."

"Do it for me. For all of us."

I shook my head, unable to comprehend what she was saying when my world was close to obliterating.

"It's so cold," she said, eyes drifting shut, and her hand dropped limp in my grasp. She appeared so beautifully peaceful, her skin so perfect and pale, but her chest . . . it was so still.

No. She can't *leave me!*

"Cassia." I shook her, but this time she didn't flinch. "Cassia, wake up." I sniffed and panic seized me tight. I quickly shifted up on my knees, forcing myself to focus, and laid my hand on her chest. It was warm, and I grasped at threads of fleeting hope, feeling a hum beneath my palm. "You're all I have," I kept repeating as if it could breathe life back into her still body.

Light began to glow where I touched, and I wondered if her soul could be returning to her form. The vampire was dead, and perhaps that meant he would give back what had been stolen.

I gasped when the light glowed brighter, breaking through her skin as I lifted my palm. Under my touch, a sphere of white and blue shone with a pulse of energy I became entranced by. "Please come back," I whispered to it, somehow—impossibly—feeling her spirit within it.

"What have you done?"

My fist closed tight as a surge went up my arm and burst in my chest as the light winked out. As if the ordeal had stopped time and was just now snapping back into motion, my eyes fell to find Cassia deathly still in my arms.

Death. The darkest force that rippled with devastation in the wake of every claim.

It slammed into me, shattering everything I was, so much so that I thought I felt it reach out a second hand in offering to me.

"Cass," Calix muttered, his low tone of dread bringing me back to my cruel reality. One that would go on without her, the echoes of death's laughter fading since it wouldn't take me too.

"It was . . ." I couldn't speak. I couldn't look at him in the doorway.

"No." Calix's steps rushing toward us made me hug her tighter in complete denial, knowing he would tear us apart. "Get away from her!" he snarled.

I gave a sharp sob when he gripped my shoulders, trying to pry me away, but I couldn't let go. Then cold metal touched my neck, and if I hadn't been crying so hard I might have asked him to use the blade. It should have been Cassia cradling my body instead.

It should have been *neither* of us.

"Let her go, or so help me, Astraea."

I had never heard such a promising threat from him. My gaze moved over Cassia's face as I blinked back tears of frustration.

This wasn't how it was supposed to be.

Yet she remained so quiet while her voice replayed in my head. Suddenly realizing that my years would skip on without her while she remained frozen at twenty-five. What if I forgot the notes of her laugh? What if the deep blue of her eyes started to fade and I forgot the smile that never failed to light up a room?

"You were all I had," I whispered. My arms loosened, and Calix didn't miss a second as his sword left me and he dropped down to take my place.

I stumbled to my feet, so beyond freezing I was numb.

"Get out of here," Calix muttered low.

I bent for my dagger lodged in the vampire's back, but I couldn't peel my eyes from Calix. The way he rocked the body of the first person to have ever seen me.

I was nothing without Cassia.

A ghost.

A forgotten existence.

"I don't care what happens to you. And I can't promise I won't kill you myself if you don't *leave*," he seethed. A beat of desolate silence passed before his head snapped around, rattling me with his loathing stare through red eyes that glittered with misery. *"Leave!"*

I tripped a few steps back. I didn't remember swiping up my satchel, but it was slung around my body, and occasionally my hand would reach for the walls that closed in as I tried to make it out.

Outside, the nip of the night wind didn't register. Nothing did. I walked and walked. Gravity didn't weigh me down, so maybe I had died with Cassia and become a breathing ghost.

No destination.

No belongings.

Nobody.

14

Time became irrelevant. My mind was empty, but I didn't stop moving. I knew it had been daylight and then darkness was falling again. I didn't care if it cloaked me. Smothered me.

I only noticed the rain when walking became heavier. When loose strands of my hair clung to my face and I was shivering violently.

Eventually, I stopped moving. I looked down at my dagger. The dark blood had mostly been washed off with the rain, but the flecks that remained made the scene replay in my head with punishing clarity. Flashes that stole my vision, my breath. I leaned over on my knees, sheathing the blade and trying to find the ground when it began to drift away.

"You didn't deserve that."

Only when I heard Nyte's voice did I remember my heart still held a beat. He eased out from the trees like a shadow.

"Me?" I breathed incredulously. "You're right. I deserve to be the one without this miserable life instead."

What surged inside me was the instinct I'd allowed to be suppressed by his enchantment. Fear. Fresh in the wake of Cassia's death. But he . . . Surely, he wasn't a blood vampire. I'd watched his shadow follow him. But I couldn't rule out the possibility he was a soul vampire with no reflection to check. Or perhaps he was a fae who also answered to the king.

It didn't matter what he was.

A seething anger rose within me. All I could replay was the kiss of death one of his kind had bestowed on Cassia. All I could see was this creature before me who was capable of it too.

Nyte edged toward me, and while my mind screamed to run, I tried to rally even a fraction of the bravery Cassia would have felt.

Nothing to lose. I had *nothing* left to lose.

He took another step, and this time my fear shook over the anger.

"Stay back."

"Astraea."

I blinked at that, turning the word over in my mind, but I wasn't so confused in my grief as to be mistaken. "I never told you my name," I whispered. "You've been following me all this time. Did you kill her? Send him to kill her . . . ?" My next breath came like a spear in my gut. "Was it supposed to be me?"

"I had nothing to do with your friend's death."

Death.

That word would never fail to slam into me with the force of the world caving in. My mind reeled. I couldn't believe him. I didn't *want* to believe him, but my thoughts waged war. I wanted to try to let rage consume me enough to fight him, but my heart was aching so badly it was already a lost battle.

Nyte took another step, and I did the only thing I knew I could.

I ran.

I gripped my skirts, pushing myself to run faster than I'd ever run before. Tears wet my temples, my adrenaline pulsed hot, and my mind taunted me with the idea that it would be over in a heartbeat. I was a lamb caught in a lion's game, a fool for even existing in a world I could not survive. And I no longer wanted to when Cassia had been my only fight, and now she was gone.

I felt like I flew through the woods as the light rain turned to snowfall, hoping the fire burning in my lungs would end my suffering before another *creature* had the satisfaction of taking my life. Ahead there was an opening in the woods, and I spied the frozen lake. And even though the bitter cold stung my cheeks, I couldn't be certain it was cold enough to have frozen the water thick enough to withstand my weight.

"Astraea, stop."

I shook my head as if it would expel his voice. I didn't slow, focusing instead on blocking him from being able to reach into my mind. Breaking past the trees, I threw all sense away, pushing on against the basic survival instinct that screamed the ice was too thin.

"STOP!"

Nyte's voice brought me to a sudden halt. I had one foot on the lake and the splintering sound confirmed that it would break long before I reached the other side. The splintering ice sounded the same as a thin arrow cutting the air. There was a certain melody to it.

In that exact moment I knew I wanted the end. I wanted to find peace. I stared down at the ice, barely able to make out my frosted, fractured reflection.

The slow sound of breaking ice became a countdown.

"Don't move." Nyte's breath sounded labored. Not with exertion but *worry.* "I can't save you here."

I don't want to be saved.

But I didn't tell him that. Something in his tone made me believe it would hurt him to hear those words. My shoulder blades locked when I felt him behind me. I didn't want the breaking ice to take him too. His reckless pursuit of me shouldn't be my concern, yet it was the only thing that stung me with regret and worry.

I shifted my foot back, wanting to see one last face . . .

The ice split beneath me before I got that chance, and black water swallowed me whole.

Never before had I been gripped so tightly and completely. Clutched within the arms of a frozen death, the pain that shot over every inch of my body was shocking. I had no will so I gave up.

Something slammed into me before grabbing me tight, and if I weren't so weak I would've wrapped my arms around it. But my body was pulled by a greater force even as I began to shut down.

I felt something warm on my lips and I gasped when air suddenly filled my lungs, my eyes flying open. Pressure beat in agonizing pulses on my chest.

I coughed, spluttering water, and that punishing grip of ice shook me violently.

I could vaguely make out my body being lifted. Some weight fell away. My cloak. Then my sleeves were peeled from my arms. When my laces were loosened, freeing my breasts, I gave a weak protest.

"You won't get to hate me for this if you're dead."

Nyte was here. In my agony, I was glad not to be alone. Though this was the second time I thought I'd heard the wavering of his composure. There was a new clarity to his voice, as though anything I'd heard from him before was only an echo of reality compared to now.

My teeth chattered violently, making me think they would break. My underbust corset came off, leaving me in only my sleeveless chemise before I was pulled close to Nyte's hard form. He was so *warm*. It was as if I was feeling him for the first time. His heat was so inviting that I burrowed into him far too eagerly. My cheek pressed up against his skin and I breathed in faint notes of mint.

"Nyte," I whispered, finding those eyes of dawn that came in and out of focus.

His palm cupped my cheek, returning the warmth to it, and I shuddered. "I've got you."

"You should have let me go."

His jaw tightened. Every light within me started to wink out. But I could have sworn shadows started to surround us. Shadows that glittered like the night fell down to wrap around just the two of us. He held me tight but it felt like we were pulled by some invisible force. Gentle but fast. All I could do was press myself tighter to his solid bare chest as if this unexplainable void could pull us apart.

"This is not the way you die. Stay with me a while longer."

Gravity returned again, though I wished to be free, flying, anywhere I might evade the tether to this world that was slowly wrapping around me.

Except for him. I wanted him.

"You're warm," I mumbled, unable to stop thinking this was *new*. He'd touched me before, but this time I couldn't place my craving for it.

"I wish I could say the same for you." His voice sounded strained as he carried me, and I was about to tell him to let me go. "It's nothing to do with you," he said in answer to my thoughts.

His exertion *had* to be because of me.

Nyte stopped walking, taking a moment to breathe, and I fluttered my heavy eyes to his face. He was so beautiful, with his midnight hair slicked around his sharp features. Droplets of water rolled down his complexion, pale as if it had been far too long since he'd felt the sun. Something about his face was different. More troubled and worn and *tired*.

"Nyte," I said though my chattering teeth.

"Starlight," he breathed back.

"I'm glad that room wasn't empty."

The confession slipped out as I thought I might not have another chance. I realized I'd run from him, but I wasn't truly afraid of him. I was afraid of living after all I'd failed at and lost, and I was *hopeful* for this to be the end so Cassia wouldn't be waiting long for me.

My palm flattened on Nyte's chest to feel his deep inhale. Then he was moving again, holding me closer, and my lids slipped shut as I forgot the wrongness of my wanting this final comfort before then.

"I plan to have you dance for me a second time."

I shook my head—or I thought I did, but a wave of drowsiness lapped at me, and my hand fell limp.

"Stay awake, Astraea."

My head became a boulder atop my shoulders, toppling off until it was jerked back and rolled to find balance. My forehead was now pressed into his neck with the adjustment, sending me off with notes of mint and sandalwood, and I decided this was a peaceful scent to die with. This felt safe despite what he might be.

"Had you ever danced for anyone before?" Nyte didn't sound in a healthy form to talk either, but I enjoyed the rough surety of his voice and the way I could feel its vibrations. It felt . . . *different* than any other time he'd spoken. So certain and promising when it should have been the opposite with my senses barely-there.

"Would you be jealous if I said yes?"

He chuckled, the sound light and staggered with exertion. It was enough to tug at my mouth, but not to open my eyes. "To a dangerous degree."

My slowing heart skipped a beat. "I'd never danced for anyone before," I whispered.

The cold became so unbearable I wished it gone in my whimper. Despite enjoying the firm grasp of Nyte's arms, I wished he hadn't come.

"Just a little farther," he said with a plea I almost nodded to.

I could make out the distant crack of branches and a rustling I confused with the rush of water I'd been engulfed in. Until the breaking stopped and so did his movements—save for his chest, which rose and fell deeply. He collapsed to his knees, relaxing his arms, but I didn't want him to let me go.

"We're out of time," he said, sliding a palm across my cheek. "You're going to be just fine."

I wasn't fine. I never had been and never would be even close to the bare minimum it took to exist without the world caving in on me with every step. *Fine.* Nyte had become this beautiful, impossible, taunting distraction I'd thought I wanted to chase away, but now I feared he was all I had left.

"Please."

I wasn't sure if the word had truly escaped my lips or why I'd really spoken it when darkness swept my mind and the shadows slammed down heavy. Before I succumbed to the numbness offered by the torture, a feminine voice sounded above the water.

As Nyte, the only sure thing I knew in that moment, slipped away from me . . .

I slipped away to nothing.

15

Whenever my lids opened a crack, blurs of color danced in my field of vision. The ice in my bones raged as if it were fire, and I wished for anything to take the agony away.

Every now and then, distant voices tried to pull me from a place I wanted to stay. I didn't deserve the warmth that seeped in, but I nestled further into it and allowed oblivion to claim me again.

When I woke, I didn't know what time it was. My fingers flexed, finding soft fur, and I was enveloped by a heat that blazed at my back. I didn't want to be awake, but no matter how hard I tried I couldn't drift off again, and I feared the silence of my own mind.

My eyes snapped open as I remembered why I savored the heat, the memory of the freezing lake biting my skin. My bones ached, and I hissed as I rolled onto my back. Lolling my head, I tried to grasp my surroundings. Fear shot through me when I couldn't recognize the room, but the finery it was decorated with forced me upright. I knew of only two places where I'd slept in such luxury. For a second, I thought I was back in the manor, but as I started to take in the details, nothing seemed similar to my elaborate former home.

"We all have fears." Nyte's silvery voice slipped into my mind, and I whirled with a gasp. *"But I don't enjoy being forced into mine."*

I was alone in this room. My hand touched my flushed cheek, remembering how it had felt to be pressed to his chest, and that caused me to look down at myself. I was in a new sleep gown of lilac silk, and around me were the soft furnishings of the bed, which had been stripped to be placed on the floor by the fire where I'd awoken.

"Where are you?" I asked, glancing out through the tall glass window to see nightfall.

A timid knock made my head jerk toward the door, and I clutched the blanket to myself as it opened tentatively.

"Oh, good. You're awake!" a feminine voice said.

I could only watch her with bewilderment as she eased herself in, carrying a tray. Nothing about her was recognizable, yet she seemed so bright and at ease with me.

"You need to eat. Get your insides warming too."

"Where am I?"

"My home. We're on the edge of Alisus." She crouched to my level, and it was only then I noticed the two small, rounded horns on her head. Her hair wasn't dark brown like I'd thought from afar; it was a deep green, and when she met my eye, the honey-brown of her own and the scattered freckles on her cheeks made her the semblance of a beautiful forest.

I must have been staring, because her movements slowed, and she tucked a nervous strand of hair behind her ear. Her delicately *pointed* ear. I lurched back with terror, yet the nature-infused beauty of her and the complete drop of her expression at my reaction quelled my fear just as fast.

"Sorry," I muttered. "I've never met a fae before. Or are you—?"

"Yes, I'm fae," she confirmed with a soft giggle.

I relaxed, knowing my ignorant assumption wasn't wrong. "You're not . . . part of the king's army, are you?"

She fixed the items on the tray as if to distract me from her wince. Mentally I was transported back to the wagon of fae being forced against their will, and the memory surfaced a true fear on this stranger's behalf.

"No. I've been able to remain hidden. I was born just after the last Libertatem that Arania triumphed in."

Over a hundred years ago.

I studied her a little more, not sure how I felt to know she appeared a little younger than me but was truly far older. "I'm sorry," I said, even though it was a pitiful offering with the threat she lived under.

"As am I," she said, tying our circumstances, which were somewhat similar with how the humans had also become the property of the king.

"My name is Lilith," she said, lifting the bowl to me.

I took the steaming broth though I had no appetite. "Astraea," I offered. "Thank you." I forced a few mouthfuls while she watched me expectantly, the delicious vegetable soup like a warm hug. "Do you have magick?" I asked.

"Of course. I feel nature. What it needs, how it fares. I can grow things faster than the Mother—a gift from her to keep our land thriving."

I smiled, fascinated by her.

"Some humans are born with magick, you know."

My brow lifted while my lips paused around my spoon.

"It's more like spell magick. They call them mages. They have gifts from their god, the Fate. Their magick is solarbound, like the celestials, however, so they were affected when the quake happened. The king sought them out at first too, but I don't think there are many of them left. They're the only ones who can spell the prized Starlight Matter into various enhancing potions."

I'd never realized before. Humans . . . they created the coveted Matter. I was becoming both thrilled and daunted by what each species was capable of. But without having told her of my embarrassingly sheltered existence, I wasn't sure if it was a bad thing Lilith assumed I needed all of this explained to me.

"Can't you have them spell Starlight Matter to hide your heritage so you might wander like us?" I asked.

"The Matter can be addictive. For humans it's no more than a taste for alcohol or a pipe. To the fae and celestials, it can consume them more powerfully and become hard to break. It can turn us into beings no better than the vicious nightcrawlers with their insatiable thirst for blood, or it can have the opposite effect and weaken us greatly."

I shuddered as my memory drew forth the grim flash of taloned wings. *Okay, so that isn't a viable option.* I didn't know why my mind scrambled to help this stranger, thinking she was too kind and delicate to remain condemned to a fate of hiding.

"I can't blame the celestial houses for protecting themselves beyond the veil, but many of my kind do, and I think it is why they join the king willingly. He hasn't stopped building his army since solar magick started to strengthen again. Until . . ."

I set my spoon in the bowl at her troubled look. "It's happening again," I concluded, casting my gaze out the window at the growing darkness of night.

"I think so," she confirmed. "Five hundred years ago something changed. Everyone felt it, like the world was cracking, like something had stepped into the realm that was never supposed to be here. I think everyone knew the Golden Age the star-maiden had ushered in was about to be shaken like the stars that began to die out."

"Would she have made herself known?"

Lilith didn't answer right away. Her gaze slipped to my chest, and I resisted the instinct to cover my markings in company. "Perhaps she's biding her time. Or fate has been biding it for her."

My head pulsed with everything I was learning. Lessons on the vast world I'd ventured into that I wished I'd known far sooner so I could be more prepared. Or perhaps I had, and they were part of the lost strings of memory I'd come to terms with never getting back.

"Your hair is like starlight."

I looked down at the strand I'd been fidgeting with in my rise of anxiety. My gaze flicked out to the sky. Nyte's voice didn't intrude, but my neck heated to know he'd appreciate Lilith's observation.

"How did I get here?"

"I found you at our gates. My parents are not home. I had to get you into something dry. I hope you don't mind."

Relief relaxed my shoulders to know it wasn't Nyte who'd undressed me fully, though my chemise, especially soaked through, didn't spare much dignity.

"I was alone?"

"Yes."

Because Cassia wasn't coming for me this time. My heart beat in shattered fragments. I lay back down.

"You must eat more."

"Thank you for helping me. If I could rest this night, I will leave by morning."

"Stay for as long as you need. Please."

I tried to force a smile, but I wasn't sure it broke on my face. Her eyes creased with pity, and I could only imagine my sorry state. Little did I care. I stared into the fire wondering what I would do next. Where I would go and who I would be. Lilith didn't speak again before she left, and I would have felt bad if I could feel anything at all with yesterday's cold recollections creeping back.

"Starlight—"

"Get out of my head if you can't face me in person."

Silence answered, but just as my eyes slipped closed, his presence slowly grew more tangible. Nyte was somewhere in the room, but I didn't seek him out.

"I don't know what you want. But I wish you would get it over with."

"Is my company so intolerable?"

"Your company is always half-there."

A beat of silence.

"Go away, Nyte. Or kill me."

The floorboards creaked, and I stiffened.

"You need to eat."

"No."

"Look at me."

"No."

I jerked back with a gasp when my view of the fire was snatched away by darkness and the devil crouched before me. As I propped myself up on one hand, he reached for the strap of my nightgown when it slipped. My reaction to pull away faded as I beheld his thoughtful look. His fingers tingled over my skin, always barely-there, running gently past my collar until he met the marking on my chest.

I watched him in fascination, wanting to know what brought on the hint of sadness as he traced each point of the constellation I wore. The flame in his eyes licked down his arm to touch me, and when I shivered he seemed to snap back into himself, retracting. Nyte met my gaze with a hard edge, and I blinked at the contrast.

"What do you want with me?" I whispered.

"Many things. But if it brings you comfort, if I wanted you dead, you would have been long ago."

His proximity heated my skin, or perhaps it was something else as fatigue strained my muscles. Familiar enough that I remembered . . .

"How long was I asleep?"

"A day."

My palm cupped my forehead and I nearly groaned.

"What's wrong?"

"Where's my satchel?" I asked, feeling the words like lead on my tongue. "I had a bottle of pills."

Nyte's eyes flexed as though he were debating before they flicked sideward. I groaned to even think of crawling to my dress, which was drying over the arm of a chair. Not caring about the scandalous piece of silk I wore, I bit my lip, my muscles crying with every movement.

My heart galloped as I sifted through the sodden things until relief flooded out of me as I felt the solid item.

"What are they?" Nyte studied the bottle I pulled out with a deep frown.

"I'm not well. I need them for my blood."

"Your blood?"

The intrigue in his tone I didn't care to answer, only offering a nod.

My shuffle back to the furs was just as torturous, but I nearly moaned at the returning embrace of warmth from the fire. Popping the cork, I tipped one pill onto my palm and stared at it. Nyte extended a glass of water from the tray, and I looked between both for longer than necessary, until he read my contemplation.

"What would she say if she could hear your thoughts right now?"

He didn't inspire me. There was nothing kind on my face when I snapped my glare to him. "You don't get to throw that at me," I warned. "Not when it was *your* kind who did this." Or was he even a soulless at all? My head spun with the new revelation that I wasn't certain *what* he was.

"You're right," he said calmly, maybe with genuine apology. "But also wrong."

I shook my head, incredulous at this male who should be everything I despised and feared, yet whom I couldn't escape. "Then *tell me.*"

Nyte extended the water to me again. I took it this time, trying to subdue the guilt that I wanted health in the wake of Cassia's death. "Just because she lost her life doesn't mean you have to abandon care for yours," he clarified.

I took a long drink of water as soon as the pill hit my tongue. I kept gulping greedily until it was empty. I caught my breath before I responded. "I might be slow at figuring you out, but at least I can take a hint. I don't give a shit about what you have to say. You didn't know her, and you don't know me. You're wasting your time, or if you're finding entertainment in this, you'll be bored soon. Then maybe you'll actually be of use to me and do what your kind does best." I set the glass aside, and he caught my arm. About to rip it from his grip, I paused when both our forearms upturned and his sleeve rolled up.

I blinked at the markings. While my phases of the moon were waxing, his were waning. As if lightning had shocked me straight from where we touched to ignite my chest, I tore my arm away from him.

We locked eyes, and I had questions about what it meant. How he'd gotten that tattoo that could lead to answers about my own. But his hard expression riddled me with the fear I should always have around him.

"You're right about some things. I don't give a damn about your friend's life, but let's call my *stalking* of you an infatuation. So hate me, fight me— the truth? I want you to fucking despise me. Your anger is my pleasure, your darkness is my light, and I hope you use it without apology to right every wrong you've endured, starting with this."

I didn't know when he'd inched closer, but his knee met the ground as he leaned into me, and his proximity was a snare I became trapped in.

"He's dead," I hushed out.

I realized I was hoping for him to voice what I felt—that the death of the soulless who'd killed Cassia was not enough retribution. Yet I didn't know what would be.

"So, what do you do now?"

That was the question I'd barely had the time to surface but knew would linger in the aftermath of Cassia's death. What would I do . . . and where would I go?

"Why did you bring me here?" I asked, having to start with the puzzle of him. Perhaps my fear of him was already trumped by the terror of being alone.

"Because it seems my challenge has become not to kill you, but to keep you alive."

"So, you're my eternal punishment."

His finger tilted my chin, emitting an unwelcome flutter. "Wrong again." He pierced me with those golden irises, and I had nothing left to lose as I allowed myself to become lost in them. "You're mine, Starlight."

My eyes fell to his neck, fighting the impulse I'd had before to discover which constellation was tattooed there when only two points were visible.

Then there was his scar. A jagged line running from his temple, just missing his eye, that finished on his cheekbone.

"If you want my clothes off, just speak your mind. Or I wouldn't be opposed to you *acting* on it."

I leaned away from him with an awareness like a whip. "I want to be alone."

"No, you don't, or I wouldn't be here." Nyte rose again, and I stared at him incredulously while he paced toward the long glass window, giving me his sculpted back in the black shirt that was tucked into his pants.

"You seem to have a way of being able to find me if I try to run."

His chuckle was smoky and sweet like a lover's touch. "As much as I thoroughly enjoy chasing you, that's not what I meant." He took up a side lean against the wall that cloaked him in shadow. Retrieving something that glinted gold, he studied it for a few seconds and then, without a word, slipped it back into his pocket where his hand stayed. He said, "You didn't step onto that ice because you were running from me." His tone grew colder, circling like the shadows that became darker around him. "I watched you as you ran, then slowed, then stopped. You saw the ice crack and knew it would break. Never again will you stare down at death and desire to take its hand."

"I lost everything," I said. "I have nothing left."

"Your loss is deep, but you will heal. It will linger, but you will keep living."

I had no need to counter his words. The wound within me had been split open stitch by stitch and there was nothing he could do to mend it. So I lay back down and watched the fire rage.

"Rest now. When you wake, the world will still be cruel and your heart will still be bleeding, but you are breathing, Astraea. And every breath is a reminder that you live for something."

16

The fire dwindled to embers and my tears fell silently down my cheeks. As much as I despised each one, I couldn't stop; the exhaustion kept me down. I barely slept and greeted the new dawn with reluctance.

Lilith kneeled by the window, muttering quiet words with her eyes closed and her hands clasped to her chest. The sun streaking over her gave off the most ethereal glow. I didn't disturb her until she'd finished, when she opened her eyes and gave the new dawn a smile.

"Was that a prayer?" I asked softly, unable to raise my head.

There had been times I'd gone months without seeing Cassia and my voice had grown hollow. There was little else that could bring joy like she did. But as I propped myself up, I felt no more than a ghost. This time I would never see her again.

"Yes. To the Mother, who has kept me safe. And to Dusk and Dawn for the safety of their daughter they blessed us with." She turned to me with such brightness at my interest. "Do you pray to your god? I know some don't."

My god . . . The question only offered more mysteries that eluded me. "I'm not sure who I would pray to."

Lilith didn't pass any judgment. She stood, brushing down her light green gown. "The vampires worship their creator, the God of Death. The humans sometimes remember theirs, the God of Fate. The celestials mostly favor theirs, the God of Dusk and the Goddess of Dawn. But most species pray to them for giving us a mortal deity for peace. I don't believe people are tied to what their birth or creation dictates. And I don't think the gods would reject anyone's will to change. For good or evil. The soul of a person has its own free will."

I didn't want to erase her hopeful expression as she talked of the gods. I was sure they had abandoned us. Or if they still existed, maybe I would curse them instead of worshipping them and making things worse for myself.

Lilith changed the topic. "Your wears are of impeccable design. Though I apologize—your dress might not be salvageable from the damage."

I wouldn't normally care for something so petty, yet my mind wanted me to suffer the punishment, feeling broken with the news, knowing Cassia had purchased the dress for me.

"Oh, it's no matter!" Lilith chirped at my sadness. I wanted to smile. She deserved it, and I admired her positive company. "We have plenty here. I'm sure we'll find you something. Come!"

Everything in me cried out in protest for me to lie back down, but I couldn't take advantage of her hospitality. I had to move on, though I had no idea where I would go. Nothing physical could touch the crushing weight of what was turning my body to steel. The effort to draw my legs up, to stand, became my penance for still being alive.

Lilith watched me, her expression falling. Then our eyes met and she beamed as if I wouldn't notice her pity. What I greatly appreciated about her was that she never asked what kept me in such despair.

I followed her mindlessly into another room, which turned out to be the biggest closet I'd ever stood in. I found temporary distraction in the clothing that had always fascinated me. There were countless dresses in here, but I gravitated toward the back, where a beautiful outfit was displayed on a mannequin.

"My mother is a fighter," Lilith said, pride coating her voice as she came up beside me. "She competed in the trials to be the Selected."

My gaze snapped to her, and she delighted in my interest. "Where are your parents right now?"

"They were personally invited to the Keep for the send-off by Reigning Lord Reihan."

I had to take a few deep breaths through my stab of grief. *Stars,* the thought of Reihan's agony when Calix would take Cassia's body back made my head pound.

"You did not go with them?" I asked.

Lilith played with a strand of her green hair as if it went with her answer. "They do not like me being in public. My mother is human, but in binding her life to my father's she extends her years. My father looked like me once. Some fae can blend in with the humans far easier, and my father . . ." She flinched, tucking a strand of hair behind her ear. "He cropped his ears many years ago and files his horns to disguise himself. His green hair could easily be the result of a human consuming Starlight Matter."

I was impacted by the revelation, sickened by the measures her father had to resort to just for a breath of freedom with his wife.

"I once thought I could do it too, but . . . it's unimaginably painful. His horns grow back, and he must do it again at least twice a year. His ears had to be cut continuously for weeks as they tried to heal themselves too fast. The points got shorter and shorter, and with some healing enhancements they are now as rounded and smooth as a human's."

I didn't realize my hand had covered my mouth with the tale. I couldn't fathom the beauty of Lilith's fae attributes being so barbarically removed out of desperation.

"You should stay here a while longer. At least until my parents are back. They will know how to help get you home safe."

I had no home. No one waiting for me. "Thank you, but I must leave today." I wouldn't be their burden. I turned to look back over the garments.

"I think Cassia Vernhalla will win the Libertatem for us. Then we'll be free to wander as we please without fear."

The room swayed. My fingers flexed against material as I caught myself on a shelf.

"Are you still unwell?"

I had been so selfish in my grief and what Cassia's death meant to me that I hadn't considered the damning fate of so many others. An entire kingdom. With their Selected gone . . .

"What happens if the Selected never makes it to the Central?" I asked with cold trepidation.

Lilith frowned. "Their kingdom's borders would be locked immediately. No citizens would be allowed to leave or choose another candidate for their realm to possibly win immunity."

My eyes closed as my vision peppered, and I crouched slowly until my knees met the carpeted floor. Lilith took my arm to help, her concern growing.

"I'll get you some water."

I took hold of her forearm. She searched my eyes, and I could only imagine the dread in mine.

"Your mother—" It was the first conclusion I frantically drew. "Could she take the Selected's place now?"

The slow shake of Lilith's head made my hold on her drop. I stared at the ground, overcome with the kingdom's heavy loss. We were condemned, without a glimmer of hope, to be at the mercy of the vampires for another century.

"The king would not allow it. The Selected's profiles are already circulating, and it would be unfair to those making the choice right now whether to stay in their kingdom or choose another—Astraea, are you all right?"

I couldn't answer while my mind buzzed. I vaguely felt Lilith slip away from me and exit the closet. I let my gaze drift up. The ensemble I was kneeling before stood powerful and beautiful, in some ways with the elegance of a dress: a bodice that hugged tight, material that crossed at the neckline to give a V shape. The cut in the skirts on each side reached right to the thick, intricate belt, and I imagined the fitted combat pants that would go with it. Decorative but with some small slots for daggers, I assumed.

Lilith returned, taking my hand and pressing a cool glass to it. "My mother said this is what she would have worn to the Central," Lilith said quietly.

I swallowed over the lump in my throat, but it only grew, so I drank fast and greedily. I slowly realized that I was envisioning being back in the black waters of yesterday, perhaps wishing, once again, to have drowned in them, and my mind turned dark with the thought. For if I had . . . I wouldn't be staring at the hopeful young fae beside me now, not knowing how to break the news that she would never be free.

It was a cowardly, selfish thought that made my eyes burn.

My chest pulsed. Three beats. A push toward something that overcame me. Something I wasn't used to. Purpose. This beacon rejoiced at the thought, heating with new determination. To a plan that seemed laughable, but the more I processed it, the less protest I could muster for the reckless course of action.

We have to win.

Cassia had wanted this. She *believed* I could do it.

Do it for me. For all of us.

I cast my eyes up. Then they fell sideward to the hopeful friend I'd made. "Lilith?"

Her eyes lit up with acknowledgment and my face creased.

I would have longed for that recognition. To be known, *seen.* The Libertatem was our one hope in a century to have the freedom we deserved.

"I need your help."

17

I told Lilith everything, though it took its toll. Exhausted by the emotions once again, I tried hard not to break down. Lilith had a calm and bright nature that I felt relaxed in, and I knew my secret would be safe with her, for when we exchanged stories I couldn't help but see a slightly younger version of myself.

"You're very brave," she said sadly, helping me tie the bodice at my back.

"When we have no choice, can it really be called bravery?"

"You do have a choice," she said.

I caught her eye in the mirror and glanced down at the ensemble, trying not to be wracked with unworthy guilt, but Lilith was insistent I wear it.

"You don't have to do this. You could flee and hide. This is not your responsibility, but you're carrying it on."

"You should move kingdoms to whichever you believe to be the strongest. Convince your parents. Will you do that?"

Lilith squeezed my arm before she went over to a new assortment. "I'm not going anywhere."

I turned to her with an insistence that she change her mind, but she smiled, holding out a deep purple cloak also styled for combat. My protest faltered in rise of my nerves as I equipped myself with it, trying not to give in to the will to shrink out of it all, as wearing such a fierce outfit felt like a mockery on me.

"Are you sure your mother won't mind?" I tried one last time as I slid into a pair of boots. There was a little extra room around my toes, but they would suffice.

"I promise," she said.

I glanced back at the bare mannequin one last time before following Lilith out.

"It's at least five days' ride," Lilith called over her shoulder, and I rushed to keep up with her giddy pace. "You'll need to push faster than usual with less rest to get there in time."

My race to the Central wasn't just for that. It would all be over if Calix made it back to Alisus Keep and announced Cassia's death first.

"In Cassia's profile her preferred weapon is a bow," Lilith continued. I admired her attention and help greatly. I followed her as she heaved open twin doors, and my mouth opened as we trailed inside. There were so many weapons I didn't know where to land my gaze. "You should arrive with one at least."

Lilith examined three bows before settling on the smallest, most decorative one I didn't immediately take.

"She taught me, but I'm no match for her skill."

What was I thinking—that I could possibly pull this off and be convincing in the role?

"Focus," Lilith said.

I blinked at her assertiveness, which shed light on how flustered and sheltered I was being.

"She also had a finely tuned skill for throwing daggers."

That was something I knew I could match her on. It had begun during my nights of boredom on Hektor's rooftop terrace, lodging my own dagger into a wall he'd never found torn up. *I can do this.* The voice of confidence was small, but I had to tune out the taunts of weakness to see this through.

Lilith handed me an armguard. I'd barely fixed the strap around my forearm when a small throwing dagger was thrust at me, then another, and another, and I fumbled with them. She didn't look back as she crossed by me, and I took a moment to slide the blades into the small holsters around my waist, then the bow onto my back.

After grabbing a quiver of arrows and stuffing a pack full of supplies, we stood in the grand reception hall of the manor. Only when I looked at the door did it hit me all at once what I was about to venture out to do.

"I wish I had a horse for you, but there's a town only an hour on foot from here." Lilith took my hand and pressed something into my palm. I opened my mouth to protest the coin pouch when I'd already taken so much. "This is not just for you—none of it. You'll accept it because what you are doing is selfless. It is for you and me and everyone in this kingdom."

My eyes burned at her hopeful passion. This stranger who longed for so much out of life that belief was all she had. It made my choice easy. For them all, I *had* to try.

"Thank you for everything," I said.

We embraced, and that comfort I savored.

"I hope we get to see each other again."

"We will," she promised.

With that final vote of confidence, no further words were needed.

I took my first steps out. The winter air nipped my cheeks, but I breathed in deeply. There was no sure end to the path I took, and maybe all I would have was the darkness to guide me, but onward I went to seal the fate of my kingdom. In Cassia's honor.

18

As I trudged through the forest, the ground layered with crisp snow, I subconsciously touched the stormstone dagger at my thigh every time I heard a noise. Including my own footsteps. I chanted nonsense to myself in an attempt to tame my skittishness. Occasionally my chest would pulse with a warmth and I'd power on with confidence, but eventually I would remember all over again how out of my depth I was. Alone and wandering through a world I did not know.

It was already exploding with more than I imagined.

Fae. Celestials. The tales of a star-maiden. All so exhilarating it pushed me to go on and discover what else made up the lands. How our society's hierarchy worked, which fears were true, and what could be fought.

My pulse was racing, my mind reeling. It kept me distracted from the burst of wings, the caw of birds, the crack of branches—everything that powered my legs on with jumpy anxiety to be back in civilization.

I exhaled in relief when I finally spied the town, and I jogged the last stretch to be away from the clusters of timber that had begun to panic me with their endless directions.

Time was not my luxury.

I headed straight onto the town path, my only mission here to acquire a horse. My pace quickened through the streets, and I glided through bodies, the task giving me the focus not to be overwhelmed in a foreign place.

Around the next bend, my eyes lit up at the two horses I found tied outside an inn. I was hopeful the coin Lilith had given me would be more than a generous sum as I knew which horse I desired. Approaching slowly, I gawked at the brilliant white beast with a long mane and hair around its hooves. The care toward it was evident from the way its mane and tail had been beautifully combed and given a few braids.

The thought of trying to climb atop a horse, however, had me mentally flipping through options for how else I could get to the Central just as fast.

"You have never ridden a horse?"

I sucked in a breath at Nyte's silvery voice, turning my head to find him close by. I was becoming accustomed to the abruptness of his presence. It never failed to stroke my spine, and regardless of all reservation, I never felt alone. Why he followed me, I didn't want to break the small comfort to find out.

I took a deep breath and reached out a hand, my rigid poise loosening off when the horse seemed to bow its head, receptive to my touch. "I asked Hektor once, but he said they were dangerous and unpredictable."

"Danger is not in the act nor the being; it arises when one does not know how to handle a difficult situation." Nyte's hand ran over the horse's neck close to mine, and his proximity didn't go unnoticed, raising the hairs all over my skin. "Unpredictability comes from a lack of preparation or observation."

In his tone I felt the warning. I had so much to learn, and with where I was heading, my only hope for survival would be to trust in whatever help I could get. Even from him.

I eyed the metal hoop dangling from the saddle. I'd watched people mount horses plenty, though it didn't translate to confidence now I was confronted with it. "The owner must be inside," I said.

"Or you could just take it."

"I have coin."

"But not time."

Just then, a man exited the tavern smoking a pipe, and I stilled as his attention landed on us. He gave no reaction, but walked over. I believed the horse to be his. I cursed Nyte for the distraction and opened my mouth to explain we were simply admiring it.

Nyte put a finger to my lips, pressing his body to mine. I stared at him in incredulity. Nyte's eyes danced at my reaction before the man approached his horse and scratched its head as though he didn't see us. My eyes widened. I knew what Nyte was doing. His gloved hand eased away from my face, but the one around my waist remained. He held my stare with a challenge to be silent. He didn't look away until the man took a deep pull on his pipe and headed back inside.

"How do you do that?" I asked, shuffling away from him.

Nyte shrugged. "That's an explanation for another day."

"Can other vampires . . . manipulate minds?"

"I've told you before I am not that. But no, they cannot. They have some magnetic compulsion to trap their victims, that is all." He contemplated my eager reaction. "Though you might say I'm particularly good at it."

I nearly rolled my eyes at his arrogance. "How am I supposed to believe you?"

"I'm not trying to convince you."

He's insufferable.

"Your eyes—they're different," I ground out.

That earned me one of those smirks that danced the line between approval and amusement. I didn't give him the satisfaction of my scowl as I reached up to the horse's saddle and strained with the height to jam my foot into the metal half-hoop. I felt childish for not knowing its name.

"Your struggle right now has me questioning who really danced for me," Nyte said as he came up behind me. "How high that leg can go is something I'll never forget."

My mouth gaped, only to snap shut when his hands held my waist. "I didn't dance for you," I grumbled.

"Bend and jump."

I did as he instructed, and my heart lunged when I soared higher than my mind had prepared for. My other leg hooked over the saddle, my thighs clamped tight, and my whole body seized at the new vantage point and how the horse huffed and dipped.

"Now shuffle forward."

I wondered why until I looked down and saw he was braced to mount the horse too.

"No way. There's another horse."

Nyte chuckled—a low, genuine sound I despised myself for enjoying the lightness of. "If I leave you to ride alone, I hope you're content with going wherever the horse decides to lead you."

"It can't be that hard." Yet I had no example to follow when I didn't know how to command the horse to even walk.

Nyte simply waited, knowing my admission would come, but I said nothing and simply shifted forward. He mounted the horse so elegantly I couldn't suppress my admiration, but I should have anticipated there would be no space between us when he slipped in behind me. He enveloped me completely, reaching over me for the reins, and my breath caught. I said nothing of his breath blowing across my ear, but I wondered if it was deliberate so he could delight in my reaction now my head was level with his shoulder.

His hand snaking around my waist made me open my mouth to object, but he kicked his feet, and when the horse jerked forward I leaned back to balance myself, my hand lashing over his. There was a second, when Nyte's fingers flexed and mine could have slipped through, that I wanted the gloves removed, if only to know if the tingling in my stomach would erupt at the contact.

I snatched my hand away as quickly as the thought came.

"I'm heading to the Central," I said.

"I know." He seemed to contemplate it. "If you were smart, you would forget this course. Head past the Central and toward the veil."

"Why?"

"You've been longing for adventure, have you not?"

That didn't seem adequate reason. I brushed off his obscure suggestion. Nowhere else could be an option anyway.

"I have to do this."

He said nothing, and I knew this leisurely pace couldn't last. I had to ride fast from here on out. I needed to make it to the Central on time, or it would all be a wasted journey of a fool's hope.

"HEY! STOP!"

I gasped at the man's call behind us.

Nyte's arm encircled me fully, and he pressed his body into me before he said, "Hold on tight."

19

I rode fast and far, leaving everything I knew with no time to mourn. As I drew closer to the Central, only the daunting fate I was about to walk into consumed my every thought.

Nyte stayed with me even when I couldn't see him. I spent a lot of my time taking short rests, eating only what I needed, and galloping quickly in the direction he'd sent me, having no other choice without a map. He lingered in my mind, but I preferred that over the distraction of his physical presence which would slow me down.

I had so many questions about him. How he often felt like a ghost in my wake but was also so promising. I wished Cassia could have seen him, if only a glance, to settle my mind.

It didn't matter right now. Nothing did. I slowed the horse on the crest of a hill and my breath shuddered out of me.

The Central Kingdom of Vesitire was so much more than my mind had speculated. In the brilliant night it glittered mesmerizingly against the full moon's rays, reflecting so much glass it could be mistaken for an ocean at first glance.

At least, the top two tiers could.

The city was built like nothing I had seen before. Three circular levels high, and even from here I could see the biggest building I'd ever witnessed: the castle dominating the top level. From this side, water fell from several points on the bottom level, spilling into the wide river circling around the city and breaking off into several rivers that weaved through the surrounding villages. A triumphant arched bridge would be my way across.

"There's a whole world before you, Starlight."

Nyte took a physical form this time, standing beside the horse as if he were reacting to the frightening beat of my heart, knowing I needed grounding in that second so I wouldn't choose to flee.

"Look beyond it," he said.

My eyes flicked up, past the huge city and beyond to the duller surrounding towns. A white line made up the horizon. The more I stared I felt a pull, my eyes drawn toward it like a magnet, magnifying it as I did when I gave my immersive sight to the stars. It moved so subtly I could see, almost *feel,* its life force.

"The veil . . ." My voice trailed off with wonder. I'd always imagined it to be black and sinister. But it made sense that something that repelled nightmares would be made of light.

"You should abandon this plan and head there."

"I would be abandoning an entire kingdom."

"You would be safe."

My attention passed to him with a frown, but he did not meet my eye. "How can you be sure?"

Nyte's jaw worked. "Do you trust me?"

"I'm barely convinced of your existence at all."

He didn't match my humor. Instead his golden gaze caught me, and I couldn't read into why his eyes became so guarded.

"I'm already late," I said quietly, more to myself to spur on my urgency. The other Selected would have arrived early this morning, and I only prayed the king would be receptive to whatever excuse I was yet to conjure for my tardiness.

"I'm right here with you."

I nodded, staring vacantly straight ahead toward the misty white veil, unable to deny I felt a longing for what could be discovered if I chose selfishness. Then I cast my sights up, hoping the stars would offer serenity as they always did. I studied them out of habit, my frown flexing.

Stargazing had always been a soothing comfort to me. Sometimes Cassia and I would spend hours mapping our own constellations, and I wondered if she saw them as in-depth as I did. At first glance, the sky was a blanket of tiny crystals, but there were layers I could measure the distance between, and the sizes, they blinked.

My chest warmed. A slow pulse that beat three times as I stared up.

It seemed a childish notion now, to believe we would eventually become stars and all I had to do was look up to find Cassia. My eyes burned, but tears didn't gather.

"What do you see?" Nyte asked.

"What do you know of the nights growing longer . . . darker?"

"It's what happens when two stars collide," he said. "Something that should be beautiful becomes an utterly destructive, devastating force."

When our eyes connected I couldn't untangle the knot in my stomach. The sorrow we shared, yet I didn't know why. I had the building urge to ask more—what it meant—though my heart was braced for a tragic tale.

I didn't get the chance when his expression blanked to stern indifference—a contrast I had to blink against as though it would return it to the momentary vulnerability he'd displayed.

"The Central awaits," he drawled.

My brow furrowed as I contemplated for a second. I let go of the reins, dismounting not entirely with grace as I was still growing accustomed to the beast. I unhooked the bow from my back as I trailed back through the woodland I'd emerged from.

"Cold feet?"

I didn't deign to respond to Nyte's sarcasm. Retrieving an arrow, I felt completely foolish, not having the first clue about how to hunt. I could hit stationary targets, but I'd never tested the skill this way.

"You just ate," he went on.

"I'm not hungry," I hissed. "Now, would you be quiet?"

Something leaped past the trees in the distance, and I crouched, nocking the arrow, but my aim wouldn't stop shaking, and it took considerable strength to hold my poise even for a few long seconds. As the rabbit bounded out of view I relaxed with a huff.

"A person might be a better bet," Nyte said, and my head snapped to him at the casual suggestion. "Larger target, slow or stationary if you pick your moment right . . ."

"I'm not killing someone for this!"

"If you stay here, you're bound to attract a nightcrawler," he went on anyway. "Aim for the wings. They tend to show off with them, and they make ample targets."

My breath hitched. I backed out of the trees slowly with fresh awareness of the creature I didn't want to encounter. I ran a hand through my hair, and when I looked at my palm I did a double take, not used to finding the stark new contrast of black silk tresses. It had taken every coin Lilith gave me to purchase enough Starlight Matter to achieve the desired effect. The silver elixir would also conceal my scent and change my eyes to a deeper blue until I stopped taking it.

The tightening in my gut wouldn't ease. I'd stolen the attributes to impersonate Cassia. Just as a precaution.

"Darkness does suit you in clothing, but I'll admit, I long to hide your elixirs for a glimpse of your silver hair again."

"The disguise was your idea," I grumbled. "Though I don't think Hektor's men are going to catch word about me here. Even if they did, I'm practically saving them the hassle of having to kill me."

"You're not going to die."

I eyed him carefully, wanting to feel the same confidence with which he spoke those words, and took a deep breath, needing to calm the racing of my heart and embody the lethal combatant they would expect. "You're certain the king never visited the Keeps to meet the Selected?"

"No, he has not," Nyte confirmed. "Feel free to ask again if three times isn't enough."

As I turned to cast him a glower, a crack startled me, and I whirled back around. I fixed the arrow back into place—a deterrent, I hoped, even if I didn't have the confidence to strike accurately with it. My eyes scanned the depthless dark furiously. I heard footsteps but could hardly tell the direction in which they were headed. I backed up to emerge on the hill again. My heartbeat thumped in my ears, and then I caught sight of a figure. I held my breath, about to pull back the string and take aim—until the first rays of moonlight revealed their face.

"Zathrian?"

The rush of overwhelming relief escaped as a whimper from my lips. I let go of the bow and ran to him without hesitation, not caring how he was here, why, or for the possibility he could be a trick.

He wasn't immediately receptive to me, as if confusion stunned him. "Astraea?"

It took a moment to realize I didn't look entirely like myself. My eyes swelled with tears, and I nodded. Zath needed nothing more. He made the last few strides until his strong arms were wrapped around me tight. Then I came apart.

"Oh, Zath, so much happened. I can't—Cassia, she . . ." I couldn't form the sentences to explain everything at once.

"You're all right," he soothed, smoothing down my nape with his palm while I cried.

This gift of familiarity and safety I clung to tight, right when I needed it the most.

"How did you find me?" I sniffed, wiping my nose with my sleeve when we parted.

Zathrian looked over me with a solemn face, and I didn't try to be brave knowing he would see right through it. "Everything went to shit after you left. I couldn't risk staying there when I was seen helping you by some of Hektor's men. But I stayed behind for a while, stopping as many as I could from coming after you, until a week went by with nothing new. I came as soon as I could, but I didn't expect . . ." Zathrian trailed off.

My brow pinched to fight the sting of grief in my eyes. "It's just me," I said.

"Then what are you doing here?" He scanned me from head to toe, my plan all but communicated by my altered attributes, and the firm lines of his skin smoothed out to dread.

I didn't think telling Zathrian my plan would go well, but he listened to everything I tried to explain, each step from the moment I left the manor. I rushed it all out despite his look of concern and horror, glancing toward the city when I spoke of my plan that seemed so much more ludicrous spoken aloud.

"Astraea, you are no fighter," Zathrian said lightly. As though I were naïve enough to believe I was.

Somehow, it stung to hear aloud what I felt within, but I didn't let it show.

"There's more to these trials than fighting," I said. "I'm the only chance we have. If I don't try, Alisus has no hope in this Libertatem."

His expression was conflicted, like he wanted to take me far away in the opposite direction, but we both knew I was right. "Are you sure you want to do this?"

"Yes," I said honestly. I had nothing to lose, and being here in Cassia's memory, knowing how much it had meant to her, made my choice easy.

"Well, of course I'm coming with you."

I smiled, so relieved not to be facing this daunting hurdle alone that I nodded gratefully. I perked up, swiping up a bow and extending it out to him. "I have a plan, and I need you to do something for me."

"STOP!"

My fear beat to the pounding of the horse's hooves. We didn't slow at the barked command. Instead Zathrian leaned into my back tighter, and I didn't think it was possible for the horse to charge faster, but my eyes watered with its speed.

"Are you sure this was a good idea?" he said, mouth close to my ear.

"Not at all."

His chuckles were swallowed by the commotion we provoked as we headed straight toward the guards posted at the gates.

The idea to make my story as believable as I could was simple, if brazen. My hope was that, in our rushed state, it would gain me some sympathy, or at least cause enough of a distraction to demand some formality where I was sure to flounder. My eyes almost scrunched shut to hide like a coward when, for a split second, I thought we'd have to trample the guards. They dove out of the way just in time. My skin was slick with sweat and my pulse raced.

The castle expanded before me, so wide and triumphantly tall I tried not to balk at the sight. Zath tugged the reins hard as we reached the end of the courtyard and some of the longest steps I'd ever seen rose up before us. Many huge colonnades supported the portico, and the tall ornate doors made me feel so small.

They weren't the most distinguishing feature. The castle was crafted of black stone and glass—not to make it sinister and frightening; it was breathtaking when the moonlight reflected off it, as if the structure were made of the midnight sky.

"Dismount at once!"

My attention snapped down to the line of guards all angling lethal spears at us, and my throat burned as the exertion caught up to me in punishment. Zathrian didn't hesitate, slipping away from behind me. My chest heaved, and while dizziness swept in, I forced my leg around the horse, knowing they wouldn't have a shred of patience.

Zathrian helped me down, and both of us held our hands up to show we were unarmed as five guards swiftly closed in. I took a few deep breaths to remember everything I'd rehearsed, forcing words through my constricted throat.

"I am one of the Selected," I panted.

Zathrian added, "The rest of our party was ambushed days ago. It is only the two of us."

They continued to assess me, and I could do nothing but stand bare to their judgment. One nodded to another then gave no words, only jerked his chin at me, before he twisted. It was an invitation to follow.

Zathrian's hand on my back was the only thing that forced me to defy the roots I'd planted to keep me still. I was so damn grateful he was here.

As we passed through the dominating doors, the grand reception hall was like something from a darkly beautiful fairy tale. I tried to keep from admiring the pristine, silver-embellished black marble. The wide space could suspend an echo for seconds, but everything was so eerily quiet. A peaceful desertion.

The grandeur of my surroundings offered enough of a distraction to slow my pulse. I was really here, in the fortress of the Central I'd only heard whispers of.

And I should be here with Cassia.

My gaze dropped with sinking despair to track my boots over the light mosaic floor that broke up the black decor. The loud groan of doors directed my head up, but what I didn't expect was for a loud commotion to hit my senses like a physical blow. It was sheer focus and determination that kept my steps from halting like my mind demanded. I wanted to turn and run far away from the gathering I hadn't expected to interrupt.

Only one guard walked ahead of us while the others stopped, and we followed his lead until we stood at the center of a table that spanned around us on each side in a U shape. The hushed silence of those seated was weighted with judgment, intrigue, and astonishment. The feast drifted so many scents at us, but I could focus on nothing but my erratic nerves trickling sweat down my spine.

"She claims to be the last of your Selected, Your Majesty." The guard bowed before turning sharply, and as soon as he stepped away as the final barrier between us, the King of the Six Realms set his intense eyes on me. Breathing became a conscious effort, and I swallowed hard, but my throat stung with dryness.

I dropped into my own bow as the king rose slowly, his broad form dominating, and I wanted to disappear with all the attention. Every set of eyes felt latched onto my skin, and the worst of all of them let the thick silence linger.

"Is that so?" His voice rumbled with intrigue.

I shivered, haunted by it, but forced myself to straighten. "My name is Cassia Vernhalla," I said, glad when my voice came steady, though my nose prickled with a note of shame at the impersonation. "Our company was ambushed. We barely made it out." I couldn't help but to survey the gathering. From their looks of disgust and horror, I knew they couldn't distinguish the blood we wore as an animal's and not a person's. Zathrian hadn't taken long to hunt the rabbit, and we'd coated ourselves enough to add merit to our story.

There were many in attendance, but from the elegance and even spacing of them, I knew I stood in the center of my competitors.

The other four Selected.

My gaze returned to the king, but I did a double take upon seeing the male on his right. My breath caught. His sharp jaw, high cheekbones, the roundness of his eyes . . . He was beautiful. Though dangerous too, I realized as I beheld his pointed ears. He looked back at me intensely, and I saw that his eyes were the color of caramel. His short brown wavy hair, held back by a gold band, met in a widow's peak at the center of his forehead.

I'd heard that the king had a son, but never any details. He'd seemed like a fable to me until now.

"Cassia," the king drawled slowly.

I snapped out of the trance I was slipping into. My cheeks flushed to realize we'd been staring at each other.

"The Selected for the Kingdom of Alisus. We feared you would not make it. But we can forgive you as the Libertatem has not yet officially begun while we enjoy this welcome evening."

I forced myself to react like I owned the name, wondering if my biggest challenge to survive would not be this deadly game but my slowly shredding heart. "Your Majesty." I dipped my head again.

My pulse counted the beats of silence, and when his slow smile curled, I almost relaxed.

"Do you have your invitation?"

Shit. I hadn't thought of that. With a glance at Zathrian, he spoke for me. "We barely fled with our lives, Your Majesty."

"Then how am I to know that you are who you say you are?"

My mind scrambled. This was about to all be over before it could begin . . . I drew a shallow gasp, and though it made my heart wrench with the possibility the king might claim possession of it, I willed my hand to reach into my neckline and reveal the seal of Alisus on the silver pendant.

The last thing I had of Cassia's.

The king's chin tilted upward faintly. He stretched out a hand, and with two fingers motioned for me to approach. My blood chilled. Zathrian gave me a small smile of encouragement before I obeyed. I stopped right before the king's table. He reached out farther and I stepped forward again, this time my thighs touching the wood. Everyone seated there watched for judgment as if this were the first of his trials.

The king studied the pendant, and my breath caught as he lifted it from my chest and held it up to my high neckline. The prince shifting in his seat drew my attention to him. He leaned forward, hand braced on the table like he was ready to intervene. His gaze shifted between me and his father carefully. While his reception to me seemed amicable, I couldn't shake the crawling wariness moving up my spine.

The king's hum snapped my eyes back to him but I couldn't be certain if it was acceptance or suspicion as he let the pendant drop. The king pierced me with a studying intensity, scanning my face, my attire, and scrutinizing me as though I'd come to him as a puzzle missing a piece.

"Allow me to introduce myself." A smooth voice of silk smothered my panic under the king's close watch. "My name is Drystan."

As I straightened with the rise of the prince, the pendant slipped from the king's hand. Mercifully, it stole his keen interest away from me.

"Yes, this is my son."

The obvious didn't need to be spoken, but I gave a bow of my head regardless.

"You may see more of him during your time here. However long."

My nerves were teetering on a razor's edge. I thought Drystan's assessment was like his father's, but without the missing piece. He smiled, appearing warm, welcoming. I wanted to feel it, but I listened to the note of caution that arose from within.

"Join us," the king announced, more to the servants, who began to move, pulling out the vacant seats to our left.

"We don't wish to put you off your fine meal in our . . . current state," I said. Blood crusted on my fingers, and it was an effort not to retch at the memory of Zathrian gutting the rabbit. All for this display, in the hope it would gain us some respect from the others when everything about me otherwise was sure to pin me as a target.

"Nonsense," the king said, more cheerful than expected as he took his seat again. "I'm sure there are none here who could be put off by the sight of blood."

I had no choice but to nod in acceptance and follow a kind woman with straight black hair, braided to the side, and beautiful large eyes, who offered the only warmth in the room. She took my bow, pack, and cloak, and I slid into the seat that was offered to me, but I wanted nothing more than for the back of the chair to open into a depthless void and drop me into the abyss for how singled-out I looked with such elegance surrounding me.

At the thought, I glanced across the space to the opposite seat and found a woman's keen gaze already upon me. She was breathtakingly stunning, and as I knew, there was only one other female Selected. Her name was Rosalind. Her light pink hair was wonderful with its natural curls, two sections pinned high and adorned with gold accessories that reminded me of Lilith's delicate horns. The lengths flowed to her ribs, complementing her glowing brown skin. Though my admiration dissipated to cold dread as the assessment in her light brown eyes chilled me.

"Please, let us resume the feast," the king said as a command for chatter to fill the awkward silence.

I looked away from Rosalind as the group became loud once more, toward a man farther to her right whom I dreaded ever having to go against in combat with his brute size. An angry scar paled his tanned skin, starting at his temple, trailing under an eye patch, and ending right before his mouth. He could be Draven from the Selected profiles I'd studied—one whose best skill was the impressive weight he could lift.

Another Selected—Enver, I thought—I wished to never have to outsmart. There was a cunning gleam in his green irises, and his cropped blond locks made his angled, pale, and slim features all the more conniving. He studied me from head to toe as if I were an item on the menu.

Then, finally, the man reclining lazily in his seat had to be Arwan, the most bored-looking man in the room and the only one still picking at the grapes in front of him. My heart lurched at the sight of his rugged red hair, but his resemblance to Hektor was quickly wiped when he lifted his brown eyes to me around sharper features.

There was nowhere to land my attention that didn't prick my skin with nerves. I didn't need to meet the prince's gaze; I was already rattling with an odd awareness of it.

It wasn't by choice but default that my stare slipped back to Rosalind. She picked up her cup, sipping carefully, but I felt the mark she made of me. While the men looked at me as bait to crush, capture, and best, I couldn't shake my unease that Rosalind was studying me carefully, with an attention that picked me apart piece by piece. With a shock of incredulity that struck me far too late I wondered . . .

What the fuck did I think I was doing?

"Eat, Cassia," Zathrian said, playing along with the name in our company. He reached over me to spear some meat onto his plate, but I had no appetite. "Despite what he might say, the game starts now."

20

The rooms they gave me were too much, even more than what I was used to at Hektor's manor. I wasn't enamored with any of the lavish furnishings or expensive wears. They were nothing more than feeble attempts to pamper a lamb before its slaughter.

The following day, I stood gazing at the sky, welcoming a new dawn, when the sight brought forth one set of eyes I couldn't shake from the forefront of my mind.

"You made it," Nyte said in my thoughts.

"You didn't," I replied, though I didn't particularly long for his physical presence in these rooms. His intrusion both ways was starting to become eerily *expected*.

"I'm right here."

I looked over the courtyard from my viewpoint, my gaze landing on a circular building at the end of a long path with grass on either side. My lips parted and my spine curved to a touch that didn't exist.

"Do you know anything of the Libertatem? All I've heard so far is unhelpful variations of what the trials could be." I'd hardly rested for more than a few hours in turmoil at the end of the grueling feast, where I'd been circled by vultures that picked at me with their eyes as much as their mouths did the delicious food.

"From this moment on, you have to play as if every step beyond this room is a step onto a new game board. You might find those in the Libertatem aren't the only trials you'll face here."

That was nothing of an assurance.

"I'm afraid," I admitted.

"Good," he said with no teasing. *"It is your fear that will keep you wanting to survive."*

"For that to happen . . . the others must die." I didn't know them, but one life for the price of four was a burden that could taint any soul enough to beg for death.

"Better them than you."

The knock at my door twisted my body and banished Nyte's echo from my mind. "It's a training day, milady."

I recognized the woman as the one who'd taken my things from the feast. Another lingered timidly behind her.

I stood in a cotton robe, pinching the top together to be sure my tattoos were concealed. "Thank you. I'll dress myself."

Training. While it would usually inspire a thrill, I couldn't stop the rise of anxiety that this might be the place to set me apart from the lifelong skilled combatants I was up against.

The timid woman moved away to begin fixing the bed.

"My name is Davina, and this is Shaye. We're here to help you with anything you need."

"Really, I'm fine. Just leave out what I should wear."

"We can't be dismissed. Orders of the king," she said with a wince.

I realized my lack of warm reception and relaxed. "Thank you."

I stood awkwardly, not knowing what else to do, while the two handmaidens fixed the bed. I watched Davina as she tucked a strand of black hair that had escaped her long braid behind her ear, flashing me a warm smile. Shaye worked around her like clockwork, her short brown hair sitting above her shoulders and her eyes focused on her task.

To distract myself, I wandered into the closet. The number of garments overwhelmed me, but I tried sifting through them to find some suitable combat clothing. Closing the door, I decided I'd change swiftly enough to have my markings covered before I could ask for any help with the fastenings.

The leather hugged my body, feeling both lightweight and powerful. I slipped into black pants and an undertop, then I swiped up the jacket.

"I just wanted to check—"

Whipping around, I blanched more than Davina as she paused with her hand on the door, gawking at me. I cursed, yanking her inside without thinking.

"You-you have markings . . ." She trailed off, eyes wide as she met mine.

"I don't want the others to know about them," I said, hushed and hoping Shaye wouldn't hear me.

"I should hope not," she whispered back, also checking behind her, her face still pale. "They would lead to all kinds of speculation. Perhaps disqualification."

She studied me, looking over over my arms and at my ears. I jerked when she reached up to touch me. She pulled away immediately at my reaction, pinning me with a look I knew all too well.

I was *not* weak. *Not* a coward.

"I had my suspicions when I looked through your things."

My eyes widened then fell in accusation. "You had no right."

"Be glad it was me and not someone else who could have turned you in! Starlight Matter is considered cheating in this. I fear for you greatly should the king ever find out."

My lips tightened. How did I know I could trust her? Her face relaxed as she seemed to read mine.

What was I thinking?

"Cassia." Hands wrapping around my upper arms jostled me, and I met Davina's look with horror.

The longer we stared at each other, the more mystified I became at how easily she could read me. It only sank my dread further.

Realization relaxed her brow. "That's not your name," she whispered, arms dropping from me.

I didn't deny. I couldn't confirm. Pacing to the back of the closet, I couldn't believe I'd been exposed barely a day beyond the castle threshold. Before the Libertatem had even begun.

"What happened?" she asked.

I opened my mouth, but no words came out.

I jumped when I heard Shaye call, "We have five minutes."

That snapped Davina out of her stupor, but I couldn't shake mine. She began to rustle through the garment racks before plucking out a few other items. "Quick!" She ushered me over when I couldn't move.

I raised my arm mindlessly as she slides me into the fitted jacket. "You're going to help me?"

"Why wouldn't I?" she said, her tone back to a casual softness as though nothing had changed.

"You don't know how I got here. Why I'm not Cassia." I secured the buttons as I turned to her.

"Right now, I have to believe there was good reason."

"And if there wasn't?"

Davina shrugged. "Then you're mad for wanting to participate in this thing so badly that you would kill for it."

I winced at the word "kill." "I don't," I muttered in defeat. "I have no idea what I'm doing, and I likely won't be here long."

"Not with that attitude," Davina scolded.

For a second, I was reminded of Cassia's firm love, and it warmed my chest as I watched Davina secure various buckles. She had the most beautiful brown eyes. She made quick work of securing me into high-necked dark leathers and various holsters.

"You arrived late and missed the castle tour. It won't matter too much as I don't imagine you'll be here a whole lot," Davina explained, focused entirely on my attire.

"I won't be?" That came as a surprise.

"A day for a feast, a week to adjust and train if you wish. Then, by week's end, you'll have the induction—the rules and what to expect. That's all you'll get, and then it'll all be down to you."

I tried to comprehend what she was saying, but she'd given me little information. "That's not very comforting."

"I'm not trying to be," she said, stepping back and admiring her work. "What matters the most is you keep your true self hidden."

I nodded, trying to make it believable I held a shred of confidence now that I'd received Davina's sparse insight.

The door creaked open and Shaye poked her head around it. "I'm to tell you Zathrian is here."

I exchanged a last look with Davina. Her small smile and nod was the only assurance I had that she'd keep my secret.

21

Astraea."

The world felt distant, but the hiss of my real name was enough to snap me back. I glanced around frantically, thinking it was bold of Zathrian to even whisper. I landed my wide gaze on him, but he only returned a disapproving frown.

"Did you hear a word of what I just said?" With his reprimand, he jerked his chin at the sword I clutched tightly.

I tried to lift it. Maybe my reaction was overly dramatic, but I was ready to give up on wielding the weapon becauseit felt too heavy and long.

Zath sighed like I was a lost cause. "Let's try the bow."

The buildup of anticipation had been for nothing. Zath was the one who'd urged me into the training room that morning, far earlier than any of the others were expected. He'd found out from the other mentors that this really wasn't meant to train our skills. What use would one more week be? No. Like the feast, this was a new opportunity for us to observe each other. Find strengths and weaknesses. I hadn't been able to focus much, my mind cataloguing everything that made me a target.

"She's the weakest one here." A feminine voice echoed through the training room.

The hall was spectacular, with a high perimeter for viewing and several stations equipped for different combat teachings. We stood on a circular platform with steps to get up to it, but there was no safety barricade should an opponent be forced out of the ring.

I spied Rosalind's light pink hair as soon as she entered the room.

"Thanks for the encouragement," I grumbled.

I watched as she went over to the wall lined with swords of all sizes, admiring how she assessed a couple, weighing their balance between her hands. Seeming satisfied with her choices, she turned to head straight for us. My spine stiffened. My gaze followed the length of the two swords she held in each hand. They were a little shorter than the one I clutched.

Stepping onto our platform, she approached, and Zath took an instinctive step in front of me. Rosalind didn't spare him a glance, but I figured the sly smirk dancing on her lips was for him.

I went even more rigid when she reached out. My hand went slack around the blade she took from me.

"Men rarely get the weight and size of a sword correct for a woman." Rose thrust the hilt of my former sword at Zathrian, hitting his chest, and in his surprise he gripped it, his hand around hers, with a low grunt.

My brow raised as I looked between them, shifting on my feet with the challenge that rose in the seconds-long stare they shared. I dragged the tip of my new sword against the ground as a distraction, and the sultry way Rosalind slipped her gaze from Zath revealed it she was trying to rile him more so than any genuine attempt at seduction.

Zathrian looked to me when Rosalind turned, and as if he'd broken from a trance, his scowl showed her success.

I merely shrugged. "It does feel better," I admitted, trying out a few of the steps and swings Zathrian had tried to teach me.

"And he doesn't know what moves are best for you." Rosalind crossed her arms, tossing him another look, and whatever was written in it this time turned him even more sour.

I pinched my lips to keep from smiling. Which was easy when any dose of humor or happiness was quickly gripped by guilt.

Rosalind clipped the blade I was using to prop myself up, and I stumbled before catching myself as the clang finished resonating.

"What are you doing?" I snapped, my irritation highly flammable at the goading I'd rather watch her inflict on Zathrian. But now it was his turn to yield a small side-smile, and I had to refrain from doing something *very* childish.

"Wouldn't you like to learn from someone who could actually advance your skills?"

Zathrian scoffed, and Rosalind's brow lifted to me, wondering if I would defend my friend. In truth, I couldn't deny his teaching was awful.

"Seriously?" he all but whined at my silence.

Rosalind smiled triumphantly, and Zathrian's blue eyes pinned her with annoyance.

"Rosalind Kalisahn." He drawled her name.

She cast him a bored look but laid a hint of a warning on him. "So you know my name. Everyone in the realm will by now. Keep yours—I have no need for it."

I had never seen this side to Zathrian, and I wanted to shrink away from the growing tension in the room. His smile was all predatory. His eyes flexed, flicking to me only for a split second as if my presence affected the far cruder response waiting on the tip of his tongue.

"We'll see, Thorns."

"What did you call me?"

Zathrian's eyes lit up like he'd found a trigger. "The beauty of a rose, but prickly like its thorns. I think it's fitting."

"The only prick around here—"

"So, uh, how can you be certain I'll need a sword?" I said, feeling awkward for sliding in but thinking the two might detonate with any more testing.

"I actually hope for your sake that you don't," Rosalind said with a hard edge as she tore her gaze from Zathrian. "Does he need to be here?"

"Kind of." I shrugged then thought back to what I'd noticed. "Did you come here alone?"

"Yes."

"No mentor?"

Rose shifted her stance and angled her blade. "No."

She didn't want to talk about it, but I had so many questions.

"Why are you helping me?"

Rosalind huffed a laugh, her smile feline, before she said, "I'm not."

She attacked without warning, and I cried out, raising the blade out of nothing more than instinct. The harsh clank that vibrated down my arms made me drop my sword and it clattered to the ground. I gasped when cool metal touched my chin.

I wasn't the only one under threat, but Rosalind didn't seem at all fazed by Zathrian's blade resting against her neck.

"I should have guessed cheap take-outs would be your style," Zath snarled.

I could have sworn the hazel of Rose's eyes flashed a shade lighter as she lowered her blade and turned toward Zathrian's. The angry glare shivered over me, but I was merely a spectator to it.

"And what about me gave you *that* impression?"

Zathrian's face tightened, in a position to swiftly end her life. "You seem like you'd do anything to win."

"You are not one of the Selected, so remove that blade before I do."

"I don't think this is going to help either of us," I grumbled, gesturing between them.

With gritted teeth Zathrian shifted the blade away, maintaining their stare down before finally backing up with one long stride. He seemed to debate whether or not to stay down here with us, until a low whistle drew our attention to the entrance.

"Sleeping with the competition won't win you points, little Rose," Draven said.

Just like that, I understood Rosalind's emotions before had been only playful compared to the cold anger that firmed her features in an instant.

While the mysterious one, Arwan, smirked at the comment, he didn't look to us as he stemmed off from Draven and Enver. They strolled up to our training platform, eyes feasting on us as if we were their next meal. I spotted three other mentors on the viewing platform above us, and I wanted to flee from the sudden attention from all angles.

Zathrian fixed his defensive demeanor *for* Rosalind rather than against her this time.

"I think you missed the turn into the parlor," Rosalind said to them, crossing her arms.

Draven grinned with sly amusement, taking a huge bite out of an apple. "Speak for yourself. Wouldn't want to damage that pretty face in a place like this."

"Grab a sword and join me." She brushed him off, backing up a few paces and preparing to take her stance. "Then if you want a second eye patch, try saying that again."

I wondered if his huge build was from his previous occupation. Once, I'd overheard Hektor talk of late tradings with the Kingdom of Fesaris for coal. Perhaps he'd worked in the mines, and the loss of his sight in one eye was down to some terrible accident.

I still had so much to learn about the other kingdoms. Only from my brief study of the map I'd found in the book did I know Enver's home kingdom of Astrinus was the highest in the North with the most mountains. And Arwan came from the west, Arania, separated by rivers from the neighboring kingdoms.

Draven's one dark brown eye slipped to me, and I stiffened. The gleam he wore sized me up as feeble prey. "I'd rather test how far this one can bend before she breaks."

Enver snickered. "I reckon we'll be one Selected down before the first week is up."

I didn't know why I wanted Rosalind's reaction as I flashed her a glance. Her look was knowing, as though she agreed with them on their observations, but with sympathy. My cheeks warmed with frustration. I couldn't even pull off the guise.

"Swordplay isn't my thing," I said.

"Oh, come on. Play with us," Draven sang, sharing in some laughter with Enver.

I didn't react to it. If there was one thing I was brave against, it was mockery.

"Thank you for trying," I mumbled when I was close enough to Rosalind.

She caught my arm, staring me down intently before her gaze flicked across the room. "You'll be their prime target out there if you walk away and give them nothing."

I looked to where she indicated. There were two options: a range for archery I was confident I could complete to a more than average degree, and another range beside it with targets of all sizes spaced at various distances around three walls like an open box. My attention lingered on the latter, but before I could decide, Nyte's silvery voice echoed in my mind.

"You could take ten throws and prove yourself as competent as them. Or you could take one and silence them from thinking you're anything less than perfect."

One shot.

I slid my eyes to Draven, who tossed his apple in the air. "Are you going to give us a show?" he taunted, noticing I'd slipped one of the throwing daggers from my belt.

"If you want a show, I'll need a participant," I said, steadying my breaths. Tracking my target.

Draven smirked, bringing his apple to his mouth, and the moment his teeth pierced the flesh . . . so did the small blade, between his fingers.

The hall fell still. So deadly still.

I wondered if I'd stepped out of line when all eyes slowly found me, still poised as the culprit who had sent that knife flying. A fraction off and I could have killed him, and we hadn't heard the rules to know if that was prohibited yet.

Draven's eyes turned furious as he lowered the apple. He plucked the blade that looked like a mere toothpick in his giant hand, dropping the fruit. "A lucky shot," he seethed.

"It's too bad her accuracy is impeccable," Rosalind said, and though she didn't seem one to give praise often, I felt her subtle nod as such.

I reached for another blade as Draven tossed the first aside and stepped forward. Enver seemed to react to his every move, copying him as Draven drew his blade too.

"Your throw was cute," he said, stepping up into the training ring. "Let's see how you hold up in real combat."

Zathrian and Rosalind stepped in front me, and though I knew I wouldn't match up to them, I tried to angle my blade to give even the smallest impression I knew how to wield it. Draven lunged for Rosalind, who crossed her sword with his twin daggers, and they entered into an exhilarating dance. I stumbled back another step when more clanging sounded and Zathrian became engaged in a fight with Enver.

I felt utterly useless and feeble, cowering back even though it wasn't my fight. I wished I could move the way Rosalind did. As elegant as the wind, but as lethal as the blade that answered her.

They parried back and back, and I thought to leap out of the way, but Enver had also been forced on the defensive after switching sides, so I had no escape. I didn't realize how far they'd pushed back until my heels slipped off the platform. I shrieked, but my flailing arms could do nothing to help as I toppled from the height.

I hardly had a second to brace before I slammed to the hard ground. Heat spread across my head at the impact, a tingling sensation dizzying me when I rolled to prop myself up. My temples pulsed and warmed, and I wondered if I was bleeding, but I didn't check as I pushed myself to my feet and took a hard blink to refocus the room.

Don't appear weak.

Every choice and movement I made to those who surrounded me now was bait for them to use later.

"Cassia, are you hurt?" Zathrian asked.

I shook my head. It was a mistake. The room tilted, and I had to shift my footing to seem casual as I rebalanced myself. "I think I've made my point here though," I said, daring a look at Draven.

I took a step to leave, and Zath shifted too.

"I'm just heading back to my room. You can stay." I hoped he'd read my tone and Rosalind wouldn't. I didn't doubt she could handle herself, but I didn't really know her, and while she was the competition it didn't feel right to leave her alone with these brutes.

Zath's jaw firmed. He didn't give Rosalind a direct look, but it confirmed he thought the same. "I'll see you later?" he asked, even if he seemed reluctant to stay.

I gave him a grateful smile with my nod and left the training hall, sparing one look across that felt like a compulsion. Arwan was already watching me, the unnerving touch of his brown irises still crawling over my skin when I was many halls away.

I hissed, reaching a hand around my head. The wetness on my skin confirmed the fall had been as bad as it had felt. Though I was certain I would be fine without stitches.

Before I turned into the next hall, a tall hooded figure caught my attention. I wouldn't have given them a second thought were it not for the high braid of honey hair they also guided stiffly along.

My heart stopped with my steps.

I shouldn't follow. I shouldn't follow.

I cursed the second voice in my head that commanded movement, the one I'd had to silence painfully on the rooftop with Cassia the first time we'd seen a fae being herded against her will. My adrenaline raced and my thoughts taunted me telling me I was mistaken. I had to be certain.

I hid behind corners, always a corridor away every time the duo dipped out of sight. We headed down then through some less lavish spaces I thought to be the servants' quarters. When they went outdoors, I cursed my lack of a winter cloak.

My muscles tensed at the freezing night, immediately screaming at me to retreat. Dipping behind a tree, I didn't think I could follow them any farther without being seen by the guards as they glided by without question.

The female fae didn't fight, but I ached for her stiff walk of reluctant obedience, feeling for her with a strong urge to help. My fingers bit into the bark of the tree trunk I cowered behind.

As they headed toward the dominating black building, my intrigue sparked anew at what could be within.

I looked up. The tree seemed an easy enough climb.

Exhilaration took over until spots danced before my eyes, my mind calculating, and my limbs stretching. Until I was high enough to find a perch overlooking the courtyard just as they approached the main doors.

My mouth dropped open as the escort raised a hand and a ripple of iridescent light answered—so faint I could have missed it with a blink. They slipped inside, and though I hugged my arms tightly around myself against the bitter chill, I wasn't leaving until I saw them come back out or devised a plan to follow them inside.

22

The piercing cold made the minutes feel like hours. I shifted, antsy on my perch and debating my climb down, taking the time to study the guards. I mapped the path I could take, hopeful I could slip past their blind spots.

What would they do to a lost and wandering Selected if I were caught anyway? It was more desirable than freezing my shit off in that moment.

Just as I braced myself, a dark silhouette appeared in the open doorway. I crouched back down. M.

She came out alone. Her escort nowhere in sight.

Walking far more confidently down the courtyard path, her honey hair caught in the moonlight.

Where is she going alone?

The guards did nothing, staying so stone-still it was only the occasional blink that confirmed they weren't garden decorations.

The fae passed close by my hiding spot, and I scurried down, heading straight after her when she slipped back inside.

"Wait!" I choked out, rattled with unease. Something felt wrong. Ominously wrong.

The female stopped, turning to me with a fright that was warranted at having been followed. I scanned her from head to toe, looking for . . .

I didn't know what I was looking for. Injury? An expression of terror? Not this. Not . . . *fine.*

"Can I help you?" she asked.

"A-are you all right?" I stumbled like an idiot.

She smiled warily, looking behind me as though confused by my question. "Should I not be?"

I blinked. She was the same fae I'd seen being dragged away from her mother—I was certain. Yet her contentment right now, considering where she was, shrouded me in a blanket of doubt.

"I'm sorry about what happened to you," I said.

Her brow knitted in confusion. "Nothing has happened to me," she replied. Not as someone covering up the truth. Not with the fear she couldn't speak freely. No—her confusion was so genuine it made my skin prickle.

I wanted to be wrong, yet I couldn't accept her reply. "You're fae. You were taken from a town called Illanoi near the edge of Alisus. There was someone who loved you dearly . . . They lost their life trying to save you."

Her smile finally fell.

Her delicate brows drew tighter together and she stared at the ground. I hoped she was searching within for the memory.

"What did they do to you?" I whispered.

She shook her head, which dispelled her will to discover what I was talking about. Instead she turned to me with accusation. "I am proud to serve our king in this war."

"There is no war," I said, my voice rising in desperation. I took a step toward her, but she backed up as if I were a monster. "He's building an army, maybe to start one. You have to leave—"

"Cassia." A smoky voice pricked caused the hairs on my nape to stand up. I went rigid when an arm wrapped around me from behind and a gloved hand clutched my upper arm. I looked up at the crown prince.

He didn't pin me with any hint of accusation or anger. In fact, it was jarring to be met with his easy smile and warm caramel eyes. "Is there a problem?" he asked smoothly.

Drystan was the epitome of unperturbed. His presence was unnervingly calming.

"No," I said quickly.

"Hmm." He slipped his attention to the fae. "You can go, Elena."

As he dismissed her, my gaze remained locked on the prince, taking in his outdoor attire. My blood chilled despite the warmth that had returned to me.

Had he been Elena's escort a moment ago?

"What had you wandering all the way down here?" Drystan asked, snapping back my attention.

I swallowed despite my dry throat, taking a step away from the proximity that felt both dangerous and alluring. "I missed out on the tour yesterday," I said as my first attempt to save the situation. "I was looking for a library and got lost, it seems." I counted my breaths, trying to catch every change in his expression that might indicate he'd heard my lie.

His brow simply lifted a fraction in amusement. "Come. I'll show you." He twisted slightly, facing the outside exit again.

I gaped like a fool at the simple yet unexpected offer. Alone time with the prince wasn't something I desired, but it was like he was testing me. I jerked

when something touched my shoulders but relaxed as Davina helped me into
a cloak.

How did she know I was here?

It was the least of my worries as I realized there was no getting out of this.
She gave me an apprehensive smile with a squeeze of my arm, and I could
hardly return it.

Strolling side by side with Drystan outside, I was glad he didn't let the
silence linger.

"I have high hopes for you to win the Libertatem."

"Why do you stake your belief so surely?"

"I read your profile. I can't be certain what it was that made me so drawn
to you without ever having seen you."

Is he toying with me, testing if I'll fall for his flattery? I shook my head at the
thought. *Why would he care about my feelings?*

"Then meeting you . . ."—he gave me a sideways look that made my pulse
skip a beat—"was most surprising."

"What about me makes you say that?" I wasn't sure I wanted to know the
answer.

"You have . . . a particular aura about you."

The mention of my *aura* was not what I expected. "That doesn't answer
my question."

His smile widened, revealing two pointed teeth, and my pulse spiked. A
vampire. He had to be. While he could pull off a charming demeanor, something about the way he tracked me felt predatory.

I cast a glance behind him, not sure if I was more unnerved or relieved by
his missing shadow.

He was a blood vampire.

Drystan didn't seem as thirsty and volatile as the soul vampires I'd come
across, and the hum under my skin was curious, if cautious.

We reached the doors of the massive outbuilding, which spanned so high
I riolted dizziness as I trailed its length. The dark wood was ornately carved as
if a garden grew from it. Stunning.

A whole building for books? My exhilaration climbed at how many I was
about to witness at once.

Drystan reached out a hand. I watched in complete fascination, my lips
parting on a shallow gasp at what I saw. A shimmering veil. When he opend
his hand fully, the veil gave off a surge of power that made me clench my fists in
reaction. Then the power slowly dispersed. The doors groaned as they opened.

"What is that?"

"A ward."

It made sense such a place would be guarded by magick even on royal grounds. I walked into an expanse like nothing I could have ever conjured in my mind, let alone visited before.

The library was so much larger than I thought possible from the outside. I took in the wonder and endless possibility. No steel or iron or craft could come close to the weapons surrounding me. It was only when I stood around more books than I could consume in a lifetime that immortality became desirable. Though I had lived many lives because of books and learned more than a sheltered girl ever could in five years, I hungrily took in everything still to be discovered with a thrill.

I walked toward the wide circular balcony. I wasn't afraid of heights, and it wasn't the long distance that made my stomach coil; it was the large center cut-out on the ground five floors down.

"What's down there?" I asked. It appeared like a black hole, but something about it felt beckoning.

"Have you ever heard of the celestial dragons?"

I slipped my sights to him, and his smile widened to a grin as though he took great delight in my lack of knowledge so he could spill the tales himself.

"They existed long ago as Guardians of the Temples. As history tells, they were hunted and slaughtered during the first war when vampires came into creation. The vampire king who reigned here before the first era of the star-maiden kept the last dragon captive below us for many centuries. Her name was Fesarah, a brilliant white dragon, and it was said that when she flew her wings were made of stars."

The void cut out of the ground pulled at me, so much so I had to clamp my fingers around the railing as dark whisperings coaxed for it to be ventured.

"Do you believe in a god, Cassia?"

As though I'd been snapped back into myself, I had to blink at Drystan to catch his words. "Am I damned if I don't?" I asked.

Drystan leaned a forearm on the railing, turning his body toward me. "Some say if you pray to the God of Dusk and the Goddess of Dawn your soul will be cycled to the stars. Pray to the God of Death and he'll make sure you don't even need a soul. His afterlife may be dark, but it is just as necessary. This *thing* the celestials encourage people to believe is the orbit to their existence—their soul—makes them slaves turning the lock on their own shackles. Do you want to know what I think? They say my father is the evil one for the control he took of a realm on the brink of ruin, but how are the celestials any better? The humans worked for them, worshipped and obeyed them, all for a promise of their soul returning perhaps a century from now, and they won't ever remember."

"You have a soul," I said, wondering why he spoke as if he didn't care what happened to it.

"Many don't. The 'soulless,' as the people so eloquently call them. Victims of a curse that was cast upon them by long-ago ancestors. Who speaks for them?"

"No one," I bit out harshly, without thought, as the memory of the soulless who had killed Cassia sliced me. "They kill without mercy. I have seen and lived through it. This whole *spectacle* is to gain safety from them." *From you.* I didn't voice the thought.

Drystan didn't move. My exhale came out hard when I realized how I'd spoken to a *prince*. "Evil exists in all beings. It is another measure of control that lingers still from the celestial reign that thoroughly warped the minds of men. Brilliant, really, to make the people believe monsters only exist outside the control of their beloved saviors." He shifted a fraction closer, our bodies near touching as he looked at me with thoughtful hazel eyes. "Even the beloved star-maiden was no exception to what it takes to rule an empire."

That heightened my intrigue, causing me to forget the proximity that skipped my pulse. "You were around when she was?"

His smile grew with delight. "I was younger, but yes. She was adored, wild and free. Honorable and just. But like all things, she was not immune to the touch of darkness."

As a distraction, I turned my head and looked over my shoulder and down. Waxing and waning moon phases adorned the hole, the waning quarter glowing beautifully. I then looked up through the glass dome roof, confirming that it was the phase that shone beautifully tonight.

"It's a lunar calendar. Created by—"

"The celestials," I finished.

His irises danced, and finally he straightened, putting distance between us so I could breathe, *think*, a little more clearly. "Yes. They are rather brilliant."

His admiration of them made something flicker within me. Hope. Drystan didn't seem entirely hateful toward the species his kind were at war with, and I had to wonder if there would ever be room in the world for both of them to exist, along with the fae and humans, in harmony.

"So, what do you like to read?" Drystan diverted, holding out an arm as an indication for me to walk with him.

I wondered if there was a right answer. Or at least a favorable one.

"Fiction, to escape."

"You can do better than that."

My cheeks heated at his challenge. Something about exposing exactly what excited me most in the books I read felt too personal. "Books are sparse. I read anything I can get." My mouth tugged upward at the playful roll of disappointment his eyes gave as he cast them away.

"Very well. You leave me to figure out what kind of topics will spark your intrigue." Wheels scraped along the ground and the hinges of the ladder screeched with age as he pushed it. "Not afraid of heights, are you?"

"Not at all," I said, giddy at the chance to climb it.

As I hiked up my skirts, I almost missed Drystan's attempt to avert his gaze from my legs. At least he had some consideration for modesty.

I wasn't used to a climb being so structured. I'd scaled rooftops and rafters, so this careful ascension felt too safe. I wasn't even looking at the titles, only wanting to taste the feeling of getting to the top, until I was there, peeking up at the endless expanse of bookshelves coated in thick layers of dust. It was wondrous.

Drystan's chuckle drifted up to me, and I looked down, wondering if the fall would break any of my bones. I found a prince with a dashing smile staring back at me, displaying no hint of the monstrous vampire I thought he should be.

I had to look away. Suddenly I found the first script on a leather book. Plucking the book from the shelf, I flashed the cover at him: *An Immortal Heart of Vengeance.*

"Do you assume women are only interested in hopeless romance?"

He could hardly feign innocence with his shrug. "That one doesn't sound hopeless."

He was right, and admittedly a part of me was thrilled by the title. Maybe I even related to it.

I began the climb down with it tucked under my arm. Once my feet were planted firmly on the ground, I surveyed the bookcases, remembering this was where he'd brought Elena—which only confused me more.

Drystan watched me with curiosity, looking so ordinary it was easy to forget what he was. *Who* he was. I had to remember he would watch me die in this game. He was the son of the man responsible for the slaughtering of the human kingdoms he'd forced to compete for safety. Just how many Libertatems had he watched. All of them? I felt myself go pale. That would make him over three hundred years old.

I didn't notice that he had taken a step toward me, his hand outstretched. I drew a sharp breath at the faint sting of his touch to the wound at the back of my head. Drystan pulled away suddenly, studying my blood on his fingers.

The prince said nothing for a painfully slow few seconds, and my adrenaline spiked wondering if it could trigger his impulse of thirst.

"How did this happen?" he asked with a new low darkness to his tone. A restraint to it that turned me tense when he could lunge for me in a blink.

"I fell," I said through my drying mouth.

When Drystan finally tore his gaze from his hand, his pupils were so large I swallowed hard. Until he fitted his gloves back on and took a long breath as if pushing back his dark instincts. My pulse thrummed, unable to find relief thinking he could snap at any moment.

"I'm growing tired," I choked. It was a lie. I never felt more awake than when the stars came out.

I wondered if I'd conjured his skeptical look that blinked to impassiveness in my mind, but I needed away from him before I risked falling for more of the kindness that wouldn't do me any favors.

"I'll escort you back," he said, leading the way.

"Is there a way I can come out here again?" I asked.

"The doors are warded. You will need me with you."

Requesting the prince's company wasn't something I was keen to do. But somehow, I had a feeling I wouldn't need to.

23

By nightfall on the sixth day, I wanted nothing more than to map the stars after a week of expending energy. Physical against Zathrian, and mental against Draven.

Throwing a thick cloak over my shoulders, I eased out onto the balcony. Each breath was a frosted cloud and I savored the icy air. I almost screamed when I saw what I initially thought was a dead body laying on the balcony stone railing. But then I saw their leg swinging purposefully over the edge, in a carefree and very much alive way.

I didn't know if I should speak. I didn't want to spook them and send them tumbling off the edge. At this height the fall would be fatal.

"You've made quick work of becoming the prince's favorite."

Rosalind.

She propped herself up and I could now see her clearly. Her skin was breathtaking in the moonlight, unlike mine, which had turned even more ghostly. Her pink hair was highlighted so stunningly it had me yearning for my silver tresses.

"I wouldn't say that," I replied.

Rosalind propped herself up on a knee, and when her arm draped over it the glint of her blade snapped my awareness. "None of us have had private time with him. He is beautiful, I suppose," she drawled, beginning to weave the hilt expertly through her fingers. I tried not to let her intimidation tactic get a rise out of me.

"He's . . . fine."

Fine? Really? I could have slapped a palm to my face. It wasn't really what came to mind when I thought of Drystan, but I tried not to let him linger there for long at all.

"The tour wasn't much. A bland show-around of an elaborate home, nothing more than a poor attempt to make us feel *honored*." Rosalind's resentment wasn't subtle. "Perhaps the prince has been the king's spy all along and knows more about us than we've been led to believe."

My heart froze still. "Do you think that's possible?"

"Possible, yes. Maybe knowing the competitors helps him to set us up for the game. A cheat none of us are aware of."

My heart thawed and was now intent on racing to a speed that could kill me. I stared at the colossal silhouette of the round library building across the courtyard, trying to reel in my calm before Rosalind could detect my absolute fear at what she suspected.

Drystan had shown no suspicion . . . or so I thought.

Rosalind smiled, getting to her feet with feline stealth. I eyed her light footing, thinking it madness that she was testing her balance now on the icy surface. But she didn't stumble or slip, walking toward me until we stood parallel. I had to look up to see her face.

She leaned a shoulder against the wall. "They say Alisus is brilliant in the summer. That your father hosts the grandest celebration."

The cold began to drift away from me under her interrogation. No—this was just idle chatter.

"He does. It's his favorite season."

Rosalind dropped to a catlike crouch. "We didn't get a chance to properly meet," she said, but I couldn't shake the hint of a test in her words.

"You're Rosalind."

She huffed a dry laugh. "People tend to introduce themselves to each other, not the other way around."

"It's obvious we know each other's names."

"Cassia," she said, drawing out the three syllables as if she were tasting each one.

I didn't know what reaction she was waiting for as she stared at me, head tilted. I couldn't figure out what it was about her that made me want to put distance between us. Maybe it was because she was so stunning. Her delicate beauty that could easily disguise how lethal I had no doubt she was.

"People call me Rose."

I found the name wonderful and fitting with the color of her hair.

"Rose it is."

Her eyes flexed, yet before I could try to sway the topic she straightened. "Cool trick the other day," she said nonchalantly. "Has me wondering why you'd bother to pick up a sword at all when you clearly have no skill set there." Hopping onto her balcony, Rose sheathed her blade.

I floundered for a response.

She kept her back to me as she said, "I thought I heard summer was celebrated so passionately in Alisus because it was your mother's favorite season."

My skin flushed further as she glided back inside her rooms and the lock clicked.

My mind reeled at her last words. They were a taunt intended to shake me.

The kingdoms couldn't cross over to each other. She never would have met Cassia or her family.

"So far, you've successfully made yourself everyone's target."

I whirled around in fright, choking when I found Nyte perched casually upon the stone railing.

"I can't say I'm surprised; you do have a natural attraction to all things bad for you."

He sat with one knee tucked up, an arm extended casually over it while his other leg dangled inside the balcony. I longed to see his amber irises, but it was likely for the best he kept them pinned to the courtyard below.

"Like you?" I said quietly.

"I wouldn't say you have worse monsters circling, but certainly more imminent ones. You must be wary around the prince."

"Why?"

When I blinked, Nyte was gone. Before I could scan around, I felt him behind me like the echo of a presence, never fully there.

"When he sees something he wants, he can be . . . persistent."

I wanted to turn around, but instead I wandered over to the railing and braced my bare hands on it to feel the biting cold, needing something solid to ground me whenever Nyte was around. I didn't want to talk about Drystan to reserve judgment and find out about him for myself.

"You said the king had never visited the other kingdoms," I said, trying to ignore the clenching anticipation in my stomach that I couldn't trust Nyte.

"I didn't say never. You were concerned he had visited in Cassia's lifetime. Astraea—"

The sound of my name was as intimate as a touch. His hand eased over mine. I inhaled when his fingers slipped between mine. It tingled.

"You have to get better with words. They are of value like steel, just waiting for the right craftsman to make them as lethal as a blade."

"I don't know if I can trust yours," I admitted.

Nyte came to me in shadow. Made of it. Like how the impression of his body wasn't as firm as I expected. "Good, because they can be as devastating as heartbreak and as haunting as death should you be so open to their manipulation."

"Are we still talking about words?"

"Every weapon needs a wielder to strike."

I swallowed hard. Nyte certainly knew far more about the *craft* than me, only I couldn't be sure why he would warn me against himself. Or perhaps he was only the demonstration.

"I haven't trusted anyone," I said.

"I meant what I said about the Libertatem not being the only game."

"You didn't warn me of the prince before. No need to start now it's too late."

"It's not too late. He cannot find out who you are. You would be wise not to allow him to get close to you. He will try." Nyte leaned away from me, and I braved a turn, staring up at the dawn in his eyes.

"He won't find much interest. I'm sure his initial intrigue will pass quickly."

His knuckles grazed featherlight over my cheek. "You're wrong."

I didn't welcome the fluttering in my stomach, needing space but also yearning for the heat that was missing from his too-careful touch. I needed a distraction, *distance.*

Nyte stepped away, casting a look at Rosalind's balcony before he turned and headed inside. I followed, closing the door behind me.

"Lock it," Nyte said. "Always lock it."

I heeded his words—something I should have had the self-preservation to do myself, but the sound of a lock clicking shut was something that always panicked me. With a breath I twisted it, flinching at the sound.

I unhooked my cloak as he sat on the bed, and it was then I noticed he hadn't been dressed for the outdoors, but didn't seem to have had a reaction to the cold.

"The king believes what led to the chaos of man came down to five fatal flaws: pride, greed, envy, lust, and wrath. Every Libertatem has been structured around testing those traits to the very edge of their temptation."

I thought on his words for a moment, trying to calculate what I could expect from such trials. None of them were areas I was confident to be tested in. "That could mean anything."

"Yes. You see, every Selected's game is different. Entirely personal to you."

My pulse kicked up as I paced the floor, and I had to undo the high fastenings of my leathers.

"The Selected train their bodies for fighting and their minds for strategizing. It's all helpful."

"I haven't trained at all," I breathed, shuffling out of the tight sleeves. There was nothing graceful about the way I undressed from the garment. I strained for a tie on my corset that dug into my back but gave up with a huff.

Nyte let go of a partial amused smile. "I recall you being far more flexible than to be bested by stubborn ribbon."

I scowled at him. "Why are you here?" Then I shook my head, wondering if I was going truly delirious as my palm cupped my forehead, which had begun to pulse. "How are you here?" I aired the question, not really expecting an answer as I scanned the room for the satchel I'd arrived with.

"I have always been here," he said, so quietly I almost missed it.

Walking to the closet, I found my satchel at the far end. Relief flooded through me when I found the bottle of pills still inside. I took one out before heading to the dining area and filling a cup with water. I wiped my mouth, and gathered my breath. When I turned back to him, Nyte was frowning hard and his eyes were fixed on the glass.

"I'm the weakest one here," I said, thinking that was his observation.

"Strength isn't only in a physical body," he said, his voice devoid of emotion.

"I don't have much of mind either." I gave a laugh, but Nyte didn't lighten up.

"Why do you do that?"

"What?"

"Underestimate yourself."

I shrugged. "I know what I'm capable of."

"I don't think you do."

"Thanks for the vote of confidence, but I don't think it's going to win me any favor here."

"Is it because of *him*?" A dark chill entered his voice, turning silver notes to black, and I looked at him, trying to figure out the nagging sensation that disrupted my mind. A gravity that pulled me toward a darkness a part of me knew I would devour given half the chance.

"I'm tired," I said, passing him as I headed to the bedroom.

"Did you love him?"

Nyte asked something that had haunted me before. Did I love Hektor Goldfell? Seconds of silence ticked by. I didn't owe him anything, but the truth was that I wanted to figure out the answer for myself.

"Maybe I don't know what that means," I said vacantly. I reached behind myself again, straining for the ribbon. My fingers grazed it just as his pulled at it first.

"You do," he said in a husky murmur. "In some part of your mind, you know exactly what it means to you."

I pressed a hand to my chest, keeping still. The laces would loosen with any movement now. My neck tilted a fraction at his touch of my collar. He was tracing the unruly scar.

"I don't know how many more times I can see this without knowing who is walking on borrowed time," he mumbled darkly.

"I don't have a name. Or a face," I added quietly. I turned to him, losing my breath for a second at those molten eyes boring down on me before I found the imperfection on his right side. "What about you?"

I wondered if this rise like acid within me was similar to what he felt as I stared at his long scar, restraining the desire to trail my fingers over it as though that might unlock my answer.

Nyte diverted softly. "Were you happy with him?"

I didn't like the switch of conversation. That he would evade my question and continue prodding at something he had no right to know the answer to.

I put a step of distance between us. "Why do you care?"

"I'm merely curious."

"Yes, I was."

I said it to silence him. And it worked, though Nyte's silence was always that of a brewing storm.

Life with Hektor had been somewhat like that. For years I'd thought his kindness was true. When my voice was gripped it was to protect me. My tether to him had a limit, and it was to save me. Then I'd learned the same hand could give the softest touch and the harshest warning.

Anger touched me, consumed me, making my whole body hot. The emotion didn't belong to me . . .

I glanced at the bed. Loneliness swept in. Not a single wrinkle disturbed the sheets. There was no trace that Nyte had ever been here at all.

24

The prince imposed his company on me much sooner than I'd hoped. As I headed to the final summons of the king, Drystan fell in step beside me, and Zathrian fell back in reluctance. He spoke about the most mundane things. I found out the prince was glad for long winters and found the nights peaceful. Small things I could relate to, yet I found myself wanting to deny our commonalities. I didn't want to know these personal things about him if it would shorten the distance between strangers, edging me closer to his waiting trap.

"Your attendance here has caused quite the stir. We have never had someone so high in status as a reigning lord's daughter competing."

I hoped we were almost there since I'd avoided the topic of my *upbringing* so far. "I've heard," I said. "My mother lost her life far too soon because of a soulless attack. You say they are bound by law not to kill, but when a human is left with only a few years of many decades, how is that not a death sentence?"

Drystan was silent for a few strides. His hands were clasped behind him in a dominant pose, but he was not intimidating. "I too know what it's like to lose a parent too soon," he said.

My breath came shallow. Of all the new customs and faces and lands to overwhelm me, I hadn't considered the absence of a queen. Before I could voice my condolences, he went on.

"Did you find the vampire responsible?"

I wasn't thinking of my lie as I answered quietly, "Yes." The image of Cassia in the grip of the soulless weakened my knees.

"Did it help . . . ?" Drystan stalled, and I shifted my gaze to find his brows drawn in contemplation. "Ending them, as I assume you did. Did it help you?"

A layer had been peeled back on the prince that was both heartwarming to glimpse and terrifying. I wondered who had wronged him so truly to have inspired this unfulfilled sense of retribution.

"No," I said honestly.

He met my stare, and for a heartbeat there was no distance. Just two desolate souls who didn't know what it would take to feel whole again. A few seconds of exposed vulnerability.

Until we firmed our guards.

We walked into a massive domed hall. It wasn't the size that daunted me, but the exceedingly large round table illuminated at the far end, hosting the four other Selected, who stood upon our entrance while the king remained seated. Their impassive gazes slipped from the prince to me with distaste.

Arriving with him was not my choice.

As if it matters what interest the prince has in me.

I was doused with a heat that slicked my skin when the prince didn't move away from me. To my horror, he escorted me right to my seat, his hand hovering on my back, just shy of touching. It didn't go unnoticed by anyone. I wanted to run from that room with their attention targeting us, wondering why he'd cared to seat me as if I were a lady of the court.

Until forms grew from the shadows.

Humans.

"My Golden Guard," the king announced.

Drystan hadn't moved from behind me. I felt his presence like a vibration through the tall back of my chair. One by one the guards stopped behind each of the Selected in the same manner. My attention slipped to Rose, but she remained unyielding to the man who loomed behind her.

Inside I was shaking. I couldn't place what was off about their stillness.

"You have each been assigned a guard to ensure your protection as you traverse the city. The vampires beyond can't always be . . . *checked*. You won't often see your guard, so don't bother trying to seek them out for help."

It dawned on me then. There were only four in the Golden Guard . . .

Is Drystan assigned to me?

I would rather take my chances, but that didn't seem to be an option. Yet why would the crown prince accept a role below his station? Amusement, likely.

My palms were clammy. A servant leaned over, placing a small ornate glass in front of me filled with a silver tonic. My gaze skipped across the room to notice the others each had one too, and that theirs were empty.

I blinked. My mind was spinning so fast that I was absent and at risk of missing important information.

"Drink, Cassia," Drystan said, though he didn't lean down; his words blew sand across my neck.

I picked up the glass, bringing it to my lips.

The liquid stung my throat, and I put in every effort not to make a twisted expression as I set the glass down. Taking a deep breath, I caught the king's small smile, not sure of why he watched me, but I curved my spine with false confidence nonetheless.

"As you are all fed and rested and have had the opportunity to become acquainted . . ." the king sang, and I couldn't have been more grateful that he'd drawn the attention of the room. The tall stained-glass windows behind him reduced the visibility, making him no more than a dark form. "I want to formally congratulate you on getting here. You represent the best of each of your kingdoms, and it is now down to you to prove the life within them is worth saving."

My fingers curled at my sides at the way he spoke of us like cattle.

"For too long humans have indulged on this land and sullied it. There was a time of peace—the Golden Age—before they turned on each other, savaged the lands, and not even those who were deemed their *guardians,* the celestials, had control over the plague they were becoming. But since the Libertatem, each kingdom has thrived on its own." The king sat dominant. I could admit I was highly intrigued by his tale, though I didn't think it factual when I'd only heard it from the evil ruler of a species who preyed upon us. "It is through these trials you will be tested against mankind's great flaws. One victor will succeed at proving humans can refrain, that they can be civil."

"The vampires are not civil," I said. It spilled from me before I could think logically. I couldn't help it when everything he said was hypocritical, and my mind flashed with Cassia's last breaths, urging me to speak out. But when all eyes snapped to me, I realized my error. I wanted the ground to open up and swallow me whole.

The king didn't react in outrage. He leaned back casually, propping his elbows on the velvet-clad arms of his chair. "Why don't you speak your mind, Cassia Vernhalla?" he said, gesturing with a hand to pass the room's attention to me.

My nails dug into my thighs under the table, but I could only blame myself. "The soulless have been killing," I said, and I had to force down an ocean of grief at the flashes of raw memory my words dragged forth. "Not just leaving humans with years, but minutes. That is against *your* law. We play this game to prove ourselves, but there will be four kingdoms still at the mercy of the soulless when it is over, and it is not just shortened time they fear now. What will you do for them?"

The room grew thick with tension, and maybe it was my lack of experience, but I didn't know if I'd spoken out of line. Only that it felt right.

"Sometimes you have to set aside what is right to be smart."

I nearly shivered at the silvery voice in my mind. My fists clenched on my lap. *Get out of my damn head.*

The king rose slowly, and I realized then what Nyte meant. He hadn't been giving me an opening to speak freely, and I was naïve to have walked right into it. Foolish. His cold eyes pinned me with a threat that rattled me.

"Sometimes a person has far fewer years than they hope for. Accidents happen when a soul vampire doesn't detect their host only has a short time left."

My heart stopped. My blood turned cold. In those seconds where time was suspended I wondered if the air had been sucked from that room entirely.

What he implied . . .

No. I refused to believe Cassia hadn't had many, *many* years ahead of her in which to experience life and turn old and gray. To live a fulfilled existence before it was taken from her. The soulless were monsters, and the king would say anything to justify it.

"There was a time when humans begged for the aid of the vampires to end their suffering. They existed in peace, working together with the celestials. But in all species there are always those who will take too much."

The king stood and everyone's eyes followed him as he walked to a robed man who approached carefully. His hair was navy-blue, tied with braids to show his rounded ears.

He was *human*.

I blinked at him as though he were some foreign species until I found out exactly why he was in the king's service. Likely not by choice.

He raised his hands and a blue glow emanated from his palms and lit up his eyes. His fingers were poised, and when I looked back over the table to where he held his focus, I couldn't believe the magick I was seeing. I'd never seen a full map of the city, but from what I'd glimpsed upon the hills, the human mage had created a top-down view of it over the round table, detailing the three levels of distinguished wealth from his proximity.

"The Libertatem will commence at dawn," the king announced. "The city is your game board, and the winner will be determined through trials no two contestants will face the same way. Each of you will have until sunrise on the twenty-fourth day to follow the clues, complete your trials, and gain every piece of your key."

As he spoke, five fragments of metal appeared in the air above the shimmering city. They joined to create the appearance of a staff, but it was far shorter. I'd never seen an object like it before. It didn't look like a key, not a design with teeth. It appeared ethereal in the way each end intricately wove around encasings that shone with a purple hue like they trapped magick within. Then it was duplicated to create five whole keys, which split off to hover before each of us. Mine was beautiful, glowing a transparent purple I refrained from reaching for.

The cityscape moved until only a long flight of broken stone steps leading up to a set of large twin doors remained.

"The first to make it here and try their key is the victor—and will have the honor of becoming my fifth Golden Guard."

My gaze slipped to the guard behind Rose again. He appeared ordinary. Human, but there was something still and cold about him. Immortal. The sun kissed his dark skin. I saw his shadow cast behind him and couldn't figure out what was so lethal and feared about the esteemed role or the price they'd paid for their immortality. It was hard to believe he'd once sat at this table, and I wondered if he'd harbored the same dark caution that was creeping up inside me. As his green eyes caught mine, I looked away.

I blinked when the room tilted for a second. My vision doubled.

"There are only two rules." The king's eyes drifted to me, tunneling into me as if this were a personal declaration. "The first is that your body belongs to this city dead or alive now. Your guard will stop any attempt to flee should you lose your composure. Second, you cannot kill another Selected unless they have their complete key."

My blood froze. I couldn't look to the others out of fear that completing the trials would be nothing compared to the final game of survival. Instead, I tried to study what I could of the massive tiered city, nothing short of three levels of a spectacular maze. The first landing bustled with trade and humans and workers. The second had a stark advance in wealth. This was where the vampires lived. Then at the top . . . the castle of glass and black stone.

My chest tightened in panic. I imagined myself as no more than a speck planted in the lost labyrinth. Though we had our guards, the thought of roaming through a level teeming with those who thirsted for my blood and soul . . .

I became hot under my dress. Too hot, and the air thickened.

As a parchment was laid in front of us, the king continued. "The castle gates will be locked every day at twilight. That is when your protection ends. The vampires are bound by law not to kill you, but I have not denied them such entertainment should you wander into their path after dark."

I shook my head against a dizzy spell. Picking up the parchment like the others, it was a mild relief to see we'd been given the map. But while the others looked satisfied by the aid, I was beginning to sweat. I had no clue how to read one.

I watched Draven wipe his brow and Rosalind give a few tired blinks. Then the empty glass before me turned to three. They'd made us drink something, and the thought of falling unconscious and being at their mercy made my skin slick with dread.

Something warm and reassuring pulsed in my chest. My hand rose there, and I calmed a little, feeling like someone was holding me back.

"I have a feeling this Libertatem will be one to remember," the king said, but his voice became distant. "Good luck. I look forward to greeting one of you at the very end."

My head felt like it was under water. I heard several chairs scrape back as the others began to leave. I wondered how they had the strength. I planted my hand on the table and stood but had to fight the urge to fall right back down.

"You're just fine," a low voice rumbled like vibrations over surface water. I focused on it for just long enough to confirm my humiliation at who it was. I didn't want the prince's help, knowing his favor could come at a far higher price than anything else in this wretched game.

"I can take her."

Yes. I wanted to be in Zath's safe embrace more than anything. But Drystan didn't let me go.

"No need." He brushed Zath off.

I cast Zath a sorry look, barely making out his full features, only his unmistakably broad silhouette. Then I caught a flicker of pink as it swayed. "Zath," I rasped. Tiredness clawed at me, but I was determined to stay awake for as long as I could. "Rose doesn't have anyone."

About the strategy of the game I shouldn't care. Yet I couldn't stomach the thought of her being alone and vulnerable right now.

Zath gave a firm nod of understanding. I'd always admired his protective nature no matter who was in trouble.

I leaned on the prince, not having much other choice.

"When you wake up, you won't have the faintest idea where you are. You can't panic. You'll be somewhere in the city," Drystan said, his breath blowing across my ear as he spoke so quietly. "You need to make it back here every twilight. It is the only place truly safe for you. Trust no one, as everyone can be bought for the right price."

"You-you're not supposed to be hel-helping me," I said, barely a slur of words. I tried to cling onto his voice, the scents of wood and vanilla, anything to stay present, but I was drifting fast.

"I've never really cared for my father's rules."

I decided I wanted to discover how many layers the prince had.

He helped me inside and I quickly recognized the layout of my rooms. I wanted to stay seated, but Drystan helped me lie back. "This one will help you far better," he said. Taking the map from my lazy grip, he slid something flat and folded into my leathers, skimming my chest—which in my right mind might have made me blush.

Drystan leaned away, and out of instinct I reached for him. My grip around his wrist was weak, and I didn't really know what I intended with it.

"You're going to get through this just fine," he said.

My lids fluttered shut, and as I was drifting away, my hold slipped from Drystan, and so did his presence from me. Because another took his place. I wasn't sure why, but I needed to know—

"The prince is right about one thing. Don't trust anyone, especially him," Nyte said to my mind. There was a certain strain of irritation in his tone. *"I'm not leaving you. You still owe me your bargain, Starlight."*

I thought I nodded, letting my head fall and my eyelids with it.

25

Awoman was running through the woods. Sharp bites stung her with every step over the rocks and fallen branches. The icy air coated her bare arms and touched her skin through the holes in her thin white gown.

Waiting for her when she awoke had been the Reaper of her previous life, and he had come to claim again. The betrayal clawed at her within, more searing than the fire of her lungs as she fled from him. Tears streamed from her eyes, but she couldn't stop running. She couldn't lose before she'd had the chance to find the one she'd come back for and to right the wrongs of the world.

A figure emerged onto her path, and she stumbled to a halt. A new threat. One who might have tracked her from the scent of her blood, which had been drawn out by the woodland's spindly limbs reaching to grapple with her.

In the dark she couldn't find a shadow to confirm whether he was soulless or shadowless. It didn't matter. They would both feel the raging desire for her blood, especially when it was all but offered to them like this.

"What a gift the gods have sent my way this night," he sang. His demeanor exuded the arrogance of a predator who knew his prey had no means of escape.

Her heart pounded furiously. While the person she ran from was another threat to her life, it would be better than having time or blood drained from her.

In her next blink, the vampire's body was pressed to hers.

"Please, you don't realize what you're doing. I'm going to help you—help everyone—"

He chuckled darkly, mocking her, as his hand curled around her nape. He studied. Her eyes, her neck, her exposed arms. "Our king said such a thing once too, yet he is just as spineless."

"He is not a king," she spat.

"Agreed. Yet he defeated you."

"He didn't, but he stole the glory of my death when the real coward never would have let it be known. My people would have turned on him." She only admitted this to keep him distracted while she reached within herself. The magick she harbored was still somewhat dormant, and she'd already expended the small well she'd mustered while escaping the first awaiting evil.

"Interesting," the vampire said, his voice softly seductive, but he didn't release her. His fingers trailed down her neck, and she turned rigid with alarm.

"You won't be able to stop," she breathed in panic. "And if you kill me . . ."

"Yes, I know," he said, but she knew the thirst in his eyes wouldn't allow him to let her go. "They would be most disappointed in me if I let you die since your existence is what helps keep the celestials weak."

That wasn't wholly true, but it confirmed one thing that sparked a bout of determination within her, along with a squeeze of yearning in her heart. He was still alive. Still in this realm . . .

"I just want a taste."

"No—!"

Her cry was choked by the immobilizing grip on her body when the vampire's teeth sank into her neck. It was hard to recall how excruciating the pain was when she'd lived it before, long ago. Unlike a human, whose bite could ease off and become pleasurable, a vampire bite torched her blood like poison.

"He-he'll come for you," she rasped, blinking through the canopy to the stars as if it were their way to each other. "He'll c-come . . ."

"My child." A feminine voice echoed through her.

She almost whimpered.

"I told you not to return."

"I had to," the woman said, answering the sky through her mind.

"He will always be your downfall no matter how much you want to see it differently. Your heart can love another, if only you let him go."

"I can't."

"This time, should you fall, it will be forever, and a reign of terror will rise. For only when falls Night shall the world drown in Starlight to usher back your Golden Era. Guard your heart, my child, for it has led you astray once and will attempt to do so again. You bargained with your memories for your return, so it may reset your way."

"Wait—!" A scream left her throat at the vampire's teeth tearing her collar as he was pulled away.

"Run north and don't stop."

She thought she recognized the male voice, but her urgency to escape had her rolling to her hands and knees without a glimpse, trying to get any distance she could from both of them. She didn't get far as memories began to evaporate from her mind.

"Stop!" She cried hard. Her images of him were stolen one by one, turning to smoke in her mind that she couldn't grasp to defy the cruel agreement. An agreement she had only made because she had been sure, determined, it wouldn't matter; that she would find him, and she would get it all back.

Still, the agony she could be wrong terrified her now it was happening.

"Please!"

The Goddess would not listen.

His voice . . . it became no more than a distant whisper carried on the wind.

His name . . . now a collection of letters she could not arrange in the right order.

His face . . .

She blinked at the sodden ground she crawled through. Black dirt was wedged under her broken fingernails, and she examined them, wondering why. She was so cold, pitifully dressed for the winter, and the forest was punishing her for it. But her neck throbbed as warmth spilled from it.

Snap. Shuffle. Thump.

The sounds rattled through her one by one. She didn't know where she was. More frightening than not knowing what threat loomed behind her . . .

She didn't know *who* she was.

26

The gasp of air I took filled my lungs with certainty. I shot upright, examining myself, saw the dark leathers I wore and felt relief. A wicked dream had chilled me. The threads of it singed as I tried to recall what I could, but there was one thing I would never forget: the woodland where I had run straight into Hektor's arms.

I jerked at the sound of a wet huff beside me.

"You're awake!"

A chipper child's voice caught my attention. I found the huff had come from a large golden dog.

The cot I was lying in was barely big enough for me, and the hues of brown around the wooden structure sparked no recognition.

"Where am I?" I asked.

The emblem of Alisus pinned my cloak to my shoulder. That was new.

"East quarter of Ground City Circle, miss," the young boy said, hopping off his chair and skipping over. "I was to wait here to give you this."

He held out a small parchment. I took it tentatively and began to unfold it as I swung my legs off the cot.

"Do you know how many days have passed?"

"It's day one of the Libertatem," he said.

My shoulders relaxed.

"The others should be awakening now too. Only fair, right?"

I refrained from saying I didn't think the king cared for fairness in any of this, but I supposed equal measures was his twisted version of the concept.

"Tobias! Those horses aren't going to muck out themselves!"

The boy jumped at the screech of an older woman from outside the small window. I wondered why they would leave me here to impose on someone's home, but I was at least glad it wasn't outdoors in the winter climate.

"Good luck, miss!" Tobias said before scurrying out of the room, and the wagging tail of the golden dog followed him.

My heart raced at the realization I was alone and undeniably a part of the game now. My world hadn't just expanded when I left Hektor's manor; it had damn well exploded.

Rallying some composure, I glanced out the window. Dawn was just shy of breaking. I finally looked down at what had to be my first clue on where to go and read the lines.

*It must not be broken.
Or your voice becomes her medley.
Some may find it peaceful,
But the smart ones know its deadly.*

A riddle.

I groaned.

Of course, the trial to obtain the key pieces wasn't enough. The chase for the locations might very well drive me mad.

I read it again as I exited the humble home. The first thing to greet me was a black cat. I didn't have much experience with animals, but I approached it tentatively since its meow felt like an invitation of trust. As I crouched it sat politely, and I reached out a hand, which it tilted its head into.

"My first ally out here," I mused.

It meowed again, and while I was oddly amused by it, I forced myself to straighten with the awareness of what I had to do.

Then I remembered Drystan tucking something into my tunic. Hastily I opened his note. No, not a note—a map.

To my horror, he'd switched the city map given by the king to one displaying the whole continent. This wouldn't help me.

My panic smoothed only when I became fascinated by the elegant details of the map. The Realm of Solanis scribed along a beautiful scroll at the top. Following the swirling lines, the border was breathtaking. Four animals were illustrated in the corners: a panther, a crow, a dragon, and a serpent. I couldn't begin to wonder what they meant.

A new urge struck me. A determination to discover more of the lands and not have this city be another cage, a final one. I would not die here.

I looked around but the frosty, dark morning was still. Silent.

"Where am I?" I thought aloud—a habit that made me feel less alone.

My brow lifted when the ink on the yellowing parchment began to erase itself. Lines moved, reforming with blots of ink, and I gasped as I watched small buildings appear as though the map had zoomed in on them precisely.

Then the scroll at the top no longer scribed the name of the realm. It read "Elgalon's Road." I blinked a few times as if it would go back to being ordinary.

"Have you figured out your riddle?"

I leapt at the silvery voice cutting through the silence behind me. "Stars above," I breathed, willing my heart to calm down from the fright. "You have to stop doing that."

"Doing what?"

"Sneaking up on me!"

"It's rather amusing," Nyte said, now right behind me, and I almost shivered at his proximity.

"That's me, the source of Vesitire's entertainment right now."

"Let me see."

I looked over my shoulder as he tipped his chin in the direction of the riddle. My stubbornness was beginning to grow around him with the cool arrogance I wanted to wipe from his face, but this wasn't the time to refuse help. I showed him the clue.

"Hmm," he said.

Only my breath clouded the frosty air as though I couldn't draw it fast enough.

"What do you make of it?" I asked.

"I don't think this is a team game."

My eyes didn't get the chance to fully express their incredulity before his grin dimpled one cheek, showing off his brilliant teeth.

"Then you only serve to distract me." I stomped away, my boots crunched against the frozen grass.

Nyte's soft chuckle followed me. I'd had more violent thoughts about that sound than anything so trivial in a long time.

I kept reciting the riddle in my mind, tuning out the sound of his footsteps behind me. Dawn's light finally spilled across the hill, making the frost glitter and the grass dance with shades of pink and orange. I wanted to freeze this moment of tranquility, just before the city awoke.

A loud chime pierced the quiet morning and I winced. My steps faltered as a realization crept up on me.

"That's it," I said suddenly. My gloved fingers fumbled with the parchment as I read it again. The answer seemed glaringly obvious. "Silence." I watched in awe as the words scribed themselves below the verse. Holding it against the glow of dawn, I beamed in triumph.

"Very good," Nyte said with genuine admiration.

"Maybe this won't be so hard after all," I said, more as a way to lift my spirits.

"Don't get too ahead of yourself. And never let your guard down."

I dropped my arms to give him a scowl. "You're not very fun. Or helpful. Why are you here?"

"You tell me."

His presence grated on my nerves, but I wouldn't admit his company was mildly soothing. I turned my focus back to the riddle, scanning it and my map.

"If you knew the city, you'd have a good idea of where that's telling you to go."

I wondered if the other Selected had been taught the layout of Vesitire. It was massive, so big that I worried about straying too far and being unable to make it back to the castle by twilight. I had no money for lodgings, and beyond needing somewhere comfortable to rest, I feared becoming a meal if I didn't make it somewhere safe.

"The most important thing is that you stay hidden. You don't want to attract any vampires." Nyte blocked out the sun peeking over the city as he stepped in front of me. His light fingers grazing my chin forced me to look up at him. "This is your biggest advantage over the others. You're agile, incredibly stealthy, and quiet . . ." Nyte paused. His throat shifted with his swallow as he scanned my face with a disturbed brow. "Though I'm sorry you had to learn to be."

His apology wasn't needed, wasn't owed, but it was so genuine I thought this was what I'd always yearned for. To be seen. More than just on the surface. Captured by his golden irises, which could steal me far more wholly than the dawn.

"Where did you come from?" I asked. Most of the time I couldn't be certain he was real.

His expression turned guarded seconds before he stepped out of my path. "Don't trust anyone, Starlight. No one except the man you arrived with."

I drew a sharp breath. "Zathrian."

"He'll find you soon."

I didn't want to ask how he could be so certain of that, and I couldn't wait for him either. The countdown was on to be back at the castle, and I didn't want either of us to be trapped out here for the night. Nor did I plan to waste my days finding the first piece of the key if I could help it.

"I'll have to ask around the city on where this place of *silence* could be."

"What if I said I could help you?"

"I'd ask what's the catch?"

"This time, only that you remember what I can do for you."

I didn't like the sound of that. "No, thank you."

His chuckle was a hollow vibration of the wind across my nape. "You could have the first key before twilight."

I ground my teeth, spinning to him. "I don't want to owe you anything."

"You already owe me. Consider this a generous extension of your side of the bargain."

I shivered at the faint note of something that wrapped promise with threat. "Fine. Where is the first location?"

"There's a temple called the Sanctuary of the Soundless."

"The Sanctuary of the Soundless," I repeated, glancing at my map to squint at any small script that would reveal it, but the words were faded with age.

I didn't have to look when seconds later the lines were crossed out and re-drew themselves in their magical, hypnotizing way. Then a tiny scroll unraveled over the page, directing me over to a tall building surrounded by rocks. From the humble, aged dwellings around it, I knew it had to be on this level. I was glad to maneuver around mostly humans for the day.

"Who gave you that?" Nyte asked, but his hard stare at the parchment told me he already knew the answer.

"The prince," I said as casually as I could, as though it meant nothing. In truth, the idea of the prince giving me such an enchanted item had shaken me with the same feeling Nyte's help was giving me.

Given, but with a lingering promise to claim, and I was so desperate and willing that I'd accepted.

"You can't trust him."

"You keep talking about trust, yet you expect me to give it to you."

"Do you forget everything I have been there for so easily?" Nyte towered over me. I thought shadows crept around him to dull the morning light. "I have so far asked for nothing."

"So far," I repeated.

All he gave was a wicked half-smile that crawled over me. Not with wari-ness or fear, but a dangerous intrigue. I stepped back. Turning away, I took off at a brisk pace, trying to clear my mind of *him*.

"Is he tracking me with this?" I asked, finally stepping onto the cobbled street, which I was grateful to find empty of bodies in the early hour.

"The map is its own enchantment. Merely a tool that could switch alle-giance."

"You say that as if it's alive."

"Magick is life itself," Nyte said. "It is its own force, as long as it can reside in and answer to a vessel. A person with magick can push it too far and it will retaliate. Magick doesn't like to be taken advantage of."

"So this map could . . . trick me?"

Nyte shrugged. "It's possible. Maybe if you took it to a tavern when it would prefer a brothel."

I went to whack his arm, but he disappeared in a blink. His low chuckle caressed my other side, and I whirled to him with a scowl.

"There are three types of magick vessel," he went on, tipping his chin for me to walk with him. "Genetic, gifted, and cursed. You'll find most magick is genetic. Strengths and talents can vary depending on bloodline, and for that reason, people can spend their lives looking for their Bonded."

"Bonded?"

Nyte gave a nod. "A match of power, nothing more. When a pairing bonds, it's a blood exchange, and they act as each other's amplifiers, sometimes gaining a new power or strengthening what they have. They don't need to be romantic. They can have children with others and will still pass on the new height of their ability."

I stumbled as cinnamon filled my nostrils, tightening my stomach with a craving at the worst time.

"A favorite of yours?" Nyte mused, following my gaze. His tone was almost *knowing*.

I shook my head merely to push away my longing for the pastries and kept walking. "Gifted magick?" I prompted. His knowledge was fascinating and a welcome distraction.

"It appears mostly among the celestials, those given a higher power by the God and Goddess when they visit the Temple of Ascension. It is how the three High Celestials were chosen and how they have continued to be since the dawn of time. Celestials can be alchemists, soothsayers, and have many other talents. Regardless of if they receive a divination, they all have a role to play in cycling souls to the stars."

I took in everything and was glad for his pause so I could store what knowledge I could.

"The vampires are cursed. Or at least that's how they came into creation, but now they are born," he went on as if knowing I wouldn't stop until I'd heard it all. "Their existence relies on blood and souls to thrive, and they, along with the fae, were not Impacted by the imbalance that's shaking the source of all solar energy." He looked up, and though it was daytime I knew what he was about to say.

"The stars," I concluded.

Nyte branched off down a narrow alley. "This way."

This section of the city smelled like coal and ash. The buildings were mostly brown and worn, but some were over eight stories high, and I had to crane my neck to see their crooked rooftops.

"Keep up unless you want to be swept up in the morning work rush," Nyte called, indicating how far I'd slowed behind him.

"I thought the star-maiden was their savior. One of them."

"She was—is," he corrected, occasionally sparing me a glance to gauge my reactions. I didn't know what my expression told him. "But five hundred years ago, what entered the world was a power that clashed too strongly with hers. Two entities that were never supposed to exist together."

"Who is the other?"

He didn't answer.

I watched a few humans exiting their homes, casting wary looks at me, and some of them widened their eyes like they knew exactly who I was already. I didn't think it was that obvious, but I glanced down at my attire and found the blaring beacon. I went to unclip the sigil of Alisus, but Nyte's hand hovered over mine.

"That is the only thing keeping you safe before twilight."

I nodded at my error though the attention was grating on me. "This . . . *other entity,* do they still live?" I asked as a diversion.

"Yes. And people are starting to notice the nights are growing darker. Soon longer."

"Because the star-maiden has returned."

"Yes," he said so quietly I almost missed it.

We walked, blending in with the humans now that their initial intrigue had passed. Or at least I blended. Yet Nyte's tall form and pointed ears didn't seem to draw even a flicker of attention. The threat of panic only lessened as I fixed my gaze on Nyte, tracking him. He led us down some less crowded streets as the morning began to awaken the district and people started their day. I breathed steadily through my constricting throat.

Nyte's hand lightly grazed my back. "We're almost there."

After a few more turns through shops, a market square, and a makeshift children's playground, we emerged into a quieter area. Beyond a stone arch stood a tall castle-like building. The architecture was unlike anything I'd admired before. Around the body of the structure gave the illusion that dark gray stone grew from the ground into sharp peaks to protect it. A work of art in its own right.

"Remember your riddle. You can't speak when you enter, not even a word. This place is home to a spirit creature they call the Crocotta. If it hears your voice, it can take it. Permanently."

I flexed my gloved fingers as I glanced from Nyte to the temple. "How will I ask for the key part?"

"You won't. It will decide if it wants to give it to you."

"That's not encouraging."

"Despite what it can do, the Crocotta is a guardian. It is safeguarding the work inside and the non-speakers who choose to stay there."

"Non-speakers?"

"Some reside there to heal from past trauma until they wish to leave. Others never do, and this way of living is their peace."

That didn't sound as frightening. Maybe I could admire this creature for protecting them even if it could choose to steal my voice.

"You should wait outside," I said.

"Why is that?"

"Because you have a habit of invoking my irritation with a look, and I can't be certain I won't break."

I didn't wait to see if he would stay behind as I headed for the temple. There was no door, only an archway past the portico, and I took a deep inhale before stepping under it. I didn't expect to be enveloped by heat and the complete eerie weight of true silence the moment I stepped through it.

When I glanced back, Nyte was gone, and I concluded some kind of spell kept out the cold air here, just like it did in the palace. Whatever I'd considered to be silence before was nothing compared to what raised every hair on my arms now. It was so quiet I was certain I'd hear a pin drop.

I wandered inside, finding myself standing in a great hall that offered various directions in which to head. There were organized rows of glass cases holding objects, and here I found the first signs of people dressed in white robes. Some stood with books splayed in their palms, looking to be taking notes on whatever it was they studied. Animal skeletons. Old artifacts. A couple spared me curious glances, but no one approached.

I bit my tongue to hold back a gasp of fright when a beast stalked out of the shadows. A panther. The two women I'd seen closed their books, scurrying off at the presence of this creature, and that did nothing for my nerves.

I turned to stone in the center of the circular hall, hoping it wouldn't decide I was a threat or unworthy of being here. As I bowed my head in submission, the black panther began to circle me. Beneath my feet, lines that had no pattern or order spilled across the entire floor like sticks thrown haphazardly.

"What an honor it is to have you standing in my hall."

Those words rang loud in the silence. A feminine voice. The panther's mouth didn't move, and I almost shook my head at the ludicrous notion, but I couldn't help believe that the creature had spoken.

"I know what it is you seek, and now it makes sense why I have it."

The panther dipped out of sight, and I didn't have the courage to track it. It didn't reappear. Instead the hall began to darken, stealing the daylight and chilling the air. A glint caught my attention, and once again I had to clamp a hand over my mouth to keep any sound from escaping.

A fragment of metal was suspended in the air. It had to be a piece of the key, but it dawned on me this creature wasn't done playing with me yet. A feminine chuckle blew over my skin.

"What a prize you could give me," it cooed. "Your voice would be delicious. One of power and strength. A voice that calls through time and awakens the night."

My voice had always felt small and pitiful in the box I locked it in. I didn't know what else to do other than stand for judgment. When the creature came back around, my lips parted to the drum of my heart.

It had taken my face. My body. What was worse was that it wasn't my disguise of black hair and deeper blue eyes; my silver hair had returned with my matching irises, and my tattoos were on full display in the gown it wore. The Crocotta examined its arms, every marking, and I couldn't believe my eyes when it lifted a hand and the silver *glowed*.

There had been times before I had thought I'd seen them flicker, but I'd always attributed it to the lights giving off a metallic sheen. But this was beautiful. The glow radiated a soft energy.

Its shimmering silver eyes drifted to me with feline delight. "You make this difficult for me to win." Its chin lifted before it began to stalk toward me as though it had found something. It was unnerving to want to cower from the image of myself, but the seduction it wore was not mine. "You can be stubborn. Your pride is found mostly in your refusal to *lose*." Fingers swept through my hair as it disappeared around me again. "But it is those with the strongest will who know when it's necessary."

Movement below made me stumble back a step. The lines shifted, reorganizing themselves. Stacking and angling. When they stilled, I was sucked into a memory so fresh, staring at a far smaller version of this game made out of matchsticks on a beaten, ale-soaked table. Cassia's phantom laugh punched me with sorrow and yearning.

"The lines will shift every thirty seconds to a new version of the puzzle."

"Please help me."

With a gasp I snapped my eyes up from studying how the lines formed. A small girl stood at the far end, in front of me. Nerves turned to trickling pressure as I realized the stakes that were about to be added to this taunting game.

"You have until the end of time on the third try to save her. Or continue for more tries to win your key."

Outrage overcame me, almost spilling from my parted mouth before a light gloved hand clamped over it. I didn't immediately meet Nyte's eye as a huge gray wolf emerged, making me jolt again. At Nyte's interception, I landed my look of horror on him.

All he gave was a slow shake of his head. A warning.

She was just a *child*.

Sweat started to bead on my forehead before it could begin. Three tries. Thirty seconds. I was fast at the inn, but not *that* ridiculously skilled.

Nyte eased away when he deemed me no longer at risk of doing something foolish.

My body strained to save the girl whose cries flexed my fists. This was sick and twisted. I glanced up at the floating key piece I needed. Then my eyes closed as I shook my head. I had to save her, and I needed that damn key.

"Do you accept?" the Crocotta asked smoothly.

I took a single breath and nodded.

"Then let's begin."

My clone walked off until it was lost in shadow. I followed the moving lines on the ground frantically until they stilled. Then thirty seconds began on a countdown above it.

"Move six to create six equal diamonds."

Shit. In my frantic state at the timer and hyperaware of the threat to the girl's life, I wasted many precious seconds before I even focused right on the matchstick puzzle. The image made a star, and just as I beamed knowing which ones I wanted to move, a ring chimed through me, and the lines rearranged.

My fists clamped in frustration.

One time, Hektor had brought me an invention of two pieces that could come apart, and the trick was to figure out *how.* The focused anxiety of that came back now. He had been unable to pull me away from it, and no matter how much he taunted me that no one could figure it out, I couldn't leave it unsolved.

It had taken me four days.

The next arrangement formed a pyramid of triangles.

"Remove five lines to get five equal triangles."

With ten seconds left, my hands lifted, the lines moved to my gestures, my pulse raced, and my body tensed, but before my final two could slide into place it began to wipe itself again. My mouth opened, but my groan of anger didn't get to spill at the unfairness of the impossible timer before Nyte spoke to my mind again.

"You have to give up."

"No."

"Astraea, it is testing you."

"I can do it."

"That is not the point you have to make here."

The new puzzle formed, and at the blink of the thirty-second marker I flashed my eyes to the girl. The wolf eased down, primed to lunge.

My last attempt, or I had to admit defeat and save her.

My mind strained with the mental tug-of-war, convinced I could do both and incredulous I even thought that was an option. *I can do it,* I repeated internally, more as a motivation to myself.

"Don't let your pride cloud your rightful judgment."

The countdown began, and I blocked him out, my palm pressed to my forehead, which had begun to throb with adrenaline.

I have to solve it.

Fifteen seconds.

I shook my head as though it would fix the damn lines into place.

Eight seconds.

"Astraea."

My teeth clenched, fingers flexing with eyes fixed on the ground.

Four seconds.

A snarl sounded across the room, and I made my choice.

Abandoning the game, I drew a dagger from my belt, shifted my stance, and sent it soaring for the wolf as it lunged for the child. The beast turned to beautiful silver dust when my blade pierced it, and the thump of metal lodging into wood stunned me. When it dissipated . . .

The girl was gone too.

An eerie feminine chuckle stroked my skin. "I feared for a moment you would let your pride win. I never should have doubted you would prevail. After all, what an ironic failure it would be."

I didn't know what it meant by that, still rooted in my stupor. With the fall of my eyes, I found the lines scattered in no order like when I'd first walked in.

A light touch trailed over my arm and Nyte turned my palm upward. From above, the gray piece of metal floated down, tingling where it hovered over my hand. Eventually the enchantment left it completely and it rested coolly in my possession.

"Not all forfeited trials are lost," the spirit said. Then, for the first time, the Crocotta spoke only to my mind. *"Only when the crown shifts will your heart and loyalty be tested. Not all written pasts are true, and not all futures told are certain."*

Each word carved a space within me, determined not to be forgotten, though right now I couldn't untangle the meaning.

When the crown shifts.

I glanced back at Nyte, who stared at me with guarded concern. He'd warned me against trusting Drystan.

"Take this," the Crocotta said.

A blonde woman approached me. Her light blue eyes smiled as warmly as her mouth as she extended something to me. It was then I understood their treasured silence. When speech was taken away it opened a person up to *feel* more intensely and see far deeper past the surface to read someone. It was both beautiful and vulnerable.

I took her offering, knowing my gratitude was received from the motion of her sparkling eyes and the dip of her head before she turned away.

Nyte stood behind me and gave a gentle jerk of his head for us to leave.

Before I stepped out into the winter air, the Crocotta's final words chilled me first.

"Good luck to you, Astraea."

27

"It knew who I was the whole time," I ranted in a panic, walking the streets with Nyte. I fidgeted with the key piece, skimming every groove and dent. It was nothing more than a sad piece of metal. The beginning of a pattern had been engraved into it, but it broke off before it could be fully admired.

"Of course it did. It had to find out what to test your pride with."

I shot him an incredulous look. "What if it tells the king?"

"It has no allegiance to him."

I didn't know if I could believe him.

"He set up the games," I said.

"No. He set *you* up. Did you not listen to a word?"

"I listened!"

Nyte scoffed. "What part of the games being personal didn't you understand? He has as little clue about where the trials lead each person as they do."

My head spun with everything I was learning about the Libertatem. "I didn't need your help in there," I grumbled.

"I couldn't take the chance. There are many tones to that stunning voice you've yet to indulge me with."

"You're insufferable."

"Yet I'm still here."

I dipped into a darker alley, not wanting to linger on the main streets with the potential to become a vampire's target now we'd climbed to the second level of the city.

I turned to him. "You still haven't told me what you want for helping me." I looked him over like scattered pieces, beginning to fear my debt to him was growing to more than what I'd be able to repay. "You either give me answers or I don't want your help anymore," I said low, sounding far braver than I felt while he towered over me. He was so breathtakingly, dangerously beautiful that it was an effort to keep my wits around him. His guise could lure me in only to capture me. Yet with the way I fought gravity to be closer to him, to touch him, maybe I wanted to know if his claim on me would be bliss or torture.

Or if the two came hand in hand, an unseen entanglement within all his darkness.

"Fine. Then leave," I said at his silence. Without thinking, I raised my hand to his chest, meaning to push him, or at least confirm he was real.

It was the wrong thing to do. He took my wrist, securing my palm and flattening it against his chest, which was clad in a thick black winter cloak. We wore gloves, and I blushed at the thought of what he might feel like without them.

"I have helped you. Saved you. Don't forget that I am on your side," he said, with a hint of a plea if I didn't know any better. "I need you to swear to me you believe that."

My heart beat hard with worry. "What for?"

The tips of his fingers grazed my chin, tilting it to lock onto his mellow pale-gold eyes. "For what I have to show you."

The sound of someone dropping down behind us made me spin away from him, reaching for a small dagger at my waist, but this assailant had been waiting for me. They grabbed my wrist, spinning us around and crashing my back into the wall. I tried to slip out of their hold, but their knee wedged into my stomach, winding me, though I managed to reach up and yank down their hood, and that was when we both stopped our struggle.

Beautiful lengths of curly pink hair tumbled out, and I stared into Rose's large hazel eyes in bewilderment. "What among the stars are you doing?" I breathed, letting go of my fight completely. "We can't kill each other. I thought we—"

I didn't know what I'd foolishly thought. That Rose was an ally? I had trusted too easily, too desperately, when she'd given me no real confidence to believe it.

Scanning around, I cursed the bastard Nyte for leaving me to face the confrontation alone.

"Who are you?"

I blinked at the question. Then my blood soared when cool metal pressed to my throat. I opened my mouth, but I knew my lie was broken, and I didn't know how she'd figured it out so quickly.

"Please," I whispered. "I can explain."

"Did you kill her to be here?" The way Rose spoke was fierce . . . protective even.

"No," I said quickly. "I have no desire to be in this game, but I had no choice."

"Clearly," she scoffed. "I've been watching you. And you're a damned fool if you think attracting the king's attention gives you an advantage. Perhaps he's onto you as fast as I am."

"How do you know I'm not Cassia?" To speak it aloud made a lump form in my throat.

"What did you do to her?"

"Nothing, I—"

Rose leaned in close, adding pressure through the blade, and my eyes welled with blurred vision. "What the *hell* did you do to her?"

"She's dead!" My tears spilled over, and I released one sob.

Rose eased off me a little but didn't remove the threat of her dagger. I watched her expression twitch with something I related to. Sorrow. "I figured as much for you to be in her place," she muttered coldly.

"There was a soulless . . . and I-I wasn't able to save her." I couldn't breathe. Not with the waves of grief flooding me over and over at the scene playing out in my mind.

Rose finally backed away.

"I guess I did kill her." I spilled my darkest confession, the guilt that would consume me for the rest of my existence. "She always came for me. And if she hadn't that night she would be here."

The stillness that fell between us was colder than our winter breaths.

"This meant so much to her, and I couldn't let a whole kingdom lose their only beacon of hope . . ." I couldn't stop. The story came tumbling out of me, and I didn't care if her blade came to swipe my throat for real. I paced the alley until I ran dry of words, emotion, and as I gazed up at the sky, I prayed it was the last time I'd have to tell this story when I felt like I was dying all over again.

I didn't know how much time passed in silence after I said the last word. I had no care for the threat Rose could still be, and regardless of whether she spared my life tonight or kept my secret, only one of us could survive this bigger deadly game.

"There you are!"

Both of us firmed into defensive positions at the voice that disturbed us. Until the familiar blond head came out of the glare of the sun and into the alley.

"Zath!" I couldn't have been more relieved to see him, and my jog to him didn't slow until we collided. "How did you find me?"

"Luck, it would seem," he said.

Rose didn't ease her threatening expression that held a hint of ire now we were in Zath's presence.

"Good to see you too, Thorns," he grumbled, dropping his arms from me.

"Is he in on it too?" Rose accused, using her dagger as a pointer toward him, which didn't settle well.

Zath stepped forward at the threat. "In on what?" he asked in a deadly tone.

"That I'm not Cassia," I interjected.

That only inspired a far more tense standoff as Zath reached for his blade. He said to Rose, "We might not be permitted to kill you, but I can arrange it."

"And I might not be able to kill *her,* but you, however . . ." Rose finished her sentence with action, feigning a right attack before switching at Zath's response, but he was equally as cunning.

I stumbled back, at a complete loss for how to stop them before they could follow through on their threats. There was nothing friendly about the way they moved. Rose landed her elbow on Zath's jaw, stunning him, but he managed to disarm her dagger, pinning her to the wall.

The victory didn't last long.

I watched with a rush of dread, calling out to them, but it was as if I no longer existed in their honed battle. They kicked discarded crates, tossing debris at each other, and I was equal parts awed and anxious at the way they seamlessly answered to each other, while flailing in my mind that placing myself between them seemed to be the only option that might stop the madness.

"Stop this before I do," a deep voice interrupted.

I turned, twisting my head to peer up at the Golden Guard. Rose's protector. I spared a second glance to check for Drystan, but he wasn't here. Perhaps giving me the enchanted map had been his way of fulfilling his obligation without needing to track me senselessly.

"Truce," Zath called finally, taking several long strides back before Rose could attack again.

She panted, locked in a beautiful position of defense as she debated his retreat. "Not even close," she grumbled, but to my relief she straightened.

"You fight well," Zath commented.

"I handed you your ass."

"Hardly."

"You two have to sort your shit out," I said, exasperated. "We have bigger issues."

"She's right." Zath sheathed his blade. "But if you turn out to be a threat to her—"

"You'll what?" Rose challenged.

I wanted to ask how she knew I wasn't Cassia and so many other things now my secret was out, and my nerves sharpened at the hold she had over me. With the guard here, I couldn't confront it now.

"We should get to work," she said. "I assume you have your first riddle."

I dipped a hand into my pocket, retrieving the piece of the key.

"Well, shit," she muttered. "Perhaps I underestimated you."

"I'm going to head back to the castle. There's something I need to do."

"Rest, I hope. You've earned it," Rose said with approval. "I'd better get going for mine."

I didn't argue, pocketing the key piece that didn't feel worthy of her praise when I'd almost failed. She turned to walk away, but I called out, "Wait! We still have so much to talk about."

"I'm sure I'll see you again soon."

Rose said nothing more as she turned away this time, and I had nothing left either as I watched her back. The moment she dipped out of sight, I turned to her guard. Spinning on the spot, I couldn't believe how stealthily he'd slipped away, just like how he'd arrived.

I focused on Zath instead. "You have to trail after her."

He gave me a look like I'd lost my damn mind.

"Please. She'll say she doesn't need help, but I don't think she knows how to ask for it without being seen as weak. Just . . . try not to kill each other."

"I'm staying with you."

"I'm heading back to the castle right now anyway. I'll be completely safe, and no offense, but I managed the whole first trial without you."

"Yet you judge Rosalind's ability to do the same alone?"

"I wasn't alone."

Zath's brow arched, and he even glanced sideward as though mocking my imaginary help. Truthfully, I had no proof to even convince myself Nyte was real. He disappeared at the most convenient times to avoid other company.

Zath gave an overdramatic sigh. "Fine. I'll go after her. But if she tries to fight me again, I'm leaving her to set up her own funeral."

I smiled, which only deepened his scowl. "I'll see you later. Make it back before twilight, remember."

"Yeah, yeah." Zath pulled me into an embrace. "Keep to the shadows."

I nodded, and Zath pressed his lips lightly to my head before he took off in the direction Rose had gone. I wasn't keen to linger for a moment, and a giddiness bubbled in me when Nyte's last words trickled back in.

For what I have to show you.

28

I stared through the glass of my balcony doors, directly at the circular stone structure that was no more than a dark silhouette in the night. The great library. I was rooted to the spot, in turmoil about answering the beckoning pull toward it. It was where Nyte wanted me to go, though he'd never said it in words. I could *feel* it.

Rose and Zath had made it back, but she was still without her first key piece. I'd heard nothing of the other three Selected and only hoped they were far behind in figuring out their first clue.

My decision for the night was made when I slung on my cloak and left my rooms with the daunting task of making it across the courtyard unseen. I had a guide, though he never spoke. My instinct seemed to tangle with the direction I could only place from some unknown influence in my mind.

Ducking into an alcove, I waited for two guards to pass before I moved again. Stealth was a skill I was adept with from my time at the manor, yet as I roamed the halls I couldn't shake the feeling of familiarity. As though I knew their path from some alternate timeline.

Outside I figured out why Nyte had given me the precise hour of midnight to arrive. There were no guards as the ones around every post on my mental map had taken leave, allowing a few minutes' window for me to make it across the courtyard. Large trees were planted with equal spacing down the long stretch, in parallel pairs, with an expanse of fresh grass between them. On either side were paved pathways.

I darted between the trees for shadow cover, only pausing by each for a quick second to be sure the new guards weren't near. When I got to the end, my chest constricted at the tall structure. I stood before two massive doors, but without Drystan, they would not be my way in.

Around the side, I stumbled at a small hatch that looked like a cellar door. "You can't possibly expect me to trust that," I whispered, but Nyte wouldn't answer.

I whined as I tested the door, and when it opened, part of me recoiled with the lost hope it should have been locked to save me from the danger of this brazen adventure. Staring down at the dark depth the uneven stairs disappeared into, I took a second to question my sanity. What was I thinking? There could be anything down there, and Nyte might be nothing more than a monster fashioned into a beautiful dream to lure me here.

"What are you hiding?" I thought aloud again, pacing as I deliberated.

Still there was no answer. That, I would have to find out for myself, and I gritted my teeth at his silence. Curiosity pricked my skin, but my fear taunted that my steps down there could be a one-way trip.

Voices raised the hairs on my arms, making me whirl my head in their direction. They were distant, but the new guards were sure to spot me here as they slowly neared.

Shit.

My decision was forced. The wood creaked as I tested it, and I cringed, pulse thrumming in my ears, as I grasped the string on the inside of the latch and pulled it shut to engulf myself in darkness. My eyes welled as I clung to the steps. I breathed hard, asking myself what the hell I thought I was doing, but it was as if cotton had filled my ears, making me unable to detect if there was anything moving below.

Gentle, calm waves smoothed the sharp edges of my panic. My heart slowed, and I gave over to the sensation that grounded me enough to think straight. Then find the courage to begin the descent.

One step at a time I dragged forth my bravery, until my next step down confirmed I was on solid ground.

"I can't see," I choked. My throat tightened, feeling confined, as if the darkness had fashioned physical walls that were shrinking and I had no escape.

"There are more ways to see than with your eyes."

Finally! I was so gods-damned relieved to hear him in my mind. Taking a steady breath, I nodded, though it was pointless. I held out my arms, testing the air as my feet pressed on. I touched stone, jerking at the first sensation to greet me in the dark. Cold and jagged, but I didn't care if it cut my skin as I used it as my guide.

I walked for what could have been seconds or minutes. The only sounds were my scuffling feet and the oddly soothing echo of intermittent water droplets. I squinted when I thought I could see a flicker of light bouncing off the wall ahead. My pace picked up with hope, and slowly my vision expanded to reveal the exhilarating find.

When I saw an opening flooding white light into the passage, I smiled and surged for it. What opened before me almost stole the air I gulped greedily. The cave was massive, and above me, illuminating the space, was a hole that welcomed the moonlight.

I shivered, pulling my cloak around me tighter. Something about this place was ominous. It radiated with an unexplainable energy that raked at my skin, and I rubbed my arms, then my chest, at the tingling warmth.

It was then I realized it wasn't the cold making me tremble.

"Where are you?"

As I said it, I wished I could take it back, suddenly overcome with the thought I didn't want the discovery. This had been a mistake, and something inside was screaming at me to turn back.

A sharp rattle shot all my senses to high alert. I snapped myself around, painfully rigid in anticipation as I watched the dark space I was certain the sound had come from. It continued. Growing louder, getting closer. I took a step back as though it might lunge—whatever it was.

A pair of black boots were the first thing I saw, emerging into the pool of light, and still the chimes followed. My gaze trailed up from them as the form revealed itself slowly, and when the figure became whole . . .

I can't have been breathing.

Time stopped. I was in complete confusion, unable to attach my sight to reality. This had to be a dream. No—a *nightmare*. Because what else would need to be chained and abandoned down here other than a dangerous monster?

Yet my lips cracked open; a few beats of silence passed . . .

"Nyte," I whispered.

He didn't smile—or really react at all—but when he responded I could have fallen to my knees, which became weak at the clarity of his voice. "Hello, Starlight."

I learned in that moment the face I stared at had three voices.

The one that caressed my thoughts.

The one that spoke aloud, but always with a note of distance I'd never questioned deeper.

Then there was this—the unmistakable surety of a real voice, and I wanted to slap myself for ever believing the others.

"How is this possible?" I took in the thick iron clamped around his wrists, attached to heavy chains I couldn't fathom the need for. He was only one male. Then there was my incredulity—because they were not bonds he could slip in and out of, and this dwelling was not a place of any comfort. His clothes were far simpler than anything I'd seen him in before: only a plain worn shirt, dirty black pants, and old boots. His hair was a little longer and far more disheveled, but still he was breathtaking. Because those molten eyes never changed, nor did the perfect angles of his face. And though it was near covered by his hair, the scar from his temple to his cheekbone was real.

"I've been here a long time," he said.

It would take some time for me to adjust to the true vibrations of his voice, but I wanted to hear it again. And again.

"Who did this to you?" My gut was wrenching, my heart aching, and I didn't want to feel these things for someone I couldn't yet know was deserving of them.

"That doesn't matter," he said, stalking a little closer, but he halted, eyes flinching. Because I'd taken a step back in response. "You said you trusted me."

I shook my head. "You can't expect to hold me to that when I'm staring at someone bound in chains in an underground prison."

His jaw worked. "Then what will it take, Starlight?"

"Don't call me that." I couldn't take it. How personally he addressed me, and now I couldn't be sure who it was I'd accepted so desperately as a guide in my vulnerability not to be alone.

I wasn't alone anymore. I had Zathrian, and what would it matter if I died in the Libertatem anyway?

"That's not going to happen," he said darkly.

"Stop that," I snapped, finding the courage to step closer.

"What?"

"Reading my mind—answering my thoughts!" My eyes scrunched shut as I walked to try to calculate what the hell was going on. "How have you been here the whole time? Even back in Alisus?" It didn't make sense, and I was close to succumbing to the waves of dizziness as I tried to sort through the explosion of a puzzle I'd thought I was slowly piecing together.

"That's not important right now."

I laughed without humor. "You're not exactly in a position to decide what's important."

The gold of his eyes turned the darkest I'd ever seen them. Impatient anger clouded them, and that was enough to confirm my wariness was justified and those bonds somehow necessary.

"Astraea." He said my name with a firmness I'd never heard. "I thought you were ready."

"For what?"

"To handle this."

I blinked, taken aback. "I'd say I'm *handling* this madness pretty well."

"You're in denial."

"About the one who's been stalking me by some impossible means? Yes, I think I'm granted that."

"I need you."

That stole the rest of my words. "What could I possibly do for you?"

"Free me."

I huffed a laugh, then a chuckle, before the eeriness of my own sounds chilled me, because he had to be fucking joking. The sternest expression remained on his face, so unlike the handsome confidence he'd come to me with many times, and I decided I liked my own version of him a whole lot more.

"When you came to me . . ." I took a deep breath, struggling to comprehend what I was asking. "How could I see you? I could touch you . . . and you touched me."

"Because you wanted it."

I most certainly did not. That was what I thought to say to wipe away his confidence. But I schooled my frustration. "That's not an explanation."

"Free me, and you won't have to fear or change for him once this game is over."

At what cost? What horror could be unleashed if I did as he asked?

"I wouldn't free a lion because it whined like a house cat," I said.

Nyte's mouth curled, the first easing of his cut features. The *real* him. "A few minutes and you've already deemed me so dangerous?"

"I might not know much of the world yet, but I'm insulted you thought me to be *so* naïve that I could look at your chains, where you're kept, and not think 'dangerous' is a tame term for what you are." My fear of him turned to anger. "Is that why you chose me? You saw someone weak, vulnerable, and your grand trick was to get me here." Then my world turned cold, and in my spike of rage I remembered I had my dagger at my waist. "Did you kill her to get me here?"

"No," he said without hesitation. "I am sorry about your friend."

I couldn't be sure. Not when everything I thought I knew about him had turned out to be a lie. His very existence had only been an illusion until now, and I needed to figure out that part before I lost my damn mind.

Perhaps that was already long gone.

"I can't trust you," I said. "Not until you start giving me answers."

"How many lives are you willing to watch end before you receive them all?" he said harshly.

I flinched, hating the bait. He knew exactly where to get to me. But I held my ground. "As many as it takes to be sure you aren't a greater threat."

His fist flexing rattled the chains, drawing my attention to them. I wished to turn them to ash for causing the thick abrasions that looked healed over many times. Then I shook my head to wipe my unexpected flash of sympathy.

"How long have you been down here?" The whisper slipped out.

Nyte withdrew, giving me his back as he leaned against the uneven stone wall, half cloaked in shadow. "You're not safe out there," he said, evading my question. His quiet voice of *defeat* pinched my chest as he refused to meet my eye.

"I don't think there is such a place."

"I told you where you should go."

Beyond the veil.

"Why?"

"You're in the Central now, Astraea. Make use of the knowledge you have access to here, but be wary. The king has not one shred of mercy for anyone. He cannot find out who you really are."

"Why have you been helping me?"

Nyte pushed off the wall, making the clang of his chains resonate through the cavernous dwelling, and my gut sank with every note. He stopped, the distance between us the shortest it had been since I arrived. I didn't balk this time.

"Will you come closer?"

The low tone of his voice was so inviting I answered to it. I took a couple of steps, each one making me feel like I was tethered to an electric pull. A hum that grew over my arms and chest and made my breathing come quicker.

"What is that?" I whispered, stopping when there was only a small measure of distance between us.

Nyte raised a hand—slowly with the weight of his shackles. A finger pointed until his restraints met their end, and his teeth clenched. My brow flinched at his suppressed pain, but I saw it then: a faint iridescent sheen that rippled with the advance of his touch.

"The only thing that's keeping me here." His hand dropped, and mine fought the urge to reach out and touch what he couldn't.

"I would have thought it was the shackles."

Nyte chuckled resentfully, and the unexpectedness of it locked our eyes.

"I could take care of those just fine if it weren't for that damned ward."

"Magick?"

"Yes."

"How did you ever expect I'd have the answer to break it?"

Nyte studied me. I couldn't understand the flicker of sadness in his subdued amber irises, now a cool honey color. "You *are* the answer, Starlight."

29

E very step back to the castle had felt like a waking fever dream. I was barely present and had left Nyte abruptly, needing time to figure out how anything I'd just discovered was real.

Lost in my reeling thoughts, the air whooshed from me as I collided with someone.

"Apologies, milady." Shaye shuffled back before dipping her head.

I smiled, laughing lightly to disperse any tension. "I'm sorry too. I didn't see you. These halls are so dimly lit."

Shaye's shoulders relaxed. "Can I accompany you to your room? Or fetch anything for you before you retire? Davina has already left for home, but I could—"

"No. I'll be just fine, thank you."

Shaye nodded, and from the fatigue in her eyes I knew it must be late. She gave another bow before slipping around me, and I turned to spy her about to leave through the exit.

"It's freezing at this hour," I called, noting she was only in her usual cotton gown. Long-sleeve, but it wouldn't protect against the chill.

"I do not mind. I live just outside the palace gates."

I had already unhooked my cloak, and while her eyes widened in protest I held her gaze, telling her not to bother. I fit it around her shoulders, and she clipped the cloak at her collar as though no one had ever offered her such a simple kindness before. I couldn't bear it.

"I want you to keep it," I said, squeezing her arm. "I'll see you tomorrow."

30

I wasted a day I could have spent searching for my next key piece by instead pacing my rooms thinking about every memory I had with Nyte. Each one threatened to become distant and cold in this new reality, but at the same time . . . I didn't want to believe the feelings weren't real.

The following day I returned from clearing my mind by attempting to train with Zathrian to find Davina poking at the newly lit fire. I checked the adjoining spaces for Shaye, but she wasn't there, and Davina's harsh sniff set me still with dread.

"Are you all right?" I asked carefully, easing toward her.

She wiped her face on the back of her sleeve before turning to me. I was striding at the sight of her puffy eyes and tear-stained cheeks when a figure landing on the balcony hit me with fright. My pulse raced as I let Rose through the door, and she scanned me from head to toe, letting out a sigh of incredulous relief.

"What's going on?" I asked them.

"It's Shaye," Davina croaked. "She—She's—"

"They found her by the gates this morning," Rose explained, her brow pinched with sympathy for Davina as another tear spilled.

"Found her?"

"Killed."

It was as if death's chuckle had seeped into the echoes of that one word. A reminder it still lingered close, taunting me, threatening those around me. I struggled for air with the swelling in my chest. Slices of raw memory opened to bleed from me all over again. Cassia's final moments . . . I wondered if Shaye would have looked the same.

"Astraea."

I was lashed back to my present surroundings with a firm shake. I latched onto Rose's unblinking eyes then slipped my gaze to Davina, whose upset shook me out of my shock. I hadn't known Shaye as much I'd hoped to have the chance to, but Davina had, and my heart ached for her.

Pausing in front of her, I gave her the chance to deny, but Davina embraced me eagerly. "I'm so sorry," I tried, knowing nothing I said could ever soothe something so deep as the wound of loss.

"I'd known her for a year, since I came to the castle. She was the first to welcome me here, and we've worked together side by side since."

The three of us settled by the fire and listened to Davina tell her stories of a lost friend. We laughed and shared tears, and the hours we passed were filled with memories that promised to carry her short life on.

"I tried to ask her out once," Davina chuckled nervously. "She didn't understand it was romantic, but we had a good time all the same."

"You never told her your feelings?" Rose asked. She wore such a gentle softness that was so relaxing to see.

Davina shook her head. "Stars, no. I took that as a sign she wasn't interested in women that way. I didn't want to shake our friendship."

I sat on the floor by her chair, reaching a hand to her lap. No words were needed in our shared smile of comfort. "We're going to find out who did this," I said.

Rose nodded, her determination as firm and true as mine.

I decided to fill the silence with a sway of topic. "How did you know I wasn't Cassia?" I asked Rose. Seeing her caution around Davina, I added, "She knows too."

Rose's skin smoothed out as she rubbed her forehead as if gathering strength. "It's a miracle you're still alive, Astraea."

I blinked, wondering how Rose was always one step ahead. "How do you know my name?"

She smirked. "Cassia was a fascinating person. She had many things she loved. I figured if there was anyone traveling with her here, you would be one of them given how much she talked about you."

The familiar pulse in my chest warmed brightly. I couldn't express my gratitude, not knowing where to direct it when all I knew was that this was a gift. Rose could be tense and prickly, and I wasn't so naïve as to think she would warm to me because of this. But here stood someone who somehow knew Cassia deeply, even if only through script, and that was one more flame to keep her memory alive.

I watched her travel through memories as she stared into the fire. Then Rose fiddled with the folds of her jacket, seeming to contemplate something before she took a deep breath and dipped a hand inside. She produced a parchment, unfolding it with careful attention, and there was a dent in her brow when she scanned it over. After a hesitant pause she extended it to me.

I was taken aback, but seeing her obvious twitch as she stopped herself from retracting her arm, I took it. I read over the words, my hand trembling.

I was wrong to think I'd exhausted my emotions; they barreled into me all over again as my fingers brushed the familiar swirls and the tilt of the writing.

When I turned to Rose with wide eyes, for the first time she showed me her smile. It was true and filled with sadness and grief, and I was overcome to have someone to share these emotions with.

"Cassia and I were exchanging letters before our kingdoms even hosted the Selected trials," she said solemnly.

I couldn't believe it. I wondered why Cassia had never told me, and it hit me with a pang of disappointment that perhaps I hadn't been as close to her as she was to me for this to have been kept a secret.

"She never spoke of you," I said.

Rose huffed a laugh. "Our relationship was a secret to most. We knew one of the king's guards who frequented the same border at the wall, and over five years he got our letters past that hurdle without us needing to go through any of the main lines intended only for formal reigning lord correspondence."

"When did you know I wasn't her?"

"The moment you walked in," she said, though I expected that as I recalled her cold glare. "I may never have met Cassia, but I knew what she looked like. I commend you for trying to fool me with the Starlight Matter you must consume, but something was off about you from the moment you walked in. I was doubtful at first, figuring you'd masterfully kept in any hint of recognition toward me with the audience we had. But the black hair doesn't suit you right. I can't place it. Then when you continued to act as if we were perfect strangers I knew you couldn't be Cassia. I didn't want to out you right away. I wanted to figure you out."

"Did you?" I shifted my weight, realizing I'd been under Rose's magnifying glass this whole time.

"Not even close. But you seemed harmless to a worrying degree. I couldn't comprehend why you'd be here and not her. I figured the worst had happened and Alisus wanted to fool the king to keep a player in the game. No offense, but you don't seem the type they would choose."

"None taken," I muttered. I couldn't be offended by the truth.

"But for what it's worth, I think it's incredibly brave for you to be here after what you went through. Cassia would be proud."

Rose said it with sincerity. I smiled sadly, but it was like she didn't know how to offer her condolences. Nor did I want them.

"She would want you to keep on living, you know," Rose said, her words unexpectedly soft. "She would have wanted that for me too. I didn't get the privilege of knowing her in person like you did, but I'll miss her. More than I can say. She was the last person I had."

My nose stung, and I wondered how she composed herself so well when it pulled me apart at the seams to think of her. "I am living," I said, though sometimes I wished I were not.

"You are surviving," Rose said, pushing to her feet. "Something tells me you have yet to *live* at all."

I swallowed over the marble that had settled in my throat. Despite everything and what we still had to do, I held her hazel eyes, which were far more of a warrior's than mine, and I understood. I was grateful, so gods-damned grateful, to discover she had known Cassia.

"I'm going to head to the training room. Helps to clear my mind," Rose announced.

"Can I come with you?" Davina asked. "It might help to take my mind off things too."

"Do you want to come?" Rose asked me. The genuine side that came out of her around Davina was a warmth beyond the sorrow we all felt.

I shook my head, following them to the door. "I was there with Zath earlier. I think he said he planned to head back after supper though."

Rose's disgruntled exterior returned, and I bit my lip to keep from a chuckle.

After they left, I stood staring at the closed door for a few heartbeats to process all that had happened. I pressed my fingers to my temples, and then, as though trying to ease the announcement of his arrival, I felt a light caress on my nape.

Turning, I was overcome with incredulity at the sight of Nyte on my bed. "What are you doing here?"

He didn't take his eyes off the item he threw and caught over and over again. Something metallic, made of brass. "I thought we went over this," he drawled as I clicked the door shut. "I am here when your thoughts are reaching and I happen to be in the mood to reach back."

"I still don't understand how . . . *this* works," I said, shivering at the notion he wasn't here. Not really. And though I could see him so clearly now, I'd been physically closer when I couldn't see him at all in the library with Drystan.

"Lie with me."

"I am *not* going to do that."

The round brass item he caught in his palm disappeared with a clench of his fist. His golden gaze slipped to me with a devilish smirk. "I'm sorry to hear about your handmaiden."

"She was more than just that."

I believed the understanding that erased his jesting for just a moment. I'd exhausted myself with grief with Davina and Rose, and maybe there was a part of me that was glad for this distraction.

"You can tell me anything while I stand right here."

"I could," he sang, "but I would much rather you lie with me."

He isn't real. There was nothing scandalous or real about obliging. I removed my boots, and knowing the tight sleeves of my jacket would strain uncomfortably, I unbuttoned the high neck too, peeling my arms free. Though he didn't watch me, the quirk of his mouth ground my teeth.

"Lose the gloating, or I'll cast you away."

"I have no need to gloat about you giving in to your wants."

He was insufferable. Arrogant. Devious.

I marched over to the bed, listing other things to distract myself from the *wrongful* giddiness rising in my stomach as I got closer. My confidence faltered when one knee was pressed to the sinking sheets, displaying every relaxed and beautiful angle of him. I knew his crisp, dark jacket with gold embroidery, much like his finely made pants, was just an illusion, but I admired his fashion sense outside the forgotten cave dwelling. As I eased onto the bed I kept a spacious distance between us, all too aware of my bare arms and the low, curving dip of my neckline. When his head turned and his eyes skimmed over me, it was as if he traced every silver line that marked me, knowing the path of each one.

"What did you want to tell me?" I asked quietly.

His eyes met mine. "Come closer."

I held back a shiver with that command. Telling myself it was to save a string of useless protests and jesting, I shuffled over.

"Now lie with me."

That smooth, silvery tone would never fail to race through me. I eased down, not even an arm's distance away, my heart thumping loudly in the silence. I wondered with a flush if he could hear it.

We stared at the navy canopy over the four-poster bed, and slowly the fire I knew to be blazing across the room died out. The amber diffused, and in its place stars came out to play, stretching beautiful color and constellations above us. It was enchantingly beautiful.

"How do you do that?"

"It's your desire. I only make you believe it's real."

I let a few beats in my chest pass before I said, "I don't desire you."

"You're intrigued. Some part of you believes I have the answers you've been searching for."

"And do you?"

"Perhaps."

"Only in the form of tricks and games."

Nyte chuckled, and though the vibrations weren't physical I felt them all the same.

"Why are you helping me?"

"You fascinate me."

That wasn't an answer, but I bit my lip against any argument. "You let me out of Hektor's manor," I said suddenly.

"You let yourself out."

I shook my head, wanting to deny the truth, but he had nothing to gain with the lie. I'd been trying to make sense of the memories I thought he featured in. Every time I remembered he was never really there I thought I'd feel lonely, disappointed . . . But he had been real to me all those times when I was desperate and reaching.

He'd answered.

"I fell from the wall."

"Yes, you did. But you're more agile than you give yourself credit for. And you undid the lock with two hairpins."

"Why did I think it was you?"

Nyte's head turned, and I mirrored him. He looked at me with an honesty I couldn't decipher. "You wanted someone to be there for you. So I made you believe I was."

My brow pinched at my own pitiful sorrow. How weak and vulnerable I must have seemed to him. I couldn't bear it, and I twisted my gaze away, but I had nothing to fill the silence.

"I believe I owe you a story," he said, and I was grateful for the change in direction.

"Why tell me anything at all? I haven't agreed to help you."

Nyte took a deep breath. My hand lay palm-up by my head, and my breath hitched when his did the same. So close it wouldn't take much of a shuffle to touch him.

"Like you, I find the nights alive. Perhaps we can both find a means of drifting off peacefully with a tale."

I didn't want to know how he'd discovered that about me. Or what other things might have leaked through the barrier I tried to keep firm in my mind.

"Once upon a time, there was a war between the stars," he began, his voice taking on a soft cadence that was relaxing to my senses. "What started as a beautiful collision turned out to have the most dire consequence for the world." He paused as if to gauge my reaction.

"Keep going," I whispered. Something fluttered in my chest like an echo of pleasure.

"The Daughter of Dusk and Dawn went against their wishes."

"The star-maiden."

I kept my eyes on the moving stars above us. They shifted, forming two starry silhouettes, and I couldn't stop the need to see them closer, propping myself up on one hand.

"Yes. And she met another of similar strength by . . . hostile means. Two who were never meant to exist in the same realm. Their powers combined were too much, and it shook the balance. Everything is a give-and-take. Our souls give back, retire as stars to keep the solar magick going. They shed, which is what falls and is then crafted into Starlight Matter. It's found in the form of stunning clear and silver rocks. Then it's turned into an elixir that can be influenced by human mages to create all kinds of things. Like the theft of your silver hair. I think people started to realize something was wrong when more fell. Too much. What was once this rare and precious material dipped in value, but that was a superficial concern. What really mattered was what was happening to the realm." He paused only to run a finger through my spilled dark tresses, skimming my shoulder. "In turn, the celestials weakened slowly at first. The ones who harbored the most power in the realm became not even a match to the vampires who took advantage of the king's careful plan to overthrow them."

I watched the scene unfold. Desolation in a thousand glittering sparkles. My adrenaline raced and my senses filled with the tale as he made it feel so *real*. As if I were right there among them.

"They had an abundance of soul energy to feed from, and the nightcrawlers and blood vampires became reckless and greedy. All together, they started the uprising, led by one male who saw it as his chance to gain the throne. They believe he won because he conquered the gods to be here by walking through worlds . . . as their savior."

"The king isn't a vampire?"

"No. He is nothing more than a fae."

I tried to process what that meant; if it could be important. "The vampires . . . could they ever coexist with us in peace?" I thought of Drystan, and with the way Nyte seemed to pause before he answered, perhaps he knew it.

"Yes. There used to be a truce. The vampires and celestials worked together to create harmony. They would feed on the souls of the wicked, those who didn't deserve to find peace in the sky, who would one day return to the realm for a new life. Murderers, rapists, evil beings . . . And then there were humans who would trade days, weeks, months of their lives with the vampires—and their willing blood. Sometimes they gave it with affection; other times they treated it like currency."

"That doesn't sound fair," I mumbled, in a trance with the story.

"The world will always have dark corners of cruelty. Life, no matter which species, will always deal unkind hands of fate. Make it more difficult for one to reach the same goal. If you ask me, it only makes their story worth more in the makings of their legacy."

The constellations broke and reformed, creating the couple once more.

"What happened to them?" I asked.

Nyte took a deep breath, and now I knew of our mental connection, I thought the notes of despair to be his. "They found themselves forced to lead on enemy sides."

My heart felt *squeezed*. "This won't have a happy ending," I said, clinging to the glittering forms of the couple.

"The star-maiden was ordered back by her parents as the world erupted into chaos and war, but she defied. She wanted to fight. But there was nothing she could do. One of the two star-gods had to die for the celestials to regain the strength of their solar magick."

My head twisted to him with wide eyes. His lips firmed and he nodded. I cast my sights up just in time to see the feminine form dissipate from the other, and he reached after the stardust she became.

"What happened next?"

Our eyes met for a prolonged, searching second. There was no next. Not for them.

I lay back down. "Being here, can you . . . *feel*?" I asked with growing anxiety. In the silence I counted my breaths, watched stars collide, and almost settled on thinking he wouldn't answer.

"It's been a long time since I've felt anything at all."

I didn't know what to say to that, nor what he was really trying to tell me with it.

"You have to want me here. The more you desire it, the more tangible it can become. It's a push-and-pull of sorts. Every touch was as real as you believed it to be because you opened yourself to me. The mind is a very powerful thing."

It somewhat explained how sometimes he only spoke to my mind. Even now I couldn't reflect on the memories as anything less than real with how sure I was that he'd been before me all those times.

I sucked in a breath when his fingers grazed mine, and though I wanted to deny it, I'd *longed* for the reality of that touch, and that was what it had become. I was drunk on the magick of it and knew this was safe. I could banish him at any moment and lock him out for good.

At least I thought I could.

"Do you feel me?" I asked quietly.

"As much as you do me."

He continued until his knuckles grazed my palm, his hand rested in mine, and I slipped my fingers through his, unable to stop my curiosity as I locked them under mine.

"But it's nothing compared to how I *want* to feel you," he added in a low murmur. "Truly real. I may have moments of peace in my mind, but you are a maddening temptation, Starlight."

I shifted my hips at the tight sensation over my skin. Finally, I found the will to rest my head toward him, immediately captured by his irises, which flickered like the candlelight he'd stolen from the room. My gaze drifted down to his neck and the gold markings peeking out from under his collar. I didn't know where my bravery came from as my other hand reached over, moving slow like he might be spooked by my advance at any second.

"You only want me to free you," I said. My fingers brushed the material and his neck tensed, but he didn't stop me.

"I do. And if I only got one true feel of you before the world collapsed, it would be worth it."

His fingers had brushed over my tattoos many times, and now it was my turn. Our hands remained within each other's, and something enchanting raced over my skin. I touched the first constellation point high on his throat then boldly traced down to the next, heading lower. I almost missed his shallow, contented sigh.

My mind sparked as if I should know what the tattoo meant. As if I had seen it before but couldn't place the whole picture. I tried to peel back another inch of his tunic but he caught my wrist.

"If you're going to take my clothes off, I want *that* to be real."

I snatched my hand back. Both of them. Propping myself up, my heart thumped wildly at the closeness we'd shared and the intimacy I'd so easily fallen prey to that would have had me lying there until the stars rested for dawn.

As I spun off the bed the room brightened again with the return of the amber fire. I didn't feel the chill of the room, being so far from it as my body flushed with a heat I wanted to douse with ice, to stop feeling at all, because what was happening within me was sure to get me killed by the demon who wouldn't leave me alone.

"What's wrong?" he asked.

I closed my eyes, gathering breath to find my rational mind. Everything I needed to find out was becoming clouded by his trance. He wanted me for one thing.

"I'm not freeing you."

A new darkness swept through the room and blew over my skin with the coolness I thought I desired. Not this kind, which rippled with danger and passion.

"Why not?" he asked in a hard tone that contained his thinning patience.

"You won't tell me what you are or why they see you fit to have you chained down there."

Nyte laughed bitterly. I turned to him, not finding him lounging on the bed anymore, and before I sought him out my chest *ached* at the sight, for the only side with crumpled sheets was where I had lain. No physical trace of Nyte lingered, and I didn't want to feel my disappointment at that fact.

"Why don't you ask your prince?"

His voice came so near I gasped, stumbling back until I met the wall, and he closed in, planting his hands by my head.

"You're scaring me," I whispered.

"Yet I'm still here," he challenged.

My mind was mocking me. Laughing and laughing, and I didn't know what to do.

"Push me out," he said like a dare, and I closed my eyes. "Do it, or I could kill you right here."

A hand wrapped around my throat, snapping my eyes wide, and the gold irises that pinned me now were burned bronze. I reacted. My hands tore his wrist from me, and I shoved his chest. Hot anger and the instinct to defend myself pricked my eyes and labored my breathing.

"Don't fucking touch me like that."

Nyte searched me, eyes blazing. Not at what I'd done, but he'd read my response too easily. He knew why.

Humiliation threatened to cast him away and never let me surface another thought of him.

Until his expression softened. So slowly. Tentatively he closed the distance, reading my every flicker of a reaction.

I didn't stop his approach.

His hand rose again, pausing at my throat when my whole body locked. Only when I relaxed, calming to his careful movements, did he continue.

He's not going to hurt me.

Why was I so certain?

"It's not the touch you fear, but the intention," he said softly, grazing a light caress over my neck that inspired a tingling warmth this time. He angled his head toward mine, dipping, and I almost held my breath. Not knowing how else to release the anticipation coiling within me, I flattened my hands against the wall behind me.

"He doesn't get to win," Nyte said, a growl of a threat so close to my lips.

I realized his hand had encircled my throat fully and I didn't have an inkling of fear. My fingers flexed against the cool wall from the *need* tightening in my stomach, heading lower. "Nyte . . ." I breathed. His proximity consumed me like a fever. I wanted the press of his body and became frustrated by the lack of heat from him even though my skin was hot. My eyes fluttered to the slip of his hand around my nape as he tipped my head back, but his lips moved from hovering over mine.

"He doesn't get to take this from you."

I drew breath as the ghost of a kiss was pressed to my neck instead. My pulse raced. Desire tingled, and I wanted—

My eyes snapped open to the grip of loneliness, my chest heaving as I sank to my knees.

Nyte was gone.

I'd wanted him to *bite* me.

Stars above, what was I thinking?

31

I sat with my legs dangling off a high roof, mulling over the sheet I'd obtained from the Crocotta that mapped the location of my next trial. It had various lines and some circles, though nothing else that could help me decipher what it was for. There was a beautiful line drawing of a flaming bird. A phoenix.

"Are you really going to keep ignoring me?" Nyte drawled, reclining lazily on his hands beside me.

I twisted, crossing my legs and giving him my back. I picked out my map instead. It was childish, but I didn't have the energy to push him away right now. "I told you I needed time."

"Time is not our luxury, and I could have told you exactly what that is by now."

His offer wasn't even tempting. I didn't want the answer I felt close to figuring out from studying my map and the new transparent clue.

"I think I'll pass."

"It's time to make our bargain official now you know . . . *where* I am."

I cast him a frown over my shoulder. "What does that entail?"

"Come back to me and find out."

I pushed back the shiver that took over me with the enticing way he spoke.

Scanning the city, I saw there were many pointed ears roaming the streets of the second level. I wondered if any of them could be fae, but that only brought about unsettling feelings of Elena, the fae Drystan had escorted to the library. Her switch to contentment at being here wasn't something I could let go of completely. Something wasn't right.

"The fae . . . they're being forced into the king's army," I said, not posing it as a question Nyte could skirt around.

"Many of them are compliant," he answered.

"What is he doing with those who aren't? Those who are hiding but are found?" I couldn't tear my eyes from observing the different walks of life below, trying to discern what could single out the fae.

"They either yield or they die."

"Why can't he just leave them in peace?" Anger seeped into my voice.

"Many of them have magick, and even those who don't provide strength in numbers."

"There is no war. Why is he still taking them?"

"War is ever-present, Astraea. There is always a hand reaching, a power growing, an opportunity waiting. It's only a matter of being prepared for a battle that could strike at any moment. The celestials have been dormant for longer than the king anticipated. He's bracing for them to finally try to claim back what he took long ago."

"Do you even know some of the *awful* things they've had to do just to stay out of his reach?" I whirled to him as if he could do something for my rage that surfaced at thinking of Lilith.

I almost missed his wince. It only passed through him for a split second before he masked to indifference.

"This isn't the end of learning the cruelties of the world we live in," he said in the most sincere tone I'd heard from him. It was a harsh truth he clearly felt disturbed by with the way he regarded the people below.

I followed his gaze to observe them again.

The buildings here were far more structured and well-kept. Very little of the bustling trade and work happened here. Instead I found establishments fit to host the elite, though this level wasn't entirely devoid of humans. Some appeared as impeccably dressed as their vampire counterparts and looked content to be by their side. I wasn't certain if it was an act of survival, and that thought didn't sit well.

I watched blood vampires roam without shadows, an eerie effect I didn't think I'd notice, but next to anyone else the distinction was more obvious.

"What does it mean . . . to not have a shadow?" I pondered.

"They have to go somewhere," Nyte said. I shivered with that notion. "There are some who believe with the blood vampire curse their detached shadows became deadly forms of their own. To keep the creatures from destroying the land they were banished to another realm. Shadow Craft is a very powerful and ancient practice."

I skimmed over the dark cast of his form as if it were alive with his tale.

Then I watched as another vampire passed a dress shop window and no reflection got in the way of her admiring the feature gown. A soulless.

"You said the king is fae," I pondered. I wanted to rant about how barbaric it was that he could treat his own kind this way, but that wasn't what nagged on my mind. "The prince is shadowless—a blood vampire."

"Why the interest?" Nyte asked, and I detected a hint of bitterness.

It was my turn to shrug, playing it off as bored curiosity. "He seems friendly."

"I told you not to trust him."

"You can't tell me to do anything."

Nyte's hard look as he straightened only fueled me with challenge. Something about him sparked a dangerous thrill in me, and I found delight in pushing his darkness.

"His mother was shadowless, if it satisfies you to know."

I blinked, processing that information. "I wonder what happened to her."

"I would rather we didn't talk about him," Nyte grumbled.

"I would rather you weren't here at all."

"That's not true, or I wouldn't be."

My mouth opened only to stall on a response. *Think of me, and I will answer. Long for me, and I'm right here with you.*

I got to my feet, pacing across the roof as the full clarity of those words hit me truly. They warmed my chest and caressed my mind, but I wanted to shake this feeling away. Nyte had come to me every time I'd needed him. So strongly did I yearn for someone that he'd become a tangible force, fooling me all that time. Because I wanted it. Him. And that realization frightened me.

Somehow, I knew when I turned Nyte would not be there. I needed to wrap sense around what was happening. He wanted to use me, and that wouldn't change no matter how much he'd helped me before.

Casting my gaze up with a sigh, I mapped the stars though they slept. I traced the constellations solely from my memory, which could project me so close to them sometimes.

I stilled.

A constellation.

"Phoenix," I mumbled to myself.

I gasped as I held up my map. The drawing formed three circles indicating the levels of the city. It was so undeniable I couldn't unsee it. There were some broken lines, streets perhaps.

"Not the bird—the constellation."

Holding both up side by side, I slipped the transparent sheet over the map and exploded in triumph when the lines fit together, connecting to the ink underneath it to create the full constellation and circle three locations.

"Which one first?" I asked.

The map answered me, revealing a tiny scroll like before, and my vision lit up.

"See? I don't need you," I muttered to Nyte's ghost. Hopping back onto ground level, I pulled up my hood in the alley and stopped to peek a look onto the main street. It was bustling during the afternoon hour. Floral perfumes and cool wind filled my nostrils in this sector of the city. My muscles tensed at the many pointed ears and how I would be far more singled-out here.

I'd nearly braved a step out when a particular figure caught my attention. His hood was up in an attempt to remain inconspicuous, but it seemed I'd already gathered enough familiarity of the prince to know it was him from the shadowed tilt of his face as he almost glanced my way.

Shouldn't you be keeping an eye on me?

Though I was glad to know Drystan wasn't constantly following me.

He dipped around a corner, and I decided to be curious about what he could be getting up to in the city. More so, why he wouldn't want to be noticed.

I followed him down two more streets, until down a dark alley I crouched behind a wet frozen crate to spy on him as he headed toward a group of tall, dark figures. I cursed the noise around me, unable to make out a word of the vampires' exchange.

They didn't talk for long before he was moving again.

I watched him enter an establishment a little farther out. From the outside, I couldn't imagine what business he'd have in such a place during the daytime: the Scarlet Rose. I shouldn't have been surprised, but I'd still figured he could request any lady at the castle or host far more elaborate gambling nights within the palace.

I threw away all sense when I entered the establishment a few beats after him.

Expecting to inhale the sting of alcohol, I was pleasantly surprised by the embrace of delicious perfumes such as peach and rose. Paintings lined the walls, and at first I almost looked away from the scandalous images, but they were breathtaking. Women whose every beautiful curve and fold had been painted with amazing realism. Some men too, and their positions heated my skin, setting off a wild foreign desire to see them locked in passion in ways I'd never imagined. I blew out a long exhale and tore my interest from them.

It was quieter than I'd hoped for. I winced at every creak of my boots against the floorboards but continued down the narrow hall, turning once before continuing down another.

I barely got two steps before I was pushed against the wall, my cry smothered by a gloved hand. Fright pounded my chest, but my mind couldn't decide if it wanted to run or if it was relieved to be staring up at Drystan.

"Am I not to be the one following you, Cassia?" Drystan drawled the three syllables of her name as if he were playing with it.

"It seems neither of us is effective in our tasks," I said.

Drystan's hazel eyes held amusement as he looked me over. I counted my pulse.

"You haven't found yourself in any precarious situations," he said. "Yet."

"The map." It was the confirmation I needed.

His head tilted with his slow smile. "I happen to be good at optimizing my time. Why trail you through every delirious trial? I'm surprised, and I'll admit a little disappointed, you haven't attracted any danger for some action."

I could only gape, though I wasn't surprised he would wish harm on me for his own twisted amusement.

He had yet to step away from me, and I hoped my sideward glance for an escape would deliver the hint. He eased a smirk. Sometimes I had to double take at certain quirks about him that hinted at familiarity.

"How are your trials faring?"

"I have the first piece," I said.

Drystan grinned, and being this close to the exposure of his sharp teeth sliced a frightening memory of the soulless through me. I suppressed my shudder, but he seemed to notice my hesitation around him.

"Are you afraid of me?"

"No." My response came so fast it exposed my lie.

"Do you need help with your next location?"

"I have it, actually."

Drystan's face relaxed with arrogance as he extended his palm. "Let me see."

I wanted to refuse so he wouldn't know all my locations in advance, but I couldn't deny the prince. He took the map and clear sheet from me, fascinated by it as if he'd never seen such a thing before. He slid a curious look to me.

"The Poison Garden," he mused.

"That doesn't sound inviting," I said warily.

Drystan gave a low laugh. "It's not. Be cautious, as the most beautiful things can be tempting, but they're often the deadliest." The way his tone dropped with the warning accompanied by the slow trace of his eyes over me inspired a crawling warmth.

"I should, uh . . . get going then," I said, making as if to move around him, but he planted his hand on the wall to stop me.

My heart skipped a beat.

"You could stay. You won't make it to the garden to complete your task and be back to the castle before twilight now. I could escort you back in a few hours, safe and sound."

I didn't want to find out what a few hours in here with him would entail.

"Thank you, but I'll head back to the castle now on my own."

"Your Highness," a sultry voice said from down the hall behind him.

Drystan kept his attention on me, his tall form blocking my view of the woman. "Another time," the prince said, finally straightening and dropping his arm. His jaw worked with ire though he'd been expecting the woman.

I nodded with absolutely no plan to be back here with him ever.

As I made to leave, I found a stunning blonde in a scandalous silk gown, midnight in color, poised in a doorframe at the end. I quickly turned the corner for the exit as my thoughts had been right. Drystan wasn't here for any suspicious reason but, I wagered, a whole lot of sin.

The winter air chilled my heated skin when I stepped out. Heading back to climb the steps to the castle level, I walked in plain sight while the daylight began to dwindle.

"Look what we found."

The leering voice stiffened my spine, so close I didn't have time to react before a large arm was clamped around me. I turned to stone as we kept walking, Draven hugging me into his side as if we were lovers or old friends, but I felt his menacing claim. At his mention of "we," my head turned just enough to find Enver on my other side.

"Let me go," I warned, praying he would decide I wasn't worth the petty entertainment.

"Do you have any of your key pieces yet?" Draven ignored me.

"I wouldn't tell you if I did."

"We could find out," Enver said, his eyes roving over me, and my panic started to rise with his meaning.

"You think I would have them on me?"

"Only one way to know," Draven said, turning me abruptly toward him.

I reacted on instinct. My knee jerked toward his crotch, and while he groaned and slackened his hold I managed to grab his eye patch, which broke as Enver clamped a hold around me from behind. I caught sight of his hollowed eye socket before his hand lashed up to conceal it. Taking his moment of floundering, I used Enver's body for momentum to plant my boot to Draven's gut and kick. Enver lost his footing with me, and we went tumbling too.

He let go to regain his balance, but I kept falling.

My calves met something solid before I was swallowed whole by a freezing embrace.

Then I was back in the lake. Floating and drifting in a numbing cold that stole my will to fight. I tried to open my eyes, but nothing glowed like I expected it to. No gold reaching for silver.

Air ripped down my throat when I was pulled with some force. I coughed violently on my knees, aware of someone beside me. Something warm was slung over my shoulders.

Warm.

Nyte had been warm when I'd felt him at the lakeside. He had to have pulled me from the water.

Yet I didn't know how.

"I guess I spoke too soon."

It was Drystan who held me. I wished for it to be anyone else. *Anywhere* else. At least he wasn't entirely abandoning his role of ensuring my safety.

"You could have been more prompt," I chattered, panting and shivering as intensely as if I were becoming ice.

"Always room for improvement."

"I'll help her."

Oh, thank stars. Zathrian was here. That forced my head up, and I found him about to crouch, but Drystan was already helping me stand.

"You seem to have your hands full already," Drystan said, drawing our attention to Rose, who was fighting both Draven and Enver.

"Damn, Thorns," Zath muttered. "I told her it wasn't worth it."

"I'll be fine," I said through my bashing teeth.

I didn't want to be left with the prince, but more so, I didn't want Rose to be alone. Especially not as three of the Golden Guard began to close in, ready to intervene. Zath's jaw worked with irritation, but his fist flexed on his sword as he watched Rose as if he were holding back from the urge to go to her.

"We need to get you warm fast," Drystan said, coaxing me to move.

I nodded but couldn't look at him in my shame at being a damsel in distress. I passed Enver groaning on the ground just as Zath hooked an arm around Rose to prevent her next lunge at Draven. I didn't turn around to see their inevitable blowup over it.

"It's humans like those who ease my guilt at the inferiority of their species," Drystan said, bored.

My legs were on the verge of locking still from the frozen bath of water I'd fallen into, which I assumed was a trough for horses, but I still cast him distasteful eyes he didn't meet. "We're not all like them," I grumbled. "Most aren't."

"Your defense is adorable, though hardly convincing."

"Of course you see nothing but a meal."

Drystan flashed me a wide grin. "Is that what you really think?"

"It's not what I think—it's what everyone knows."

"Are you offering?"

I stalled, shrugging out of the arm he had around my shoulders. At my look of outrage, his laughter grated on my nerves.

"Relax. Fuck. Human blood isn't like a *meal* to us—not something so bland and routine." He kept walking, and I was so eager to be back at the castle that I followed him reluctantly.

"Then stop feeding on them."

"I didn't say unnecessary. We do need blood to survive, and animals can suffice. But human blood is far more desirable. Taken by force it can be painful, but if they're willing it's pleasurable for them. Humans cycle new blood. It's harmless."

"They savage without care."

"Just as humans dominate without care?"

I realized what he meant immediately. To think of all vampires like that was hypocritical when I'd argued not all humans were like Draven and Enver. *Devious bastards.*

"Fine. You're right."

"Was that hard for you to admit?"

"No."

I scowled, though admittedly I was glad my conversation with Drystan wasn't tense and frightening given who he was.

As we walked in silence toward the castle gates, I couldn't stop replaying the memory of the lake with a new rush of urgency to question the clue.

When we got to my rooms, it almost seemed like Drystan was about to follow me inside. I blanched at the thought. I wouldn't be able to shed any layers in front of him or I'd expose my tattoos.

"Thank you, but I'll be fine from here."

As I faced him, the ringing alarm of Nyte's warning not to trust the prince replayed in my head, but it collided with a desire to believe I could.

I was so damn confused and exhausted.

"I should make sure you get warm enough—"

"No."

The shift on his face at my quick dismissal skipped my pulse. It was something like ire, yet it blinked into nothing but understanding.

"My handmaiden will be here soon," I added quickly. "We might stir speculation if you were to be seen leaving my rooms. They'd think I have an advantage in the Libertatem."

Drystan scoffed, an unusual bitterness entering his tone. "The damn Libertatem is nothing more than a hollow distraction. I thought you would have figured that out by now. No one really wins."

"A distraction from what?"

Drystan leaned in close. "There is a sixth key," he all but whispered though we were alone in the hall. I took a single step back, but my palm flattened against the door. "That's the one he truly wants. No one has ever found it." His eyes bore into mine, a slight curl disturbing his mouth as if we shared a secret. "I have a feeling this Libertatem will be a marker for history."

Before I suffocated trying not to share breath, Drystan leaned away.

"Why this time?"

He reached for me, and while I would usually have balked, I blamed the cold for keeping me stiff and shivering. Drystan twisted the handle of my door, pushing it open.

"Let's just say it's been a very interesting beginning."

32

I cursed the sad, cold firepit. Stripped of my extra layers, I tried to no avail to spark flames. It was hopeless when I hadn't a clue how to do it, and I was too damn cold to keep trying.

My eyes lit up as I remembered the castle had running water. Hot water. It had to be magick, or perhaps a marker of wealth Hektor hadn't reached yet. A pain clenched in my stomach to wonder if that was what he sought: *more*. The life of power and luxury he had would never have been enough for him while there was always more to gain.

I cast away the thoughts of him as I watched the tub start to fill. I dipped my hand in the warmth. My teeth clenched against the pain, but as my skin adjusted to the drastic change in temperature I moaned contentedly.

"This isn't how I imagined I'd be hearing those sounds from you." Nyte's voice interrupted my peace.

On my knees, I barely had the energy to cast him a scowl. All I cared about was the tub filling with water so I could throw myself in. Though I had to have been thinking of him. More specifically, recalling one crucial fact.

"You saved me," I said, staring into the water's rippling reflection just as I did on the icy lake. I turned my head then, needing his reaction in case he evaded an answer. "You pulled me from the water. I wouldn't have been able to do that myself. I didn't want to—"

"I know," he said sharply.

To detract from the tension he made ripple through me, I stood, searching through the cabinets for some soaps. I poured various delicious scents into the bath, attracted to the honey and lavender hitting my nostrils. The water turned a milky white while the flow created bubbles. I smothered the noises in my throat so as not to give him the satisfaction.

"I was alone on that ice," I went on, "and even if your chase wasn't real . . . you pulled me out of the water."

"Are you sure?" His voice echoed in a taunt, rattling the confidence I'd mustered.

"Yes."

Everything I reflected on I could now see in a new light. The things that gave him away. How his touch was always featherlight even when I was sure his body would feel firmer the times he pressed himself to me. The variations in tone missing from his voice even when I believed him to be speaking aloud. I was now aware of the echo that put distance in it when it was only his illusion standing right before me.

"Before then . . ." I struggled to go back. While I was certain he had been there at the lake, everything else was cold and blurry. "In Hektor's cell?" I couldn't believe that every memory I had now required reassessment. "There or not there?" I asked.

"That is for you to decide."

I squinted, hoping he wasn't hell-bent on driving me to madness. "Were you physically there?" I amended. I already knew his answer, but my heart squeezed tightly, wanting to be wrong.

"No."

I turned to him, studying his finely made black jacket, this time with no color but beautiful black embroidery. Not a mark scuffing the boots over his fitted pants. An illusion. My face pinched as I looked him over from head to toe, admiring his clean face and tamed midnight hair. A lie.

"Don't look at me like that."

"Like what?" I whispered.

"With pity. I don't need it."

That wasn't what I felt, but I only dropped my eyes. What grew inside me was something like anger crossed with heartbreak, so strong I didn't know how I'd allowed myself to care this much. All we shared was a means to an end if I decided to agree to his *partnership* deal.

"Hektor's men who grabbed me . . . they died. You-you had to have killed them."

"If I were there, they would have died the second they touched you."

I snapped my gaze to him, not expecting such cool certainty, for him to have decided so surely he would have killed for me. His features remained cut like steel, no teasing or taunting. Nyte leaned against the doorframe. I couldn't stop my gaze from following the hand he slipped into his pocket, remembering the heavy iron he wore.

"Does it hurt?"

His lips firmed, deliberating every word he shared with me. "When you've lived through the worst pain invisible to the world, that which can be in-flicted on flesh becomes insignificant."

The hurt in me this time touched upon something deeper. So much more frighteningly deeper. I wanted to know so much about him. Things that should be meaningless. What color attracted him most. What he enjoyed doing. What he liked to eat. Everything that felt like a dangerous venture to find out.

"The soulless who would have killed me too . . ." I trailed off with the sudden horror of my realization. "You killed him?" I dared to look, and his grim expression gave me my answer.

He wasn't there.

"You killed him," he confirmed.

I leaned a hand on the countertop, feeling my heart beating and seeing shades of black. Darker and darker. I met my refection only to realize I too was a walking lie with my fake black hair and deep blue irises intended to imitate my best friend . . . who was gone.

I didn't look at myself in denial when the memory replayed and it was there, reconstructing itself from what I'd *wanted* to see in all its dark, bone-trembling reality. I flexed my fist with the phantom feel of the dagger, how I'd been so overcome with grief and rage that perhaps I'd blanked it from myself all this time, unwilling to remember that second and final plunge through the vampire's heart. Wanting to believe in a savior instead.

Nyte lingered, not stepping closer, and I had to ask.

"If you were really here . . . would I see your reflection if you came closer?"

He contemplated. "Yes."

It wasn't a comfort because it confirmed he wasn't a soul vampire. Rather, it was a relief. I thought he deserved that assurance of being a living person after having spent so long as a ghost in people's minds.

I reached behind myself, my back arching as I strained to find the loose end of my corset ribbon.

"You are exquisite," he said, his voice barely audible as if he hadn't meant to speak.

I pulled the string and my emotions soothed to something tender that stroked me within. This reaction I gave to him I wanted to deny, but I enjoyed it too much. I needed anything to distract myself from all that was lost and lonely within me and had been for some time.

"You are more of a survivor than you know, Astraea. It does not make you a monster."

"How can you say that?" My anger and disgust built, tasting like bile on my tongue and coursing hot over my skin. I saw his chains, and for a second they weighed on me instead. That was what I deserved. How could I pretend to be any better than him? My life was one step forward only to be knocked two steps back. Every thread of hopeful discovery came with frightening truths about myself that darkened the path too much for me to see anything *good*. I was nothing but volatile fragments of an existence desperate to find my whole.

I sniffed. I would not cry in front of him. Unraveling my corset, I held the loose material to my chest before looking at him expectantly.

He didn't even give a teasing smirk as he turned around. I thought about casting him away, but I didn't desire solitude.

The leather dropped to the ground, leaving me bare-chested, and I quickly unbuttoned my pants.

"Knowing you are naked right now is the most riling madness I've felt in a very long time."

I trembled at the low, silvery gravel of his voice, easing over to the water and dipping my toes in first. I couldn't bite back the soft sighs as more hot water caressed my skin.

"And those *sounds* you make, Starlight."

Nyte turned when I was submerged. My body relaxed under the hot water, bringing on a sleepy aura. I wasn't shy to have him present, real or otherwise, while I bathed. The gaze we shared only added to the heat, sparking a tension I needed a distraction from.

"I found the location of the next key piece." I tipped my head back, slipping my eyes closed in contentment. "All of them, actually. Turns out I don't need you after all."

"Yet you didn't gain another piece today."

"I, uh . . . got distracted," I admitted. "I ran into Drystan in the city."

Nyte was silent for long enough to make me peel open an eye. His expression had locked firm, looking not at me but *through* me as he pondered something.

"Are you disregarding my warning on purpose?"

I huffed. "Don't flatter yourself."

"Then what are you trying to prove?" he asked, edging on a dark challenge as he stepped closer.

The knot in my gut tightened. "Nothing. I can make my own judgments and want to give him a chance."

"For what?"

"For me to decide how I feel about his character, not what you want me to."

We stared off. His molten gaze was electrifying, sparking over me more intensely with the water.

"Astraea."

Something about the way he spoke my real name tightened over my skin. It felt like a warning, a dare, something I wanted to provoke further to see what he would do, and that was perhaps more deadly than any trial I could face out there.

"You warn me about the prince, yet I'm to trust you?"

"No. As I don't trust you."

I gave a humorless chuckle, but Nyte remained serious. "I didn't ask you to."

"You owe me a bargain."

I decided to *push*. "I said I don't need your help anymore."

"After you have already accepted so much of it," he growled. He stalked closer, right until he touched the edge of the tub, and then he lowered. "You don't get to back out now, or let me tell you . . . unfulfilled debts will always become a penance."

It felt like a threat. It was. Something I had provoked in him. Nyte was dangerous, dark, and perhaps capable of vicious things that had bound him in iron and sealed him behind an impenetrable veil. But that was only the surface of him. Every time I was around him he built my compulsion to discover *more*.

"You'll get your bargain," I said, and that seemed to relax him.

"Good."

I slipped under the water to my neck. "Do you know what the next trial will entail?" I might as well test how much he would offer.

"You've faced pride. Next you'll be tested against greed and envy. When you've discovered the things you desire the most and managed to resist the temptation, how will you react when you watch someone else have it all?"

I thought over the concept, and even in my right mind my gut sank with want.

Jealousy.

That hideous, tormenting emotion I had felt trickles of before while watching the freedom of the dancers at the manor, how people had effort-lessly enjoyed the night's entertainment while I was an invisible tourist to the main attraction.

"How do people fail the trials . . . ? What happens to them?"

"If you had continued the puzzle and not broken your pride to save the girl, it would have been reset, and you wouldn't have remembered the last attempt. Every time you failed you would have forfeited a year of your life. Once you are in the game, you either win or you die."

"The king didn't tell us that," I breathed.

"Why would he? There is only one he keeps at the end even if you all make it. If a player is killed in a trial, the game completes their key, and it will await them outside the temple for another player to try."

I had only passed one trial, and the new daunting outcome didn't inspire me with confidence. "How does he give the Golden Guard immortality?" I asked.

Nyte canted his head to the side. "They started off as an experiment. A way to build his army faster. To transition humans . . . into vampires."

Stars above.

"But there is always a consequence. Their hearts do not beat, and they are cursed never to attract true love. They are perhaps his most deadly weapon as they keep their shadows and their reflections. Their ears are round, and a human would never know the new bloodlust that walked among them."

"Who would choose that?"

"None of them do."

This event had become so much more sinister than I'd originally thought, and I didn't know what to do with the information Nyte revealed.

A new, unwilling breed of vampires . . .

It couldn't continue. I couldn't fathom such a heinous act being forced upon me, especially not on Rose. There was no glory in winning; it would be nothing but another manipulative gain for the king, and I loathed him more powerfully than I thought myself to be capable of.

He had to die.

"Drystan said there's a sixth key—that's what he's truly looking for," I said, calculating while trying to keep my calm.

Nyte's eyes narrowed a fraction. I couldn't decide if it was the prince's name or the knowledge he was reacting to. "Yes. The star-maiden's key."

My spine straightened at the mention. "Why does he think we can find it?"

"Because long ago the star-maiden made sure that should anything happen to her, no one would be able to wield it. She broke it into five pieces and scattered them throughout the city. Every one hundred years, anyone with even a shred of magick can feel the pieces awakening. It's a very powerful tool, and it can only stay dormant for so long before it has to expel something. The king didn't create these trials; he was the first to ever participate in them. Over and over, until he had five whole keys, and it almost drove him to madness. But none of them opened the temple door he's been trying to get inside for three centuries since. He started the Libertatem as a brilliant political structure to keep the kingdoms obedient and under his control in exchange for their safety from the savage vampire attacks that were close to wiping out entire human populations. At the same time, he has five people playing the star-maiden's trials, hoping each time the real key will be among them. He kills four Selected out of nothing more than spite and rage, and one he keeps to form his Golden Guard to keep up the pretense of a reward for the victor. That's all the Libertatem is for."

My fingers gripped the edge of the bathtub, not realizing what I was doing as I sat forward. Only the bubbles concealed my upper half, and Nyte's golden gaze flashed a dark shade, but he did not look down.

"You're hardly being fair," he said huskily.

I stifled a shiver, but my mind was reeling with the information. "What is beyond the temple door?"

Nyte remained at eye level, and when his hand reached for the water I almost barked out a protest. But this wasn't real, and instead I tracked the fingers he danced across the surface of the bathwater with some intrigue as to how they would feel.

"It's a place to summon the God of Dusk and the Goddess of Dawn."

"Why does he want that?"

"He has always craved magick as someone without it and despises that he has always needed someone else to keep his empire under his control. The king has found a way to call the God and Goddess to mortal form, and with the star-maiden's key he would hold the greatest weapon. They might very well grant his wish in exchange for it."

I didn't want to know really, but I asked, "What is his wish?"

"To become a god, and he plans to kill them."

"He can't."

"Agreed," Nyte said, his voice still low and distracted as if our conversation were about the weather: insignificant compared to what truly held his interest in this moment. "Which is why you must free me. I can help to stop him."

"I'm afraid," I said honestly.

Nyte's head tilted, his hand dipped past the water's surface, and my lips parted. "Of me?"

"Of what you could be capable of."

"You should be." His fingers grazed my calf, and I breathed steadily.

Not real. This is not real.

Yet the more I chanted it in my mind, the more tangible it became. My body betrayed my thoughts to want it.

"That's not convincing me."

"What if I promised I would never harm you or your friends?" he said.

"You would bind that in the bargain?"

"Yes."

Zathrian would be safe, and I would make sure Rose and Davina were too.

"I want answers," I said.

Nyte's eyes flexed, debating. "Deal."

"I want to know how you saved me on the lake."

"That, I might give you *after* you free me."

"You haven't told me how I can do that."

"We find the key."

"He's been searching for it for centuries—we might not find it."

Nyte inhaled deeply and his fingers moved higher. "Don't worry about that. Just get through your trials."

I wanted to argue, but all I could think about were two things. His touch, so believable it was frustrating to remember it wasn't real, and the bargain with the devil I was slowly being seduced into.

"I need to know you're not going to be a threat."

"What people see as a threat often speaks more about them."

He was impossible.

"Turn around."

Mercifully, he did.

I stood, grabbing a cotton robe to sling around myself.

Nyte kept his back to me, his tone dropping a few sinister notes as he said, "I can slip into your mind. What makes you think I can't do the same to the king or prince?"

His threat to out me turned the mood sour.

"You would have done so by now," I said. For the first time I felt like I'd won a challenge against him. "If you could reach their minds, you would have tormented them until they released you. Something is protecting them. You need me, and if I die you lose that."

This time when he turned I couldn't read his emotion. Annoyance locked his jaw, but maybe he fought approval on his mouth.

"What makes you think I can't find some other like you?"

"Another fool to answer to you?"

"Something like that." He shrugged, but the bastard was enjoying vexing me.

"Then I hope you haven't been down there too long. It may be some time before you lure another to *bargain* with you."

33

Balancing on the precarious edge of my balcony railing, I enjoyed the exhilarating view and the freedom that raced through me with the height. I stalled my attempt to leap across to Rose's balcony. My hand kept glued to the wall and my feet planted with reluctance when one miscalculated jump would result in a plummet to my death.

My body believed it to be ridiculous that I'd been debating the jump for so long, but my mind taunted me, stretching the gap wider with the illusion it was too far. With a huff to myself, I firmed my stance, preparing to leap . . .

The shallow creak of the door bounced my heart up into my throat. My balance wobbled, and I clung to the wall as though it would save me.

"Shit," I choked.

"What the hell are you doing?"

"I think that's rather obvious."

Rose looked me over with disgruntled disapproval. "Get down before you make this Libertatem one person easier for those bastards." She walked over to her railing, hauling herself up as I retreated to the safety of mine.

Rose leaped across as if it were as easy as a step. My mouth snapped shut at her smirk.

"I wasn't hesitating for long," I grumbled.

Her chuckle followed me inside. "If I'd had to wait any longer for you to try, I would have considered taking a nap."

"You make it look easy."

"I've trained my whole life. It *is* easy if you've leaped rooftops at least three times the distance like me."

I turned to her, wracked with unease to be in front of such a skilled person. To be in *competition* against her, though I didn't want to think about that.

Rose crossed her arms after closing my door. "Want to tell me what you thought was so important in the middle of the night to be intruding on me?"

"Did you find the first key piece?" I asked. It had been over a week since I'd retrieved mine.

Rose dipped a hand into her pocket, and I relaxed with relief at seeing the metal. She began a casual toss of it into the air. "Three days ago. You can call off your guard dog—he's grating on my nerves."

"Can't you just accept help?"

"I didn't ask for it."

"You don't need to."

Rose curved a brow at me. "I didn't pin you to be so assertive." She paced to the firepit.

"Why did Cassia write to you?"

That was what had truly been on my mind since the first mention of it. I'd been trying to figure out what else Cassia might have kept from me and what she already knew of the Libertatem.

"I wrote to her first, actually." Rose's tone took on a somber edge as she sat in the armchair by the fire. I copied her, desperate to hear this tale. "When her mother passed, everyone heard about it as the Reigning Lord of Alisus's wife. I lost my mother around the same time, and I guess you could say it was my weak child's heart that was aching for someone to reach out to."

"I think that's brave," I interjected quietly, but my clasped hands tightened when she seemed to reject my words.

Her jaw worked and she stared into the flames as though trying to deny I was here at all while she spoke of her past. "I was orphaned, and I had nothing to lose by writing that letter. I begged a border guard, offering what little coin I had left, and I guess he took pity on me. He became our way to pass letters from then on."

Of course Cassia would answer her letter. My eyes watered, but I smiled, fighting the tears from falling when my chest clenched painfully with the memory of her.

"We decided we were going to win our trials and become our kingdoms' Selecteds for this barbaric parade."

"You didn't come here to win it," I said, my voice barely audible as my adrenaline raced even though I couldn't figure out their alternate plan.

"Neither did she."

My heart could have stopped with the revelation.

Rose sat up and looked around the room as if the walls had eyes. "Have you ever heard of the name *Nightsdeath*?"

I blinked, haunted by it. "Yes," I breathed.

"He's the reason the king is so feared. He doesn't just kill people by ordinary means; he *is* death. Some say a God of Death, able to kill masses and fulfill horrors in the minds of men. He is what keeps even the vampires afraid, and he leads most of the king's armies. His heart is black and he does not know mercy."

I turned so cold I had to stand and pace to the fire Davina had lit for me earlier. "What about him?" I dreaded to ask.

"Without Nightsdeath, the king is nothing."

"How do you expect to find him?"

"We already have."

My pacing stopped and my heart lurched up my throat.

"The prince. It has to be him."

I almost relaxed as the face with warm caramel eyes didn't register with the chilling name. "I don't think you have that right," I said.

"Why? Because he has leaned in close and flashed you a dashing grin? I need you to be less naïve if you're ever going to help carry this through."

"I'm *trying*," I defended. Running a hand of exasperation over my face, I tried to think it over. My mind kept rebelling against Rose and Cassia's conclusion, but she seemed so sure.

So did Nyte.

If this were true, his warnings settled with a new clarity.

"Cassia and I have been figuring this out for many months."

"Wouldn't people have seen him? The kingdoms would know the prince is the notorious *Nightsdeath*." I could hardly say the name without shivering.

"They say a person rarely lives past getting a glimpse of him. He's only known to arrive for one reason: to kill the king's problems. What better way to hide than in plain sight? He likes secret weapons."

Yes, he does. I turned nauseous as I recalled Nyte's insight into the king's transitioned vampires. I didn't think burdening Rose with that knowledge would be helpful to her game right now.

My head spun, and I sank down into the chair, trembling with cold sweats.

"You need to keep yourself together," Rose said, firm but with a note of understanding. "You chose to take her place, and I'm holding faith you can handle the plan we've had set in place for years. Fate isn't fair to cast this on you, but it is our only hope."

I didn't voice that I'd come fully prepared to die here. Scheming to take down the face of the realm's nightmares was not a part of that plan.

"What was your plan?" I asked because it was too late for anything else now. Still my blood roared, unwilling to hear the answer.

"When falls Night, the world will drown in Starlight," she recited.

I was beginning to think everyone knew of this damn prophesy but me.

"Cassia is so certain it refers to Nightsdeath, that his fall will be what we need. She didn't come here to play games—they were a distraction to get close to the prince. Win his heart . . . and end him."

I shook my head. "I'm not Cassia."

"You *have* to be."

"I *can't*." I dragged a hand through my hair, trying to process what Rose was implying. "I can't light up the room with a laugh like she could. Or stand up for what's right no matter what like she would. I wouldn't walk into the line of danger like her. I'm not as beautiful or extraordinary. She's *gone*!" A single tear slipped down my cheek, and I swiped at it with the anger it brought forth. "I'm not brave like she was," I whispered. Each time I placed her in the past knowing her present was gone and her future wouldn't come, it cut fresh wounds.

"You are." They were the softest words to ever leave the stern exterior Rose always wore.

"I don't need your pity."

"Nor am I giving it. Because really, you need to get yourself together. Cassia's life was already on borrowed time, and she wanted to use the last of it to bring an end to the evil that took both our mothers. She would be honored to see you doing the same."

My brow furrowed, and suddenly the room was too cold with the same kind of ice as lingering death. I didn't know if I'd survive the weight of whatever made Rose's face twitch in confusion as she watched my reaction.

"What do you mean 'borrowed time'?"

Rose matched my expression as though I were playing her for a fool, but whatever she read on me turned her features to dread. "She never told you," she barely murmured.

I was so close to crumbling. The ground didn't feel so solid, and I didn't care if it caved and swallowed me to hell when the pain building in my chest could kill.

"Tell me," I pleaded, nearly a whimper. I thought I knew, but it didn't make sense.

Accidents can happen if one has far less time than initially thought.

The king's warning.

No. It couldn't be true.

"Astraea, I'm so sorry."

I believed her. I'd never seen such sadness sweep over her.

"I thought you knew—"

"Just tell me," I snapped.

The blade was lodged, and I needed it pulled free—even if I bled and bled and never stopped.

"The only reason the Reigning Lord of Alisus agreed to his eldest heir even *trying* for the Libertatem was because Cassia wasn't supposed to live to see her twenty-third year. Five years ago she got the confirmation from a healer, one with genuine magick, and only with their infused remedies was she given more time than everyone thought. More than anything, she wanted to make it here and have her legacy be for her mother."

The world stopped spinning.

One year, Hektor had gifted me a small ornate globe that sent flurries to the stars when it was shaken. Then, when he caught me disobeying his order, he'd shattered it right in front of me, and never again would those stars dance and shine. Now I felt myself drifting with no direction, no place, only shaken through the skies without a care about where I would land. Just like a broken constellation in that globe. That was the impact I suffered at the news of the existence I was condemned to as Rose finally clarified her meaning.

"Cassia was dying."

34

Time faded when I heard the three words that collapsed my world. *Cassia was dying.*

I couldn't remember what I'd said to dismiss Rose after that. Nor how I'd stealthily eluded the castle guards to cross the courtyard. Only when I broke through the darkness of the underground passage below the library did my senses return and I realize where my soul-shattering grief and anger had led me.

I stumbled to a halt in the massive cave as the resonating clank of chains trembled through me.

"What happened?" Nyte asked in a low and deadly growl.

Cool air breezed along my cheeks, but I didn't sob over a single spilled tear. They just wouldn't stop *falling*. My teeth clenched with the bite of my nails into my palms. I walked toward the veil he stood in front of until no more than an arm's distance remained between us. He studied every inch of me, and I wondered if he was looking for any signs of physical harm that could have caused my pale and ugly appearance.

"I will bind your bargain," I said, not recognizing the ice-cold detachment of my own voice.

"You didn't answer my question."

"I don't need to."

His eyes flexed, and for the first time it was like he didn't know who he was staring at.

"I will free you, but in exchange I want to know everything about the prince—the one they call Nightsdeath."

Surprise lifted his brow, but I also watched a dark flare of recognition, which I took as confirmation he had the information I needed.

"Where did you hear that name?" he asked.

"It doesn't matter."

"That's not how bargains work, Starlight. It's give-and-take."

"Fine. Cassia and Rose figured it out, and you're going to protect her too."

Nyte gave a single mocking chuckle. I was so fucking far from being able to tolerate his jesting.

"Are you sure you want to keep stacking conditions on your end? How much are you willing to owe me in return?"

"What else do you want?" I didn't care anymore—whatever it took for him to give us the advantage.

"Careful," he said, the word teasing down my neck like a caress of shadow. His head tilted as he observed me through molten eyes. "There are many things I could want, and you are too vulnerable right now to agree to something you might regret."

His prod at my *vulnerability* only blazed the fire growing inside me. I didn't want to be *weak* or thought of as naïve and foolish. Not anymore.

"What. Do. You. Want?" I repeated. I wasn't in that cage. And when the time came to unleash him, I wouldn't care what he could do to me as I would have achieved what I wanted. Cassia's legacy would be fulfilled if I killed Nightsdeath for her.

For that, I didn't care if my selfishness damned the world.

"To be freed, of course."

I waited, watching his contemplation.

"My other request will come after that."

"That's not a fair bargain."

"No one said I played fair."

"You think I'm desperate enough to agree to *owe* you?"

"Seems like you are."

For a second, the thought of crossing him passed my mind. I could use him, gain what I needed, and never free him at all.

"Do you think me such a fool as to allow that? No. I've gone too long aiding you with no sure return." He answered my thoughts, and I shook my head, taking a long step back.

"I want to know how to block you completely from my mind," I snarled.

His mouth curled cruelly. "Your thoughts are frantic right now. You're practically screaming them at me, and it's bringing on a headache."

I glared at him, but he was right. My mind was blaring, but I couldn't get it to stop.

Pacing away, I tried to calm myself, taking deep, steady breaths to be sure I knew what I was doing. What I wanted. But I could see no other way to ensure both Rose and I survived this. Nyte knew things. He could know how to end the prince, perhaps the king too, and guide me through the remaining trials to see the end.

"Do we have a deal?" he called, a note of song taunting me from the darkness. My spine curved with it. Maybe I even enjoyed the thrill it awoke in me.

"What do I need to do?"

Nyte's smile showed teeth, revealing two longer pointed ones I'd never noticed before. It made me recall the moment they'd come so close to my throat. What awoke in me at the thought of his bite wasn't terror, but an unexplainable sinful desire.

Which was even more frightening.

He cast his gaze up and I followed, knowing now what surrounded the circle through which we could see only the sky. He looked through the gap in the cave as if he could see the stars from here, and I watched his eyes map a set pattern like it was a habit the moment his dawn irises touched the sky.

"We should take a walk through many worlds," he said.

In the library, it felt jarring to walk side by side with Nyte now devastation had been added to his impeccable appearance as I knew the *real* him was still chained below our feet.

He turned to me halfway down a row of bookcases. "If you keep staring, I'm going to assume this bargain is unnecessary as we already find our desires aligning as one."

My breath hitched when he shortened some distance. I backed up until my fingers skimmed along the spines, and he leaned in close enough I should feel his warmth. He was cold and still, yet his energy hummed through me, and I focused my mind to banish him before he could stroke his knuckles along my cheek.

I breathed then clenched my teeth in frustration at his sly attempts at distraction. Storming through several rows of books, my irritation stirred because I needed him.

"You're getting better at knowing how to shut me out. It's good." He crept back up to walk side by side with me. I didn't give him any attention, but I relaxed with the assurance I wasn't completely at his mercy.

"What are we looking for?"

"Up here."

I whipped around, blinking with disorientation as he called me from seemingly so far away. Skipping over to the railing, I looked up to find him three levels higher and cursed the fact *I* wasn't an illusion who could appear up there with a thought. Instead my legs were protesting by the time I reached that floor, and I made a note to myself to get back into some regular exercise.

"*The Book of Bindings*," he said as I found him gazing at the top of the case. "I would pull over the ladder for you, but . . ."

My eyes rolled as I gripped the wood, driving it toward where he indicated. I paused with one foot ready to ascend, trying to bite back my wonder when I felt like giving over to my petty side and being silent. I mentally scolded myself. I had poor resistance.

"There were times you did things, passed me things, or—" I couldn't recall everything, but each time I lingered on a memory I struggled to believe he'd never truly been there.

Stepping down, I turned to him. The flickers of emotion he showed often pinched me within, enlightening me to the fact even dangerous things could feel.

"Everything you thought I did was because you *wanted* it to be real." He took a step toward me, always like he didn't even realize he was doing it.

My fingers curled around the ladder again as my spine curved to the slant of it.

"You have no idea the agony it was. To watch as you did it all craving for someone to help, to be there for you. So no, I didn't remove your face covering at the manor. I didn't hand you the glass of water. I didn't pull your dress ribbon, but, *fuck,* as enthralling as you are when you stretch, I wanted to unravel every ribbon from you that night so badly it torments me still."

Stars above. The eruption in my stomach wasn't a welcome one. The *need* clenching in places I had to breathe hard to ignore. Nyte was a wicked sin.

"Nor did I do anything else when you believed me to be interacting with physical things. I am limited still. What if I said in all my time locked here, being unable to have your true touch has been the one thing fueling my rage to be free beyond sanity?"

My eyes pricked as Nyte leaned over, gripping the step above my head. My heart was slamming in its cage. I didn't breathe too hard, aware he might feel it against his lips from this perfect angle if I did.

"The lake . . ." I didn't yet know how it was possible, but one thing I refused to believe wasn't real was his warmth then. His real skin against mine. "There or not there?"

Nyte's jaw flexed. His hand slipped across my neck, his thumb on my chin parted my lips, and for a second I wondered if he would kiss me. "There."

Even though I'd been sure of it, hearing him confirm it flared something warm and beautiful within me.

"How?"

Nyte shook his head. "I told you that part might come *after* you free me."

I didn't like the unsettling thought he could dangle that explanation over me. But right now, my care for it slipped away.

My fingers loosened on the ladder, unable to stop the impulse to reach for his face. The scar that never failed to draw my attention—not for its beautiful imperfection, but for the unexpected surfacing of my anger to know what had caused it.

Nyte remained utterly still, watching me while I memorized every jagged line. My skin touched his, tracing the raised scar with a faint vibration of energy, but not the real warmth I was growing a frustrating, careless craving for. It spiked my awareness to realize how much I wanted him to be whole and physical. To know what he would feel like, since the only recollection I had was hazy with a frozen death.

"How did you get this?"

His phantom hand curled around my wrist, guiding my hand away to snap my wandering thoughts. "Doesn't matter."

I wanted to tell him that wasn't true, that he mattered, but it felt like a dangerous confession that I cared. Needing a moment to collect myself from my reckless thoughts, I banished Nyte from them. He disappeared in my next blink, and the air to my lungs came easier.

Climbing the ladder, I searched all the spines, trying not to get distracted by so many intriguing titles. I didn't succeed when one in particular caught my attention: *Daughter of Dusk and Dawn.*

Taking one extra book wouldn't do any harm, would it?

I plucked it out, tucking it under my arm as I kept climbing. When I reached the very top I realized Nyte hadn't been exaggerating about the height.

There it was, in brilliant gold metallic text.

The Book of Bindings.

It took several tugs to pry the heavy tome from its long-forgotten wedged position on the shelf. In my arms the surprising weight shifted my balance, and my heart leaped up my throat, making me clutch the ladder tighter. The fall was sure to hurt, even to break bone if I landed wrong.

Once again, I found myself climbing a few more steps until I was looking over all the tall shelves. Instead of heading back down, I thumped the book on top of them and then braced to lift myself onto the wide width of the bookcase, uncaring of the dust creating dark smudges on my purple dress. My legs dangled over it, and I grinned at the exhilarating vantage point.

"Beautiful."

Nyte's silvery voice was barely a whisper that touched my chest. He was nowhere near, sitting opposite me atop the parallel bookcase. When his compliment registered, my cheeks stained pink. I averted my gaze to plant a hand on the book.

"You know, most would find comfort on the ground," he said, reclining back on his hands.

I shrugged, glancing at the vast expanse of the library. "There's something peaceful about the height. Private and secret. Not a place to hide, but to explore thoughts without distraction."

"And what are your thoughts right now?"

I heaved open the heavy book. "You should know. You only exist here because of them."

"Not entirely true. And I would never violate them," he said, closer now, and I jumped at his presence beside me. "I would never read your deeper thoughts without consent. If it gives you further peace, you would feel me if I tried. The temptation to answer your loud surface thoughts I can't deny when it's like you want me to hear you. Unless I put effort into blocking you, but I'm not that morally bound."

I didn't tell him I believed him, instead swallowing over my dry throat. "How do you do that? Creep up on me when I don't will it at all."

"Sometimes you do but don't realize it. But your mind can also bend to *my* will." Nyte shifted closer again, until he could drop to a convincing whisper against my ear. "Believe what I want you to believe, and you are oh so willing."

As though I had something to prove, I reimagined his place, and when I found him once again opposite me his wicked smirk was delighted.

"But there are far more exciting things I would like to watch you bend for me," he continued.

My mouth dropped open; his deviant smile only spread wider.

"Once you free me, of course. I'm sure we could both make it convincing like this, but it wouldn't be nearly as satisfying."

I flipped through the pages fast as if they could fan away the heat crawling up my neck. "I would rather break."

"Oh, Starlight, that's the best part."

I shut the book, loud enough that it resounded for a few beats before I stared Nyte down. "I think I've changed my mind about this *bargain*."

"No, you haven't."

"You're insufferable in my mind. You'd be intolerable if I couldn't banish you with a thought."

"Has anyone ever told you how attractive your anger is?"

I huffed a humorless laugh. "You haven't seen a fraction of my anger."

Even from this distance I thought his gold eyes flashed like the first rays of sunlight. He disappeared again, only to reappear by my side, leaning in close, and in my shock I gasped, shifting around until I was reclining, and my back met the wood in an attempt to keep some distance.

Nyte hovered over me, strands of dark hair curling into his eyes. "Show me," he said in an alluring gravel tone.

"What?" I breathed, bewildered by how sudden and impulsive he could be.

"Your anger. I want to see it."

"You're twisted."

He chuckled, so low and smooth my eyes nearly *fluttered*. "Perhaps. Because the thought of you beautifully unleashed is driving me wild. Like I said, darkness becomes you." His golden gaze flashed to the spilled tresses around my head, and he hooked his finger around a strand. "Except this."

"I quite like it dark."

"I never said I didn't. But your glittering silver hair is more befitting."

"You seem to have an obsession with my hair."

"I have an obsession with *you*."

Clearly. Stars, I was slipping. Losing what had become a game between us.

He added, "Your hair is an alluring attribute. Though you've certainly drawn the attention of the prince without it."

"You sound jealous."

The darkening of his eyes switched to a swirling gold. "I don't have to be when you don't truly return any affection he shows."

"And with you I do?"

"You tell me."

"I don't."

He leaned down until I couldn't hold eye contact anymore. My breaths came shallow with the proximity of his lips.

"I still don't need to read your thoughts to know that's a lie."

Suddenly, Nyte's gaze flicked up with an alertness that cooled the heat flushing my body.

"Stay down and don't move," he said.

The groaning of the library doors rattled through me. I could already picture the face that might be walking inside. Though with what I knew about the prince now, this new *name* he carried, I couldn't decide if the king would be a slightly lesser threat.

My head tipped farther back, but I wouldn't be able to see, and when I straightened Nyte had eased off me. I was too stunned to order him to hide, but he didn't need to. Only I was truly there, and that fact would never fail to drop in my gut when I looked at him.

Rolling carefully onto my stomach, I crawled awkwardly to the end of the bookcase to peer over it.

"Do you ever listen to instruction?" Nyte drawled.

I didn't answer when my words might be heard by the intruder. Tentatively I peeked, and sure enough, Drystan was strolling around the balcony perimeter, heading toward . . .

"He's here to see me," Nyte confirmed.

There was a bookcase that featured a hidden trigger into the passage I had climbed to get here. As Drystan pulled the faux book and dipped away, my eyes widened with realization.

"The ward . . ."

"It's likely what brought him here earlier than usual. I wasn't sure if it would set anything off since you technically didn't breach it from the outside. The door you came through is just outside its protection. But being in the main library, perhaps he felt something."

"Seems flawed," I said.

"The ward is only for common measure. There is a hoard of weapons in here. Knowledge that has been safeguarded for millennia. The ward they keep me behind is entirely personal." He said the last word with sarcasm.

"So he thinks it's you?"

Nyte shrugged. He didn't respond, but I studied the tunneling look on his expression, wondering what Drystan would be saying to cause every flicker and shift. His lips were pinched and his eyes firmed with ire, but before I could ask he was gone.

35

W e don't have much time."

Nyte's true voice echoed through the cave with a touch of irritation. I wasn't sure if it was his impatience for me to get down here after the prince left or whatever they'd spoken of that lingered with him.

"What did he say?" I asked, realizing how out of shape I was from rushing down here with the heavy tome.

"All I remember was an irritating buzz."

Stopping close to the veil, I dropped to my knees with the book, cutting him a look, though he hardly appeared in the mood to talk about it. "I know the feeling," I muttered, flipping through its pages.

"Astraea." His tone of warning stopped my movements. Then he crouched in front of me, and my gaze traveled along the thick chain that clanked along with him, its links disappearing into darkness. "He can't find out you know I exist. If there's a moment of suspicion, you have to sway it completely."

My eyes flicked up to his then, catching a frown of turmoil I didn't expect.

"Most importantly, he can't find out who you truly are."

"I'm no one," I whispered.

He pressed his lips into a firm line, the flinch around his eyes revealing he was suppressing his next words. Instead he looked to the book. "Drystan is going to seek you out. We have to do this now."

"Why would he be looking for me?" Dread flushed my body.

Nyte's mouth curled with the flash of his honey eyes. "It seems you're doing well to draw his attraction. Is that what you wanted?"

I refrained from a childish scowl. "Only if it can help me end him. If he is what Rose says he is . . ." I trailed off with the rise of horror at what I was planning to do. What I thought myself to be capable of. Killing a prince. Or a king. That was Cassia's goal, and I'd promised to follow it through.

Flicking my eyes to Nyte, I felt it somewhat ironic to ask for one evil's help to take down another, but I wondered what it was that made me want to side with one at all.

"With this bargain, you'll help me kill them . . . ?" I had to shake my head to expel the desire to exclude Drystan. What I'd seen and felt of him didn't match the malicious persona he was said to have, and perhaps he deserved a chance to explain . . .

"Yes." There was no hesitation, and Nyte didn't break my stare so I would feel his promise. "Because you're going to help me."

I shook myself out of my stupor. I had to give to gain—of course that was how it would be. I also had to remember that after it was done, he would be done with me. Nodding vacantly, I flipped through a few more pages until I found the one I'd come across while searching above.

"The Binding of Bargains," I recited. "It requires blood."

"Mm-hmm," Nyte hummed, and my eyes widened with realization.

"You knew how to make the bargain this whole time!"

"But we had a lovely time together, did we not?" He was prodding at my irritation, and the sparkle in his amber irises switched to tell me he *enjoyed* it.

Standing, I closed the book, and maybe it was childish, but the frustration he'd triggered needed some physical release. I threw the book at him, not even remembering the veil until the book collided with it, echoing a high chime, and I winced with my stumble back. Then it *passed* through it.

Nyte straightened and side-stepped effortlessly to avoid it as the old book skidded across the stone. "How considerate of you to provide me with tedious reading material."

I blinked at the rippling veil as it lost its echo and stilled to near invisibility once again. "Can you pass it back?"

"No," he said, retrieving the book. "You'd best hope no one goes looking for it."

Shaking my head, I wished I'd scouted for a book on wards too, if only to figure out their magick. "If I passed through . . . ?"

His eyes skimmed from the pages to me. "As tempting as that is for me, we would have a far bigger problem on our hands."

"You've been wanting me to touch it."

"Have I?" he taunted.

I didn't respond.

"It may hurt to pass through. Or kill you. I can't be certain."

I gaped at him for how close he'd beckoned me toward it several times knowing the danger. Nyte didn't pay attention to my incredulity, continuing on.

"As much as your true voice here is highly desirable, you have to get back. So here." Nyte crouched again, leaving the book open on the ground. "You'll need something to cut yourself with. Then recite this phrase."

A blood oath suddenly felt like the most damning commitment.

"Starlight—"

I stood abruptly. "How can I trust you?"

He didn't straighten. Instead he held my gaze with a coaxing sort of patience that confused me. He was concerned, but he wasn't pushing me into this.

"Come here." He spoke the soft words I already felt in his gaze.

I obeyed, lowering myself back to my knees. Taking a few seconds to breathe, I couldn't decide if it was the real proximity between us or the pulse of *power* I felt drawn to that set my pulse racing and my veins catching low fire.

"You're not going to like this part," he said.

"There's a part I should like?"

While his mouth curled, the smile that stole my breath was what sparked in his eyes instead. "If this ward didn't exist, I would make sure of it."

I took one breath, collecting my sanity. "You can just say you're lonely."

"That would imply I seek others' company."

"Doesn't everyone?"

Nyte tipped his chin to the side, and I found a sharp rock. My skin pricked with what he wanted. A bind there would be no coming back from.

"This past century has had its perks in solitude. I haven't slept so well for so long without a single demand or duty."

I didn't hear anything past the small kernel of information he let slip so casually despite it falling with the weight of stones in my gut. I swiped the rock. "You've been here a century?"

At the flex around his eyes, I realized it was something he hadn't intended to tell me.

"What part of 'the prince is looking for you and will be more suspicious the longer he doesn't find you' didn't you understand?"

I didn't react to his tone, thinking it only sharpened as a deflection. I fixed my attention on the task. "You still haven't told me why I can trust you."

"Because it matters not what I say, but what you feel."

That inspired me. Frightened me. I suddenly wondered how long I'd been fooling myself.

"What happens if I don't free you?"

"Only I get to decide your consequence, and you will have until the end of the Libertatem."

"I don't understand. Why me?"

"You don't need to understand."

Still, I hesitated.

Nyte looked up as though praying for patience. "Or walk away now. But you are on your own, and I warn you, the lamb will never survive in a cage of lions. Perhaps it will outsmart them, remain hidden for a while, but on its own its fate is to be devoured."

I didn't want to be the lamb. I didn't want to depend on anyone, but that wasn't what this felt like. Nyte guided more than he saved; he encouraged more than he told.

"What do I have to do?" Reckless words, but I had nothing else to lose.

"Cut your palm and pass the rock through to me with the drops of your blood on it."

The first nip spiked my adrenaline. I had never felt so brazen or darkly seduced. My teeth clenched as my skin broke and the sting intensified. A little deeper and I whimpered.

"Good," Nyte said, and it was enough of a distraction to steal my sight so I could slice fully.

"I don't need your praise," I hissed. I squeezed my fist and the warm trickle of crimson slipped over my pale skin, landing on the rock.

"Maybe not here."

"Not ever."

"But you would enjoy it." He said it with such certainty and promise I wanted to drown in the lake all over again to smother the heat creeping over me. Nyte fought a devious smile that triggered violent thoughts.

My blood stopped dripping, and with a huff I slipped the rock toward the veil. So close we almost touched. Sparks skittered over my skin, and I retracted at the electric shock when it was through enough for him to retrieve it. The drumming in my chest beat harder, louder, as I acknowledged there was no going back now.

I had officially signed myself over to the devil.

Nyte picked up the stone with a small pooling of my blood on it. Those eyes of dawn I swore darkened to a burned amber, so filled with hunger and desire, and I might have made the biggest mistake with the darkness I felt creeping toward him.

I didn't know what I expected he would do with it. Draw a marking, chant a spell. What never crossed my mind . . .

Was that I would watch in horror as his lips parted and three drops of crimson landed on his tongue.

I was transfixed.

Every move he made was a danger of the most lethal kind. Because it was alluring, desirous, and even though he drank my blood my horror was quickly subdued as pleasure relaxed his face. The thought of what it would feel like for him to take it directly . . . to *bite* . . .

I launched to my feet in shock at my thoughts.

"You didn't say you would drink it!" I choked.

"You didn't ask." Nyte's voice took on a darkly enticing tone I shivered at. He kept himself turned away from me, the back of his hand resting over his mouth as though he were collecting himself. "Recite the words on that page. Now."

My mind roared to object as my body locked itself in place. Only when his eyes flicked to me did my knees weaken enough to ease back down. His irises came alive, burning brighter than I'd seen them before, but the fire in them was sputtering out quickly.

"Now," he growled.

I saw the words but knew no meaning. I spoke them but I couldn't hear them. This was wrong, so dark and wrong, and I was a fool out of my depth to have placed my trust in a chained being as my savior.

My forearm tingled as I continued to recite the words. Then it burned, and I stumbled on the words as I whimpered with pain.

Nyte crouched before me. "Keep going. It's almost done."

I breathed long and deep and finished the final line of the verse.

The silence echoed with the impact of a siren.

The same heat scorched hot on my skin, and I cried out, needing to see what it was. I undid the sleeved garment I wore over my dress, peeling out of it, and stared at the silver constellation that had been etched over the moon phases I wore.

The shift of material drew my attention to Nyte as he finished rolling up his own sleeve. The waning moons on his skin had also been decorated with a constellation.

A damningly familiar one that made me raise my hand to my chest.

Nyte said nothing, but his look was all-knowing. He reached behind himself, and the air around me grew humid as he unfolded himself from the torn shirt he wore. Every muscled contour of him came to moonlight-flooded glory before me, and I didn't know what to hold my attention on. Every dip and angle of him was honed like a warrior, his strength reflected in the many scars he wore.

So. Many. Scars.

My eyes welled to map them. I wondered if they were memories of battle or if malicious hands had inflicted them. Then I found what he wanted me to see—what had always drawn my intrigue when I'd caught glimpses of it.

The constellation that spanned over his neck and chest in a metallic gold.

"Constellation Phoenix," I breathed. It was what he wore—I was sure of it. And now I did too, in silver. "What does it mean?"

I was so swept away by the beauty of him that all caution toward the bargain now branded on our skin dissipated. He wore other gold markings over his arms in a different style from mine, but for the first time . . . I didn't feel my existence was answerless.

"You'll have to be more specific," he said, so quiet and *vulnerable*. He hadn't hesitated to show me this part of him, but his whole body tensed as though my eyes were stones of judgment.

"Nyte," I whispered, but I didn't know what words to follow up with that would be enough to make him believe he didn't have to hide. "I'm not afraid."

There was only a split second of deliberation—all I needed—before his defenses hardened. "You should be."

I shook my head.

"Astraea . . ." He said it like a plea as his knees met the stone. "You have to go back now, but you are right to be wary of the prince."

"Are you . . . a blood vampire like him?"

Nyte debated his answer before he said simply, "Not exactly."

"Then what?"

"Does that really matter to you?"

"Yes."

Nyte's jaw shifted, reluctant to explain. "I have never been where I am supposed to be."

"That doesn't answer my question."

"It does. You're smarter than you know."

My lips pursed, and I didn't press. I was unable to stop my attention from dropping to his naked torso, wanting to memorize every mark on him, and that was a frightening desire.

"Are you cold?" I asked.

Nyte's brow furrowed as though it was a question he'd never heard before. "Not like you think," he said. "Nothing is the same behind the ward. I don't need food nearly as often, and I don't feel the winter as it thickens."

My sadness still rose for him in this isolated place, especially now I'd learned just how long he'd been here.

"I've known many centuries of torture," he said, so quiet it touched me gently. "And yet the greatest agony is you."

That stunned me. A thrilling but sorrowful tug, and I knew in that moment what I wanted.

I wanted him.

Just for a moment, if that was all I could get. With the only true memory I had being only half-conscious, it wasn't nearly enough for me to know if what I'd felt was something I could taste and forget.

"I don't spare your thoughts because I've gained some moral code; it's because I don't *need* them. One look in your eyes and you don't even realize you tell me everything. Like right now, you have no idea the punishment you're inflicting with that look, knowing should this veil not exist, one touch would make the stars collide, and neither of us would care if we collapsed the world with it."

Part of me acknowledged the distant drum of alarm. The danger I had sworn a blood oath to. What drowned it out was the impulsive, careless side to me creeping in as if it had been locked away for too long and I'd forgotten its addictive adrenaline.

We stood simultaneously. I didn't think I would feel this yearning to stay. I knew I could see him the second I stepped out of this cave, but it would never compare to this *realness*.

"I need one more thing from you," he said as I backed away to leave. "A vial of your blood."

I opened my mouth, but the refusal wouldn't form. It was right there, but I couldn't spill it from my tongue. I tried again and again, my hand rising to my throat until it dawned on me.

My gaze snapped to him in horror. "What did you do to me?"

"Nothing but what we agreed."

"Why can't I say no?"

"A precautionary measure."

"You *tricked* me!"

"No," he growled.

"I can't refuse you anything . . ."

"Are you afraid now?"

I wouldn't give him that satisfaction. At least not in a confession, but perhaps he'd stolen that from my mind already. Any inkling of sympathy I had for him was now snuffed out completely.

"Now I see why you deserve the chains you're in," I hissed, trying to rein in my composure so as not to let him win a damn thing from me again.

Nyte's irises flickered, displaying maybe a flash of *hurt* before the burning amber subdued it. I tore mine away from him to storm for the exit, casting my sharp final words behind me as I went.

"And this place seems exactly where you belong."

36

I stood outside the Poison Garden, reluctant to step past the tall, ornate iron gates. They were open, but there was nothing inviting about the scene. The blackness was not that of decay; but of beautiful death.

With a deep breath, I strolled in, the hairs all over my body standing up at the sense of something sinister. It was so silent, no other bodies to be found. All that disturbed the quiet was the faint crunch of the frost under my boots. I was somewhat expecting a creature like the Crocotta to greet me. Nyte had yet to show at all despite our deal, and I wondered if I was succeeding in blocking him out, reluctant to face him after the cunning trick he'd pulled.

A garden was a fitting term for the decoration around the stone maze path, only this garden was like nothing I had seen before. I thought I recognized some of the flowers, but they bloomed a stark, unnatural black.

My gaze trailed up the dark timber of a tree, finding gleaming black apples that made me want to itch the impulse to reach for one. A butterfly that almost glowed with a trail of gold against the gloomy background flew close to a low-hanging apple. I watched its beauty as it landed, but my awe was smothered when it tensed and shuddered until the blackness from the apple seeped over it and it turned to dark dust that caught on the winter wind.

My face fell in sorrow at what should have been an insignificant death. But I couldn't help but to think the insect was part of a far bigger story.

"I was looking for you yesterday," Drystan said, encroaching on my silence.

I hadn't expected his intrusion out here. With everything I'd learned, I couldn't help my new coating of unease around him. He could turn on me as the notorious name he carried the moment he discovered I knew of it.

"Oh? I was training, then I took a walk, then I joined Zath in his rooms for supper, then—"

Drystan cut off my rambling. "He's very protective of you."

I swallowed, reading his hint of a question. "He's like the older brother I never had."

"Hmm." Drystan reached up.

"Wait—!"

He plucked the apple carelessly, and I gaped at the black fruit in his gloved hand. Was that enough protection from the poison? Drystan revealed two pointed teeth with wicked delight at my reaction, then he brought the apple to his mouth.

I jerked to stop him on instinct, my hand just shy of brazenly grabbing him when his teeth sank into the ripe flesh. My breaths came hard as I watched him tear out a large bite, waiting on a razor's edge for him to choke and splutter to the ground.

He simply chewed.

I blinked from his hand to his face, but nothing happened. The apple remained black, though inside was an ordinary, glistening pale yellow-white.

"I didn't know you held such regard for me," Drystan said casually, tossing and catching the apple. "I'm touched." He stepped closer.

Too close.

"Try it."

I shook my head, but it didn't seem like he would accept that. "What are you—?"

An arm slipped around me, bringing our bodies flush, and my blood roared against it. I tried to strain, but his grip was firm. His other hand held up the dark apple, and I balked at the proximity of the false allurement. I didn't know how he ate it with no affliction, but everything in me was screaming it would not have the same mercy on me.

"Just one taste," he said with a low, seductive edge.

My lips parted, almost willing to oblige if it would get him to release me. I almost closed my eyes as the apple came close enough to bite, until it slipped from his hand, and instead his mouth came down on mine.

Wide-eyed, I braced flattened palms against his chest. Drystan held me for a few more long, torturous seconds before yielding to my push.

My hand rose to my mouth in utter shock at what he'd done. Then he *laughed*.

Anger boiled in me, and I spun to him with a deadly glare, uncaring if it was Nightsdeath instead of Drystan I saw after he'd made such a deplorable mockery of me.

It was neither.

The last of the prince's form caught as black smoke in the wind, and I stumbled at the sight of it.

A trick.

Drystan hadn't been here at all.

On the ground lay the apple. Missing one bite.

I shook my head to pass a wave of dizziness. A bitter, ashy taste filled my mouth, and I pulled off my glove to raise a hand to my lips. "Shit," I breathed, smudging the black soot-like substance between my fingers. It was poisonous. My mind had been played with to have eaten it.

The trial's timer was now set with the need to find the antidote.

I focused on my steps, my breathing. Why did it have to act so damn fast? I thought the stark roses were crying. Soft wails carried through me, and I mourned with them, not knowing what for, but I became so weighted with sadness. Their vines grew, reaching to share their condolences, and I leaned toward them.

"They are beautiful," the ghost of Drystan observed with me. "The black rose blooms when death lingers near."

The first scratch pierced my skin. I gasped, snapping out of the illusion to stumble back, and their sorrow turned to merriment, so overwhelming and eerie it cut through me.

I broke into a run away from them.

At least I tried to. Fatigue turned my shoes to lead instead, until lifting one foot in front of the other became a heavy burden. I almost gave in to the wobble of my knees until I came across a bench.

I needed to rest. Just for a moment.

My breath frosted the air desperately as I slumped down. I rubbed my eyes, trying to rally some focus. I couldn't fall asleep. I had to find the antidote.

"Something made from the same place," I thought out loud through a labored breath. I tried to calculate. "Another plant."

Movement caught at the edge of my vision, and I leaned back, jerking away from the long black stalk that grew from the bush beside me, thinking the roses had followed me.

Until it stopped reaching. A black flower bloomed magnificently, more like a lily of death. I blinked as though the illusion would vanish or turn into another cruel trick. It stayed still except for a flicker dangling from the top of the stem.

I reached for the dark paper tentatively, reading one word:

I was *not* about to trust that.

Groaning, I massaged the dull ache forming in my head. I scanned the three letters carefully, but their placement was off. The "T" sat highest, then the "e" slightly slower, and then "a" a farther fraction below. My final observation was to wonder why the "e" and "a" were in small letters while the "T" was uppercase.

Seconds ticked by.

My mind rearranged the letters. Then my brow relaxed, and a small smile curved my mouth.

"Tea," I said to no one.

I swallowed hard, conjuring what might have happened if I'd eaten it as the instruction prompted at first glance. Making tea, however, must be a way of canceling out whatever poisonous effects the apple had.

Down the path I spied a quaint hut. With nothing to lose, I plucked the flower and sluggishly headed for it.

My first knock made the door creak open, and I slowly eased myself inside. "Hello?" I called out, but from the rundown interior I figured it to be long abandoned.

The floorboards groaned under my weight as I walked over to a small kitchen area. No place for running water. I had to pause and stop myself from cursing the gods for their sadistic humor. To add insult, the firepit mocked me as I slumped before it. I tossed some of the piled wood into the dark space.

"You'll want to add the dried leaves and moss."

My teeth clenched at the sound of Nyte's irritating voice. "I can figure it out for myself," I grumbled.

He was the last person I wanted to see.

"You might have to come back to this tomorrow to make it back before twilight."

"In case you haven't noticed . . ."—I winced at the ache in my muscles— "that's not really an option this time."

"You'll be fine if you take the flower back to the castle. Try again tomorrow."

"Not going to happen," I said, barely a wheeze as I tossed the final log onto the pile. "I want these trials to be over, and I'm getting a damned key piece If I have to sleep here."

"You need to be back tonight—"

"Then command me," I bit out, finally turning to cast him a glower.

He didn't ease his hard frown that looked prepared to fight me on the matter. "I won't do that."

"Then why add the condition to the bargain at all?"

"To protect you."

I scoffed, my smile pure bitter resentment. "You don't do anything unless it is to your benefit."

Nyte crouched slowly, sparking a hint of challenge in those molten eyes. "My benefit and my desire are that you stay alive."

I stuffed dried leaves into the firepit, trying to ignore him.

"Good. Now use your dagger to carve out a small wedge in the log and grab that stick."

My petty side didn't want to give him the satisfaction of obeying, but time wasn't my luxury. At Nyte's instruction I was up on my knees, braced and trying to roll the stick between my hands to create a spark. I whimpered pathetically on my fifth try, finding it far more labor-intensive than it looked.

"Don't stop—you almost have it," Nyte encouraged.

When the first glow of amber against the darkness ignited, I could have cried with joy. Then, after a few more tries, a flame sparked to life. I continued to follow Nyte's guidance, gathering the leaves and gently blowing until it caught on the wood.

I smiled with relief at the fire that licked across the tinder, growing like a precious heartbeat. I was transfixed. Nyte remained silent, and when I turned I found him watching me with a softness I didn't want to see. The kind that stole all past tension just for a moment.

"There's a water pump outside," he said gently.

I wished he wouldn't look at me like the helpless person I was right now.

It took the last out of me to return with a crooked pot of water. I set it over the fire thinking I wouldn't make it to standing again. The heat of the fire enveloped me, further dragging on my consciousness. My eyes fluttered as I watched the blazing tango.

Nyte sat beside me, one knee bent with his arm resting over it, while the other he angled flat and propped himself up with one hand. So casual and beautiful. My gut sank.

"What will you do when you're free?" I asked quietly, setting aside our animosity for a moment.

The flames danced across his thoughtful features as he stared through them. "I've had a long time to think of what I'll do," he said, not meeting my gaze. "It's recently come with some reassessment, and I'm not entirely sure where to start."

I shuddered. He spoke as if he held many promises to fulfill. Someone had wronged him truly, perhaps several people, and I would be the one to unleash their looming fate.

"I'm trying to figure you out," I admitted.

He slipped his golden gaze to me, and it was alive with the flames marching in them. "How is that going for you?"

"I think you're afraid."

"I have little to fear."

"Except yourself."

A beat of silence. Then his mouth curved a fraction. "You fear what I might be capable of," he said.

"Yes."

"Good."

"You like people to fear you."

"I need people to fear me," he corrected. "It is an easy feat. Once I touch someone's fear, I can destroy them with it. One thought from me, and they bend to my mercy."

"Can I tell you a secret?" I whispered. My lids grew so heavy I had to close them.

His answer came in the form of a growing energy. I felt him as though he'd snuck up behind me, and with my neck inclined in my sleepy, delirious state I believed the warm lick of the flames was his breath across my skin.

"I fear myself sometimes," I said.

A phantom hand tipped my hair away for his words to purr close to my ear. "Tell me."

I shouldn't want his touch. Yet I *craved* it.

"One time I wandered through a part of Hektor's manor I shouldn't have. Many places were off-limits, but I was curious, and he was out of town. It happened to be a private lounge for Hektor's highest-ranked men. I was found by one of them, and though he knew who I was and how his life would be forfeited if I spoke, he was confident enough that I wouldn't speak out for risk of Hektor's wrath if he discovered I'd left my rooms while he was gone. The man was huge, and I was so scared I didn't know how I would escape. He tried to force himself on me—" I had to pause, not at the recollection but at the waves of *anger* that washed over me, so raw and shadowy that for a moment I regretted sharing the story for Nyte's reaction.

"You can tell me anything," he said. I had never heard his tone so restrained. "Add the petals."

I nodded heavily. Sweat slicked my skin.

The black petals gave off a hiss when they touched the water, like a cat priming to strike, and my heart galloped. They shrank, dissolving into a mist that turned the water dark.

"I had my dagger," I continued. "And until then I never truly believed I had what it took to wield it. Even now I hardly remember the slice across his throat, nor the several wounds in his chest he was said to have been found with. All I remember is my blood-splattered reflection and the dark, sinister way I was *exhilarated* by what I'd done. Not only that, but I knew I had to clean myself up to get rid of any trace that could relate his death back to me. Yet for a long moment, I didn't want to. I wanted Hektor to find me that way. Blood-soaked and near savage, I wanted him to see what I was capable of. Not his weak little pet. Not deserving of a cage, with or without bars. Because I could do the same to *him*."

At Nyte's stillness my head turned. The light graze of his hand across my cheek pinched my brow.

"You are perfect."

With three words he set me free. Maybe I shouldn't have found comfort in being *his* kind of perfect—something of danger and unpredictability—but I didn't want to be anything else. Our darknesses touched, understood each other, and the only thing that frightened me was how content I became.

My head slumped, and I cursed the tightening of my throat as the spell of sleep overcame me.

"The tea, Starlight," he said as though pained he couldn't truly aid me.

I thought I nodded, though I couldn't be certain when I could barely reach out to wrap a cloth around the pot handle. My hand shook the boiling water dangerously, but I managed to pour enough into the cup.

"This is safe?" I asked with blurred vision, hoping the black water was a mistake.

"It won't taste pleasant, but yes. And if you're still wondering, the plant would have killed you if you'd consumed it raw."

It wasn't the right moment to tell me that; now I was overcome with the notion I hadn't boiled it for long enough and it could still be deadly.

"Your time is running out," Nyte urged.

I took a deep breath, letting it blow over the cup to cool its surface before I took a sip. Cringing, I pulled away, coughing at the bitter taste of ash and water.

"You have to drink it all." Nyte was behind me again, bringing a hand under mine to coax the cup back to my lips.

I tried to shake my head, but the cup reached my mouth and I drank again. I gagged, but Nyte's hand remained there, determined to make me drink it all despite the water pooling in the corners of my eyes.

It burned, and I wanted to vomit with every gulp I took.

"That's it," he soothed, his voice becoming distant.

The last drop sliced my throat, and I panted. The cup dropped, shattering as my hand caught me from falling, but the world was spinning.

"Lie down."

I didn't have a choice when my arm gave out and I fell.

37

I jerked back up with a gasp. I didn't know how I'd gotten to my feet, but my disorientation began to clear, and I walked a few vacant steps.

"Nyte!" I hissed down the dark hall I was standing in.

He didn't answer.

My hand caressed my neck, certain it had been on fire seconds ago, but now I felt normal. My shoes echoed as if it were marble beneath my feet as I walked toward a light with flickers of color. Voices sounded now, though distorted, like I was underwater, and I became desperate to push through to the surface.

Until a bustling room unfolded around me as my focus came back. My hands shielded the burst of light.

It wasn't the sudden commotion that stilled me. A slow chill crept down every notch of my spine before beginning to coat my skin.

I felt him, and I wanted to race from this place I thought I'd escaped.

"My darling," he said in a sultry tone.

Hektor's hand touched my waist, and I couldn't move.

Oh gods.

He'd found me. I couldn't believe I'd thought I could ever escape this hold, ever run, when my chain to him would always have a limit.

"I missed you." He pressed his lips to my bare shoulder, and my eyes pricked.

I examined my gown. It was a dark purple, hugging my body. The cut at the top of my thigh let air breeze over my legs while sheer sleeves fell from my shoulders, attached to a low, heart-shaped neckline.

"I'm sorry," I whispered. It was all I could do when what I'd done rushed in with a daunting horror. I'd run from him, and now he'd found me I would face punishment. "I didn't mean to—"

"Shh," he silenced me, easing me around until my head leaned back to look him in the eye. Those green eyes I'd hoped to never see again. Yet in that second, maybe the pang in my chest was relief at the familiarity and the fact I hadn't killed him.

"I want to give you the world, Astraea," he said, running his hands up and down my arms, but it felt so *wrong* it grated my skin. "Everything you have ever dreamed of."

That had my thoughts drifting to wondrous things, unlocking every desire I'd ever had and knowing there was one key to having it all.

Hektor's hand dipped into his pocket, and while he'd gifted me jewels and trinkets before, my heart stopped with the purpose of this.

He took my hand. "Marry me, and it will all be yours."

There were no limits to what I could have. I thought of every precious stone and beautiful garment. All the delicious food and expensive wine. I spared a glance around the room and realized how much he meant it. I had only ever glimpsed this room from above, but here I was—public, known. I wasn't hidden anymore, and these people looked at me as if I were a *queen*.

The cool metal drew a gasp from me as it was slipped onto my finger, and as I stared at it, I realized the price. The rock on my finger spoke of a lifetime of wealth, but there was a distant tug in my heart.

Hektor didn't release my hand, instead guiding me gently, and I followed.

When I looked up, the purple velvet throne he led me toward was triumphant, though it felt somewhat familiar—but not in this room. It dominated the place with power, and I wanted to know what it would feel like to sit upon it and have the eyes of the room regard me as royalty.

I turned with his coaxing and sat, looking over the adoring crowd and noticing their gifts. They wanted to extend them to me. I met eyes with Hektor and his sparkled wide with adoration, giving me everything I could ever desire.

"Not everything."

I gasped at the intruding voice. He couldn't be here—not now. I tried to shake him, but it was like he fought to remain. He wanted to take it from me.

"Leave me alone, or I'll order you gone."

Nyte's chuckle was darkly smooth, and a featherlight stroke along my jaw invited my head to turn to my opposite side. "This is not what you want," he said.

I tried to shake him again, but he grew roots in my mind, and they had claws I would have to pry free.

This was everything I wanted. The power pulsed with exhilaration, the gifts and jewels more than I could crave in a lifetime.

I was seen, and I would be heard.

"Greed comes at the price of losing something," Nyte said distantly, observing the crowd with me. *"For this, it would be your heart."*

His enlightenment had me glancing at the hand Hektor held out. I looked at the diamond now, feeling the weight of an iron shackle. I could have every luxury with him, but not love.

"No," I said, the word barely a breath as I knew it would inspire the sinister look in Hektor's eyes. I pushed to my feet, backing away from him, and tried to pull the ring free, but I cried out when it clamped down harder.

"I offered you everything. Why won't you take it?" Hektor's voice became unrecognizable, a dark vibration, as shadows engulfed the room.

My answer was there, lodged in my throat, and I knew it had been for some time. Growing and suffocating, and now I wouldn't breathe until it was out.

"Say it," Nyte taunted.

My head was spinning. The ring around my finger squeezed tighter, and I yelped with pain before lowering to the ground. My hands clamped over my ears, trying to expel Nyte's presence so I could focus.

"You have already beaten the trial—now end it."

I looked up, trying to find him, though I knew he wasn't here.

"I can make it all go away, darling. Give yourself to me." Hektor's hand reached out again, and I looked at his palm. The offer had me contemplating the material things once again.

What was one harsh hand to a world of many?

My mind broke with anger, surging powerfully through me. There was nothing I wanted, nothing I could be bribed with, more than the freedom and strength to never feel another harsh hand again.

"I don't love you," I confessed. "No number of diamonds in this world could make me love you truly." My heart was cleaved and I was bleeding. "That was all I wanted, not your wealth. But your love is condemning."

I didn't want to mourn for him, but I was. The darkness faded and his face turned to something I'd never seen before. Pleading, regretful.

"I love you," he said, voice soft, and the temptation to fall for it was too much.

Tears fell for the years I'd spent with him, the gifts he'd showered me with, and the illusion of safety he'd built around me. As the one who harbored the only memories I had.

I could change that now.

"This isn't love," I said. I held up my hand. The band cut into my skin and warm blood trickled, dripping off my elbow.

On his face, sorrow snapped to rage.

"We don't need her."

Both of us whirled at the woman who spoke. My knees almost buckled.

Rosalind sat like a goddess atop the throne.

I closed my eyes, shook my head, but when I looked at her again her smile only widened. She held out her hand for Hektor, and he went to her.

The people all looked to Rose with the same adoration they had showered me with. She would have it, while I . . .

My pulse skipped as I examined myself. The stunning dress had vanished, and now I wore torn rags and had bare feet. My hands were dirty, my silver hair tangled. Rose laughed, but I couldn't believe the haughty sound. She wasn't warm and kind, but this cruel mockery I couldn't have predicted from her.

I wanted to take it back. Switch places.

"No, you don't." Beside me, Nyte observed the scene. "Look at your hand."

I did, and no longer did the diamond ring cut my flesh.

"You are free now. You don't truly envy what she has at the price it would cost."

We watched Rose as she drank from a golden chalice. People gushed at her; Hektor doted on her. And here I stood, with nothing, as a nobody.

Nyte was wrong.

I took a step forward, but a hand curled around my arm. I snapped him a hard look, but Nyte's golden eyes held firm.

"Walk away."

"Let me go!" I cried, trying to pull free, but he only drew me closer. Standing flush against his tall, firm body, I stilled, hypnotized by his irises.

"I'll be damned if you lose a single year of this lifetime. Walk. Away. Now."

Something moved me at the command. I couldn't deny him.

The bond.

My body turned, and the laughter at my back grew, taunting me that it was the wrong choice. I could have everything Rose had. I *deserved* it as much as she.

My eyes burned at the ridicule as it echoed after me because I'd chosen to remain as no one instead. The lights dimmed in the hall and the sounds plummeted as if I'd walked through glass.

In my despair I didn't see the floor end, and I fell into a black void that swallowed my miserable existence whole.

38

I awoke with a pounding headache. Opening my eyes, I found the fire before me sputtering its last embers, darkness falling around me. I lay against the unforgiving ground, my temple to the cold wood hardly a bother compared to the ache in my soul that kept me down.

"You're getting too cold. You need to get up." Nyte spoke gently.

I couldn't move. Both because of the drumming in my head and the helpless sorrow that had clouded over me in my pitiful state. Would I ever truly break free? I had tried to be brave and strong, but I was hiding from the frightened girl who still lived within me. The one who harbored regret for leaving, because while the rafters of Hektor's manor were a lonely place, they were safe and warm, and a part of me still yearned to be there. I was a fool for ever thinking I could be something more. Something on my own. Hektor had been right.

And I'd killed him.

"Astraea."

I pushed myself up when I knew it was dangerous to stay here. The cold would kill me if I gave in to the tiredness weighing me heavy, and as soon as I was sitting, I realized . . .

"I need my medicine." I barely got the words out, but I was doused with dread when I looked out the small box window and spied the fleeting waves of the sun's rapid descent. I had been too caught up in the trials to remember how much time had passed since I last took a dose, and now my body was punishing me. I hadn't been this long without it, and I feared I wouldn't make it through the night if I was locked out of the castle, unable to get to the pills my mouth had dried out for.

"Shit," Nyte cursed, so close I tried to blink him into focus. I hadn't seen such worry on his face since the lake. "Come on—you can make it if we go now, but we have to be fast."

As my hand shifted, a chime of metal rang. My fingers curled over the item with a sigh of relief in my dire situation. Then I noticed the other broken shard.

"Two key pieces," I said, holding them up then patting my side to confirm I still had the first in my pocket.

"Greed and envy. You passed them both," Nyte confirmed.

I pocketed the pieces, and it gave me the surge of triumph and hope I needed to push myself to stand.

Nyte's expression became desolate as he watched me. He moved, trying to help me, but maybe my mind was too weak to allow it to be as believable as I wanted. I knew I was alone and there was nothing he could do.

Then I feared more than anything that my condition would cast him away completely if I couldn't reach back.

"I'm right here," he soothed, so close I bit back my whimper, wanting it to be real. To lean into him.

"Please don't leave," I said pitifully.

"Never."

I stumbled out of the hut and clung to every illusion that Nyte was right beside me. Helping me. Using walls and tripping over discarded crates and debris, I made my way through the streets. I couldn't pull out my map for the way back, but I didn't need to as Nyte was showing me the way.

Looking up, I shook my head at the growing twilight. "I'm not going to make it," I breathed.

"Keep moving," he commanded firmly.

I couldn't disobey as he used the bond that tied us. I cried out, forcing my body forward against the need to collapse. "You're a bastard," I said.

"If it gets you past those damn gates in time, I can live with that."

"I wish you were real so I could slap you."

"I shouldn't find your violence so attractive."

If I had even a shred of energy to spare, I would have attempted a glare. It didn't help that the temperature was dropping and the paths were becoming more dangerous, freezing over. Then a white flurry filtered into my vision, and I was sad I couldn't enjoy the snowfall.

I saw the gates and could have fallen in relief, but the sun was gone, and I realized then I was too late.

They were closed.

I walked up to the guards anyway, hoping in my desperation I could plead with them.

"I need inside—please," I panted as though I had run without pause to be here, but that was just the exertion my body felt.

The guards remained as still as stone, not even voicing a denial.

"I'm not well. I just need my handmaiden to fetch something for me," I tried.

Still no response.

The throb of my head became too much. I didn't want to fall in front of the emotionless vampires. I shuffled away in defeat, until I found an alley I could rest in just for a moment. I slumped onto a crate.

"You can't rest here," Nyte protested.

"Just for a few seconds." All I needed was a moment to gather myself, then I could find somewhere warmer and hope my illness wouldn't take me during the night.

"Astraea, you need to get up. Please."

I didn't think Nyte would plead for anything, but when I found the golden dawn of his irises, he seemed so at a loss for what to do that I couldn't stand to be his burden.

"It's okay," I tried to say. I shivered with the snow melting over my face. I couldn't feel my nose or cheeks or mouth. "I'll be okay."

"No, you won't. Come—I can guide you somewhere you'll have warmth and shelter at least." Nyte reached for me, but he couldn't really pull me up.

My head lolled against the building as his hand reached for my face. My lids fluttered closed. "I wish it were real," I mumbled, nestling into his hollow palm anyway.

"You're killing me."

My lids lifted heavily. His beautiful face had become so sad, and I reached for it, but my hand didn't make it before the weight became too much to bear.

Steps crunched beside me down the street. Nyte swore, shifting as though he could shield me with his body from the three forms—or were there four? Six? My vision kept tilting, so sometimes the figures doubled. Though it wasn't the fact there were so many of them that brought doom to my inevitable fate.

It was their wings.

Nightcrawlers.

The only color to pierce the darkness was red. Near glowing sets of red eyes.

"Astraea." One word of utter strained misery and desperation. "I can't protect you here. You have to get up, love."

His tender agony sliced through me. I had thought his main concern was to make sure I stayed alive to free him, but this . . . it was something more urgent and personal, and I *had* to try.

"You can't fight them. *Run.*" The last word was a command striking through the bond.

I sobbed before my body reacted, turning and breaking into a stumbling jog.

It was helpless.

Tripping, my gloved hands slapped the snow-dusted ground. I breathed heavily, but I wasn't afraid. Not of the creatures who stalked me. Lifting my eyes, I didn't expect the only emotion to slither through my drowsiness and suffering would be for him. A gut-sinking sadness that I couldn't make it out for Nyte.

I sat back on my knees, and Nyte crouched down with me.

"You're so brave, Starlight," he said, slipping a hand across my cheek.

I had never witnessed such a livid threat glow in his golden irises as when they flashed up.

"We found a prize," one of the nightcrawlers said, so close behind me I turned to stone.

"We shouldn't," another interjected.

Nyte's breaths were calculated. I studied his every flicker of rage to gauge the vultures who circled me, too cowardly to see them for myself.

"Just a taste wouldn't hurt," another said. This one was the closest as he eased around me. "We are granted a little playtime if they fail to make it back."

"I'm going to kill them all," Nyte said, so low and promising.

My hand rose to my cheek over his. The nightcrawlers couldn't see him, but that didn't matter.

Finally, I braved meeting the red eyes watching down over me behind Nyte. They weren't just hungry . . . they were *starving*. His wings had hooked talons at the top, and over the leathery texture were various tears that added a savage edge.

"You don't look so good," the creature mocked. "I rather like it when my meal has a little *fight* in it."

My stomach churned at the grim notion.

Nyte took my hand. "I wish there were any fucking person close by but him," he muttered darkly.

I was about to ask what he meant when a new voice, a true voice, came toward me.

"What the fuck do you think you're doing?"

Drystan.

A sigh of relief left me. Even with everything I knew about him, Drystan was safer in this moment.

The nightcrawler's eyes flashed with fear. He didn't get the chance to stand fully before the prince was upon him. I fell back in horror watching how fast he moved, then without hesitation, Drystan didn't just snap the vampire's neck, he tore it from his body that hit the ground before his head followed lazily from the prince's hands.

I didn't realize I'd shuffled back in my numb state until I gasped, touching something solid. My heart choked in my throat peering up at blood-red irises of sinful amusement.

"We happened to find a little mouse," the vampire behind me said.

"Get away from her before I make an example out of all of you," Drystan snarled.

He dropped down to my level, tilting my head with a hand under my chin. "You look awful."

"I need—" My speech faltered.

Witnessing the cold murder he was capable of exposed parts of him I had refused to see. My sickness fogged my mind beyond being able to be anything but relieved I wasn't at the mercy of these nightcrawlers anymore because of him.

Steps shuffled away, and as I swayed, an arm curled around me, and I was lifted.

"Tarran thinks you're hiding something," the same vampire said.

"Tarran had better watch his accusations before I come for him," Drystan replied.

My head came to rest on his firm shoulder, and it was the first time I'd come close enough without a racing mind to notice his scent of leather and something earthy, maybe even faintly familiar. I managed to steal one last glance at the nightcrawler whose blood-red eyes lingered on me, narrowing before they returned to Drystan. Whatever he read on the prince's face made him decide it wasn't a confrontation worth provoking. I wasn't sure of the control the king had on the nightcrawlers, but I could make out five of them and knew they could have challenged Drystan.

Until I remembered the sinister alter name that turned me stone-cold in his arms. I had now seen a glimpse of what could have attached such a reputation to him. Perhaps it wasn't the prince they feared, nor the king, but *Nightsdeath.*

"This would all be rather anticlimactic if we lost you this way."

"Are you locked out too?" I asked sleepily.

"Yes. Looks we have each other's company for the night."

"I need . . ." I couldn't get the words out. They became lead on my tongue as I lost all sense of myself.

"Shh," he said. "You're going to be fine."

39

Consciousness returned in waves. I didn't know how much time had passed.

Giggling was the first thing to make my senses trickle back in. My mind was foggy. Cracking my lips and trying to swallow, I winced at the painful dryness and peeled open my lids to find the source of the feminine voice.

Several things moved. Several *people*.

Then I remembered the last face before I'd fallen unconscious.

Mercifully, my headache had dulled and wasn't punishing me for the luminance that flooded my vision. It adjusted, and I wished I hadn't bothered to try to enter my surroundings at what I saw.

There was a beautiful red-haired woman straddling the prince. Another, a dark-skinned woman with stunning large eyes cast seductive looks at him from his side, and a handsome man with a pale complexion trailed a seductive hand over his shoulder to his nape. Drystan reclined casually, the top of his shirt undone, but thankfully everyone was clothed to some scandalous capacity. Their wears were light and elegant, reminding me of those from Hektor's establishment, only far sultrier.

Drystan was yet to notice I was awake, and I kept deathly still, only peeking, as he leaned forward. The woman angled her neck, and my skin blazed at what I was about to witness. The prince's teeth sank into her neck with the ease of a ripe apple. She tensed against him for only a few seconds before she relaxed and *moaned,* pressing into him and moving her hips as if it aroused her.

I twisted around, my breath spiking as I pushed up, scrambling for a way out without being noticed.

I was too late. Drystan's low groan rattled through me, and I stared at him through a mirror I couldn't avoid. He caught my eye, and his were only wild for a blink before he let go of her neck and eased a slow, wicked smile.

My skin torched. Yet I couldn't break his stare.

He wiped a trickle of blood from the corner of his lips with his thumb. His tongue swept over it too.

Stop staring.

Was he trying to look so dangerously seductive?

"You're awake," he said, his thick voice coaxing the woman off him. "Good." He gave those around him a look and a nod of his head, and they didn't even glance at me before they left.

"Where did you take me?" My cheeks were burning. I tried to look anywhere but at him while his clothes were disheveled, the open top of his shirt revealing a muscular chest. I had no business seeing him in this state. Clearly, I was interrupting his pleasure, and there was no way I was going to give the impression I would continue what he'd dismissed.

"The Scarlet Rose. The establishment you followed me into the other day," he answered.

"What time is it?"

"Almost dawn."

I scanned myself, relieved to find nothing had been taken from me. I still wore my cloak and boots, ready to walk out of here. "The castle gates will be opening again; I'll be able to get—"

I stopped myself. I felt fine. In stark contrast to how weak and helpless I'd been at twilight. A soft purring drew me to a black cat, always around at the most unexpected of times. I was surprised they'd let it in here.

"Your handmaiden happened to be outside the gates with your pills. I assume that's what had you so much the worse for wear. Truly, you had me worried for hours. I thought you'd touched or eaten something you shouldn't have in the Poison Garden."

I blinked, stunned, and wondering how Davina could have known. It didn't matter right now. I would find her later for that explanation. All I could be glad for was that she had been there.

"Why did you bring me here?"

"Where else was I supposed to take you?"

"A separate room from your . . . affairs would have been appreciated." I got to my feet, and Drystan approached me with a glass of water I took eagerly. When I finished, he held me with a studying look I turned stiff at. Even when his hand rose, I didn't stop the brush of his thumb against the beads of water on my lower lip. "I should get going." I rushed out, sidestepping him, but Drystan mirrored me.

"Pull out your map."

I blinked at him. "What are you—?"

When I didn't oblige, he seemed to think it appropriate to do so himself. I caught my breath at the proximity as he reached a hand into my cloak, knowing exactly which pocket held my map and overlay. He didn't look at them, instead fixing them together and holding them out to me. It didn't take me long to see and realize . . .

"I happened to remember this was marked in your destinations."

The tiny scroll appeared over another circle on the overlay: the Scarlet Rose.

"You've done well. But I happen to know Draven is collecting his final piece now. Enver is dead. Rose is heading for her final. And as for Arwan, he's been difficult to track, but I don't doubt he's close to the end of his trials too."

It seemed I wasn't making headway against the others as much as I'd thought. "How did Enver die?" I asked. This was news to me, and I blanched at how casually he mentioned it.

"Draven. There is no such thing as an ally in a game with one winner."

"He stole his key."

The prince nodded, and my blood ran cold.

As my mind reeled, I didn't register Drystan's advance. My breath turned sharp when my hair was tipped over my shoulder, and he stepped closer. I meant to protest and put some distance between us, but my gaze turned to his face. He didn't meet my eye. Though I was fully covered to the top of my neck, Drystan's attention lingered on my neck.

My first impression was that he was reflecting on his indulgences with the woman from earlier, and my refusal formed with a spike of fear knowing he didn't need permission to take what he wanted. It wasn't until I allowed his fingers to trace my collar, right over the exact points of my scar, that I was sucked through a portal to another dimension of time. It stole the ostentatious pink decor and lavish furnishings, snuffing out all bright color to replace it with something ominous.

Searing pain erupted in my neck, and all I could do was stare stunned at the black canopy of trees. Then I was falling, landing with force, and every movement cut my palms, my legs. A ringing filled my ears from shock, but shallow voices echoed above it. Trying to scramble to my feet, I was so unequipped for the nighttime forest setting, but all that raged within me was survival.

I could hardly draw breath, but an instinct to run coursed through me. To know if I had the slightest chance to make it, and to find out why he'd let me go.

I turned around.

The hooded figure had his back to me. I couldn't feel the claw of branches tearing the skin of my feet and ankles as I tried to gain distance. He turned to glance at me over his shoulder, and I sucked in a gasp that began to pull me back. Speeding, racing time forward.

The familiar caramel eyes latched onto me as he raised his hand to wipe the blood from the corner of his mouth . . .

I stumbled back as the bright room of the Scarlet Rose exploded around me. *Us.*

Those eyes from the vision didn't change, and I knocked into a table, items clattering to the ground as I tried to gain distance.

"Are you all right?" he asked, canting his head curiously.

All this time . . . Drystan had held the other end of the tether to my memories. Which only made one thing blare through my mind with even more clarity. Rose and Cassia had to be right: Drystan *was* Nightsdeath. Somehow I clung to the notion the title wasn't befitting of his subdued and careful exterior. But now I remembered a trickle of that night before I'd turned and run into the arms of Hektor . . . how could I continue to deny it?

Drystan fastened the top of his shirt and righted the rest of his clothing. "This trial can wait; you should head back to the castle and get some rest. I'll accompany you—"

"No." My response came too fast, and I scrambled to tame my racing heart, which choked my airway. He couldn't know what I suspected. It would remove my disguise in an instant. "The others are well ahead of me," I said. "I have to get this one today."

His tight jaw eased in understanding as he reached for his cloak.

I jerked as something grazed my calves until I found the black cat, an oddly soothing comfort right now. When Drystan turned to me as if to come closer, it hissed. The prince's gaze fell to it with no reaction.

"I'll send a carriage for you once you're done here," he said. "Draven won't kill you unless he can obtain your whole key, but you're hardly in a state for the exercise."

I didn't argue or say anything. My mind was still reeling with the haunting vision of someone who wore the prince's face while hiding a malicious glare I couldn't picture on him right now.

How the hell was I supposed to kill him?

When he left, I slumped down onto a plush couch.

"How are you feeling?"

I whirled at the silvery voice.

Nyte stood in the corner of the room, cloaked in shadow. His tone was distant.

"A lot better," I replied. "Thanks for helping me."

Nyte huffed a bitter laugh. "I did nothing for you. I could do *nothing* for you."

That fact pinched my chest. Judging by the way he kept his distance, I figured it pained him too.

"Only two pieces to go," I whispered as though on the other side of that goalpost things would be different. As if then he would truly stand before me, no barriers.

Gold pierced the darkness he stood in as he finally looked at me. "Did he touch you?"

I suppressed a shiver at the threat in those words. "No," I said. It wasn't a lie. I knew the distinct type of touch Nyte was asking about.

His lips pressed together, and all he gave was a small nod.

I took a few breaths to collect myself, staring at my lap until a large, scarred hand, a phantom touch, tingled over my thigh. Nyte crouched before me, but I didn't look up.

"Your heart is racing," he said softly.

I couldn't calm it. "It's been eventful," I muttered, which was putting it too damn lightly. "I'm going to get this trial over with." I needed to get away from him. These dark, lamenting feelings that tore through me with him near were beginning to tangle themselves with the horror that still clung to me from a moment ago.

Out in the hall, I decided to take the stairs, hoping to find someone I could ask for any indication of where the next clue was. The landing widened far more than the halls below it. My steps stumbled at the eight doors, four on each side, seeing the white and purple stars on them. Breathing steadily, I tried not to allow my mind to project me back to Hektor's manor. Perhaps it was a common enchantment for this type of venue.

They were all purple—which meant "occupied" if the spell was the same— except for one white star. I headed for it and stepped into the low-lit room, which coaxed me inside with familiar, gentle notes.

40

I knew the song. It had played at Hektor's manor. I had danced for Nyte to it. It couldn't be defined to me as just a melody anymore; it was an embrace, a soothing and beautiful comfort. As I glided into the room my body felt weightless. I wore no weapons, and the lightweight material further coaxed my desire to move.

I wasn't alone.

Sounds emitted from across the space, and I found the flowing white bed canopy to be hiding two silhouettes. I headed for it, my skin pricking that it was wrong to intrude, but they wouldn't know of my presence if I was silent.

Soft gasps accompanied by low groans disturbed the song, and though part of me knew what I was about to witness, I couldn't stop.

As I neared the sheer material, I found a slight gap through which the full clarity of the passionate affair was exposed. The beat in my chest slammed hard, and a heat tingled over my stomach only to tighten lower down. Suddenly, my skin felt tight and my body lonely.

The woman straddled her lover, moving her hips with such sensuous grace I was as transfixed as he was, admiring her with a face painted with lust.

"Why do you watch?"

Nyte appearing behind me sparked a wild thrill.

"It's . . . interesting."

His chuckle was low and taunting. A hand slipped over my bare midriff, and I leaned back into him. "Interesting," he repeated, his mouth lingering by my ear. "What about it do you find most curious?"

The sounds she made, amplified by her ecstasy. The slow strokes she made that began to turn more urgent. It was like I could imagine the chase she was racing toward. But it was the man who fascinated me the most.

"His attention," I said. It was as if his pleasure were tied to hers. He left no part of her untouched. I'd never known that kind of exploration of my body.

Both of Nyte's hands were upon me now. His lips traveled lower, then they pressed to my neck, and I parted my lips with a suppressed sigh of bliss. "You deserve to be worshipped—every damn inch of you."

His words against my skin felt the realest they ever had, and I didn't want to lose this moment. Nyte's groan only tightened the need between my legs.

"As much as I want to oblige, you can't give in to your lust. You need to deny its pull this time." He tried to step away, but my hands went over his, easing between the gaps. I couldn't remember another moment I'd felt this alive. Nyte awakened new and exhilarating thrills I was near desperate to explore to their fullest.

"Please." It was all I could do.

Nyte took me with him this time as we drew away from our sinful observation of the couple.

Then he slipped away.

I spun around, but thick darkness cloaked me. My chest rose and fell deeply at having been abandoned in the pitch-black.

"Are you afraid of the dark, Starlight?" Nyte encouraged my feet to move in the direction I thought his voice had come from.

"No," I answered honestly.

"Come find me."

My blood drummed. His voice changed direction, and I walked again.

Until I stopped.

"I already have."

He was the darkness. The night. Right now, I was wholly consumed by him. It wrapped around me tighter, energy humming faster. Then his arm slipped around me, and I drew in a soft breath when he brought our bodies flush.

"How do you find me so easily?" I asked, barely a whisper with my thundering heart.

His hand brushed my jaw, slipping over my neck. Every touch ignited new heights of pleasure in this beautiful darkness I wanted to bathe in for eternity with him. I didn't need to see his desire, nor hear his affirmation. I felt everything with certainty and confidence now the light was gone.

"Because you are the brightest star," he said, a murmur over my lips. "And the brightest star needs the darkest night."

My chest exploded. I ran my hands up his black tailored jacket. "Kiss me. For real this time."

In the manor it didn't count, not when I'd considered it the first bind to our bargain.

"The trial is heightening your desire right now. It wants you to fail," he said.

I shook my head, not wanting to hear what felt like a rejection. "You want this," I told him.

He tipped my chin. "More than anything I've wanted in my long and torturous existence."

It was too much. His words this close were sure to send me over the edge.

"Trust that this is straining every last damned tether of my control. I'm a selfish bastard for enjoying that this is what the trial has found to tempt your lust. That you'd want this as if nothing else in the world mattered. But it is not the whole truth."

I closed my eyes when his mouth hummed closer, thinking he would kiss me.

Then a breeze whipped around me like an acknowledgment and I was standing alone.

This darkness felt hollow.

"It's time to break out of it," his voice echoed.

I snapped open my lids, my chest rising and falling deeply. My need raged, and frustration became entangled with it. Candlelight now spilled over my surroundings, and I yearned with a pitiful desperation to rewind the last moment.

Then I found him again. Sitting half-cloaked in shadow like the day our paths first crossed. I strolled up to him, and after a pause, a tight coil in my gut that he might deny me, I eased down onto his lap.

"Astraea, don't." Something darkly possessive rattled the air. He used the bond, but I strained to defy it. "It's not me," he said.

I ignored him as, contrary to his words, his hands traveled up my thighs. My head tipped back. I couldn't stop—this was what we both wanted. When his arm encircling my waist pressed our bodies tighter together I could have whimpered. My hands tangled in his hair as my head straightened, needing to feel his lips on mine. I knew the detonation between us would be a devouring bliss and I'd become intoxicated by it. My mouth leaned closer. So close I almost moaned with my need for him.

"Astraea, stop. Now!"

The harsh command pulled me away sharply when it surged through the bond Nyte had tied to me in the cave. My eyes snapped open. It looked like him. But something wasn't right.

The cunning smile wasn't his, and the scent . . .

When I blinked, horror doused me all at once.

I pushed off his chest and stumbled back. Ice froze anything of lust and desire, replacing it with repulsion and incredulity that I'd been so thoroughly tricked as the intruder's red hair now eased into the light.

Arwan stood with arrogance, brushing off his clothing as he straightened.

"How did you get in here?" I spluttered, blinking as though he too could be part of the illusion.

"I've been following you."

"Clearly."

"For longer than we've been in the Central."

I backed up with every step he took toward me, trembling as those words settled.

"You don't recognize me. I don't blame you, for you fled before we had the chance to properly meet, leaving your kin to fight for you."

I shook my head. "You must have me confused with someone else."

"It had me wondering why he wanted to protect you so urgently and why you didn't stand to fight—until I discovered how powerless you are. Though I'm yet to figure out why."

"Stop," I breathed, having nowhere to flee as my back pressed to the wall.

Arwan didn't come closer. Instead he studied me from head to toe, and I was glad to feel myself back in my full leathers now the trial had set my mind free.

He dipped into his pocket, and I inhaled with surprise at what he held up. His full key.

The pieces looked similar to mine, even though held fully together I could still see the breaks, as if the key remained too defiant to become whole again. It wasn't a key like any I'd seen before. It was beautifully carved and too straight, without teeth at the bottom to unlock something.

"Have you tried it?" I asked, but I dreaded why he would show me. Why he was here at all when he should be waiting for the other Selected at the temple to try theirs, even if it meant taking them by force like Draven.

"No," he said, but his smile crawled over me. "Because you're going to."

He advanced, and all I could do was tense, subtly reaching for my dagger, but Arwan didn't attack. Instead I felt a weight enter my pocket. I stiffened when his finger slipped through my hair, observing the black tresses as they slipped from him.

"Like you, I know how to remain hidden. And how to kill a Selected to be here."

"I didn't kill her." The confession slipped out of me too fast.

Arwan smiled with triumph. "It doesn't matter how you came to be here, only that you are. The king is looking for a particular key, and I plan to get it before he does." His eyes drifted to my neck, and I pressed further into the wall with a flash of recognition at the look.

Hunger.

My gaze flicked behind him, and I turned to ice as I glanced in the distant mirror only to find my own horrified reflection. "You're a vampire," I said. *Soulless.*

His brown eyes met mine as he reached up, tucking the red lengths that framed his face behind a delicately pointed ear. I swallowed hard, wondering how he'd eluded the king so easily.

"Why do you think I can get the key?"

Arwan chuckled then laughed. Each note of it grated against my skin, and my eyes pricked at the ridicule. He reached the chair he'd sat on and retrieved something. I gasped as he tossed it to me, catching it clumsily.

"Find your final piece, then I'll take care of the other Selected so you have their keys too. From there, you'd better hope you can figure out how to use them." He strode for the door, casting a look over his shoulder. "I'll be waiting to collect. If not the true key, then your capture as a consolation prize."

When the door clicked shut, I was left with nothing but a hammering chest from the explosion of so many unanswered questions. The world swayed. I needed a moment to brace myself against the wall.

My mind reeled over everything he'd said. Doors opened and images flashed, nothing of sense, but I was missing something crucial, and my thoughts were bursting to find it. Arwan knew things, and he goaded me like I should too.

In my barrel of anger and frustration, my palm slapped the wall with a cry. I had felt like I was making strides in this game, completing the trials on my own, and perhaps I wasn't a hopeless contestant. Now I couldn't be certain of anything. I had another Selected's key—no, he wasn't a Selected, and I spared a second to mourn the life I didn't know that had been taken for this vampire to have claimed his place.

"The king isn't powerful at all," I thought aloud. "How did Arwan get past Nightsdeath? Why does it seem like Drystan doesn't care?"

All these questions battered me, and I rubbed my temples. If Drystan was now refusing to be Nightsdeath, the one they feared, then maybe that was why the king's control over the soulless was slipping, and maybe he wasn't even aware of the uprising against him.

I laughed. A delirious, drained sound as I slumped to the floor. This was the biggest puzzle of my existence, and I was constantly holding the wrong clues. I breathed in and out, making it my only focus. Nothing would be solved with the current lattice of my mind.

Eventually, I peeled myself up and stood outside.

It wasn't only the shock run-in with Arwan that had kept me down. I remembered what I'd done before. How I'd imagined Nyte and what I'd wanted from him. It buried me. I had to know what he thought, but embarrassment kept him locked out of my mind, and he didn't seem eager to try to push through.

Stars above. I had all but shamelessly confessed my attraction to him. My desire for him I'd spent so long trying to deny. It was infuriating, and I wished

I could let go of what had taken root within me, but in truth it had only grown with every appearance he'd made, and now I feared what it would feel like when he inevitably needed to be ripped free.

A carriage awaited, and only then did I remember Drystan saying he would send for one. I couldn't complain about the special treatment when I was in no mood to trek back on foot anyway. I needed a full night of rest before I set out for the final key piece.

"Don't mind if I do," an irritating voice sang.

My objection stumbled in my throat as Draven shoved past me, his brute form nearly knocking me off-balance. He flashed a cruel grin before opening the door to the carriage.

"You're welcome to join me," he said, making a show of mock chivalry for me to go first.

I kept my face blank. "I was planning to walk anyway." As if I would spend even a minute locked in a confined space with that bastard.

"Suit yourself." Draven disappeared, and I couldn't see him through the curtains of the carriage.

When it took off, my shoulders slumped and my eyelids weighed heavy.

"Will you come with me?"

I turned to find Nyte standing a few paces behind me. An eruption in my stomach jolted me wide-awake. I thought I'd feel embarrassment at seeing him, the need to insist that what had happened earlier was simply lust fueled by the trial to get me to break. But as soon as I looked at him, the return of those feelings stole my denial in fluttering echoes.

I glanced at the sky. It had to be around midday. "Okay," I said, knowing I would follow him even if twilight were falling.

41

Where are we going?" I asked after too long in giddy silence.

"Always so inquisitive," he mused.

I watched him as we walked. Nyte had never felt like a stranger. He'd never treated me like one either, and I couldn't place what it was that made me gravitate toward him. He slipped his gaze down, but there was something pained in his eyes at whatever he found in mine, and it dissipated my growing thrill.

"I didn't think you would object to a climb," he said, stopping, and I followed his line of sight.

We stood in a dead-end alley, and the climb he indicated was a rather precarious venture up the side of a building. My mind mapped the route too easily.

"We won't have much time if you stare at it," Nyte called—from above now.

I grumbled a curse since I was the only one needing to put in physical effort to scale the building. But as soon as my legs were stretching to find the next ledge and my fingers were grappling with each crevice and stuck-out brick, freedom became me.

I spied Nyte standing on the roof across from me and realized the jump it would take to join him. I'd hesitated on Rose's balcony, but this jump I was somehow more confident I could achieve. So I ran.

I cast out my arms, and in those seconds I felt nothing but air. An overwhelming sense of what it would be like to fly higher, soar longer, made me tumble to my landing. I caught myself on my hands and knees, breathing deeply but wanting to do it again.

"Are you all right?" Nyte crouched, examining me for any injury.

I was more than all right. Straightening, I looked over the distorted array of rooftops, wanting more than anything to fly above them all.

"Come," Nyte said gently, and I felt the brush of his hand against mine.

I watched our palms meet. My fingers slipped through the spaces between his, and though he didn't grip me with the realness I wanted or emit the warmth I craved, I was glad when he didn't immediately pull away. Instead he continued to lead with my hand locked with his, and I ignited inside.

"Try not to fall," he whispered from behind me, bracing his hands on my waist when we came to a small wooden ladder attached to the outside of a tall tower. "I can't really catch you if you do."

I nodded, bracing my hands to climb, but Nyte pressed himself to me closer, his phantom form so tangible I wanted to lean back.

"It's killing me," he added in a low murmur against my ear. "I wish I had the strength to stay away from you."

My head turned, and our lips came so close I should have been able to feel his breath, but all that embraced me was the cold winter wind. I ached inside—more than what was safe to feel for him. "I don't want you to stay away."

In my next blink Nyte was gone. On instinct I looked up, finding him perched in the opening, but he didn't look down. I began to climb, though a part of me was crying out not to follow him any farther. What sped up my heart was sure to shatter it, but I didn't think it belonged to me anymore.

Nyte wasn't waiting for me at the top when I finally gripped the ledge and hauled myself over. I didn't expect the warmth to hit me with the open archways as windows. My breath was stolen by the space.

"We're in the city bell tower," I observed, walking around the perimeter of the huge brass bell in the center.

"Yes," Nyte said from within a break in the stone, and when I found him, he dipped into the shadows.

I followed after him. The drop down from the narrow plank I walked across turned my stomach. I wondered about the magick that was keeping the outside chill away. Daylight broke again at the end of the hall, and I walked into a room set out like a person lived here. A large four-poster bed took up a lot of the floor. Black silk sheets and cushions dressed it with dark beauty. There was a bathtub and a fireplace, humble but with a personal touch it felt wrong to intrude upon. Though nothing could steal my interest like what I found positioned by the large open archway window.

"What is that?" I breathed.

It pointed to the sky, a large cylindrical invention on three legs.

"I would show you, but it's for the stars. It's called a telescope. I have a great depth of field through the stars without it, but this is unparalleled."

"So can I." Wandering around the telescope, I laid a hand on it, wishing it were night. "See through the stars, I mean. Sometimes I wonder if others also stare for long enough to feel pulled between them." My eyes were drawn to him in the silence. He watched me so thoughtfully I wondered what was on his mind.

"You were born for the sky," he said, so quietly it was like a slipped thought.

My pulse picked up. "The owner might come back," I said.

Despite my concern, Nyte sat on the edge of the bed. My gravitational pull to him became so strong as he watched me. Turmoil swirled in his golden irises.

"What's wrong?" I asked.

I couldn't be certain of what he was thinking or feeling, only that it was something vulnerable I wanted to discover more of. I crossed the space to him. Reaching out, I slipped a palm across his cheek, and my stomach flipped when his went over mine—not to reject my touch, but as though he longed for it to be true as much as I did. His brow drew tighter as his eyes closed, and I'd never seen him look so heartbreakingly lost.

"You can tell me," I whispered.

"I told you not to give me your soul, Starlight," he whispered.

"I haven't."

His eyes closed and an arm circled around me, drawing me closer to him with a sigh. "Do you know what a soul is?"

I could hardly think with his palm flat on my back, coiling slowly around my waist.

"It is the very core of what we are. The truest form of our emotions. It is always reaching for something lost. The beholder can refuse what it reaches for, but not without a lifelong depression for their denial."

My fingers slipped over his neck, feeling the soft back of his hair. "How do we know when it's found?"

I drew a shallow gasp when he looked up at me and pulled me in gently. One knee eased onto the bed beside his thigh. Our lips hovered shy of touching, and I wished I could feel his heart under my palm to know if it raced as much as mine.

"When you turn the key on the past and stop looking to the future. Because there is nothing but now to be found. There is nothing more certain than the need to treasure every second of the now as if there won't be a tomorrow."

I nodded, the need for release swelling in my chest. *Nothing but now.*

"I need you to cast me away," he said. "You know how to do it. To my dismay, you've been getting damn good at it."

He felt so real against me, his chest firm, only missing warmth, but I didn't let that waver my focus. I wanted him here. My hand trailed higher until he tensed when my fingers brushed the skin of his neck, and maybe my desperation to have him conjured some heat at the contact.

"I can't," I whispered. I met those fiery eyes, seeing the last of his restraint snap right before he broke.

"Fuck," he said as his lips crashed to mine.

Our mouths moved feverishly, his hand cupping my nape to keep us close. I whimpered at the absence of something, but I tried to forget where he was and that this was only as good as a dream. Nothing had ever touched me with such exhilaration like this, and I wondered how I would even survive the true feeling.

He hooked me behind my knee, pulling me over his lap completely, then reached under my cloak, but it wasn't enough. I needed his skin against mine even in this blissful torture of a ghost reality.

"I have waited so long for you," he murmured, pressing his lips to my jaw, then my neck, and I moaned softly, clutching his hair in my fingers. "I would have waited an eternity for this."

He was too convincing. Too addictive. As maddening as his mouth was along my collar, I brought his lips back to mine, and we erupted.

I straddled him. His tongue slipped into my parted mouth, and he groaned, switching our positions effortlessly. His hips ground against my core, making me moan softly. That seemed to encourage him. He pressed harder, raising my pleasure, and I arched into the blissful torture. Not enough. I whimpered in frustration at what was building too slowly for me to chase it.

"When I fuck you, it will be real," he murmured huskily in my ear. "You know how to find your pleasure. You've done it before, thinking of me."

I gasped. My eyes flew open as I realized what he meant, but Nyte's lips continued to trail down my neck. "You were in my mind," I breathed.

"It was one of the easiest times to be with you from afar. How much you wanted me there, and, *fuck,* Astraea, I was both thrilled with your thoughts and absolutely murderous not to be the one inside you."

"I wanted it to be you." My lust-hazed mind let slip the confession without care.

Nyte chuckled sinfully down my throat. "I know."

My thighs tightened around him, but he stopped moving, leaving me needy and breathless.

"Slip that hand down your body, Starlight," he coaxed thickly.

Realizing what he wanted me to do, I took a few heartbeats to decide. His irises were all fiery challenge.

So I did.

I undid the laces and buttons of my pants, pulse thrumming as he watched my every movement. I couldn't believe I was doing this. Nyte fixed his attention between us, where he was still positioned against me, but I managed to dip my hand under my waistband, finding myself slick with arousal. My head tipped back, and his groan only added confidence. More than that. Knowing he was devouring everything I was doing, and it was bringing him pleasure too, built on an impending climax.

"Look at you," he growled. "So beautiful as you touch yourself for me."

My hips rolled, knocking against the strain of him in his pants, and his arm slipped under my arched back to press us tighter together.

"Oh god!" I cried, chasing the pleasure scattering over my skin.

Nyte's mouth came down on mine, hard and only once, before he mumbled against my lips, "Say my name, Astraea."

It was already dancing on my tongue as I circled the sensitive bud of my apex harder and faster to his sinful whispers in my ear.

"That's it. Use me."

My pants were too tight for me to curve my fingers inside myself, but imagining him above me, what it would feel like to take him, compensated for it. Blood rushed through me, flushing my skin and making me pant with the chase of pleasure. I whimpered with the frustration of being restricted by my clothing, wanting to shed it, but I couldn't stop.

More so, I wanted it to be *his* hand between us. Relieving the ache he'd caused. *Stars,* I even imagined his head between my thighs to *taste* the arousal he ignited through me, what it would feel like to have his fingers curve into me.

I boldly left every one of my sinful thoughts open to him.

"I plan to savor every taste of you," he purred close to my ear. "Feel every perfect inch of you, hear every sound I'm going to draw from you, and watch––" His head dipped down to where my hand disappeared. His growl was low and primal, dragging his sight back up. "Watch when you take me beautifully." His hand slipped up my side, phantom teeth nipped my lobe, and I unraveled.

With how much I wanted it, the feel of him was too real, and I ground against him as I reached the pinnacle of my climax.

"Nyte!" I cried out, trembling violently with the first hit, unlike anything I'd experienced in a similar manner. I breathed hard, trying to collect myself while the tremors shook through me.

Nyte didn't ease away, planting soft kisses over my neck and jaw as I came down. "That," he said, squeezing my thigh still hooked around him, "was the single most exquisite thing I've seen and heard in centuries."

Now the cloud of my lust was dispersing, I lay in utter surprise at what I'd done. In front of him—part of me had done it *for* him. *Stars above,* who was I? This new air of confidence I wasn't ashamed of.

I was thrilled.

I fastened my pants, but I didn't want to leave this place regardless of whether the owner came back to find me here or not. Nyte lay beside me, grazing his knuckles over my flushed cheek.

"Perfect," he murmured.

My eyes fluttered as I rolled onto my side. I could have lain in this peaceful silence with only his touch for hours.

Nyte stilled. I became alert to the shift in him. The lines around his eyes tightened. He stared off to the side as though he were in two places at once, and I realized where I'd seen that look before: in the library when Drystan had visited.

He backed off the bed abruptly, and I followed his alarm, scooting to the edge.

"Nyte," I tried carefully.

His eyes closed and his jaw tensed like he was in pain. I stood, slipping my palms over his face, desperate for him to look at me and explain what was happening. He only gave a strangled sound as if trying to suppress it, and panic bubbled inside me.

"Is someone hurting you?" Adrenaline coursed hot through me. Then fear. Then rage.

Nyte fell to one knee, and I went with him. He clutched my arm, held my hand, but he could hardly move.

"What's happening?" I tried, desperation seeping into my voice. I couldn't help him here.

"You can't go back," he said at last, his voice so labored and pained my heart cracked. "To the castle. Promise me you won't."

"I have to."

He gave another groan, and I held him tight, but it was hopeless. Not the comfort he deserved, and not the help he needed.

"I'm coming."

I tried to straighten, but his hands tightened. Finally, he lifted his broken eyes to mine, and my body became weak with it.

"Astraea, they know. They know who you are, and he can't have you."

"H-how?" This couldn't be right. I was so close. It couldn't end here.

And I was not leaving without him.

"We have always been cursed from the start," he said, brushing the loose tendril from my braids. "I need you to leave the Central, Astraea. You'll find the key another way."

"No—"

"Remember the monster you saw chained. There is a reason."

Nyte didn't feel so firm anymore. He was fading, content to leave me behind when I was not.

"You don't get to decide what I see as a monster."

"There is so much you don't know. So much I'm sorry I never got the chance to explain to you. It wasn't the right time."

"Nothing is ever the right time. Except this. Us."

"Stop."

"You don't get to push me away. Not now."

Nyte appeared so tired my chest clenched, near suffocating, with thoughts of what they were doing to him. "I order you to leave the city."

"No!"

I knew what he'd done seconds before my body reacted to the command through the bargain we'd made. "I will fight it," I said, already straining against it. "I will fight you, Nyte. You can't win this one."

"Once you leave, the bargain will be broken. You won't see me again, I promise you."

Tears filled my eyes as I tried to hold onto something that was slipping from my grasp too fast. What was once whole and firm was now drifting like sand . . . until Nyte was gone and my palms flattened against the wood.

I sobbed. A tether running through me tugged with agony and heartache, and I couldn't ignore it to leave. But the bargain was stretching another way. Far away from Nyte.

Fuck your promise.

Anger built within me, raging-hot, enough that I cried out with the force it took to defy his command. He would not get to order me away. He wouldn't suffer alone. Not anymore.

Against all that was slicking my skin in my battle to act against it, I settled on my destination.

The castle.

42

Every bone in my body fought the direction in which I ran against Nyte's command to flee the city. Tears streamed from my eyes to defy the pull of magick enforced from his bargain.

I couldn't stop.

My fire of my rage overpowered that which torched my blood as punishment for my defiance. Maybe it would kill me when I finally got there.

I only needed a moment, just enough to hope my arrow or blade could stop whatever harm was being done to him. The last look of agony on his face wouldn't erase itself from the forefront of my mind. It drove me, making me soar through the city streets. As I wove around the bustling pedestrian traffic some people shrieked, stumbling out of my way. Others called after me with curses. Some looked inclined to come after me, but I blocked it all out. My feet slapped the stone, running faster than I ever had before, and my lungs tore in protest, my throat freezing with every breath of winter that speared it on its way down.

Yet still I pushed on, thinking the road ahead stretched farther than I remembered, mocking me that I wouldn't get there in time, taunting that it would take no small attack to inflict pain on Nyte. He'd suffered so much it was branded on his skin, and what reaction he yielded to me was still a mask. He didn't want me to witness the extent of what was happening to him.

Could they kill him?

The beat in my chest became a war drum, increasing to a climax, and I wasn't sure what I was capable of. This kind of retribution might have been a shock even to myself, but I couldn't explain the *need* powering me. It unlocked something from a dark past, an event I knew could consume me with its discovery, so I sealed it tight, only focusing on this task.

The castle finally came into view. I could have collapsed with relief. When I finally slowed—from the exertion of my sprint and my defiance against the magick—nausea rose, and I couldn't stop the need to double over and splutter through my hard breathing.

I found an inconspicuous vantage point from which to peer into the main courtyard. I couldn't enter that way—I needed a route around it to get to the library on the other side. But something caught my attention before I could move again.

The carriage Draven had taken here.

I stopped in place as a few guards surrounded it. One leaned in, struggling for a moment, until my hand covered my mouth at seeing what he dragged out—*who* he dragged out.

Stars above.

I didn't care for Draven in the least, but seeing him hauled limply from the carriage inspired a chill as if death were laughing behind me, stroking my nape as if to say, "It should have been you in my arms." Then that caress turned to a scorch of fire around my neck, and I gasped. I cast my eyes over the dominating stone structure, somehow knowing the pain was an echo of someone else's.

Nyte's.

Too many unraveling spools threatened to tangle around me. I had to cut them off one by one, though all of them felt dauntingly close to coming together to reveal something I wasn't ready to know.

All that could matter right now was getting to that damned library.

I made it around the black castle perimeter fence. The bars, I thought, were wide enough to squeeze through—I just needed the guard to look the other way. Unhooking my bow, I nocked an arrow.

My aim targeted him, and my hand tingled with what it might feel like to rid the world of one more vampire. I shook my head. I'd watched them wander the streets among the humans here, and maybe it was through familiarity that they didn't always scurry from them in fear. Or maybe I was learning there could be a whole different side to the world—a glimmer of coexistence.

My aim drifted to the trunk of a tree in the far distance. The guard, to his credit, was alert before it even made its mark. As soon as he was out of range I darted for the fence, wincing at the tight fit, but I forced myself through.

Keeping to the shadows, the sight of the library, its doors ajar, pierced me with such a rush of adrenaline my movements became a drift of wind, as easy as breathing and honed to calculate the quietest, darkest route. If there was one thing I could be glad of in my years of being Hektor's sheltered, fearful pet, it was the stealth and careful observation I'd gained while being a fly on his walls.

Yet all it took was one keen eye to swat me. And this one I should have known had a target on me all along.

"I had a feeling you would come."

The voice that halted me could have made me crumble. I was so close. *So fucking close.*

I turned. The four guards around him were unnecessary when my fight had already been stolen. "Drystan . . ." I breathed, wishing I were wrong.

The alarm had been raised about him many times, but I wouldn't listen. Even now I wanted to reject what was right in front of me. His cold eyes held nothing in them.

"What are you doing to him?" I tried, still aching to sprint to Nyte.

There was a time I would have balked at this confrontation. But I had been too late, too weak, and too cowardly to save Cassia, and Nyte was the sole thing that had kept me from following after her so many times I hadn't even realized.

"Nothing but what he deserves for his interference. I knew he would find you. All this time, you thought yourselves cunning."

"You're a spineless coward," I spat. It was a dangerous test, and one I paid for in blood when a guard stepped forward so fast I didn't have a second to brace. With his immortal strength he only held back enough not to snap my neck from the force of his slap across my cheek. It exploded over my jaw, and my eyes swelled with hot tears as I clutched my face. It left behind a cut that bled on my cheekbone.

I had never felt such anger. Such a dark desire to fight back.

To do so, I had to kill the girl who'd spied from the rafters. The lost soul who'd chosen silence and compliance. She died with the movements I didn't remember making until the guard who struck me choked, a small blade piercing his neck. A second was already in my hand, but it was only a temporary possession as it flew toward the next movement to my right.

"Stop," Drystan ordered. Not to me. His guards halted their advance, but I was pinned by many sets of threatening eyes.

I mapped the ground. They were all shadowless. Blood vampires like Drystan.

"The king will be most livid when he discovers he had you in his reach and you toyed around him." He took slow steps, a venomous snake priming to strike.

I thought to deny his accusation, but that was a coward's response. So I tipped my chin high, owning what he thought I was capable of.

Drystan stopped only a few inches from me, and I stood firm. He lifted his hand to my face, twistedly tender until his thumb brushed over my cut, and I hissed. My chest rattled watching him examine the blood, and my teeth clamped hard when he brought it to his lips. His eyes closed briefly, and when they snapped back to me, I could have sworn they flashed a frighteningly brighter hue.

"So your father sends his prized hound for me," I hissed.

Drystan's mouth curled, the kind of leering smirk that made men tremble at the cruelty to come. "Precious thing," he mused, tipping my chin, but I shrugged off his touch this time. "I don't want the game to be over yet. My father doesn't know. I, however, knew who you were the moment you stepped into the banquet hall. An excellent disguise, I must say."

"Then how?"

This time, his grin widened to reveal his lethal pointed teeth. "We all have our secrets." His hand curled around my waist, guiding me away from the library, and within, my soul cried at the wrong direction. I couldn't fight them all, and even if I did, how would I free Nyte?

The game wasn't over.

43

I couldn't become that frightened girl again. I couldn't allow her to crawl from the fresh grave I'd laid her in.

That was all I chanted to myself as I equipped myself for the final day of the Libertatem. I hadn't slept. My room was surrounded on the prince's order, and I didn't stop watching the building beyond the balcony.

I knew who you were from the moment you arrived.

I couldn't shake the prince's words. Not out of incredulity that he'd seen through my disguise. No—there was something deeper nagging at me. Since my library visit with Nyte, I hadn't touched the book I'd been drawn to before reaching *The Book of Bindings*.

I flipped through the pages of the book I'd taken that day, lifted away on some otherworldly road as I read, absorbing words that should have shocked me, pummeled me with fear, but each page was like a story that already lived somewhere within. I squeezed my eyes to think of that day in the library, struggling with hard breaths to come to terms with what I was learning. Then my thoughts quickly became consumed by him.

I feared the worst.

No—Nyte couldn't be gone.

I hadn't realized how familiar I'd become with his presence, but I'd never felt so hollow in his silence. Even when he hadn't spoken, he was always there in some echo.

I left the castle. Retrieving my map and overlay, I knew the final destination. A place called—

"The Maze of the Mad Serpent."

I nearly crumpled the map at Drystan's approaching voice. "Doesn't sound pleasant," I said flatly.

"Would you rather a slaughterhouse be called a rose boutique?"

I cast him a glare, but I must have done a poor job at hiding my fear beneath it because he chuckled lightly.

"Merely a point."

"Are you following in case I decide to run instead?"

"You wouldn't get a foot past where you're supposed to be if that were your intention."

"Then leave me the fuck alone."

"Where have you been hiding this feisty nature? I rather enjoy it."

I ground my teeth. Ignoring him might have a better impact. "He told me not to trust you," I said, unable to stop the slip of anger. "I never did, but I wanted to believe they were wrong."

"They?"

Shit. I couldn't implicate Rose.

With a flush of dread, my palms clammed at the thought of her, unknowing of where she was, which also made my stomach twist. I wondered if Zath was safe too.

"I hope the king kills you for this betrayal," I sneered as a diversion.

We weaved through the paths that were eerily quiet despite it being daytime. My eyes caught flickers on the roofs, sometimes down alleys—the Golden Guard were tracking us too. All except Rose's, unless he was exceptionally elusive. I prayed to the damned gods it was because he was still tracking her.

"My father is nothing more than a puppet who can't see the strings."

Drystan was the true puppet master.

"What do you want?" I asked.

"Everything, my dear. And you're going to get it for me."

It seemed we were both dancing around calling each other out. I didn't use his *other* name. I didn't want to give him the satisfaction.

It took coming down to the center of the human city level to stare up at the curved sign:

The Maze of the Mad Serpent

A shudder ran thought me at the thought of what the name could mean, and even more so for the destination that led *down*. Down and down until nothing but darkness engulfed the entrance.

"The trial awaits," Drystan sang. "I'll be here to escort you afterward."

"Charming of you," I muttered.

Drystan slipped in front of me. I tried to move away, but he gripped the folds of my leathers. My hiss at him was smothered when I beheld what he slipped into my jacket one by one.

Three keys.

"Try not to take too long."

I met him with incredulous eyes, wondering how he knew I had Arwan's key and had found it. He must have taken possession of Enver and Draven's keys too now they were dead.

I decided these weren't answers that would do me any favors right now.

Every muscle protested my journey down. My throat seized, and swallowing became painful but necessary to combat my dry mouth.

Down and down . . .

It reminded me of my first time venturing to find Nyte. My chest squeezed as his face appeared at the forefront of my mind when I entered true darkness. But he wasn't here—not even a hint in my mind. This darkness clawed with despair instead of comfort.

Down and down . . .

Until there wasn't another step to take. Ahead my vision was broken by a flicker of amber. Come threat or relief, I had no choice but to head for it. No sound but my boots against stone disturbed the silence, amplifying the thump of my heart.

At the end, the open archway led into a room. Torches lined the windowless stone. A firepit expanded across the far end, where it played host to tall chairs. I thought I was alone in the stillness. Until a musky scent with notes of whiskey filled my nostrils and within me roared an instinct to keep my distance.

I saw their polished, pointed boot first. It uncrossed from their knee, and as they rose my mind wanted to paint their hair a different color, switch the irises that finally turned to me, dancing for my reaction against the flames. I wanted the image to change to anyone else in the world except this one impossibility.

"Hektor," I choked out. Just to be sure I could speak.

"Hello, darling."

I shuffled one step toward his advance, shrinking right back into the terrified pet I was to him. He may as well have brought a leash since I was a fool for ever believing I had torn off my collar.

"You're not real."

Hektor tipped back the contents of his glass before setting it down. "Then come here and feel how *not real* I am. I have missed you more than I can say, Astraea." His tone was so soft, familiar. Reminiscent of those times when I'd been too frightened to move and he'd had to coax me back.

"How did you survive it? I-I killed you."

His expression flashed with an anger I knew all too well. With Hektor's next step toward me, I freed my stormstone dagger. It only fueled more rage when he spotted it.

"I wanted to give you everything, Astraea. I was prepared to risk *everything* for you."

"You were going to sell me."

His fist clenched. "I had a plan for both of us, and all you had to do was be *compliant*."

That boiled something inside me, taking my cold fear and turning it into a wrath that could match his. I clutched my dagger tighter, not afraid to have a second try at ending him.

"I am not *property*," I seethed. "It felt good to drive this through your chest the first time, and now I'm granted a second."

His smile teetered between rage and amusement. "Do you know what saved me?" he taunted. "You. More specifically, your blood."

My blood. Something even the soul vampires thirsted for.

I'd spent five years in the arms of betrayal.

"You've known all this time there was something different about me. That's what you kept me for."

Hektor laughed—a mocking, resonating sound that pricked my eyes with humiliation. "I think only you could look in the mirror and be convinced you weren't special, darling."

"Because of you!" I shouted. Pitiful tears for the girl I'd let down so badly threatened to fall.

"How easy it was," he said.

"Did you ever truly care for me?" I whispered. Why did it matter? It wouldn't stop the pain within me at knowing all this time I'd been nothing more than a possession. Knowing my own poor will had succumbed to that existence, perhaps I was desperate for anything to explain why I hadn't broken free sooner.

Love, even in its most manipulative form.

"Of course," he said, brow pinching with disturbance now, and I believed him. "I care for you now, which is why I am here. It is not too late." He extended his palm to me, coming close enough for me to take it.

A flicker in my vision caught my attention. I hadn't known there was another presence with us, concealed behind his tall seat, and when he stood, reality mocked me, threatening to unravel what I believed to be real and true in that moment. This was a trial—was it possible for both of them to be a twisted illusion? I prayed it was, but something felt too *real*.

My lips cracked to whisper, "Calix?" I posed it as a question in the hope he would deny it or turn into some other beast, because anything was better than believing his cold hatred was true. The last memory I had of him threatened to pull me to my knees. The heartbreak and misery of his final look as he'd cradled Cassia's body. It would forever haunt me.

"How dare you pretend to be her?" he seethed.

My mouth opened, but I floundered for a response, my gut twisting with a sickening guilt. "I'm so sorry," I said. "I did what I had to do. I had to try to do this for her."

"I never knew what she saw in you. You're weak, a coward, always appearing in her path like a weed."

"Stop." I couldn't take it. The hands he sank into the wound Cassia's death had opened tore it wider with every word, exposing the lie I was within.

"I'll make it all go away and it will just be us again," Hektor intervened softly. "No punishment. I promise."

I studied the lines of his hand. I'd felt its softness and its harshness.

Calix took careful steps forward, face firm with loathing. A glint off the fire drew me to the blade he freed slowly.

My heartbeat measured the countdown to decide my fate.

"You are the punishment," I whispered to Hektor.

Then I struck.

Shifting one foot back, my hand sliced down, and Hektor's cry was my victory. The palm he'd extended to claim me clutched his bleeding cheek instead, and I took off running.

"Go after her!" Hektor snarled in the distance behind me as I hurtled through dark corridors with the fleeting light.

Calix's footsteps already drummed my pulse with their fast, scuffling advance.

"Stop running, Astraea. We both know you deserve this."

I wanted to drown out his taunting call, wondering if I'd ever overcome the part of me that fed greedily on such nasty words. The part of me that believed them so easily it threatened my adrenaline in a chase of survival.

With the tight corner ahead, I had no choice but to slam into the wall, wincing with the sharp impact that ricocheted over my shoulder before I pushed off it again. At the end of this hallway I burst into light as though the roof had been peeled away. The walls still climbed so high I couldn't see over them. Above me, two levels of a square perimeter where I imagined spectators would gather.

It was an arena of some sort. No—with the walls, I stood in a maze.

"I should have killed you long ago." Calix's snarl reached me.

I turned out of his path too late, crying out at the burn across my arm when his blade sliced down. Crimson leaked through my fingers where they pressed on the wound.

I glared at Calix. "She would be ashamed of you now."

I expected the flash of rage on his face, but this time I was not afraid. I slipped a small blade from my belt, and Calix groaned when I lodged it into his side.

Then I ran.

My hands reached out for the walls as if they would answer me with a sure direction. I turned and turned, growing dizzy as if I were running in circles.

"Astraea!"

Stars above!

My head snapped up, and I could have fallen with a flood of relief at spying the pink hair spilling over the balcony Rose leaned over. I scanned around her, trying to focus, but all I could make out from this distance was the deep rise and fall of her shoulders as if she'd exerted herself.

"Where's Zath?" I called.

"I lost him in the maze," she said. When she held something up, my face relaxed with pride to see the full key. Until her gaze tracked something behind me. "You need to run!"

It wasn't footsteps that licked cold fear down my spine; something *hissed*, the sound bouncing off the walls to confuse the direction it had come from. Just as I turned with a shiver, I was tackled. Thrown against the wall. My head slamming into the stone peppered my vision.

"You didn't deserve her," Calix snarled in my face.

I blinked a few times to reorient myself. My teeth clenched, hot retribution pulsed through me, and my knee jerked up into his abdomen. "Neither did you," I hissed.

He doubled over and I pushed him hard.

He wasn't winded for long. When he lunged for me, we both fell to the ground. He straddled me, and I thrashed violently.

I was *not* weak.

I fought him with everything I had.

Not a helpless coward.

Calix clamped my wrists, pinning them by my head. He reached for a dagger, but so did I. I hooked my elbow, jabbing it up under his chin. He choked, losing his hold on me, and I used his imbalance to my advantage. My hand formed a fist, and I acted in some out-of-body instinctual state. It connected with his jaw, sending him sprawling off me, and I was upon him in a flash.

My knee dug into his chest, and I stared at him with such anger I didn't know how to reel it back in. This side of me that wanted him to keep fighting back when the storm was still gathering within. The spells that had been unleashed were not enough.

"You want me dead? Then keep fighting, you coward!" I punched him again, though it struck pain up my arm, and I knew my knuckles would bruise along with his face. Blood pooled in the corner of his mouth, and I delighted darkly in the sight.

"Astraea, stop," Rose called, but her voice was a nagging note to my need for violence that was far from quelled.

Calix groaned, but he caught the next pull-back of my arm. As he flipped us, my dagger clattered out of my hand.

"It's your fault she's dead," he snarled, hands clamped around my throat, and I clawed at them.

My vision blackened; the pounding in my head became amplified. I let him go. "No," I choked. My arm fell, straining my reach. "It's yours."

His release of me drew out a greedy breath, and as Calix fell back my dagger slipped free from his side. My throat caught fire, but the wrath pulsing through me rolled me to my knees. I crawled to where he clutched his bleeding wound, stumbling with the exertion, but I wasn't done.

Not until he was dead could I be done.

I straddled Calix, the promise of death in my eyes. His own were wide as though he was now seeing his. But I had no mercy as I raised the blade in both hands, my breathing deep and heavy.

"I forgive you," he let out in a labored breath.

Three words I hadn't realized were the stitches to stop my bleeding within. My determination faltered. "I forgive you," I echoed.

This wasn't me. My hands lowered slowly, disbelieving that I'd almost killed Calix in this trial that had toyed cruelly with my wrath. Yet he was no illusion. He remained firm beneath me. His wound still bled too much, and I had caused it.

"I didn't mean it," I said, laying down my surrender. I stared into his pine-green eyes as they filled with agony. "You did deserve her. You protected her, loved her, and she never got to tell you that she loved you back. But she told me. Her last thought was of you." I stood, returning to myself fully. My mind was a place I didn't want to be, but never one I could escape. "Cassia loved you, Calix," I croaked. "And I'm so sorry."

I looked up, trying to find Rose, but she was gone.

Seconds ticked by, and this time, with the next hiss to vibrate, I thought I heard the distant clamor of footsteps. We had to get out of here, but I was still short of the key piece despite completing the trial. At least, I thought I had, having broken through the wrath before killing Calix. I didn't think I could take much else now I was close to crumbling inside.

"I came after you . . ."

I winced at Calix's groans of pain as he stood.

"When I heard the Selected of Alisus had arrived at the castle, I knew it had to be you. I came after you to say I forgive you. And to help. I saw Hektor heading here and joined him, convinced him I was on his side to get you back.

I guess he used me anyway. He's been to the king, Astraea. He slipped out to this trial and used me, made me drink something, and afterward all I could feel was *anger*. So when I saw you, it came out all wrong. I don't want you dead, though I can't say I didn't mean some of the things I said."

A sharp sob escaped me. The confession drowned me. "It's okay," I croaked. "Thank you for coming."

We stared at each other with a new kind of grief. One that wanted us to comfort each other, but we didn't know how to reach out a hand.

Neither of us got the chance to break before a large form skidded around the corner.

"Zath!" I called, but my brightness at seeing the head of dark blond hair racing toward us faltered at the ghostly expression he wore.

"Lovely reunion," he panted, not slowing as he reached us. "Now both of you fucking *run*!"

The ground shook, and nothing could have prepared me for the sight of the huge coiling body that slithered around the bend Zath had come from. He hooked my elbow, and my horror didn't get the chance to stun me before his pace sent us flying. Calix came into himself enough to turn wide-eyed at the sight and race from it too.

The giant serpent rattled with a hiss, so close now the sound rippled over my whole body, almost making me falter in my desperate attempt to keep up with Zath. It stroked like temptation, daring me to stop, to fall to its mercy. Its long body hitting the walls in its chase boomed through the space, vibrating under our feet.

"Why do you run?" a voice taunted with a melodic feminine hiss.

What a wild question. I didn't deign to answer. There was fire in my lungs, and I didn't dare look back.

"How long have you been running for?" I asked. And where the hell was Rose?

"Too fucking long," Zath panted. He let go of my arm, and I pushed my legs harder than I ever had before. "Rose woke It getting her key piece—after she expended her wrath on me in the trial. Then I saved her ass again from *that*."

Well, shit.

"Then you know where I have to go to get mine."

"I'm not a maze-mapper, and frankly, I've been more concerned about not being eaten alive. I have a debt to collect from damned Thorns."

I couldn't feel the disruption of the ground anymore, and the last crash had been some time away. I finally slowed my pace and braved a look around.

"It's gone," I said, coming to a stop.

An error. A foolish, costly error on my part when, in the space that stretched between me and them, a blast through the wall had me shielding my eyes.

My arms flailed as I fell back into the giant mouth as it opened, twin fangs dripping with venom lunging toward me. I expected to slam to the ground first, but the impact never came. Instead, I was engulfed wholly by the darkness of the serpent's jaw.

44

A peculiar thing you are."

The first thing to trickle into my senses was the curiosity of an old man. With the flashback of lethal fangs promising a painful end, my eyes snapped open at the jarring sound. I shot upright, registering I was lying on stone, but heat crept over me. Beside me I found a humble fire. The room looked similar to the one I'd left Hektor in, and in my panic I searched for him.

"You will not find him here," the old man said.

I followed the voice to the armchair, and its gentle tone quelled my fear to stand steadily. "Where am I?" I asked, looking for Zath or Calix or Rose, but it was just us.

Just us, and as I surveyed the room again to discover why my throat had begun to tighten, I realized one thing that sped up my pulse.

There was no door. No windows.

"Where do you want to be?"

A tap against stone turned me around. I took a step back when the man revealed himself. His yellow-green eyes were sliced by vertical pupils. The irises of a serpent. Around the edges of his tired, pale skin green scales crept out, starting at his silver hairline and traveling up his neck. Despite my wariness of the large beast who had chased us, I couldn't be fearful of this man's presence.

His cane tapped the ground as he came closer, the top of it carved into a snake. He waited, and I remembered his question.

"Does it really matter where I want to be?" I asked back.

His smile curled with warmth. "Of course. This life can drag us to many places against our will. Destiny is a sea, and the boat that fights it will drown. That which rides the storm finds the strength to conquer it."

I thought on his words, staring at the back wall that had become a depthless void. I wasn't sure whether it was the way out or a trick that would claim me for good.

"I am where I want to be," I whispered. It kindled something inside me. Threads of memory that led into a space as uncertain as the one I stared at.

"Then you made a brave choice to come back," he said.

"I'm not sure destiny wants me here though."

"Waves can seem high and they fight with direction, but no storm is eternal. Venture the path that calls to your soul when the sea calms enough for you to see what lies ahead. That is our want, though it is never without challenge."

My eyes closed with the liberation he lifted from me. The glimmer of hope that dispersed shadows of uncertainty. "Your serpent attacked me," I said, wondering where I truly was.

"Many have faced the Hasseria, but she is actually very peaceful. Like the Crocotta, she is a spirit guardian protecting the thing at the very center of the maze people have come from far and wide to attempt to retrieve. It is impossible, however. A masterful illusion that lures those with ill will toward it into her lair. It keeps her fed and entertained."

I shuddered at the casual way he spoke of it. "What is it?"

"Why don't you see for yourself?"

I really had nothing to lose. If I'd died from being swallowed by the Hasseria, then this passing would be inevitable.

"What about you?" I asked, turning my head back as I stepped closer to the wall. I blinked at the empty room, raising a hand to my forehead with the dizzy spell. I couldn't keep up with the tricks of this game.

Is he just another illusion?

I reached out to the wall, and when my hand passed through it, I forced my body to follow. The darkness that guided me was weightless. A void of nothing. Calm like an ocean at peace. While my feet still walked on firm ground, my form drifted. Then, slowly, my anchor was sinking, gently drawing me back and reminding my soul to abide by the laws of gravity.

Light broke to reveal the steps I climbed, and I felt oddly spirited and lightweight as though coming out of a trance. At the top, I was encased by four walls, but casting my sight up I knew from seeing the square balconies that I was back in the maze. In the distance I thought I heard voices, but I paid them no attention as my sight fell to the podium only a few strides away.

I turned back as if the old man would appear to help explain, but the stairs were gone.

They didn't exist.

My hand cupped my forehead. I couldn't handle any more obscure conjurings, or I was sure to start slipping from my grasp on reality. I breathed slowly, making my only focus to feel through my senses one by one and confirm that what was unfolding around me was real.

Calmed, I was drawn to the podium again. It whispered in a language so

ancient and beautiful, moving my steps and stealing the world around me
as I stared at the most magnificent thing I had ever laid eyes upon. Resting
beautifully on a cushion of blue velvet was a giant, scaled black egg with silver
etchings. I thought I could hold it in both palms, but as I reached, a familiar
hiss coiled up my spine.

"Where have you been?" the Hasseria asked in that serpentine voice. It
moved like a slow lap of water toward me, circling me and the podium as
though it wasn't done deciding my worth. "You fled in your cowardice, and
now you come to claim as if you didn't abandon us for centuries."

"It wasn't my choice," I pleaded, overcome with sorrow though I didn't
have a full recollection of what for.

"You should have stayed away."

"No."

It began to rise, towering over me, and this time I didn't think its attack would be so merciful. "As soon as what dwells within you is released,
history will begin to repeat. You think the stars are dying now, but if you
are unleashed, the nights will fall for longer . . . the darkness will shroud.
Without the sun, the fae and humans will be powerless. Without the stars,
the celestials will fall again. The moon will thrive eternal, and the reign of
the vampires will begin."

I fell to my knees. "There has to be another way."

"It is unfair," it said, almost with pity. "That the one who belongs is the
only one who can be destroyed to stop the plague."

"What is the plague? What is making the stars die?"

"Search your heart and you will find it."

I shook my head with a surge of denial, not knowing exactly what for,
only that my world might be cleaved in two if I discovered it.

"I have a duty, just like you," it went on, and I balked at the threat looming over me. "I too am a protector of the celestials, and right now, you are a
threat to them."

"Wait," I breathed, reaching for my dagger, but it looked feeble against
the mighty serpent.

"Goodbye, maide—"

I winced at the high-pitched screech that pierced my ears, smothering
the human cry I'd heard right before it. But I'd seen the flash of pink, and
out of fear for Rose I snapped my eyes open, incredulous to find her atop the
serpent's head, two hands wrapped around the hilt of a blade she'd plunged
between its eyes.

Stars, I didn't know how she'd climbed the wall to leap down, nor how
she'd gathered the unwavering courage I watched in awe of.

"Shit," Zath swore, passing me just as I surged toward the battling duo as they came crashing down. He got to her before she hit the ground. I winced at the impact that slammed them both down as he wrapped his arms around her to take the worst of the fall.

The Hasseria withered, still shrieking.

"How did she do that?" Calix said beside me.

I couldn't take my eyes off the fascinating beast as it turned to sparkling gold dust. Beginning at its tail, its whole huge body dissipated until it floated like wisps, a snake of the air that soared high, and my momentary sorrow turned to wonder, somehow knowing . . . it was not the end for the guardian. Only the end of this form.

"You're going to be the death of me," Zath groaned, pain straining his voice as he rolled onto his side.

Rose was already standing, frowning at him as if she were debating whether or not to help him. "You shouldn't have done that," she grumbled, bending to hook her arm through his.

Zath glanced at her touch, and I felt the need to look away from them, instead occupying my attention with the egg that remained.

"You're welcome," Zath said without a thank-you.

"What is that?" Calix asked, coming up by my side.

I reached for it, but Zath grabbed my wrist.

"Oh, hell no. We are not taking that to hatch a baby serpent demon."

"I don't think that's what it is," I said.

He let me go, but his wariness remained.

My palms went to cup the egg, skin pricking with anticipation. I hesitated in awe when it changed color. Texture. It became gritty white with fiery red hues like it had been born of flame. Though it was equally as mesmerizing, it wasn't the one I wanted. It switched back as if posing a question.

A choice.

Though the brilliant, warm-toned egg was beautiful, it didn't feel right in this realm. So when it changed twice more, my hands flattened on the black-and-silver etched egg.

My heart skipped a couple of beats.

Nothing happened, but it did not switch again.

"It's probably dead," Zath muttered.

The shell was cold. My fingers moved over the thin, glittery scales, tracing the silver swirls that reminded me of my own. I marveled at it with a flare of protection, but Zath's assumption dropped in my stomach. I lifted it fully, momentarily bracing as though the walls would tumble down with my claim on it.

"I send you for the key and you retrieve trinkets."

My blood chilled at Drystan's voice from above. Our attention whipped up to him, and the others braced. The prince leaned over the balcony on his forearms as if we were an amusing spectacle.

"I can't say I'm surprised, but he's right. It's nothing more than an ornament. Perhaps worth a pretty penny though. Now dip into your pocket, Calix, and give her what she needs."

Calix frowned, patting his side, and his eyes slipped to me as he retrieved . . .

My final key piece.

"You might want to hurry along. I would have killed that past lover of yours, but I'm trying to remain unseen, and it seems he has the protection of guards, which only means one thing: right now he's heading to my father, and if he already knows about you, you'll have to trust I'm a lesser force to fear."

"Hektor is here?" Zath growled.

I shivered at the lethal glare he cast Calix in accusation. My brow furrowed in apology to find Calix still clutching his wound.

"Calix needs help," I said to Zath.

"I'm not leaving you with him," he snarled.

"You have to. It's almost over."

I approached Rose, and she seemed to read me as her hands reached for the egg. I released it to her with a dash of reluctance. She wasn't one to express her concern often, and I could only smile to ease whatever pinched her expression in protest. We both knew there was no other way. This was the sacrifice Cassia had been willing to make.

Rose extended her key to me. "Good luck."

I nodded, trying to appear brave for them. "Don't let the king capture you. It might be best to find somewhere in the city to lie low for a while. I'll find you all after," I promised.

When I scanned the space above, Drystan was gone.

"Stray—"

"I'll be okay," I said at Zath's pained objection. Taking the final key piece from Calix, I braced. Held my breath. As the world engulfed me in light.

45

The moment the key piece slipped into my palm I was taken from the maze entirely. Maybe I'd traveled far away from the realm I knew, pulled through a dark void of starlight and wonder. I thought I'd been here before as my body moved with no time or direction. Only for a few beautiful, fleeting seconds before everything stilled.

The shadows dispersed, and the first thing to greet me was a wickedly smirking prince leaning sideways against magnificent twin doors that eclipsed him.

"Took you long enough," Drystan said, straightening.

The black stone was carved with ancient intricate swirls and decorations behind him, so tall I would never glimpse the beauty of the top. A long, iridescent dark flight of stairs led up to them, and I took them slowly, savoring my surroundings in a place that radiated unearthly, exquisite power. But it was only an echo of what lay beyond those doors. Not the darkness of evil or ominous beings; this was the kind of power and cosmic beauty.

The pieces of my key floated from my palm, and I watched in a trance as they fixed themselves together. My skin tingled as I reached for it. Until I had possession of all five keys.

It was about to be over.

"Bravo. I almost thought you would kill him in there, you know."

I cut him with a look of hate. "What do you want from this?"

"Believe it or not, I have no interest in getting beyond those doors. I only need to ensure my father never does."

"Then you should have wanted me to fail."

"Oh, no, for the key is a very powerful tool I would very much like to have possession of." He stalked to me with slow attention. "It can make gods bow."

I shook my head. "Power. That's all this is in aid of. It will corrupt you."

"I am flattered you consider me not to be already."

I shouldn't have been so naïve, yet I couldn't let go of the confliction in his words. It lived like a kernel of belief inside me so I couldn't believe the warnings against him—not fully.

"And if it's just like every other time . . . ? What if none of these are it?"

Drystan paused, searching my face, and I tried to read the emotion in his, but he put up his guard quickly. "Then I have no further use for you."

I wasn't *that* foolish to think his threat was empty. "Let's get this over with then," I said, dipping into my leathers for the other keys.

I tried them one by one, my heart thundering, my palms slicking, my grip trembling. Four of them didn't work, and I held my breath as I slotted the last one into place . . .

Nothing.

Dread sank me. I tried them all again, cursing and chanting and praying.

Nothing moved.

My anchor lowered me to my knees.

Drystan growled in annoyance. "Think, Astraea. There must be some other way to try them."

I shook my head. I was just another failure. "I never told you my name," I whispered. My racing pulse had nothing to do with the lost hope of the keys anymore. I feared lifting my head as I remained vulnerable to him.

Drystan crouched, but still my fear stopped me from looking at him. "What a tragedy you have become," he said as if it were a sad, slipped observation.

Whatever he thought I could do differently with the keys, he was wrong.

I breathed out in disbelief. I'd thought for a moment it would work.

The keys slipped from my grasp in defeat, chiming to the floor as dull, scattered pieces of metal. The Libertatem was nothing more than a cat-and-mouse game, a complete ridicule of collecting meaningless trinkets while the king fooled the land to be at his mercy.

I couldn't take my eyes off them.

Drystan's thinning patience was audible as he stood abruptly. I scanned each key over and over with growing rage and frustration at what they represented.

It had all been for *nothing*.

The keys were whole, but each one kept their serrated breaking points, ready to split again and be cast out for the next Libertatem. A never-ending cycle of puzzles and trials.

The king was right. There would always only be one winner.

Him.

I picked up one key, shaking with the desire to throw it while I frantically tried to reassess how to end him. And Drystan. It had to end with Nightsdeath.

As I calculated how to fight or escape Drystan, my fingers flexed over the key. My eyes traced it carefully, over and over, until it became soothing . . .

hypnotic. But every now and then the trance would stumble . . . because something about the intricate design wasn't right.

It didn't perfectly match.

Grazing the piece with extra detail on its design, I blinked at the shimmer. My first instinct was to conclude it was my own desperate conjuring for *something,* but against my skin it gave off the faintest tingle that crawled up my arm and awakened my mind.

"Puzzles," I breathed. Glancing down at the other keys, I let go of an incredulous laugh.

"I've never been fond of them myself," Drystan drawled.

I laughed again, a sound to mock him. Them. Everyone. I didn't hesitate with the theory that erupted in my mind. Drawing my arm up, I smashed the key to the ground, wincing at the loud crack that vibrated like power colliding through the space.

"What are you—?"

The next key plummeted from my hand to the ground, then the next, over and over, until all five keys were fragments around me. I stood smiling with adrenaline as I scanned them all like a scattered jigsaw.

"You had it from the start," I said wickedly. I wanted to laugh with irony in the king's face. "Every time you had it."

There was never a sixth key. There had always only been one.

One hidden among five.

I found the single piece from each key I was looking for, and this time when they snapped together, they fused with a metallic glowing silver.

Piece by piece.

Five of them.

Until the final one slipped into place, and I had to shield my eyes from the blast of power. When it didn't stop, I opened my eyes to watch the brilliant flare expelling from the new key as it became whole. My hair whipped around me, and only then did I notice the glittering silver strands. The Starlight Matter that changed my appearance must have been counteracted by whatever energy was coursing through me now. My blood roared to life, skin torching, and I marveled that *I* was glowing. Light peeked out from the cuts in my leathers and the cuffs of my sleeves. It was as if my markings were flaring in answer to the key I held.

It grew, becoming like a small, decorative metal staff. Each end was weaved with metal filigree, and a purple stone was protected in a beautiful cage. Holding it horizontally, I marveled at the length as if it balanced two halves of a beating heart. Yet somehow I knew that while this was the true form of the star-maiden's key, it was not the only weapon—or tool—it could become.

The power in the air sucked back into itself all at once, and I remembered I was still breathing. I knew the key would open the grand doors if I could will its transformation, but I didn't head for them. I met eyes with the prince, who stared at me for the first time in awe, like he'd forgotten everything before this moment and was gawking not just at the key, but me.

Time began to tick in my ears. I had a choice. I could discover so much by visiting the God of Dusk and the Goddess of Dawn, everything I had been searching—*longing*—for my whole life. But my destination was set. My mind was already made up.

"Astraea, you can't go to him."

"Did you order the harm on him?" I asked, surprised by my own lethal calm.

He didn't respond.

My palm heated around the key.

"You don't know how to use that. It could kill you as easily as it could me right now. Let me help you."

"You have given me no reason to trust you."

"Have I not? I've known who you are this whole time and kept your secret."

"Why?"

"Because you deserve far better than the misery he will always cause you."

My heart skipped a beat. "Nyte? Why is he locked down there?"

"The same reason any beast needs to be contained."

Maybe it made me a fool to deny the prince's claim. As he slid a step toward me, I cast out my hand on instinct at seeing the glint of a blade.

In an instant power surged for him, and all I could do was brace against the key—against what *I* seemed to command. The flare of purple light hit Drystan, and with the impact of his body slamming against the wall I lurched with regret.

He fell, and I winced with a thundering heart as he lay unmoving.

The beat of a countdown was drumming. The king could arrive at any moment from Hektor's alert, or maybe he would have felt the awakening of the key, which hummed with an energy through the air.

I had to make a choice, not knowing if I'd fatally harmed the prince. Though it wasn't without a new seed of guilt that I turned . . .

And ran.

I chose Nyte.

46

It was the second time that I was sprinting faster than my lungs could cope. I didn't have the luxury of leisure. When the king discovered the shattered keys and found me gone, he would figure out where I'd headed.

I clutched the key tightly, feeling its desire to aid me, but I wasn't sure how to answer it, use it. I only prayed through my exertion it would hear my desperate call to free Nyte.

The castle came into view, and I took the same route around it. I had no bow this time and no choice but to dart right past the guard. He called out, alerting the others, but his large body couldn't chase me through the fence. I tried to keep out of sight as more guards grew alert and the courtyard became a hunting ground.

The main doors were sealed, so I darted around for the cellar entrance. Fire tore through my thigh, and I cried out, falling instantly. My palms froze against the snow. It seeped through to the skin of my knees, and though it stung I was glad for the contrast that distracted me from the arrow protruding from my thigh.

Raising a shaky hand, I whimpered. Dizziness swept over me as I realized I needed to pull it free the same way it had gone in since it hadn't struck right through.

I was running out of time.

With a cry I tried to pull the arrow out, but with the resistance and pain I swayed on my knees. Instead all I could muster was wrapping both hands around the arrow to snap the length with a sob.

Calls around me surged my adrenaline, smothering the pain enough for me to get back to my feet. I took a limp step.

Then another.

And another.

Then, with clenched teeth, I ran.

It couldn't end here.

Voices grew, and I knew the guards would be closing in. I could have cried with relief as I made it to the hatch, hauling it open and slamming it shut behind me. I didn't have a chance to notice if anyone had seen where I entered. I hastily descended, my grip tensing as my wet boots slipped.

Only a few meters down, my clumsy, slick footing became my downfall. I braced in time for the impact. The vibrations slammed through me, stunning me still and jolting a wave of disorientation through me that didn't pair well with the dark. My body ached so badly I wished for it to be gone. For a second my mind was content to give up here in the lonely dark.

Drip, drip.

I tuned in to the familiar sound of leaking water.

Drip, drip, drip.

My chest warmed, pulsing in time with that sound. It grew, becoming urgent, and with the next pulse it stole my breath as if it had almost broken free from its cage.

"Get up."

I turned entirely still as those two words came in a voice I'd thought I'd never hear again.

"Get. Up. Astraea!"

I surged upright. "Cassia?" My eyes filled, but I couldn't see a thing. My chest was so warm and bright.

"You're almost there."

Her voice didn't sound full. Not even close. It was like a whisper from within, and even if it was my own mind shaping my will to live and a determination to see this through, I clung to it with everything I had.

The wound on my leg was still bleeding and my pain grew intense, but I got to my feet, and without using the wall I walked, then jogged, then raced, down the passage. I was so close to Nyte. And even though he hadn't shown for some time, I had to believe he still cared. That this wasn't all a trick, and he would be able to save us all.

Light broke through the darkness, and a sharp sob escaped me. I didn't stop to find him, somehow knowing he would be there waiting.

He wasn't the only one.

I didn't think I'd ever be able to explain what overcame me at the sight.

Nyte on his knees.

Three guards.

All holding a whip that restrained him like some animal.

By his wrists, stretching his arms wide. And around his neck.

I saw white. Both from my all-consuming rage and the key that flared to life. As the guards turned at my intrusion—shadowless—I detonated.

The key became a blade, so featherlight it was as easy to direct as a throwing dagger. My speed—I didn't know where that came from, but they didn't fall from the strike of the blade; a sheet of light surged from the key I'd made, and I watched in fascination, then horror, as it cut through all three of them.

I didn't get a chance to react to the gruesome sight when the power that had sliced through them kept flying. It hit the veil, and my hands covered my ears at the high-pitched collision.

My blood raced as I watched the iridescent sheet crack like beautiful glass. This was it.

As Nyte freed his wrists and unbound the whip around his neck, I was running again. Braced, exhilarated.

Clutching an arm around himself, Nyte rose weakly. Those beautiful amber eyes flicked up to me, momentarily stunned as if he didn't believe I'd truly come.

A current began in my fingertips. My markings flared with the streaks of silver and gold that swirled around us. As if we existed in our own time. Our own void.

The electricity grew, the veil rippled to distortion, and my palm grew hot.

The key glowed so brightly I didn't know how I was doing it, but I twisted it in my hand and didn't think twice as I braced, slicing at the veil.

The world erupted.

White light stole my vision. I couldn't feel the thump of my heart. I was floating, and during those seconds where I was suspended I wondered if this was death. Peaceful oblivion. Until I was unwanted by its claim, cast out to face my punishment instead, and then I was falling . . .

And falling . . .

So fast I thought the impact would shatter me.

Something wrapped around me like a tether urging me to reach back and slow myself down. So I did, giving over to the aid, and then all at once I was caught. Breath returned to my body, too much to inhale at once, and I spluttered. The sensations of the real world returned to me one by one. And they were all *him*.

The scent of mint and sandalwood. I thought I'd known it before, but this was so much more embracing. My fingers flexed against the thin material, but beneath I shivered at the solid feel of him that was unmistakably real compared to every other touch we'd shared.

I feared opening my eyes, but the moment they fluttered and I saw my hand on him, my pulse returned as a racing beat. I shivered violently with the cold that came back, demanding in its force.

As he shifted, I panicked. My fist clenched his torn shirt as though he would drift away, and so would the only thing I craved in the world.

His warmth.

I realized with a flood of emotion it was all that was keeping me from break-ing against the agony of the freezing ice. Nyte pulled my cloak tighter around me and I fought the desire to slip my eyes closed, encased in his heat. Instead I finally looked up to find twin suns staring back at me. Concern and rage waged war as a fiery tango in those irises that burned so ethereally bright.

"Nyte," I whispered.

His firm brow eased. "Starlight."

He spoke with such clarity, and I didn't want him to stop talking with the vibrations I felt under my palm.

"You're real," I said, my teeth bashing together.

Nyte tried to hug me closer as though it would transfer more heat. "After all this time, did you still doubt it?" he mused.

I chuckled, my vision blurry.

"I need you to keep your eyes on me," he said.

I did, but my face was pained when I felt his hand approaching my thigh. "It hurts," I breathed through the panic of him reaching for the arrow.

"I'm going to take it all away. Then kill every hand responsible for harm-ing you."

My teeth clenched as his hand curled around the broken end, but pain didn't explode like I anticipated. Instead gentle notes lapped over me, a sense of calm and numbness.

"That's it," he said.

All I focused on was what he offered me within. I winced at the sensation of the arrow slicking out of me, but it only stung superficially.

He tore the cloak, wrapping the strip tightly around my thigh to quell the bleeding. Nyte remained on his knees, and I shuffled upright before easing up to straddle him, my heart galloping at the position. I was too greedy for his heat, pressing our chests together, and he didn't move—not even when my frozen hands touched his face. He didn't even flinch, allowing me every decision and action.

Under his collar my breath stuttered. He tensed when my fingers brushed the abrasions around his neck.

"What did they do to you?" I choked out.

He took my hand, brushing his lips to my bruised knuckles, which he noticed with a flex of wrath. His tender care fluttered in my chest. "Nothing I haven't felt before."

That didn't help the ache that swelled within me. I pressed my forehead to his, not knowing how to release all my hurt for him. "I'm sorry they did that to get to me. I think I know why, but I don't know how they knew about you. How I feel—" I stopped myself, stumbling with the confession I'd almost let slip, too afraid of what it meant.

Nyte took a deep breath, his fingers tangling into the back of my hair. "Don't ever say you're sorry. Not to me. There are still things you need to know."

I shook my head. I couldn't hear anything else right now. Drawing back, my eyes dropped from his golden gaze to his mouth. I'd kissed him before, and though it had been a masterful illusion that bent the laws of reality, this would be different. *Stars,* there was nothing I wanted more.

Maybe he heard that thought, because finally his hands touched my waist. They moved over me with careful precision, and I came alive at his touch.

Gravity needed no words, and as we both gave in at once . . .

The stars collided, and the sky became our palace.

Nyte was right. In this moment, I didn't care if the stars fell and the world cracked. I didn't care about anything but him. The taste of him, so raw and passionate; the way we moved as if centuries of resistance were pouring out violently. I whimpered against his mouth, opening mine for our tongues to clash feverishly. A low groan of pain emitted from him as our bodies pressed tighter together, my hands fisting his hair, and the same ache of explosive yearning tightened inside me. I didn't want to ever part from this salvation he'd become.

Nyte took my pain and thawed the ice of my skin with blazing desire. His hands dipped under my shirt, and my brow pinched with his warmth. *His warmth.* I didn't think I could get enough, and despite where we were, I wanted to feel every inch of his skin on mine for the heat we would create.

The hard length of him pressed to my core as my hips moved against him. He groaned into my mouth, and I shamelessly chased the pleasure. He hit my apex with every stroke.

"Astraea," he breathed, leaving my lips to kiss my jaw, my neck. Though he'd told me he wasn't a vampire, I couldn't explain my urge for him to bite, feeling it was his desire too. His teeth scraped along my collar, and I moaned softly. "Not here. But *fuck,* I can't tell you everything I've thought of doing to you."

"I want you to tell me," I said. Feeling bold, my fingers released his hair to travel over his shoulders and chest.

Our mouths collided again, turning demanding like time was fragile, both of us consumed by the fear something could pull us apart at any moment and we were prepared to be defiant.

Nyte slowed our kiss, turning soft and searching before his lips trailed along my jaw, and I caught my breath. Our hearts hammered against each other's. My thighs tightened around him with scattered desire as he planted kisses back down my neck.

I had never felt like this. Never before had I been so wholly compelled that Nyte became a need, not a want. A dangerous drug to desire, but a sweet addiction nonetheless.

"I would have waited an eternity just for this," he said.

I shivered at the delightful gravel of his voice blowing across my skin. My palm slipped from his nape to hold his jaw. He pulled back to allow me to look over every inch of him. Though we had come this close before and it had felt exhilarating, it was nothing compared to the real feel of him. As I reached my fingers toward his scar, his gaze remained thoughtful, pinched with notes of sorrow and vulnerability.

Brushing a strand of his midnight hair, I traced the long scar from his temple over his cheekbone. "Where have you been?" I asked quietly.

"Right here," he said, reaching for a tangled silver strand, which he tucked behind my ear. "I've always been right here. Waiting for you."

My mouth impulsively leaned down to meet his. I moaned at how easily we came together, the flutter in my stomach sending me flying, and my rage of desire burned against him.

Nyte gripped me, sure and tight. When I felt a familiar pull, I tightened around him as if we would be torn apart in this void. It stilled just as fast, and when the shadows dispersed we broke apart.

I knew exactly where we were.

The bell tower.

"Why did you bring us here?" I asked, not stepping away, but my attention was stolen by the view. The sun was setting, spilling serene warm hues like glitter on the top level of the city, and this time nothing in me surged with the urgency to be somewhere I'd never wanted to be anyway.

The castle glinted darkly alluring in the distance.

Right here and now, with the sky bleeding orange and pink, I was thrilled to welcome the twilight, then nightfall. I wanted to spend every hour of the stars awakening in the arms that held me now.

"Don't tell me you forgot where we were interrupted," Nyte said huskily.

My eyes fluttered with the warmth of his breath across my ear.

"Because I haven't. Not for one damn second."

47

Nyte barely let me go. A touch to my back, a soft kiss on my shoulder, as though he thought I could turn to stardust any second. I craved it all. More than that. A desire to have his skin on mine climbed within me so strong. But he was so careful, always catching my eye as if to ask for permission before he laid his hands anywhere new.

Occasionally my eyes would prick. My nose would sting. Because this kind of affection I'd been so wrong to think I'd known before.

I stepped toward the dresser, remembering my injury with a limp that made me clench my teeth.

"Sit on the bed," Nyte said, his voice full of an underlying wrath as he glanced at my leg. Then, meeting my eye, he brushed his soft knuckles over my bruised cheek. His silence was furious but composed.

He let me go reluctantly, and I shuffled over to the bed, perching on the edge.

Nyte maneuvered through the space, opening cupboards and retrieving a bowl, a cloth, liquor, a needle, and thread. He knew exactly where everything was.

"This place is yours . . ." I observed.

Nyte barely gave a sad smile at my observation as if he wanted to correct me, to say something, but he'd thought better of it. "You're going to have to take those off." His chin jerked toward me, and knowing the arrow wound on my thigh was his highest concern, my cheeks flushed to realize he meant my pants.

Sliding open another drawer, he retrieved a feminine nightgown. An ugly rise of jealousy stirred a protest as he came over to extend it to me.

"You want me to wear something that belongs to a past lover of yours?"

Nyte's mouth curled with amusement. "I would rather you wore nothing at all."

I held out my hand for it with a scowl. "Look away."

He leaned down to pass me the lilac gown. "As you wish." His lips brushed mine with the stroke of his fingers under my chin.

I melted under his true touch.

Nyte focused his attention on the bathtub, running the water and finding liquid soaps that wafted welcoming lavender and honey through the air. The scent was so embracing it tugged on something within me.

I didn't waste time folding out of my combat wears, hissing at the sting of my leg and then remembering the long cut across my arm. As I slipped into the sleeveless silk I tried to examine the injury from Calix.

A soft touch landed on my arm before I could see the full extent of the wound. Nyte's emotions were becoming so palpable they had to have entangled with mine. This time his rage was wrapped with vengeance, reflected in the hard lines of his face as he continued to look me over for other marks.

"Who did this?"

I shivered at the dark tone. His sight became fixed with scary calculation on my neck, and I remembered Calix's hands tightening around it as I swallowed.

"He didn't mean it."

"That wasn't what I asked."

"I can't tell you." Because I feared what he would do.

Nyte stepped forward, forcing me back until my calves met the bed. His arm wrapped around my waist to lower me slowly before I could fall. "I don't need you to tell me, but I would rather it came from you."

Our eyes met, a challenge radiating between us.

Nyte lowered, never breaking my stare as he dragged the bowl of water over. "You faced your wrath," he coaxed. "It's always something physical, though not often truly real."

"Stop trying to figure it out."

"You can enjoy puzzles, but I cannot?"

My mouth tugged at that. Nyte dipped the cloth into the basin.

"This isn't a puzzle. And I don't need you to seek vengeance on my behalf. I will heal."

"The act won't be erased when it leaves your skin."

I was pretty sure it would scar, but I didn't voice what would fuel the fire in his irises. "No. But forgiveness is just as healing to the wound within."

His fingers curled around my calf, trailing up slowly. Sparks shot to my core, making me all too aware of every inch of my exposed skin. My breasts tightened. He would see them through the thin silk fabric, but he didn't look. He didn't have to.

"You have far more restraint than I do," he said. "Keep your eyes on me."

I did, and as he poured the alcohol over my thigh I hissed, reaching to clutch his wrist, but the sting was surprisingly faint. My body relaxed.

"How do you do that?" I asked.

"By tricking your pain receptors," he answered casually, bringing the warm cloth to my skin.

"I understand that," I muttered. "Your magick . . . what is it?"

"Many things."

"You have to tell me *some* things about you," I pleaded.

His movements were so gentle as he cleaned the blood from my leg. My breathing occasionally stuttered at the slow strokes when they reached the hem. My hand over his made him pause.

"Why were you trapped down there?" I asked quietly.

His golden gaze flashed up, so vulnerable I didn't think he'd ever exposed this side of himself. "I stopped being what he wanted me to be."

"The king?"

He flinched. "Yes."

Nyte retrieved a needle and thread. My stomach turned at what he was about to do.

"Don't look," he said.

My breathing became labored. "It's hard not to when I know there's a needle through my skin."

"I didn't think you'd be so . . . weak-stomached." He held my thigh in both hands, and I panicked, sitting up and bracing my hands on his shoulders.

"Wait."

He did. Instead of the sensation of the needle, his lips pressed down. My mouth parted, eyes fluttering closed, and I tipped my head back. His hand squeezed, massaging as his lips pressed higher. Both became a maddening distraction I moaned softly at, the space between my legs heating up. I wove Nyte's midnight locks through my fingers, and he chuckled darkly, reading where my lust-hazed subconscious mind wanted him to reach.

His teeth dragged along my flesh, sharper than I expected, and before my breath of pleasurable surprise could leave my mouth they were replaced by soft lips. Higher, and the material began to bunch around my hips. I became weak to his hands and mouth exploring me.

Then he stopped.

As I straightened, Nyte's teeth snapped the thread. I stared at my leg in bewilderment. He'd managed to stitch the wound so precisely while distracting me.

"How did you do that?"

"It wasn't hard to divert your attention. Do you want me to continue?" He wrapped a strip of bandage several times around my thigh, catching my gaze as he tied it tightly. "One word. I wouldn't just oblige, not when I've been thinking of tasting you for so fucking long that the scent of you is straining the last tether to my already pitiful willpower."

I could admit that the sight of him on his knees, so close to the building ache between my thighs, was clouding my mind with powerful need. I'd imagined this too, and it had been nothing compared to the real thing.

"Your bath is ready," I said, nerves gripping my confidence.

"There are more enticing ways to get my clothes off, Starlight."

The nickname settled in me with a new tug toward something.

"What's wrong?" he asked, tipping my chin up to seize my attention.

I wondered what he'd say to it. If he could help me to discover the truth in it. But I didn't want to lay that burden on him just yet. One night. I wanted one night to bask in the peace I felt at being in this secluded tower with him.

"Tomorrow," I said. "Can we talk about it tomorrow?"

He smiled—a smile of such genuine *happiness* it showed something in him I'd never seen before. Nyte rose, reaching behind him to fold himself out of his torn shirt with no warning. I tried to avert my eyes, but it seemed my willpower was just as damned as his.

The sight of his scars would never fail to rile something heartbreaking and vengeful in me, but what consumed me with a foreign rage was seeing the fresh dark bruises peppering his ribs. He masked his pain so well, but when he turned toward the bath . . .

I stood, my hand covering my mouth.

"They did that to you?"

His back was raw with wounds. Whipping wounds. My body tremored at the sight of it. An anger so pulsing and hot overcame me, and I didn't know what to do with it. The king had ordered that because of me . . . or had it been Drystan? He knew I'd found out about his secret, and this confirmed I'd begun to fall for his *monster* enough to care about the harm he inflicted.

"It's not the first time," Nyte said as casually as if he were speaking of verbal discipline. "Not even nearly the worst," he added, reaching for the buttons of his pants, and only then did I turn away. "There are a few skeletons on my side of the veil from when they couldn't let go fast enough before I caught the strike and pulled them through."

I couldn't tell if he was joking. Fuck, did I want him to be? When part of me relished in but also felt sickened by the grim notion he could talk about killing so easily. Then again, hadn't I believed I'd killed Hektor? And even now, all that twisted in me was disappointment that I hadn't.

The gentle splash of water told me he was dipping into the bath. Then, with his hiss from the sting of his raw skin, I imagined him submerged in the milky water beyond sinful distraction.

"You should have let me tend to those," I said as I turned around.

Nyte waved a lazy hand as if it were nothing, and that splintered something deep in me. His head tipped back contentedly, eyes slipping closed. He propped his arms up on the too-small bathtub and, *stars above,* his glistening torso was godly. Mapped with scars and gold markings. He was mesmerizing.

"I'll heal in a few days," he said. "Maybe a week."

"How?"

"My fae blood will start coming back around now I'm out of the damn ward. Paired with the small vial I consumed of yours—I only needed it so I'd have enough strength to get you out of there when you came."

"You're fae." It was all I heard, greedily adding pieces of him to the map I was charting.

He slipped one eye open as if to gauge my reaction. "Sort of."

That made my eager expression drop, and as that eye closed again, a slow curl of amusement grew.

"You need a haircut," I said flatly.

Nyte didn't even look, pointing his finger across the room. "There should be some scissors in one of those boxes if it disturbs you so much."

As it turned out, he could be just as insufferable on this side of the veil.

I wandered over as he dipped his head underwater. I looked in several containers, finding the scissors, but I paused, drawn to an ornate purple box. I unlatched it, and when I lifted the lid musical notes began floating from it. Two dancers spun while the song played, and I watched, mesmerized. The inside of the box was navy-blue, beautiful constellations decorating the fabric, so it was as if the figures were losing themselves to each other in the sky. And the song . . .

"I've heard this before," I said vacantly. Then I was transported back to the market, back to holding that tiny box while cranking the lever, and these were the same notes—I was sure of it. I looked over my shoulder, momentarily distracted by how devastating Nyte looked with droplets falling off his midnight tresses while his face gleamed with the light of the moon that had replaced the sun.

"You have."

"Was that . . . you?"

His jaw worked as if he were debating the answer. "Yes."

I closed the lid with more force than necessary. "Why?"

All this time he'd been following me, helping me. Soothing my doubts and making sure I never felt truly alone. And I'd accepted it all as a desperate, tragic soul. What I didn't want to confront was the *why.* Why he'd chosen me.

"I hoped you would remember it for times I could not reach you."

It didn't answer my question; his reply only weighed down on me, pricking my eyes with unexpected tears.

I asked again. "Why?"

"We have one night before the world goes to shit. I'd rather not waste it on the past."

I was reluctant to let it go so easily, but more so, I shuddered at what he meant by that. Of course the king would be hunting for me. He'd be hunting for Nyte too when he discovered he was missing.

"Come here."

It was unnerving how easily he could read my emotions. Perhaps my rise of fear was written all over me, but I snapped out of it, finding myself distracted by my racing pulse the moment I stood by the bath's edge. I got to my knees, close enough that Nyte could reach out a hand and slip a finger through my hair, watching the silver curl of it.

"Much better," he purred. "You could join me."

"You hardly fit in there yourself."

"Is that all that's stopping you? I'm certain we could make it work."

"Just . . . let me cut your hair." I could hardly handle the giddy thrill taking over me. The thought of our wet skin against each other's with no barriers was too tempting. *Too* damn tempting. Before he could read that too, I shuffled behind him.

Dark locks fell away as I cut, and soon I became lost to the feel of his hair. My fingers combed through it, and I delighted in the low noises he occasionally gave off that tightened my skin.

"Your hands . . . *Fuck,* you don't even know."

I slipped them through tighter, adding pressure, and the vibration it drew from him . . . My eyes *fluttered. Stars,* I was losing every sense of myself to his reactions.

"Tell me," I whispered close to his ear. Feeling bold, past the point of being coy, I slipped one hand down his neck, tracing the raised imperfections along the way, until I could feel the beat of his heart under my palm. Hard and fast. Not enough.

I wanted him undone for me.

"I've had fantasies about these hands," he said, taking mine. He guided me up and around to his side without turning. "You don't want to know all the depraved things I've fantasized about you."

My heart lurched. "Maybe I do."

This version of me wasn't someone new; it was someone found.

By him.

Nyte leaned forward, planting firm hands to my waist and soaking my nightgown. I gasped. He paused, waiting for me to object, but I didn't.

"I'm not wearing any underwear," I whispered.

"I hoped not," he replied in a low gravel tone that was utterly sinful.

Sparks shot through me as his lustful gaze trailed over my body. Bracing on his shoulders, I eased myself into the water.

I hadn't been wrong to think the bathtub was too small, but he didn't seem to plan for there to be any space between us, and I didn't want it either. My pulse was in my ears as the warm water lapped at my thighs, my ass, drenching the nightgown I still hadn't removed. I swallowed, licking my dry lips, which made a sparkle of hunger flash in his eyes like he was waiting to devour me.

I sank down, inch by inch, until I was hovering just shy of letting my apex press against him. My brow pinched, and I felt over his chest, combing my fingers through the new shortened lengths, now similar to how he'd always appeared to me when our minds were entangled.

This was so *real*.

With the last acknowledgment, not wanting to revert to how he'd been so close but so far before, I pressed myself to him fully, letting out a soft noise at the hard length of him I was thrilled to finally meet.

"Do you feel what you do to me?" he mumbled huskily, leaning forward until our chests were flush. He took a deep, devouring inhale from the crook of my neck.

"If you're not a vampire, why do I get the impression you want to bite me?" I breathed. It rushed through me, and I'd seen the sharp points disturb his smile before.

"I do," he purred, pressing his lips to my throat. Then teeth. Pinching enough to make me fist my fingers in his hair with a gasp that turned into a moan. "It's one thing of yours I would kill to taste again."

My hips moved near subconsciously, lapping the water, and his hold slipped to my ass tightly.

"Would it heal you faster?"

His breath grew staggered across my neck, and I knew his response. "Yes. But I won't take it for that."

"I want you to."

"You're driven by lust right now."

"I think that's part of the point."

I could feel his smile against my throat, and I needed it then. So badly I was close to abandoning all shame and *begging* for it. I couldn't do that. No—that felt like he would win when I wanted *him* to beg.

"Suit yourself," I said, lifting but only getting a fraction of space between us before he pulled me back, nearly spilling the water over the edge.

"Don't do that," he said darkly.

"Do what?"

"Be a damn tease."

It was my turn to smile.

Nyte tucked a strand of silver behind my ear, irises of honey delighting in the game. I drew a shallow gasp at the water flowing over my shoulder right before he dragged a soft, lathered cloth along my collarbone. His fingers lingered on my bruised neck, his chest rising and falling with calculation under my palm.

"I'm okay," I hushed out.

I became transfixed watching every flicker of his reaction as he mapped my body, soaking the nightgown so completely I might as well have taken it off, but this moment was too precious to disturb.

He washed the dirt from my skin and kissed the blue and purple peppering my knuckles. Then I stopped him, taking the cloth and adding more honey-scented soap. Nyte sighed contentedly, eyes fluttering, when I began doing the same to him, marveling at every imperfection and gold marking, wanting to discover the language of him I thought would be sacred to us.

"Astraea, you made your mark on me long ago and I vowed never to remove it. Even if it became my greatest punishment to carry."

Something about his declaration flashed past to present.

Past to present.

Past to present.

I didn't know what it meant, only that this felt right. Nyte was what I wanted, and whatever was shadowing his face with doubt I needed to erase.

I kissed him hard. Needy and wanting. He gave it all back and more. The water sloshed with my movements and how he aided my slide against his cock. Nyte gripped my ass, then my nape, tearing his mouth from mine with a groan of satisfaction, and my neck inclined as if on instinct.

"Are you sure?" he said, voice strained and unrecognizable at my throat.

"I've never been more sure of anything in my life."

Gods, I was so close to climaxing at the thought alone, so primal and dangerous I craved it as if *I* were the one who was starved.

"Just remember you're in control. The moment you want me to stop, I will."

I nodded, still chasing my pleasure against him.

"Words, Starlight."

"Yes."

"You are in control."

"I am in control. I want this."

He pressed one final kiss to me, and I braced with a held breath.

Then his bite eased into my skin.

My eyes snapped open as the two lines of pain made me seize like an electric current from my neck down my arm, locking me still. It only lasted seconds before it faded away, turning to something possessive. A fire that didn't just burn; it consumed.

Nyte drank from me, his teeth inside me reminding me of the ache of emptiness I felt below. I rocked against him harder, now frustrated with the challenge of water, but the heat and our slicked skin was so sensual I didn't want to leave.

His groan while still buried in my neck made me whimper for the end I was just shy of reaching. Nyte's hand fisted tightly into my soaked nightgown, strong arms crushing us together, and I held him back, never wanting to disentangle myself from the safety he shielded me with or the warmth of him that carried me.

"Nyte." I sighed his name, so deliriously high.

His teeth sliding out of my neck made me shudder violently, breaking me out of an otherworldly trance. I wanted to do it again already.

"Fuck," he panted. His tongue lapped my neck and a burst of trembles shot through my every nerve with the sensitivity. "Are you all right?"

I held his face, in a state of rapture as I nodded. "Far more than all right."

His irises were alive again, near glowing, and something thrilled me within at seeing the effects of my blood. Trailing fingers over his neck, I noticed the raw marks were gone. The relief I felt was immeasurable, but it didn't erase the memory of it that gripped me with a vengeance.

Nyte kissed my jaw. "You are so brave. So magnificent. But I hope this isn't the end of your desires tonight."

I shook my head. It wasn't even close to enough. I needed so much more from him I couldn't even form a sentence with the scattered words in my mind.

"May I . . . ?" Nyte's fingers lingered on the hem of the nightgown clinging to my skin.

My chest ached at his tenderness, not used to this kind of attention. It flooded me suddenly, and once again all I could give was a silent nod.

I raised my arms as he peeled the material away, but he locked eyes with me even when I was finally naked before him. He shook his head, scanning every inch of my face, and my gut twisted at the anger and disappointment locking his jaw. My barriers rose until Nyte moved so abruptly I yelped, clinging to his neck, my legs clamped around his waist as he stood from the water.

Nyte carried me to the bed, and my heart slammed. It felt as if my skin were the only thing stopping it from breaking free.

"I was going to list all the things you deserve, but fuck that—it's not good enough. So here are my promises instead." The black silk bedsheets clung to our skin, but all I could focus on was the fiery passion in his eyes. "I'm going to kill him. I will never say his name because I plan to wipe it from existence on this realm so you may never hear it again." His cock slid against me, and his hand hooked my thigh around him to bring us closer. "I'm going to right everything he wronged. Give you everything he denied you. Worship every inch of the goddess you are, starting right now. Do you believe that?"

My brow pinched with every press of the tip of his cock against my apex. "I believe you."

"Good. Now I'm going to fuck you, if that's what you want. This night won't end with once or twice if you tell me yes. There won't be enough time to fulfill every promise I make to pleasure you either. But this night is yours. I am yours."

"I want this," I said. "I want you."

Nyte had been a pain in my ass but a longing I'd always reached for. Even the night I'd stumbled into the dance room and discovered him there I'd wanted him.

He wasn't just a lustful craving. Never had that been all I wanted, but I couldn't place what it was. Something our language didn't know, that didn't begin and end with our time. And I wanted to take it slow to figure it out so I wouldn't miss a thing of what was unraveling between us.

"Just know this ends any second you say. You are in control." His lips on my jaw scattered everything, and I arched into him. "Say it."

"I am in control."

His tongue trailed over the bite mark he'd made, and my legs tightened around him. My whole body surged with a current of pleasure, and he smiled, heading lower.

"Your blood is incredible. But I've dreamed far more of tasting you in other places."

Teeth nipped over my peaked breast, and I inhaled sharply. My fingers tugged his hair when he sucked instead. Every lap of his tongue and placement of his lips was so precise, leaving nothing of me untouched. Nyte trailed torturous kisses over my ribs, down my navel. Realizing where he was headed, my eyes opened, but my head tipped back. My blood was roaring. I'd never had someone—

My hands grappled the sheets tightly as his tongue slid slowly through my folds. He gave a groan of pure gratification that vibrated over my core, and I was in a state of utter pleasure. He licked again and again, so slow my teeth dragged over my lower lip, wanting to beg for *more*. I didn't know what to ask for, only that this was bliss and torture combined.

"Watch me as I pleasure you," he purred.

Stars above.

I wasn't prepared. Nothing could have braced me for the surge of domi-nance I felt witnessing Nyte on his knees off the bed, hands curled around my thighs as he gave a dark smile of satisfaction between my legs. He locked my stare, planting a kiss to my inner thigh as he said, "Good girl."

Then he devoured.

I didn't know what I expected, but Nyte knew how to unravel me. He touched and licked and sucked so meticulously every movement raced me toward a high edge.

"Are you going to come for me, Starlight?" The rumble of his voice over my apex accelerated my sprint. My hand unfurled from the sheets to slip into his hair, my hips rocking against his mouth, and he chuckled with satisfac-tion. "You feel like you are. You taste . . . fucking incredible."

I couldn't watch anymore, throwing my head back at the finger he slipped into me. My body curved, and I moaned when he added a second. He worked them with a slow hook, building speed, until I teetered on the edge of some-thing so euphoric.

"That's it," he praised, and those final vibrations threw me over.

I cried out with the climax that shattered me. He kept devouring, and I was helpless against the grip of his hands digging into the flesh of my thighs. I hoped it would mark. I wanted him imprinted on every part of me.

This experience would never compare to anything I'd done before with Hektor. Nyte was taking every memory of him and setting it ablaze so I would never think of it again.

Only this.

Only Nyte.

"The sounds you make, Astraea—" He climbed back up my body, and when he was close enough I couldn't stop myself. His lips glistened with me, and I claimed them. A low growl emitted from his throat as his tongue swept across mine. "I'm going to be hearing those noises on repeat on my damn deathbed."

"That was—"

"Only the beginning."

My chest rose and fell deeply, and though my body still tingled warm with the aftermath of his wicked assault, I was thrilled with those words.

"How shall I take you?" he murmured. "Here? The wall? Braced against the open arch so the whole city can watch me fuck you?"

I'm in control. What awoke in me was a dominating need to feel that.

When I planted my hand on his chest, Nyte pulled back immediately. Those molten eyes blazed over me, waiting. I pushed him and he answered, lying on his back, and my leg hooked over him. He ran his hands up my thighs, a curl of delight forming on his mouth.

"Like this," I said breathily. "For now."

His eyes closed as if that aroused him. Only then did I finally look between us, and for a second I balked at the size of him. My mouth watered
unexpectedly with a rush of want to taste him too.

"Another time," he said, reading my thoughts. His strained voice accompanied the squeeze of his hands. "Because right now I need to be buried so
far inside of you it's driving me wild."

My breath shuddered on an exhale as I reached for him. At the first feel of
my fingers curling around his cock, barely meeting, I couldn't help but work
him slowly.

"Fuck . . . those hands," he groaned, hips jerking into my play, and I relished in the power I felt, owning his pleasure.

Then I positioned him at my entrance, brow pinching as the tip prodded
my body with a demand to take him whole. But he was more than what I
was used to, so I had to go slow, sliding down another inch. Back out. Another inch. My breathing hardened as the tightness grew. A faint pain with a
stretch under the waves of pleasure as he filled me.

"You're perfect for me, Starlight. So fucking perfect the gods reject it out
of spite."

I needed nothing more. I couldn't wait any longer as I braced my hands
on his chest and sank my hips down to take him fully. My cry mixed with
his growl, and we stilled for a few seconds. At least I did, to remember my
own damn name, when this completeness consumed me far deeper than lust.
I became entangled with him, wrapped in his essence. I didn't want to ever
be a separate soul again.

This felt like the calm before a battle with so much bottled up inside of
me straining to be released. Raw and furious, because Nyte would wage this
war with me.

I began rocking my hips slowly, powerfully. His cock left my body right
to the tip, only for me to take him all the way back in with one quick thrust.
I kissed him as I picked up pace. His hands aided my movements, roaming
along my spine, my hips, my ass.

"You are so—*fuck*." I slammed down on him hard.

I began to feel a caress over my navel, snaking around my back like new
hands pleasuring me, though his didn't move from my hips.

"You once asked if I command the shadows," he said thickly.

That tingling, featherlight caress trailed over my breast before building in
pressure. I moaned as so many sensations exploded over my skin, his shadows
like feathers falling around me. Then those hands of shadow massaged, teasing
my nipples while I rode Nyte with his aid. My nails dug into his chest, and now
I'd had my fun I needed him to take over with something more *demanding*.

Nyte read what I wanted. He sat up, still seated inside of me. "My turn," he whispered against the base of my throat. "As much as having you fuck me is like witnessing a goddess in power, I'm going to take you my way now."

"Please," was all I could muster.

"Your plea is music to my ears, but unnecessary." He lifted us from the bed, and I suppressed my moan with every step that became a gentle thrust, unable to focus on where he went. "I've had a particular fantasy, if you will indulge me."

A flutter erupted in my stomach.

He took us over to a wall before slowly setting me down. I sighed at the cool breeze between my legs as he slipped from me. Nyte met my eye as though asking for permission. I nodded, anticipation building for what it could be.

"Once upon a time, a woman stumbled into a room." His hand curled under my knee, lifting. "She didn't just dance. She moved as the most exquisite thing to have ever lived." His hand flattened against my calf, and I held his neck tightly for balance, realizing what he was doing as he tested my flexibility with care. "And there was a male . . . who fell completely at her mercy that night. Who would have trekked through the fiery depths of hell to see her bend like that again." My ankle rested against his shoulder. He stepped closer, and while the stretch burned slightly, I knew it would pass and this position would be worth it.

"Is that why you've followed me since?" I teased.

The tip of his cock pressed into me, and I whimpered. "I followed you . . . because I can't stop."

Nyte slammed into me with one powerful thrust that strained my toes on the ground, and I cried out. He gave a few long, slow strokes that shot sparks of pleasure through me. Then he kissed me once and let go.

He pistoned in and out of me, and I couldn't be sure what sounds came from him or myself. Each rut of his hips driving into me over and over scattered everything I knew about myself. What built was wild and desperate, like centuries of war waging against us at once. He slipped my ankle from his shoulder, hooking it around his waist as he lifted the other.

I didn't realize he'd moved us until I was set upon something solid. My arms slipped from his neck to plant themselves on the dresser behind me, rattling everything upon it and sending some things tumbling off when he didn't stop his merciless thrusting. Nyte's expression was pinched with desire and fury, watching where he fucked me hard. His thumb brushed over my apex, and I threw back my head.

"I need you to come for me now," he rasped.

I was so damn close, and his words were as sinful as his touch.

"Look how beautiful you look wrapped around my cock."

Stars, I was undone. Completely and utterly *his.*

"You're squeezing the fucking life out of me."

The cliff he pushed me toward was higher than the last. Impossibly higher, and I feared and braced for the intensity of the fall, knowing it would tumble through me. My body tensed, and my climax this time shook the stars of my world.

"Good girl. Fuck, *Astraea*—" He called my name with a tight grip as he released himself.

I continued to soar. Nyte's arm hooked around my back when I couldn't hold myself up anymore. I was flying, only to tumble back down and remember where I was. *Who* I was. Pieces of me snapped back one by one, reforged with the essence of him.

Our skin was slick against each other, heated and glorious.

"Of all the times I imagined this, none of it comes close to what you have done to me," he panted.

He lifted me off the dresser. I was still catching my breath when my back met soft sheets. Lying down brought on a sweep of tiredness, but I wanted to fight it.

"Can you promise me something?" he whispered, planting tender kisses over my collarbone while pulling a blanket over my cooling skin.

"Yes."

"It was all real, Starlight. Everything we've been through. Everything I feel for you is real. When the dawn comes, please remember that."

"What happens at dawn?"

Nyte lay beside me, and it was an effortless, near subconscious movement to tuck myself in close.

"We face who we are."

I inclined my head to look at him, and I reached my fingers up to brush the lock nearly touching his eye. "We have to kill the king," I said.

I couldn't stop now—not when Nyte had said he could help me and this was what Cassia had wanted to achieve. But selfishly, I wanted nothing more than for Nyte to take us somewhere far.

He took my hand, planting a kiss in my palm. "There are a few more on my list," he murmured, eyes flashing to my cheek, then my arm, then down to my covered body. "But yes."

"I killed this one," I said quietly, touching my cheek. "I struck another too, though I don't know if he's dead."

I didn't know what to think of how fast I'd acted. How it had been so easy that recalling the moment felt like stepping into another person's body. Discovering these things I was capable of . . .

"Good," Nyte mumbled, lips pressing to my shoulder as I lay on my stomach. "He met a faster end than he would have had from me." His touch traced between my shoulder blades, adding pressure down either side, and I turned my face into the sheets to suppress my moan.

He stopped.

I flicked a glance up at him.

"Don't deny me your reactions. It's absolutely wicked."

I smiled, so content and genuine it stopped all teasing from him. Nyte mapped my face, running a hand up my back as if to be sure I was there.

"What's wrong?" I asked, wanting to smooth out the furrow of his brow.

He shook his head. "It's how *right* things feel that is most frightening."

His words inspired trepidation. Invited in a trickle of the cruel outside world I wasn't yet ready to face.

I hooked my leg over his waist, coaxing him to lie down fully. Desire sparked anew in his amber irises, and beneath me I was thrilled to feel him wanting again.

"What did you say about overlooking the city?"

48

I t pains me deeply to say this," Nyte mumbled against my bare shoulder, "but you have to get dressed."

I stood watching the sunrise wrapped in nothing but a black bed-sheet. Turning, I found him impeccably dressed. His black jacket was embroidered with gold, and his pants were crisp and tucked into expensive knee-high boots.

My eyes fell to the bed, where he'd laid out a beautiful purple gown. I was in too great a mood to wonder who it belonged to.

We'd only slept for a couple of hours, but it was all I'd needed. Nyte had taken me again and again, fulfilling his other desire as the city turned to star-light and he took me overlooking the empire. Moments from last night kept replaying in my mind, and I cursed the rise of the sun and how the orange glow split the horizon with reality.

I dressed, expecting the gown not to fit in places, but it hugged me per-fectly. I stood and looked in the tall mirror, reaching for the corset ribbons, but Nyte crept up and brushed his fingers over mine as he took over. With the first tug I arched into him, tipping my head against his chest.

"Can you promise me something?" I asked.

His lips pressed to my temple, and we met eyes in the mirror. He contin-ued to fasten my dress without looking.

"Anything."

"No more secrets. You can't scare me away now. And I'm afraid . . . you won't see me the same after mine when I'm not even sure *I* see me the same."

His lips thinned, contemplative. "I suppose you mean we have a lot to talk about."

I nodded, and when he finished his tie, his large hands on my waist twisted me around.

"You are the same. Now and always," he said. His palm cupped my nape, and he kissed my forehead. "I'm so sorry, Astraea. I didn't mean for it to turn out this way."

The change in his tone threatened to crack the globe we'd crafted around ourselves.

"Sorry for what?"

Nyte pulled back, and I watched his face as he seemed to travel elsewhere. His jaw twitched, anger flashed his irises a dark amber, and I tried to search for the cause.

Footsteps sounded, growing louder, and only then did Nyte turn toward the opening of the room. No doors. He used his body as a shield against whatever was coming, but he didn't transport us away.

A single person, I thought, from the pattern of steps.

But I never could have imagined the person who walked into our safe space . . .

"Drystan," I whispered incredulously.

Though he'd planned to use me, I couldn't deny the lift of relief he wasn't dead from being struck by the power of the key. It had retracted to a smaller version of itself, which I reached behind me to take from the dresser.

"You're bold to seek me out," Nyte said with a threat I'd never heard before.

The prince didn't even appear wary, but as a bystander a chill crept over my skin. His caramel eyes slid to me, scanning me from head to toe as though he'd arrived as my savior.

"Astraea, come with me," he said.

"Quit the act," Nyte snarled.

"He's going to use you. Trust me, I can help you."

"You have to be insane to think I'd go with you," I said. I didn't know the full extent of his capabilities, and I feared Nyte was still too weak to stand against him.

"You should leave," I warned, feeling my palm heat slowly, but I didn't want to attack him.

A muscle in the prince's jaw flexed. "After all you've seen, you would really choose him?"

"You used me." It hurt. I didn't know why I'd allowed myself to care enough to believe there was good in him.

"Did I? I *pushed* you, and look at what you gained from it. I knew you could do it—find your key."

His word choice rang through me.

My key.

"I didn't need you for that."

Nyte remained deadly still. I'd known there was animosity between them before. No—that was too tame a word for what locked Nyte so still as he pinned the prince with a calculating glare, primed to strike in a heartbeat.

"He will always hurt you," Drystan said.

"I'm giving you this one chance to get the fuck out of here," Nyte said, his voice so low I shivered.

"You didn't scare me chained, and neither do you now, brother."

Time paused. My mind scrambled to rewind, replaying the jarring word I couldn't possibly have heard right.

Brother.

I blinked as though I could still be asleep in Nyte's arms.

Brother.

Brother.

Brother.

It couldn't be unspoken. As Drystan's gaze slipped to me, it was as if he were mourning the death of someone before it had arrived. It had always been right there, and now it couldn't be unseen. Some of the angles of Drystan's jaw; the shape of his eyes. It made the idea of them being kin so undeniable I couldn't believe I'd missed it.

"You didn't tell her," he concluded, likely reading how stunned I was as I stepped away from Nyte's back. "Did you tell her anything before you decided to fuck her?"

Nyte crossed the space so fast my fright knocked me into the dresser. Drystan let out a groan as he was pinned roughly to the wall. "She has nothing to do with this."

Drystan dared to laugh, and I winced as Nyte drew back his arm and connected his fist with the prince's face.

"Stop!" I cried. Maybe it wasn't my place to intervene, but this violence between them I couldn't stand by and watch. Most of all, I couldn't comprehend such hostility between *brothers.*

Drystan wiped the blood from the corner of his mouth as he straightened. His eyes of hatred and pity met mine. "You are everything to do with this."

Nyte clamped a hand around Drystan's throat, and it was chilling to witness how effortlessly he could overpower him. A blood vampire. Nightsdeath. With a reputation to instill fear in entire nations. The prince should have had the strength to push him off.

"What did you hope to achieve by coming here alone? Except your death," Nyte taunted.

"You won't kill me."

Nyte *squeezed.* Drystan choked, and I stepped forward, floundering with what to say that would get Nyte to think about what he was doing.

"He could have told the king where we are!" I tried. "We should go."

But Nyte wasn't the male I thought I knew anymore. He was someone unforgiving, and now he was perhaps giving in to the vengeance he'd spent a century building.

"My first drop of honesty for you, Starlight. He is only my half-brother."

That blazed something in the prince, who tried to attack. He barely got to move before Nyte hit him again, forcing him to his knees, and he gasped.

"Please stop," I whispered.

It was as if I no longer existed while this dormant battle was reforged between the brothers.

"He killed my mother," Drystan rasped.

Nyte kneeled, grabbing Drystan by the collar.

My mother. It confirmed what I feared. Shifted the world.

The king was Nyte's father.

The thought was dizzying. I wanted to escape, but they were blocking the only exit. Except for the open archways for windows that led a very, *very* long way down.

"Did he even tell you what you are?"

Nyte's fist connected with Drystan's jaw again, his fury rising with every test.

Drystan didn't stop. "Did he even tell you what *he* is?"

"I know what you are," I blurted, my pulse thrumming in my ears as I confronted him.

Drystan had the audacity to look confused.

"You were there that night, right before Hektor found me."

The slight widening of his eyes was all the confirmation I needed.

I shuddered to say, "You're Nightsdeath."

That fell all shock from his face. His mouth began to pull upward in amusement, and he got in one single laugh before Nyte grabbed his jacket to haul him back up. He was so furious shadows leaked through the room, circling and priming.

"I see your power is coming back," Drystan mused. As though he had no regard for his life when Nyte was so dangerously sharp right now.

"You were *there*?" Nyte seethed.

"Yes."

One word, and it was enough to snap something in Nyte.

He reached behind himself, and I was frantic, unsure of what to watch as it all happened so fast. The shadows answered him, swirling like a starlit void. Familiar. When he pulled back, I swayed at the dagger he now held.

My stormstone dagger.

"Are you going to tell her, or shall I?" Drystan taunted.

Nyte aimed the blade for the prince's chest, and it didn't look like he would hesitate to drive it through—

"Nyte!" I called his name, the cold air breezing behind me as I stepped up onto the ledge.

That seized his attention.

I was still trying to process what I'd seen, because I was sure I'd done that before. Been so desperate for my weapon that I'd somehow conjured it.

"What are you doing?"

Nyte's voice snapped me out of my memory. He advanced for me, but I shuffled back, my heels close to slipping off the edge. He paused. Rage fell to deep concern as he watched my feet and read my expression.

"Astraea, come down. Please."

"What is he talking about?"

"I'll explain everything, just—" His jaw locked when he tried to reach for me again and I moved a fraction. Behind him, Drystan chuckled breathily, getting back to his feet.

I watched war wage across Nyte's face.

"I'm seconds from turning around and killing him."

My heart skipped a beat. It wasn't even the prince's life I cared for most; it was the thought of the regret that would forever plague Nyte if he killed his brother. I didn't know their history, but something in the way Nyte had winced—if only barely-there—when he hit Drystan . . . What was pouring out of him now was a century of being wronged, and it was volatile to every-one in his path.

So, I took his hand. Watched his face relax and his shoulders loosen when he was able to slip an arm around my waist as if I might change my mind in a split second.

"You're making a mistake, Astraea."

I wished I could expel the pang of sympathy I felt at meeting the prince's final look before shadows stole us away.

Nyte placed his hand on my waist, and I followed his line of sight to watch him slide my stormstone dagger into a belt on the dress I hadn't noticed before. I didn't have the mind nor the minutes to ask how he'd retrieved it.

"Use it. Even on me if you ever feel the need. The key is volatile even to you right now." His hand cupped my cheek, a thousand words swirling in his irises, but time was slipping away too fast. "You are safe."

I met Nyte's golden gaze and couldn't be sure why I felt the urgency to kiss him one last time. Like this had all been pretend and our globe was about to shatter.

When everything stilled we pulled apart. I dared to glance at where he'd taken us, but it wasn't close to anywhere I might have expected. I'd hoped he'd take us far, somewhere we could pretend a little longer.

Not here.

A grand hall with pillars lining each side. Iridescent black marble floors and a red carpeted center leading all the way up long stairs to . . .

Nyte had taken us to the throne room.

"Why are we here?" I asked, my words filled with foreboding.

Guards began to flood the room, but they faltered when they took in the sight of us.

Nyte took my chin, looking like he wanted to say something else, but our time was up. Coolness wrapped around me as he stepped away, and I watched his face, his poise, seeing how the room darkened with his demeanor as it slipped into something of nightmares—stripped of any warmth, and least of all . . . *mercy*.

Nyte turned, scanning the guards with purposeful threat, daring them to challenge him.

They didn't. The guards *balked*. Seeing their reaction inspired the same fear in me, but I couldn't be certain of what it was for.

Until one of them spoke. One word.

A name.

One that shook dormant stars and announced to the world nothing was safe now.

"Nightsdeath."

49

It had been right there. And he had tried to warn me.

You need to get better with your words.

They were weapons. Tricks. Somehow I was always tripping over them.

Nightsdeath.

His shoulders tensed as if he knew what I was thinking. I tracked the way Nyte moved, so confident and different, nothing compared to the casual, lax way with which he carried himself below. Now he was a dark force to be reckoned with.

"Good. You remember."

I shook at the cold tone of a stranger.

"So why do you not bow?" He raised his hand, and when his fingers stretched and poised like a master puppeteer, strangled chokes echoed through the room.

My blood ran cold.

All at once, over two dozen guards were forced to their knees by some invisible force.

Nyte.

Stars above.

He let them all go, and no longer did any of them seem like monochrome statues. For the first time, they shed real emotion. True terror. As did I upon witnessing the scale of what Nyte was capable of. And I'd been the one to unleash the deadly monster.

As Nyte strolled over to one guard, he shuffled to his feet.

"Bring me the one who fired the arrow that hit her. If I have to go looking for them myself, many more of you will die in my path."

The guard nodded. "Yes, lord."

I couldn't believe the title, the way everyone in the room reacted to Nyte, and I had been so clueless all along, so content to believe my visions of him were the only reality. Not this cruel depiction.

Nyte stalked around the room as though looking for his next victim while they all tried to avoid his eye, on their knees. My throat turned bone-dry, but I wanted to speak, to ask him to take me away so we could erase this nightmare.

"I want Hektor Goldfell," Nyte commanded to the next vampire he stood before.

I trembled, suddenly not wanting to be here at all. Not near him when I was about to witness something so dark and bloodthirsty.

When that guard scrambled off, he stopped again. "I want Calix Salvier."

"Not him," I said without thinking. My heart leaped up my throat as I realized I'd interrupted this being I couldn't recognize right now.

He didn't even pretend to hear me, allowing the one he'd tasked with Calix's delivery to scurry away like the previous two.

Nyte drew a deep breath, casting his eyes through the glass roof as he walked to the center of the hall. He turned and took the few steps up the dais toward the purple velvet throne. Nyte passed me, but he didn't spare a glance down, and my heart ached, wondering how I could have been fooled so deeply.

He traced a hand over the back of the seat—an unlawful act and a mockery to the royal bloodline coming from someone who wasn't a part of it.

But Nyte was.

I swayed with the realization that hit me too late.

A prince. One who had been captured, held, and tortured by his own father.

Against the cage of my chest my heart was a furious beast. Could Nyte really have the power to overthrow him now? Nyte was undeniably powerful, but Nightsdeath had once been an ally to the king, and I couldn't piece together what had gone wrong to see him chained and bound behind a magick veil.

Had he tried to overthrow him before?

"No," Nyte said coldly.

I shuddered at the answer he gave to my flailing thoughts. I couldn't bear to look at him, riddled with the same submission and fear that had kept every guard down after he'd forced their bow. I didn't believe him. Not when his freedom thus far could only be explained by his thirst for power.

"Leave us."

The guards scrambled from the room, unable to squeeze through the doors fast enough.

My eyes pricked. This was all my fault.

Nyte was before me, emerging from a shroud of smoke and stars, and my gasp was strangled. I backed up until I'd taken one step down the dais. It was the wrong thing to do; now he towered over me more dauntingly that ever.

His jaw flexed at my reaction. "Ironic, isn't it, how much more monstrous I seem without the enclosure and chains?"

"You weren't capable of so much then," I said.

"I was capable of so much more, thanks to you."

My blood. Even the first few drops had done something to him.

"Tell me you didn't know about me—" Breathing became difficult, my heart so desperate to see the male who had helped me, saved me. This was not him. "Tell me you only realized at some point during the games. Not this whole time."

He didn't drop my stare of misery. Maybe for a split second he even matched it.

"I can't."

My head bowed in defeat.

"I knew exactly who you were long before you ever stepped into that room of the manor."

I was slowly breaking. My existence had always been a fragile one, but nothing had been able to shatter me completely.

Except him.

I sharpened the edges of the pieces he'd made of me with my searing anger. "You're a despicable liar."

Nyte chuckled without humor. "I am many things, and yes, despicable might be one of them." He stalked to me, and while I still feared what he could be capable of, I didn't retreat. "But I never lied. You were not ready to hear it. You would have faced it with denial and been helpless in your own game. Though there were times I thought you would see it, *feel it*. Times where it was like you'd never left at all."

Nyte's betrayal bled through me. But hearing that stole my fight.

"What happened to me?" I breathed. I wanted to rage and scream and fight him. But Nyte could be the only person to hold answers I longed for.

His fingers grazed my chin, and something like sadness managed to crack through his cold exterior, making a warm honey flicker in his eyes. "Once upon a time, there was a war between stars."

A riddle I'd known this whole time.

"Did you . . . ?"

"I would *never* harm you. Do you believe that?"

I wanted to say yes as my heart cried out to the memory of last night. How safe and warm he'd felt, and I would have locked myself away in that tower with him for years.

But I whispered, "No."

His hand dropped, and I was glad to see the pain crack more of him. Piece by piece I thought I might be able to break him and not have to lift a weapon at all. Words would be enough.

Then he raised a barrier against me, and a slice of the past shocked through me. Nothing whole or clear, only a sense of war . . . and we stood on opposing sides.

Nyte said, "The king might rule as the face of the people. I never wanted that. But they feared him because of me, and since he locked me away his empire has been crumbling. The vampires have been rising against him to find a new leader. He might not care for the human lives at stake, but he has been letting slip the control he spent so long chasing. His hunger for power was always doomed to be insatiable."

"Why did he lock you away?"

"You seem to be making fine judgments on that yourself."

"Because you haven't given me anything else."

What made him flinch I could only decipher as *hurt*. I wanted to believe it, if only to keep the hope there was some human feeling in him. Morality.

"I thought you were different," he said, his voice barely a whisper. "Yet just like that, you have forgotten everything that came before now." Nyte extended his palm to me. I stared at it as if his flesh could be poison. His touch I knew would set me alight, but maybe that was the trick.

"How do I know it was real?" My chest began to constrict so tightly I thought I might stop breathing. "You've been in my mind. You've altered how I see things."

"You've felt me there every time."

"How can I trust there were times I didn't—?"

"I can't answer that for you. I have told you my truth, Astraea. There is nothing more I can say. The doubt you cling to can only be let go of by you."

Nyte didn't drop his hand, and the moment I slipped my palm into his I wanted to sob. From the warmth, the sparks that shot over my arm, and because I wanted to be back down in that cave, still in denial of the monster whose hand I held now.

I hadn't decided to trust in him, but I had to figure him out. To end him.

Cassia had come here to end him.

With our joined hands, since his expression had turned to steel seconds before arriving in the throne room, Nyte finally resembled the male I thought I knew. It was unfair how much I wanted him to pull me closer.

Instead he guided me back up the dais, much as my body wanted to lock against it. If the king saw me here, there would be no hesitation on his order for my death. Yet Nyte moved over the imperial space as if he owned it, until we were standing before the throne, and only when he coaxed me forward alone did I finally root myself to the spot.

I shot him an incredulous look. "You can't expect me to sit there," I said, blanching at the thought.

Nyte gave way to a teasing dark smile. "A queen doesn't sit on a throne; she owns it. How exquisite you would look doing so."

I was caught between spluttering with embarrassment at his mockery and laughing in astonishment if he was being serious. "You're out of your mind," I said, coming to the conclusion it was the latter from the way he stood firm with the offer.

"Don't you recognize it?" he said, casting a glance back over the tall, ornate seat clad in purple velvet.

A thread was being pulled in my mind.

"Your trial of greed and envy."

My hand slipped from his in shock, but I couldn't peel my stare away from the throne, recognizing it in every perfect detail, the memory unlocking in my mind.

"That's not possible," I said vacantly. I had never been in this room before now.

"We're only just getting started on the impossible, my Starlight." His fingers grazed my chin, just enough for the sensation to drift my horrified look to him. Nyte remained so calm and in control.

My hand pulled back before I knew what I was doing, and my palm stung with the force with which it connected with his cheek before I could stop myself. "I'm not your anything," I hissed.

Nyte's ethereal eyes darkened a shade. He remained silent, as though he knew it would trigger the impulsive rise of my hand again, and this time he caught it. When he twisted us, the backs of my knees hit something solid, and I had no choice but to fall.

The moment I sat on the throne . . .

Time sucked me through into a new dimension. A new version of this room.

It was bright with the moonlight flooding freely through the dome roof, and as my eyes chased to find it my breath caught. Constellations floated across the ceiling by what had to be some influence of magick. They moved—so slightly most would miss the ever-changing shift of the stars. One would give its final flicker before beginning to fall like stardust. Then another few would be welcomed anew.

A vibration along my cheek yanked me back, and I blinked away the beautiful image to set my gaze upon the twin blazing suns looking down on me instead.

"I'm sure you would like to try that again. This is the one time I'll warn against it," Nyte said, uncurling his hand from my wrist and dropping the other from my face.

I wanted to launch up and strike him. Fight him. Break down and demand why he'd brought me here to witness his retribution, the first victim of which was being dragged through the doors. A single flailing guard, dangling a bow in his grasp, was pulled in by two of his own companions who didn't appear any less afraid.

Nyte descended the few steps, and I couldn't move—could only watch with a chilling sense of foreboding, his lethal calm making his every move entirely unpredictable.

"I-it was a mistake, my lord! I-I swear it! I never would have if I'd known—"

"I understand," Nyte said in a low taunt.

He reached for the discarded bow, examining it for a second only to grow the suspense. Then Nyte moved fast. All I heard was the snap of the wood and a strangled choke before my eyes fell to the source.

The broken bow was now lodged fully through the guard's chest.

"Unfortunately for you, my mistakes are a lot more accurate." Nyte pushed against the wood and the guard fell back.

Dead.

The other two backed away slowly as though Nyte would lunge for them with the same lack of hesitation.

He didn't. Instead he shuffled back, sitting on one of the steps, reclining to prop his elbow a few steps up as though he were lying there observing the end of a disappointing show. Crimson pooled out from under the guard, and the others dragged him away.

"Was that really necessary?" I asked blankly. I wasn't sure what I was feeling. Numb. Shocked. Maybe afraid.

Nyte cast me a bored look over his shoulder. Without company, he didn't wear his arrogance. He looked tired, like he'd lost so much more than a few nights' sleep. It was in these glimpses I continued to fall for the guise of something *real*.

"Your judgment of me is still yours to make. But the moment someone harms you, they die. If it's while I'm not there, they'd best enjoy their borrowed breaths."

Once again his expression firmed, but it was like every new time he had to slip on the mask it wore him out more, and I feared what would become of him if he lost the strength to take it off. If he fell prey to the beast he could portray.

The next victim to be dragged in swayed my vision, and I braced a hand on the throne. It only added to my spike of nerves and adrenaline to remember I was sitting upon it and how laughable I must look to him.

To Hektor Goldfell.

The rage that coated the room in ice sent a tremble through me. Nyte rose as Hektor was hauled in casting colorful curses to his captors.

"What is the meaning of this? I have a deal with the king!"

I stood slowly, frightened by the shadows snaking around the corners of the room like looming death.

"Nyte," I whispered, hugging myself, but he didn't even flinch.

Instead he slipped one hand into his pocket as Hektor was shoved to his knees.

"He had an oath to the king," Nyte said, pointing a careless finger at the blood left behind by the dead guard. "It didn't help his case. In fact, every time my father is mentioned it makes me far more murderous in my judgment on how to kill."

Finally, Hektor's pride and outrage blanked completely as he took in the sight, and when he cast his green gaze up to me I could have collapsed under the stroke of terror. It would never fail to catch me with his attention no matter how much bravery I tried to grasp.

That seemed to invoke something in Nyte, whose hand lashed out to Hektor's jaw, tilting it back awkwardly until he yelped.

"Wait! Astraea, please let me—" He yelled again at the added pressure Nyte squeezed around his throat.

"You dare to speak her name?"

"I loved her," he panted.

A skittered beat moved in my chest. Green eyes of pain tried to slip to me.

"I lost my temper sometimes, but it was only because I feared your recklessness would get you found, and there were so many who would do you harm. I wanted to give you everything. I did everything for you."

The conflict in my mind was almost too much to bear. Seeing the man who'd sheltered me for five years confess his wrongdoings even with a morsel of desperation . . . it was enough to drag me back. I wanted to forgive him, thinking he could change . . .

"Is he telling the truth?" I whispered to Nyte.

Maybe it was vile of me to ask him to search Hektor's mind, but I had to be certain.

"Yes," Nyte said. "And no. He would have done it again, and while there were times he regretted his mistreatment of you, there was always a dominant side that found power in it. Your submission to him." Nyte spoke so calmly, but it was the most terrifying kind of rage that invoked the shadows to claw out from the corners of the room. He slipped his golden eyes to me, and the fire in them almost leaked out. His other fist trembled at his side as though he were trying to hold back from something.

The something dangerous he could become.

I nodded. It was all the closure I needed.

Nyte turned his focus back to Hektor, and I had to look away as terror paled his face with the realization he was staring at his mark of death.

"I wanted to string out your end for everything you did to her," Nyte said. Calm. So chillingly controlled.

A sickening *snap* resonated. I flinched back. Hektor cried out, and I couldn't stop the sob that escaped me with it. His arm was now bent at an angle.

"But every second you're still alive, even in pain, makes me murderous to a degree the darkest things can't come back from. They're going to take your soul so it may never plague this land again. I will grind your bones to dust so you become nothing. A mere blink of meaningless existence, while she will take everything you ever dreamed of and torment your last moment with what that will look like."

I was so cold. My blood, my bones. I sank to the ground helplessly, wishing I could be brave and face Hektor with my own vengeance, but all I wanted was him gone. All I desired was everything Nyte offered, and I wondered if that made me a coward as I bowed my head, shivering against the marble.

Hektor began to scream, and I winced, forcing my gaze up, but there was no physical torture. Nyte had moved behind Hektor but still held his neck. Hektor clawed at his skin, and I didn't want to know what torture Nyte was conjuring in his mind.

A guard approached, and the moment Hektor locked eyes with him he was entranced. The kind of vacant stare I would never forget as the vampire consumed his soul.

"I said to aim for the heart, Starlight. But next time . . ." Nyte's other hand plunged into Hektor's back, retracting in one smooth motion. Sickness rose in me so fast I spluttered despite my empty stomach. "Make sure you can see it."

I didn't know what hit the ground first. Hektor's limp body or his heart.

50

My breath left me and I felt both liberated and soul-crushed.
Hektor was dead.

His blood dripping from Nyte's fingers started to wisp away to shadow before it could touch the dark marble. Darkness engulfed his hand, spilling down into a wave of mist that grew over the floor to cover Hektor's body.

I didn't think I was breathing, hardly present as I watched it turn his body to smoke . . . until nothing was left of him at all.

No blood. Not on the ground or in Nyte's hand.

I blinked as though I could have imagined him being wiped out so easily. Perhaps this was a nightmare.

But then a shuffling behind me rattled my senses and I drew a long inhale. When I turned to see who had entered, nothing else mattered. My eyes widened as my feet raced for their salvation. Toward Zathrian, who marched into the room, face lined hard, and Rose, who looked just as braced for battle.

I collided with him, and Zath tried to pull back to scan every inch of me, but I couldn't stop pushing him. "We have to go," I said desperately. Maybe it would be futile to try to outrun Nyte, but I couldn't risk him finding some reason to kill Zath too. "We need to *run*!" I demanded when he held me but didn't move.

"Who is that?" Rose asked.

I stopped trying to steer them back, and something about Zath's stillness coiled a knot in my stomach. I dreaded to look up. Zath wore a face of anger, but in his pinched brow I didn't want to see the pity, the *sorrow*.

"This isn't like what you think," he said, sparing a glance at Rose.

Her brow wrinkled with accusation. "What are you talking about?" she asked, freeing a blade from her side. "You said we were coming to get her before . . ." Rose paused, and fresh dawning relaxed her firm face. Her hazel gaze shifted sideward.

"*He's* Nightsdeath?"

She didn't hesitate, but her step to Nyte was intercepted by Zath. The look she locked on him spoke of deadly promise.

"Please wait until I can explain. You're safe—both of you. I promise you that."

The way Zath spoke as if he were defending Nyte . . . I shook my head with dizzy confusion. *Something isn't right.*

"What are you doing to him?" I snapped my head back to Nyte, who stood watching us carefully.

"Nothing," he said coldly.

"You're tricking him!"

Dark ire flexed around his eyes at the accusation. Shadows began to swirl around him like he would use them to strike or leap the distance to get to me. I left my thoughts wide and free, and something he heard eased back those primed arms of smoke.

"Do you truly believe I would be capable of hurting you?"

I said nothing, still seething at the fact he'd manipulated Zathrian to stop our escape.

Nyte growled low, and I thought to brace against him as he lashed out, but it wasn't at me or Zath. He spun instead to the next commotion to enter the room.

My alarm rose this time. My protest and fight returned for this.

"Let him go," I said.

Zath hooked my arm, stopping my near step forward.

I turned to him with pleading eyes. "You have to snap out of his control. We can't let him kill Calix."

"I'm not under his control."

Zath sounded so convincing, so normal, that my mind wanted to collapse me again. But it couldn't be true. The Zathrian I knew wouldn't be content to remain here with such an unhinged adversary loose. He wouldn't betray me.

"Even after all your cowardly treatment of her, she still pleads with me to spare you," Nyte said.

I whirled then, yanking my arm free from Zath to watch as he circled Calix, who was on his knees. Calix didn't look at me. I didn't expect him to, nor did I need his warmth.

"He came to help me," I said. "You have to have known that."

Nyte spared me a look. "Do you forget so easily he would have let that pitiful man's dogs take you before you even made it out of the main city in Alisus?" He stalked to me, and I held up my chin in defiance. "If it hadn't been for Zathrian, who followed you to make sure you made it out safe, he would have let them take you."

My breath caught. Why hadn't Zath mentioned it was his arrows that had killed those men?

"I won't deny, even the words he spoke to you before and after have made me itch for his throat for some time. Then he gave me far more just cause when he led a threat on your life."

"He was protecting Cassia," I protested.

Nyte stopped before me. "That I could understand. Truly. But will you still want to protect him when you know the truth of the attack that claimed your friend's life?"

Calix spoke, a quiet declaration of defeat. "It was supposed to be you."

I blinked at him as everything began to cancel itself out around me. Everything but my focus on him. It didn't hurt to hear what I had wished for too—that it should've been me instead. But that wasn't what Calix meant, and my mind began to scream with a desire to hide from the truth that was about to bring the world down around me.

"What do you mean?" I dared to ask.

"Foolish human," Nyte said to him. "So much magick in the world you believe anything is possible and never stop to realize it comes at a price. Fate is such a fickle thing." Nyte paced around Calix, and it was the longest I'd seen him stave off his clear desire to kill. "You see, there can be many courses to one's fate. A soldier wounded in battle may die there, or they may switch paths to live and come to the crossroads of many more if a healer gets to them on time. Choice and timing have great influence. Cassia Vernhalla had no other path. No more choices. No crossing of time with someone else who could save her. Her fate was to leave by her illness, and the extra years she got were only stretching the limits of mercy on that."

Nyte knew about Cassia. Far more in-depth than he should. Everything I thought I knew was drifting away from me piece by piece, deserting me to a void of nothing.

His golden gaze came around, still pinning Calix with dark resentment. "There would have been a way to save her. I'm sure whatever they offered you to set up Astraea was not false. But it would have been at the cost of another life, and no, you would not have gotten to act her hero and take her place. It would have been someone innocent. Someone who would have otherwise lived a long and healthy life, because dark magick does not play fair. You might have still been willing if you knew . . . but I doubt she would have ever forgiven you."

"That's not true." The denial that left my lips burned on my tongue. Because I believed it. In the way Calix merely bowed; didn't try to deny or even apologize.

My heart was obliterated.

"Why?" I broke. So much rushed to the surface, and I was drowning. "What did I do to make you hate me so much?"

Still Calix did not move. He showed no flicker of emotion or reaction. All he did was await the verdict.

"I believe she asked you a question," Nyte said.

With gritted teeth, Calix's head was yanked up by an invisible hand. My lip wobbled as I met his cold eyes. They didn't hold hatred or resentment or bear anything but a hollow existence that stole my anger.

"I had to try," he confessed. "They said all I had to do was make sure you were alone, and they would take care of it. They said they would save her."

"Who did?" Nyte coaxed.

"I don't know."

Calix choked, and I couldn't stop my hand from reaching for Nyte, pressing his chest. Somehow it worked to stop his attack. Instead, Nyte became distant, his eyes fixed on Calix. Searching, calculating.

I realized then he was looking for the truth himself.

"All I see is the man and the vampire you killed," he said. Frustration flexed in his jaw. Nyte blinked and the present returned to him. He glanced down at my hand, and with a flush I dropped it. "It's not the first attempt on your life. One night, you gave your handmaiden your cloak. She was mistaken for you by scent. Then your competitor took your carriage—another opportunity where you would have been completely alone—and he was murdered within it instead."

The blame for their deaths was a blow to my gut. "Who would want to kill me?"

"A lot of people," Nyte said. "But most imminently, and the one who is trying so hard, I can't be sure. It has been my greatest torment, but I will find them."

"I hate to break up a moment," Zathrian said, "but the king is almost here."

I was torn between staying with the inexplicable safety Nyte radiated despite everything . . . and running so far from him.

"Take him to the tower," Nyte instructed. "For now."

Calix was pulled to his feet. He didn't meet my heartbroken stare or see the step I took toward him before Nyte stopped me with a hand around my waist. I wanted to speak with him alone, unable to see evil when he'd acted out of desperation for the one he loved. For Cassia I had to *try* to find forgiveness.

"You've spared him for a while. It's more than he deserves."

I tore myself away from Nyte, spinning to him with a heated glare. "You will not kill him," I said, letting the threat linger in my tone.

I waited for him to mock me for it, but his face only drew a line as if he wanted to go to war with me, not against me. Trickles of last night threatened to become entangled with the other ways I knew his passion could be un-leashed.

Torching my thoughts, I kept my composure to level with him. "At least let Zath go."

Nyte relaxed as though the request tired him.

"He's not holding me, Astraea."

I looked at Zath. This man I had grown close to over a year. Someone I trusted as much as I did Cassia . . . I saw no struggle. Nothing that gave away that his words and actions weren't his own. His face fell with apology.

My throat was too dry. Tightening. I couldn't breathe.

"Have you come to your senses, my son?"

The chill of the king's voice locked me still. Who he referred to . . . My emotions switched so fast I couldn't stop them. A cool wrath turned me to him, and I wasn't much, hardly a threat, but it didn't stop the step I took to side with Nyte this time.

The king eyed us both, lingering a look on my hand as it tightened around the key.

"Hand it over and we can forget our past grievances."

Guards flooded into the room behind the king. So many, and these ones didn't seem to yield to Nyte as easily.

"My brother always did take after you with his bold stupidity," Nyte said. He looked over all the opposition and some shifted, exposing their wariness. "I see you've created your own personal ensemble against me with Starlight Matter. It's of no consequence."

The odds were far too great. I couldn't fathom where his confidence had come from.

"You can't kill me. You'll never find a way back," the king spat.

"You're wrong. I'll admit I was a fool for believing I needed you. I let you dangle that over me for centuries. But I have a way now, and you . . . are no longer needed."

Nyte stripped the king down from a dark and feared leader to a frightened soldier in mere seconds.

"You'll erupt chaos with this. You have no idea what has been building in your absence. Let me help you, Rainyte."

Nyte flinched at the name.

It repeated itself back to me with a foreign taste. I realized the face I'd spent so long with also had three names.

One of birth.

One of reputation.

One he chose.

Rainyte. Nightsdeath. Nyte.

All of them correlated to the one thing that couldn't be denied. He was made of the night. He moved with shadows and stars, his aura always dark, but with a wandering soul.

"Don't call me that," he said, distant, cold. "You took me from the one who named me that."

"I *saved* you."

"A slave passed from one monster to another still wears shackles."

"I never wanted you to be that. I wanted you to be everything."

"You wanted a killer while you took the glory."

"I did what I had to do," the king seethed, turning vicious once more. "For *us*. Your brother saw that."

Nyte laughed bitterly. "You have no idea what you created out of both of us."

"I couldn't be the father you wanted, but you became so much stronger because of it."

"You're right." Nyte turned to me unexpectedly. Our eyes met, and I didn't know what I felt. Watching the exchange with his father had been crushing my chest slowly. Maybe no one else could hear the faint split in his voice that gave away he was hurting despite the cold loathing. Or maybe there was no one else who truly cared to hear it, and that almost collapsed my knees.

"Another truth for you, Astraea. I am the son of two of the most villainous, power-hungry beings to have ever existed across two fucking universes. I am not *good*. I was not born to be, nor do I think this world deserves it." His confession cut through me. "But you deserve it. And I wanted to be *good* for you though I can never be. Do you believe that?"

My heartbeats filled the silence. "Yes," I breathed.

His pain . . . I felt it. Wanted to take it despite everything.

His gaze dropped like defeat—only for a second before he twisted back to his father.

"If we keep her alive they will remain weakened," the king said, trying to reason with him, but it had the opposite effect. "I planned to protect her."

"She is not the problem. *We* are. I should have done this long ago."

As Nyte stepped forward, bow strings groaned all around the room. My pulse spiked, triggering the key, which warmed in my palm. Nyte dared another step despite the lethal iron tips that tracked him. Zathrian's singing blade was the only thing to cut the tense silence as he closed in behind me.

I didn't have a second to react when, just as the king's gaze slipped from Nyte to me, so did the points of more than a dozen arrowheads.

And they released.

All I could do was brace, clamping my eyes shut on instinct, but instead of crying out at anything piercing my flesh, I was engulfed by waves of pure, undiluted *power*. The spectacle when my lids flew open to find the luminance was breathtaking. Wind tangled my hair with the wall of rippling dark starlight.

Then there was Nyte. Standing before it so still and calm, but careful . . . controlled.

Splintered arrowheads littered the floor, and I gawked at the display of magick, wondering if I would ever truly know the many layers to the power he harbored.

"Don't provoke me again." Nyte's tone was chilling as the wall came down like a cascade of black smoke.

"Are you afraid of what she will think when she sees the true version of what you are?" the king taunted.

"What you *made* me," Nyte snarled.

The king's mouth curled. He stared at his son as if he'd created the perfect monster. "Yes. And you have always been an ungrateful coward."

Never before had I truly been afraid of Nyte. Not until now, as I witnessed his unparalleled magick and listened to the king goad him for *more*.

"Zath," I whispered. His touch was the only comfort in the room.

"You're going to be safe," he said.

"Get her out of here." Nyte's low command came from strained tethers of control. He didn't even turn to us.

Zath tried to pull me, but I stood firm.

"I'm not afraid of you."

His back was to us, his shoulders rising and falling so steadily. A calculating, lethal calm. A glow broke from the cuffs of his jacket like gold spilled over his tightly clamped fists. Nyte's hand dipped into his pocket, and I thought I'd seen the round brass item in his possession before. He flipped it and let the king's eyes dwell on it. Whatever he found etched on the item widened the king's eyes.

"Where did you get that?"

As the king stepped forward for a closer observation, Nyte's fist clamped, and it disappeared in a cloud of smoke.

"I'm going to find out the truth," Nyte said calmly. "And there is no reason for you to be alive anymore. You have been a parasite of realms for too long."

"You think your mother is any better?" The king *chuckled*.

"Stop provoking me," Nyte warned with trembling restraint.

"Why? Because you're afraid to face the truth? The danger you will always be to her."

Nyte didn't respond.

The king laughed again, and every hair on my body stood, anticipating something sinister was about to erupt.

"Your own mother didn't want you. And neither will she once you show her what you are, *Nightsdeath*."

"Do you really think I'm vulnerable to your words after all this time, Father?"

The king's head tilted, then his eyes shifting to me locked my spine. "No, but you might be able to save her."

A cool breath of metal met my throat, pinching before breaking skin . . .

The ground rumbled like a quake beneath us.

It happened so impossibly fast, and my stomach reacted first, twisting with a sickening crack. A few splatters of warmth fell over my collar from behind.

"You really want to die by the hands of the villain you made me?" Nyte said in a cruel voice I didn't recognize, so close behind me now I stood deathly still. "Fine."

My compulsion to turn won against the urgency that screamed at me to run.

The tattoos on Nyte's neck glowed, and his eyes . . . I'd seen them alive before, but this . . . it was as if the sun were leaking out from them, unable to be contained any longer. It diffused like gold mist from his irises. Black vines crawled up his neck, over his jaw, and to the delicate tips of his ears.

Not human. Not vampire. Not fae. Not celestial.

I couldn't be certain *what* Nyte was.

He was still there, somewhere beneath it. And despite the frightening change to his appearance I still thought him to be the most beautiful thing I'd ever seen. Though I was unchanged . . . it was like he was slowly slipping in his recognition of *me*.

A hand grazed mine, and without breaking Nyte's tunneling stare, I was guided carefully away from him. Only when I'd taken a few steps did I look down. My hand rose at the gruesome sight of the beheaded guard who'd held the blade to my throat.

"He once told me something about him," Zath said close to my ear. "That he has this *place* his mind goes to. It only recognizes darkness. It wants to side with it, and anyone with light it wants to eradicate."

I couldn't understand what he was trying to tell me.

"It's true," Nyte said, his tone near taunting, but it was as if he still fought himself. "And your light is *insufferable*."

Nyte almost took a step toward me until the king's merriment caught his undiluted rage.

That was the moment he let go.

I faintly heard Zath's curse before he pushed me behind him, and a heart-beat later I was stumbling out the way of his blade clanging with a guard's.

My heart thundered, and I stepped after the flash of pink hair, but Rose was too fast and already fighting just as lethally by Zath's side.

Then there was me. Weak, unskilled, and all I could do was watch on in horror as my two friends fought against so many who outmatched them. And Nyte . . .

Stars above.

He was mesmerizing in the way he moved. I should have been horrified by the ease with which he killed, blinking through darkness, snapping necks, shredding flesh. It was the most dark and twisted thing I'd ever admired.

My palm heated, growing almost too hot, as if something were gathering in the key, and it was either unleash it or let it consume me.

Forms rushed past me, and I cried out to warn Zath and Rose as I realized they were the Golden Guard—but the sound died in my throat when the guards started fighting *with* them.

What the fuck is happening?

A touch on my shoulder made me whirl with an attack I didn't get to unleash as I found familiar dark eyes smiling at me. I didn't think I could be more dumbfounded.

"Davina?" I examined her from head to toe. She wasn't dressed in her usual cotton gown; her hair was styled in neat braids, a beautiful coronet. What she clutched I had never seen before: a fan crafted of metal. Even folded the points were lethal.

"I'm sure you have a lot of questions," she said, too soft and out of place for the commotion erupting behind us.

"That's putting it lightly."

Davina winced, but her eye caught on something behind me that switched her delicate expression to one of steady focus. I could only stare in bewilderment as she shifted her stance, snapped the metal fan open, and cast out her hand.

At the noise of choking close behind me, I turned just in time to watch the vampire fall and see the hiltless dagger protruding from his neck. Davina's fan was now one metal piece less, and I became fascinated by the weapon.

"We need to get you out of here," she urged me.

"I'm not running."

Not again. Not ever again.

The heat crawled up my arm, tuning to a hum over my skin, and as I glanced over at him I found a similar affliction to Nyte. From the cuff of my sleeve glowed *silver.*

I'd spent so long wondering who I was, and I couldn't cower from it now I was so close to getting my answer.

I surveyed the room of blood and flesh, enemies tearing at each other, and though they were outnumbered, those who fought on Nyte's side were not outmatched.

It had erupted into a scene of savagery and destruction, and though I harbored no warmth for the king or any vampire, this couldn't go on.

I answered the key.

Like giving over to a slow lap of sleep only to be pulled under all at once, the key grew to a staff, twisting between my hands, and I headed for the raging battle. Not to join them, but to end it.

Clutching the staff in both hands, I cried out, slamming it to the ground, unsure of how it knew of my wishes but pouring all I had into making sure it kept our side safe from the blast. What exploded was time and space itself. Otherworldly beauty that could kill, birth, and transcend. My body rippled with the gales of light coursing through me. My teeth clenched and my stance firmed, and I wondered if this was how I would die.

The energy was sucked back to the key all at once, and as I held it with little knowledge of how to wield it, I was slammed into by a force so powerful I thought I could travel through realms this way. I panted on the ground, trying to disperse the light that stole my vision so I could be sure I hadn't harmed Zath or Rose or Davina. Even . . .

The first thing to break through my void was an alluring mist of gold from the irises that targeted me.

"Nyte," I breathed, shuffling back on my hands as he stalked to me.

The expression he wore was nothing of kindness or recognition.

The throne room was gone. All that surrounded us was my light fighting the darkness that hissed and primed against it.

"It's me, Nyte," I tried again, my panic rising.

What have I done?

In my next blink he was in front of me, and I gasped, holding the key staff in both hands as a block when I fell to my back. Nyte gripped it too, straddling me, bearing down with a weight I began to tremble against.

"Nightsdeath," I whispered.

He canted his head.

Not just a name; it was a part of him.

And this being had only one goal to achieve with me: to end the light.

"Such a fool," he said, so low and cold. "I told you to leave. I warned you—" His teeth clenched, eyes scrunching shut, and I grappled with the hope that he was *fighting* himself. "Gahhh. Everything would be so *easy* if you just died. Died and didn't come *back*."

"This isn't you," I choked out when he pushed down further, sure to crush my chest if I let go. Tears pooled in my eyes. "I think . . . I think I came back for you. And you . . . you waited."

Confusion drew his brows together. The gold of his irises diffused every time he looked to be trying to find himself. "Lies." He shook his head. "So many lies. And so much fucking *light*."

Too much light.

I closed my eyes with a whimper when he pushed again, and my arms trembled with the pain to hold him off. My elbows gave in, but instead of allowing the key to crush me, I listened to it clamor away right before hands clamped around my neck.

I grappled with his hands.

"You once told me something," I wheezed, not opening my eyes to focus. "You said the brightest star needs the darkest night. And I . . . I understand now."

The pressure eased, but not his threat that could strangle me in a second.

"People fear the dark because they think it's where monsters thrive. They're wrong. The dark belongs to the stars who can't shine without it. It's where passion burns brightest. It's peace and it's company. The darkness is you."

I dared to open my eyes, braced to find the loathing stare that would slice me again.

"The brightest star needs the darkest night," I repeated, finding him through words that bound us like a promise. "I need you. And I'm not afraid of you."

Nyte blinked and the gold mist expelling from his irises dissipated. The glow died out. The black vines against his skin reversed, fading until the paleness returned.

My sob of relief escaped when his warm palm released my throat to cup my cheek, and Nyte leaned his forehead down to mine.

"I'm sorry," he said. The pain in his voice cleaved me. "I'm so sorry, Starlight."

I opened my eyes but couldn't see him. Because the light was gone—but we were content.

"It's okay," I said, reaching out to touch his face. "I'm okay, and you're going to be too."

"It's not okay. Not even close." He panted, exerted after everything it had taken out of him. "It's been so long since I gave over like that. I didn't mean to because I knew the target you could become to that . . . *thing* I am. But the moment that blade touched your neck I couldn't stop it . . ."

I pushed up, tangling a hand into his hair to kiss him, and while I wanted to erupt in the void we created, Nyte pulled away far too soon. Light penetrated our cloak of darkness, and my anxiety spiked to banish it again, but Nyte pulled me to standing.

"I'm in control," he assured me, but there was something distant, broken, about his tone. He let me go, and I couldn't stop watching the luminance flood his features when he wouldn't look at me. Nothing about him glowed anymore as the throne room expanded around us again, and I couldn't shake myself out of my stupor.

"Thank fuck," Zathrian said, but I was barely aware of his touch as he took my arms to scan me over.

"What did you do to her?" Rose snarled, blade angled, and she braced against him.

My chest tugged for her fierce protection. I didn't know what I'd done to deserve it. Even against her greatest enemy.

Nyte didn't respond. He watched her with steel features, but he didn't move.

I surveyed the destruction. So much death. The dark marble floors were glistening around the torn bodies of the fallen. A winter breeze wrapped around me, and I shuddered, casting a glance at the shattered rows of windows from the blast.

It all came back to me, and after confirming the safety of Zath, Rose, and Davina I looked for the key.

The purple glow had winked out peacefully, and it lay as a still, solid staff. I thought to retrieve it, but a hand reached out to it, and I gasped.

"She will be your ruination," the king hissed.

"No—!"

Light flared to life from the key, so bright I had to shield my eyes from the waves of power too. It lessened when a form twisted in front of me, and the hand touching my waist I knew to be Nyte's.

When the air no longer hummed I pushed his chest gently.

The king was gone.

He'd taken the key.

"Well, shit," Zath said, his labored voice drawing my attention to him. He clutched his abdomen, bracing a hand on his knee, and only then did I see the crimson staining his tanned skin.

"You're hurt," I said, casting out the horror of what had just happened to head for him.

"Just a scratch." He waved it off.

"Hardly," Rose muttered. Her hand around his arm was an unnecessary aid, and though her face remained firm with ire for him, it was laced with concern.

"It'll heal," Zath countered.

"You need stitches."

"Your thorns might do the trick."

Rose glowered as she let him go, and they continued their bickering as my attention slipped from them. I was compelled to find the source of something cracking slowly within me. A silent kind of suffering.

I found Nyte.

He didn't take his gaze away from the exact place his father had lain. I expected him to be angry at the loss, perhaps even fearful of what it meant now the king had the one thing he needed for the most terrifying of deeds.

Yet all he was locked still with was *pain*.

For a moment, he was a child. One who had not only never known the love of a parent, but who had been hurt so truly by the two people who were supposed to shield him, protect and care for him, most in the world.

For a second, Nyte might not have known how closely I watched him, wanting to *see* him, to witness something he'd been holding onto within . . . finally break.

51

My chest ached from the pounding of my heart, waves of grief and confusion waging a storm inside me. I was so, so tired. I didn't lift my eyes from the ground even when I felt Nyte's approach, too exhausted to argue. Or move away.

I gave myself over to his plans for me.

"Starlight."

He spoke so softly I thought I could close my eyes and pretend to be in the bell tower. Everything I'd witnessed from the moment Drystan imposed would be a horrible nightmare Nyte could soothe me from.

This wasn't a dream. Gravity was pulling me to the ground, and before it won, an arm went around me.

"I'm sorry for everything. This wasn't supposed to happen."

I cast pleading eyes up to him, a vibration skittering over me, and my panic spiked.

"And I hope you'll believe me when I say I am so sorry for what I have to do."

"What are you doing?" Zathrian called.

My protest began to rise as I tried to shrug out of Nyte's hold.

"You knew this would have to happen," Nyte said to him.

Casting Zath a pleading look over my shoulder, I saw his lips purse as if he understood but it twisted disturbance in him. Rose flared, taking a step toward me that was intercepted by Zath.

"Get the fuck out of my way," she snarled.

"Can you just relax for one damn moment to hear an explanation?"

"You're a *traitor* if you let him take her."

"Please let me go," I said.

I hated it.

I hated him for reducing me to a role I'd tried to break free from. The helpless girl from Hektor's manor.

"I don't have a choice."

Damningly familiar shadows began to snake over me, and I whimpered, struggling against Nyte's hold.

When we stilled it was dark. I dared to look up, and the grim walls of our surroundings made my blood run cold. What would have toppled me if he let go . . . were the iron bars behind him.

"Let me out," I breathed.

No. Anything but this. Confinement.

"Let me OUT!" I screamed, not caring about dignity as my fists pounded his chest.

He said nothing. Not at my pleas. Not at my tears.

I couldn't see through them.

I couldn't breathe through the lump that swelled in my throat, taunting that the air was limited, and I would die here.

Nyte held me until I exhausted myself, reduced to nothing but a frightened girl who clutched him instead, choosing to accept the warmth as something to ground myself with, as much as I despised it. His hand stroked down the hair over my nape.

"Don't leave me alone here," I whispered.

"I won't."

It didn't make sense, but right now it was a relief.

"I want to go back."

"I can't take you anywhere yet."

My struggle began to rise, and I pushed away from him. This time he let me go. I seethed at him as though he could turn to ash from my stare alone.

"You're a fucking hypocrite."

Nyte's frown turned dark. Daring.

"You killed Hektor, but you are no better than him."

That made something lethally frightening cloud his face. But I was beyond caring about his damn feelings.

"It is because of him I have to do this," he said as cold as death. "If I could kill him again I would. Even now, I'm tormented that he's dead but also glad for it. Soon you won't be able to speak his name because it will no longer exist to anyone."

"You can't erase a name from the minds of everyone in the realm," I spat.

Nyte smiled. A slow, villainous curl I couldn't believe I'd missed before.

"You underestimate me. Though I have never underestimated you, and it is why this measure is so necessary." Nyte dipped a hand into his pocket, and what he drew forth made my mouth water. I took a step toward him, but in a blink of starry shadow he appeared on the opposite side of the bars.

"I need them," I said in a panic, reaching for the bars to curl my trembling hands around them. A desperate *pain* grew in me now my pills were within reach. My head throbbed wildly.

"He's been suppressing everything you are since the moment he found you," Nyte said, controlled wrath filling his tone that stopped my frantic thoughts to listen. Taking a capsule from the bottle, he looked at it as if it were an enemy he could kill. "Drugging you with these, so it will now be a very difficult two weeks while they leave your system." He crushed the pills between his fingers, spilling a silver liquid. I knew what it was, except this was darker than any I'd seen before. "Starlight Matter. Enhanced with such a powerful, forbidden suppression spell that your body has become dependent on it. It won't kill you to stop it, though you may very well feel close to death at times."

I shook my head, dizzy with the thought, because I couldn't hear much while my mind drummed with want for what he was denying me.

"Give them to me," I said. I didn't care about power or anything. I didn't care about what I was or could be. "Give me the damn pills, Nyte!"

Pain turned to agony in his eyes, but I gave a breathy laugh. A sound that didn't wholly belong to me. Something volatile overtook my outward reactions, and at the same time I cowered into a helpless heap in my own mind.

"You don't have to pretend you care. I'll leave; you'll never see me again. Just give them to me."

It was all my blood roared for, slicking my skin.

"You're already at your limit without them. I'm hoping the worst of it will pass sooner than I think. I am sorry this happened to you. Sorry I didn't see it sooner. I knew he had to be doing something to keep your power locked. There are other ways, but this was his method of keeping you weak enough to think you needed him and that he was helping you."

I turned around, unable to keep looking at him with my murderous thoughts. I leaned my back to the bars.

"There is only one master deceiver in all this," I said. With my world collapsing anyway, the realization couldn't harm me any more than it already was. "You—Nightsdeath."

"It was humorous to watch you conclude it to be my spineless brother."

I gave a bitter laugh. "You're the realm's worst nightmare. They speak your name as if you exist in every shadow. Yet it seems even the darkness can be captured."

He advanced to me slowly, stopping so close behind me I closed my eyes with the faint warmth, knowing he could draw me to him if it weren't for the cage he'd put me in. "There is no being on this earth that exists without a weakness," he said, the words traveling like a lover's caress over my collar.

I turned, curling my hands around the bars just below his. "You are every part the monster they speak of."

His jaw worked with the flinch of his eyes. There it was: a split-second glimpse of his vulnerability. My depraved side had found a weapon.

"There is a monster in all of us," he said, hiding any emotion from me as though he knew my wickedness at the forefront would use it. "Those who pretend they don't harbor one are the ones who end up slipping. At some point or another it comes out. And the longer it is denied, the harder it will be unleashed all at once."

"You lied to me."

"No, Starlight. I have always been right here."

I had no answer for that.

"If I had told you who I was, corrected you when you assumed it was my brother, you would have forgotten the Libertatem completely. You would never have trusted me."

The mention of Drystan once again slammed into me as if I'd forgotten. Another unfathomable truth, the discovery that they were brothers.

"How can I trust you now?"

"It won't happen today—maybe not ever. But it is your choice once this is over."

My forehead pressed to the cool metal.

"You need to rest now," he said. "I'll be right here with you."

I shook my head. "I want to speak to Zathrian."

"I think it's best he stays away for now."

My fists tightened. It was another deception I couldn't comprehend, torn between wanting to rage and demand *why* or to break down in utter heartbreak that I had no one.

Absolutely no one.

"Rosalind?" I asked with a beat of dread.

"She'll be fine. Though if she keeps rampaging things, we may have to detain her until you're well too."

"You won't touch her," I snapped.

"I have no desire to. Zath is . . . *handling* that one." The nickname he used further sliced through me.

"How long have you been using him?"

"I have never used him. I gave him a purpose he accepted willingly."

"All this time."

He didn't answer.

"I want to be alone."

"No, you don't."

My glare heated, rivaling the fire in his irises. I took a deep breath to calm myself, turning to pace away from him.

"I'm going to get out of this cage, Nyte. And when I do, the first thing you will feel is my dagger in your chest."

He hadn't taken it from me when he could have. I didn't accept it as a kindness because it wouldn't have mattered if he had; I would have found some other way to kill him.

"I'm looking forward to it."

What an arrogant, deviant *asshole*. The shuffle of his boots walking away from the cell I hoped was the sound of him leaving me the fuck alone.

I couldn't think straight with him near me.

I couldn't begin to process a single thing as my small world expanded to be more than I could comprehend all at once. Pieces I had longed for, but which were now buried, confusing me so much I couldn't sort through them all. My hands tightened through my hair as I paced the cell back and forth. Within me, calming waves lapped over the sharp panic stabbing at my head as if I were bleeding internally. Then my chest. Fuck, it hurt so badly each breath became a spear attacking my heart.

I curled into myself on the cot. More tranquil notes aided the pounding of my head, and I was both so tired and reeling with maddening thoughts I couldn't sleep.

"Make it stop," I begged. It was all I had. I needed it all to stop chanting and humming. "It hurts."

"I'm going to take it away, just for you to rest," he said softly.

I nodded, laying down the fight against him to accept this because I feared I wouldn't have the chance to achieve my retribution if I didn't.

"You're safe, Astraea."

In my mind, a shadow engulfed the troubles bartering for my attention. One by one it silenced them.

"Do you believe that?"

I shuffled down until I lay as my body became weightless. My eyes fluttered with the drowsy waves. Through the grim gray, all I saw were flickers of gold. Flickers that had once made me believe . . .

"Yes," I whispered.

52

"I wish that room had been empty," I said.

I didn't know how many days had passed. Each one dragged me deeper and deeper into the greatest test of physical endurance I'd ever felt. I was so fucking *angry*.

Sitting with my back to Nyte, I tipped my head back against the cell bars. We hardly spoke. But he never left. He sat against the wall behind me.

"No, you don't."

I laughed, mocking his confidence. My head rocked—barely a shake when it felt like a boulder atop my shoulders. My limbs were weak, arms limp at my sides. "I had an uncomplicated life," I reflected to myself, closing my eyes as even the moonlight I loved added to my throbbing headache. "Why couldn't I have just been content?"

"You were dying slowly. Your spirit. It was never destined to be contained. You were surviving, not living."

"You don't know that. You don't know anything about me."

"You know that's not true either."

"Then it's not *fair*—!" My palm stung against the stone as I slapped it. My emotions were exhausting. Triggering. I couldn't contain them. "You promised no more secrets. Everything we had was formed of them."

"Does it not speak truer to your feelings now there is nothing to influence them?"

"Not when everything I was falling for wasn't real. You were never real. Only what I wanted you to be."

"You don't believe that."

I smiled though he couldn't see it. Something dark and ugly within me wanted to take his notes of hurt, amplify them, and kill him with them. "You're just like him," I drawled. "He would lock me away and say it was for my own good. That he was helping me."

"Do not compare me to him." The threat that crept over my shoulder broke a shiver. I delighted in it.

I went on, "You all like to think you're different. Everyone believes their intentions are the right ones. But you are all different faces of the same monster."

Shuffling sounded behind me. I didn't care to move. Maybe I hoped he would reach his hands through the bars and wrap them around my throat to end my misery instead.

He didn't.

I felt him behind me, sliding down to sit until the warmth of his back seeped through mine between the iron bars.

"You're right," he said calmly.

My brow pinched. I was in so much pain I wondered if heartbreak could kill.

"Sometimes . . . I wish I wasn't the villain I was born to be. I think that is life's true challenge, to make us want things that were never meant to be ours, and to be anything other than what is paved for us in destiny."

A tear slipped down my cheek and my eyes closed. "Do you think destinies can change?" I asked quietly.

Nyte let a few seconds of heavy silence pass. "I used to."

"What happened?"

"You died."

My palm remained flattened close to the bars, and then sparks caught on them as Nyte reached back to brush my fingers with his as though he needed to be reminded that I was there. I didn't move, but a fist clenched in my chest at the first contact he'd made since locking me in here.

"The story you told me," I whispered. My harsh exterior was breaking. "In my rooms as we lay . . . It was us."

One beat of silence. The kind shattered souls were made of.

"I have waited more than three hundred years for you to come back," he said, equally as hushed. "I came to terms with believing it wouldn't matter when I couldn't find a way to break the curse of our clashing existence. Then, when I became trapped . . . I can't deny there was a selfish part of me that didn't give a fuck about the world, or that my father and brother had betrayed me, because I would get to see you again."

I thought back to the moment we'd met, finding myself reflecting on everything in my mind and from when he'd become physical to me. He was my night. The embrace of darkness that whispered through the stars.

"When did you realize?" he asked carefully. "That you were the star-maiden?"

It was a question I had posed to myself.

"I think a part of me has always known," I whispered. My nose stung. "I didn't want to be different; I just wanted to be seen. My markings . . . Hektor made me believe they were nothing, yet he wouldn't allow them to be seen, and

I thought that was the reason. Sometimes I'd see similar metallic tattoos on others, but there was something *different* about theirs, and I wondered if they found beauty in them to have had them cast by Starlight Matter. Then there were things I discovered about myself that I didn't think I should be capable of. I could throw daggers with great precision—even archery I found easy, as if these skills were already learned. And then . . . I've always braced for the dawn and yearned for the night. I found I didn't need as much sleep as others."

"It's a lot to believe at once."

"I don't remember much. I don't remember you."

"Do you want to?"

Another tear fell. "I don't know."

We stayed like that for a pretend moment of peace. Until I broke it with my most terrifying doubt.

"Did you kill me?"

"No. But I condemned you."

My fingers flinched against his. I debated pulling away if I was holding the hand of my killer. There was something twisted and wrong with me because I didn't.

"What does that mean?"

"It means I failed you even if it wasn't my hand to wield the weapon. You were always at risk because of me."

More questions surfaced with every answer, but I was too tired to learn it all right now. Too gods-damned exhausted and focused on only one thing that could take it away.

I was a pitiful fool and beginning to see exactly how I'd lost the war with my weak heart. There was no reason for me to be back.

I stole my hand away from his. "The world will be better without me. You can have the key when you get it back. Give it to whoever can use it to save people. There is no point in giving me power."

"This is just your withdrawal speaking."

My teeth ground together, rage boiling my already sweat-slicked skin, yet I was fucking freezing at the same time.

He said carefully, "You should be keeping warm to break the fever."

My heavy eyes rolled to the bed. The cot was feeble, but he'd brought me more soft blankets and pillows than necessary. Such luxury appeared ridiculous against the gloom of my cage.

"And you need to eat," he added.

There was a broth now cold on a tray near me. I hadn't touched it, only drinking the water when I couldn't take the scratch of my throat any longer. There was only one thing I craved to consume, and he denied it.

"I don't want power." I tried again, this circle we'd gone around in many times now. "Please, Nyte."

"You're doing great, Starlight."

"Don't call me that!" I ached in my heart to hear it, and I didn't want to feel for him.

My head lifted only to slam back against the iron in my frustration. It vibrated through my skull, rippled my vision, but I did it again. And again. Until hands slipped around my head to prevent the harm to myself, and I broke. My sobs unleashed themselves, and I hadn't realized how close they'd been to flooding me.

When Nyte pulled me to my knees I didn't resist. I clutched him tightly, as if he were a lifeline, crying into his chest though every heave hurt so badly, so deeply, it tore my soul.

"Why did Hekor do this to me?"

I was *dying*.

All that kept me here was Nyte's gentle strokes over my hair, his warmth holding me tight. I was too exhausted to put on a front that I didn't want it. Because I *needed* it.

"You have no idea, love," he said, a crack in his voice slowing me from hyperventilating, "how I would tear my own heart from my chest if it could help you right now."

I pressed my ear to his chest and floated back to the fast cadence of his heartbeat, pounding with what touched me like panic and guilt. "Why did *you* do this to me?" I croaked.

"I didn't mean to." Every time his voice was reduced to such an ache I couldn't bear it. I wanted to believe he couldn't feel such pain to make it easier to kill him. "I wish my father never brought me here. To save you, maybe I wish we'd never met."

Coming from him, that notion silenced my world. It seemed unfathomable. Not now. I hadn't meant what I'd said, but he'd confessed it with a clear, certain mind . . .

"You wish we'd never met?"

It was all I could take from it. His words pummeled into me worse than my withdrawal from the pills. I didn't need them. No—the only thing I needed was him.

"I'm too much of a selfish bastard to truly wish that."

I relaxed. These dark thoughts kept taunting me, and I couldn't tell what was truly my feelings or those of someone depraved as the Matter left my system, twisting my mind to something murky and resentful.

"What happens when it's all gone?" I asked with trickling trepidation.

Did I want to know what had been lingering under my skin? What I could be capable of?

"Truthfully, I don't know."

"What if I hurt someone?"

"I won't let that happen."

The fact he didn't rule it out made me shudder.

I shook my head. "It's not worth the risk. Just let me take the medicine."

"It is not *medicine*," he snarled.

I whimpered at his tone, at my desperation for the Matter still rising in me, trying to suppress the manipulation that would test all his emotions and spark something to get him to break for me.

Pushing away from him, I stood, my teeth bashing together. My slicked skin didn't want the wrap of the blankets either.

"Let me help you again—"

"No!" My hand fisted around my dagger, but as I lunged for him my slice cut through dispersing shadow.

"Fucking coward," I mumbled. With a spike of anger I threw the dagger across the cell. Then exhaustion took its toll, and I covered my face.

"What are you thinking right now?" he coaxed.

"That you were right," I said. Defeat lowered me to the cot. I curled away from him, mapping the cracks in the sad gray wall. "I don't like the monster I've denied for so long it's taking over."

"No, it isn't. You're almost through the worst of your withdrawal. Your emotions are exhausting you, and they are not true."

"They are true," I said. "They don't come from nowhere, Nyte."

He didn't answer. I listened to him sit again. He hadn't brought a chair. He hadn't brought anything of comfort for himself.

He never left.

53

The next few days, maybe even a week, passed in a blur of color and gentle touches. My eyes fluttered at the hands pressing a damp cloth to my forehead. Black locks around a beautiful pale face came into clarity. Davina's large eyes creased with her smile when they met mine.

"You're coming around well. I think another day or two and you'll be up and about."

Relief at seeing her flooded through me. "Are you all right?" I croaked, trying to sit up, but her soft hand on my shoulder refused me.

"Yes. I have a way of remaining out of the king's sight if he tries to go looking for me before everything." Her expression was cunning, but I didn't question it when I had so many other buzzing thoughts to voice. "Oh, Astraea, I'm so sorry I kept things from you. I hope you'll let me explain—"

"It's fine. You can tell me later," I said, trying to muster a convincing smile while inside me the twist of betrayal wouldn't relent. I diverted. "Zath—is he okay?"

Davina's face fell, and my nerves rose. "He's healing. We've set out to find a human mage who will help him along faster, though, and for you. Zathrian has been helping to calm Rosalind, which isn't doing him any favors. They had to detain her. She was rather *spirited* in her demands to see you. She's owed a lot of explanation too, but it's difficult to get her to listen." Davina gave a chuckle that was partly amusement, partly to cover her nerves at speaking about Rose.

"I don't understand what's happening."

"You will." She gave my arm a gentle squeeze.

I didn't think I had ever truly *seen* her. Not this version that had been lying beneath the surface. While Davina was gentle and kind, witnessing even a glimpse of her in combat had been like ripping off a mask.

"You're not a handmaiden." I stated the obvious.

She curled a guilty smile. "It's not my first occupation, no. But I like to help people."

"Did you know . . . about Nyte this whole time?"

It only took a heartbeat for me to read the confirmation in the flinch of her brow.

"He isn't always the monster he's painted to be," she said.

Not always. I cast my eyes to the ceiling. How could I trust that? Sadness swept through me with the realization I didn't know if I could trust Davina either. Another spy for *Nightsdeath.*

"Zath was never under his control," I whispered to myself, the truth finally settling despite my denial.

I couldn't trust anyone.

"No," she replied softly.

As if I were made of glass. That was exactly how I felt as each new revelation cracked my fragile world.

I felt him before I saw him. Shadow always caressed the room when he was near, and something distant within me tugged. Davina looked over her shoulder. At seeing Nyte there, she gave me one last smile—as though she longed to say more but she answered to *him.* Without even a command, the world answered to him.

Davina left, and I looked at the open cell door. My mind filtered through the many ways I might elude him to reach it and run free, but my body had become too heavy to stand. All I wanted to do was sleep. No longer did the craving for those pills I now despised torment my most wicked thoughts.

Nyte came by the side of the cot and crouched down. I couldn't fully decipher him, but there was always a note of pain.

He dipped into his pocket before producing a small pill my mouth salivated to, but my sight targeted him in bewilderment.

"It's not the Starlight Matter, of course," he said, voice so gentle. "Your blood levels are low. I think it's from the years of taking the powerfully suppressive dose and how often he took your blood. Too much of it, too often. I can't be certain if this deficiency is permanent, and I never would have drank from you if I'd realized sooner."

My neck tingled with the mention. In pleasure. Sparks that skittered over my collar and rushed heat between my legs. Nyte's eyes flared a fraction as if he sensed it but his regret remained. I had to bite back my insistence to him I would have asked for it even if I'd known. *Stars,* my sickness-clouded mind protested it wouldn't be the only time I felt those sharp teeth inside me.

Nyte went on, "Your blood is very powerful. There's no fae or vampire alive who wouldn't crave it if given the opportunity. And none of them would stop until it killed you if given a taste."

I shivered to the slip of protection that wrapped like something tangible from him to me.

"What did he do with my blood?" I dreaded to ask. My arm pricked and I rubbed the phantom pain.

"He traded it to vampires in exchange for keeping his establishment clear of them. They obeyed because it would have become a lifelong addiction and he was good at keeping you very hidden."

"He was taking it himself . . . it's how he survived my attack." From Hektor's taunts to me in the maze, I knew it was true.

Nyte nodded. "He wouldn't have survived a stormstone blade in his heart, but you were a few fractions off. I won't forget we need to work on that." His mouth quirked but it was short-lived. Between us his palm extended to me. "This will help the deficiency in the meantime while your body is adjusting from the Matter. Though it should be manageable with the right balance of diet and care."

I stared at the pill with cutting memories of Hektor. How long I'd let him place a similar capsule in my mouth unknowing it was a slow poison of control.

I shook my head. When I met his stare, I braced for his insistence. Nyte's brow only flinched. He understood. So his fist enclosed around it and when his fingers relaxed again the pill was gone.

"Do you trust me?"

I huffed a laugh, but it turned to a violent cough that ended in a pitiful sob. My ribs felt bruised and my throat like some beast had clawed free from it.

Nyte's hand was on my back as soon as I pushed myself up to curl over the bed in case I threw up. I didn't have the energy to protest what he was doing when he took the opportunity to slip in behind me. I craved his warmth as soon as I knew how close it was, and I didn't fight it when he gently took my shoulders; I lay back against his front.

"I trust you won't kill me," I answered, so tired I could barely stay awake.

Nyte's fingers brushed slicked strands of hair from my forehead before he pressed the cool cloth there again.

"Like everyone else, you want to use me for something."

I couldn't care anymore. I was no more than a chipped game piece for the highest bidder. Or the most cunning winner.

"After we won the war, I spent two centuries under the control of my father. I killed for him. Terrorized for him. I didn't want the praise of a crown for it, but everyone knew I wore the face of their fears—as Nightsdeath. It was only supposed to be for one century, then he would let me go. Until he demanded another, and when the next arrived I refused. He had pushed me so far past any morals that I threatened to kill him instead. I didn't want the crown. Maybe I simply would have rather watched this world burn itself to the ground. Yet he finally agreed to give me what I needed." Nyte's fingers combed through my hair. "A way home."

"You said you've never been where you're supposed to be."

"No."

"Then where?"

"Somewhere far, and there was no guarantee I would make it back. But I had nothing to lose anymore. I didn't kill my father sooner because he brought me here, and he was the only one who knew the place where I could attempt the leap back. He held that over me, and I exhausted every lead and resource I could to figure it out myself, but it was hopeless. Until now."

My brow pinched and my slick cheek met his chest as I rolled stiffly. Nyte kept the damp cloth from falling. His tender care was agony.

"This isn't because I've forgiven you," I mumbled, settling on my side. "You just have an annoying . . . certain type of warmth."

I could practically feel him smiling.

"Your fever is breaking. It'll be over soon."

I tried to nod, but my head felt like stone. "If you figured out how to get home, why not leave sooner?"

"My father trapped me before then. Led me to the library, beneath it, and told me it was down a passage. I knew what I'd fallen into the moment I stepped past the veil. He'd used that to trick me too, because from it, I felt you."

"Because I'm the star-maiden." I finally said it aloud, still not truly believing the weight of what that implied, but it burst with what I had been searching for my whole short life. Something that was *mine*. It would be a long road to figuring out what it meant, and the past that was attached to the name frightened me even in the small fragments I was gathering. But I wanted to know.

"That's not what you are to me."

I hadn't felt much of my heart at all these past few days. In my sickness, there were times I'd hoped it would die to spare me the misery. Now it fluttered, something light and warm echoing from within.

"How did you save me on the lake?" I tuned in to the hard beat in Nyte's chest, moving with his deep inhalation.

"I didn't think I could. When I watched you run onto that ice something dormant awoke in me. A desperation I'd only felt helplessly once before. Until that moment, even during the times you yearned for me so hard the world felt convincingly tangible, my physical body was still always behind that veil. The ice broke and you fell, and I don't remember anything except my complete determination that I couldn't lose you. Not again. And maybe there was an answering from the gods who otherwise despise me that bent the law of magick for a suspended moment. Just enough for me to push through the Starlight Veil, and then there I was."

"The Starlight Veil," I muttered. "Is that how you move? How you retrieved my dagger."

"Yes."

"Do you control it?"

"That dimension cannot be controlled. Some things are far too powerful, grown into their own living thing, so that even the gods have no influence on them. It can be used, however—mastered. The celestials can use it to hide their wings. It can be used to transport, but that is not something to try lightly. It can be dangerous if you don't know how to use it."

I didn't mention that I had before. That had to have been how I'd reached for my dagger in Hektor's cell. I stored the other possibilities.

Nyte continued. "I pulled you out of the water, and believe me, I felt it just as punishingly as you did, except my adrenaline pushed me through it because you were faltering and I wasn't sure if I was too late. I felt you—the first touch I'd truly had in a century. The first I'd *wanted* in far longer than that. I couldn't believe it. I thought maybe we'd broken the spell and I was free, that you would never have to come here, because I would have taken you far, somewhere safe. But as I carried you through the woods, I started to feel the resistance. I fought it. *Gods,* I fought the magick with everything I am, desperate not to leave you there when you wouldn't make it on your own with your body shutting down. I managed to transport you a small distance to where I knew there was a manor with a fae who would help you."

Despite the ache in my bones I pushed myself up against his chest, needing to see his face. Nyte had never looked so soft and agonized. I couldn't believe his story. I'd thought this tale would be something of arrogance and nonsense, that he hadn't been there, and he'd convince me I somehow saved myself or conjured an epic savior in my loneliness and delirium.

But this was the truth. Nyte had been there.

My fingers flexed, curling into the material of his shirt, recalling the warmth I'd craved from him in my frozen state. At some point my vision blurred. A tear must have fallen because Nyte's hand rose to brush it away.

"Don't do that," he pleaded.

"Do what?"

"I've already crossed too many lines with you." He shook his head, pain written in his eyes, making my panic surge as if he would disappear. "This wasn't supposed to happen."

Before he'd come, I'd spent my day in misery cursing him, not wanting to be anywhere near him. I couldn't explain what it was that had dissolved all of it the moment he walked in, but I didn't ever want him to walk away.

I leaned in to kiss him. Nyte didn't push me away, but I could sense something was wrong.

"I can't do this to you again," he said against my lips.

Then suddenly I wanted to take back every time I'd wished him gone.

"You already have," I bit out. "You came into my life long before you ever showed your face. You have a history of me that I don't have of you, and I *need* to know what it was."

He tucked a strand of hair behind my ear, his brow furrowed as he looked me over, then traced a thumb down my tattooed forearm. My skin tingled under his touch.

"I am the reason your stars are dying. Then and now. I am the reason you will always be in danger, because there can only be one."

"One what?"

Nyte took my wrist, and I shivered when he tenderly rolled up my sleeve before doing the same to his. He held our forearms side by side, and I marveled at the different but similar tattoos we shared. The constellations still crossed over our opposite moon phases despite the bond being gone.

"God of Stars," he muttered as if it condemned our fate. "So much energy that it's failing altogether. Magick is weakening—it is why the celestials hide. I can't bear to live an existence against you."

"Did we . . . ? Were we at war?"

"Yes."

"You won against me."

"Won," he huffed—a pained sound of resentment. "I lost everything. Everything that ever mattered to me." His heartbeat kicked up under my palm.

"I don't understand how . . ."

"A god can only be killed by something it is made of. I'm not of this realm; there is no weapon that can kill me here. But you—"

I had never seen such a ghostly expression pass over his features. So stilling I trembled with it.

"The key?"

I took the drop of his eyes as confirmation.

"I think you knew it could be used against you. So you spelled it. When it took your life, the whole world felt it. The key broke. Five pieces. Then they vanished. You made it so the only person who could find them was you. Those who tried to take on your trials were tested, or they would die for ever thinking themselves true-hearted enough to make it through. My father never spoke of how many times he'd failed the trials, how many years you'd drained from him, before he finally made it to the end. I think the world heard his rage when he realized you'd mocked him with it after all that. Until the game awoke again and he turned it somewhat to his advantage with the Libertatem."

I stilled with disbelief. The smile that cracked on my lips was a break from the weeks of misery, imagining the king's torment though I couldn't fathom myself cunning enough to be responsible. "I don't feel like her," I admitted.

Nyte searched me slowly. "I don't think you've had the chance to yet."

"What if I'm someone else . . . ?" Would that change what he thought of me? This person he believed I was.

"You are whoever you want to be. You should know there are no expectations of you to remember—to be anyone other than who you are right now."

"People are counting on her return. They think she will save them."

I thought of one hopeful fae with deep green hair and small horns. Lilith had been so dedicated in speaking of the *star-maiden* that I sank with dread to know I couldn't be that savior.

"You don't have to be anything for anyone." He took a contemplative pause. "It has never influenced anything for me. I sought you out only to make sure you were safe when I knew there would be others searching for you, and not all of them good. But these past months getting to know *you*, as who you are now, have been the privilege of my existence."

As he pressed his lips to my forehead my eyes wanted to slip closed with the wave of contentment, but something in his tone didn't settle right.

Then he slipped away from me.

"Where are you going?"

"You need to rest."

"Wait—" I stood after him, but the cry of the cell door closing rattled my senses, bringing back his betrayal.

"I will always be your enemy, Astraea. You will see that. As soon as you are fully well, there is so much more for you to learn, and you will see."

"I do see," I said firmly. He was not getting to walk away so easily. "I see you, Nyte. I want to see you as Rainyte. And I'm not afraid to see you as Nightsdeath."

"I only guided you here to free me. Now I will be doing everything I can to find my way home, and I won't look back."

I gritted my teeth. I didn't care that his words cleaved through me, nor for the coldness in my anger at his rejection. "You're a coward!" I spat as he started to leave.

That caused him to spin back around, storming to me so fast I didn't get a second to react before he reached between the bars and his hand encircled my nape.

"Do you want to know what I am?" he growled. His chest heaved, but I didn't feel his storm was directed at me or anything. It was raging at himself.

"That day, Hektor didn't lock the door. The balcony door, yes, and you un-locking it was real. The other door was always open, and I made you believe it wasn't. That he had locked you in there for no goddamn reason because he had done it before."

"That's not true," I said, but the denial mocked me. So instead I asked, "Why?"

"Because you never would have left. He would have finally broken you in that cage you believed could one day turn into a palace. I forced you out and I tricked you. And I asked Zathrian to go along with it too. Everything." He searched my eyes, and I traveled through his, wishing our circumstances were different, wanting him so badly, yet feeling the desire like a knife that wouldn't stop twisting with every new fact I learned.

"I thought I could stay away. I did—for five years, though I could have infiltrated your mind sooner. Then the chance for you to come here crept closer, and I had to meet you. I had to see for myself what I had only glimpsed through Zathrian and Cassia before, because I knew the moment I stepped into your mind I would be selfish. I thought I could do it, open your mind to me, and that it would feel convincingly real for both of us. I thought I'd have the strength to look at you and not fall. But I looked at you . . . and I plum-meted. I didn't stand a chance."

My heart shattered. I wanted him to lean down and kiss me like he was fighting against, but the opposing side won, and his hand slipped slowly from my hair.

"Cassia . . ." I breathed, leaning my forehead to the bars as the pieces slid together. "Did she know?"

"No."

My breath of relief didn't even settle before he continued.

"But I knew Cassia's course was to come here, and you never would have met if I hadn't guided her onto your path. Your relationship was real—every part of it. She knew nothing about me."

My eyes filled as I whispered, "You sent me Cassia."

"I only wish I could have seen the danger to you both sooner. I managed to slip into her mind to wake her up when I saw it, but I was too late."

I could hardly breathe, slowly lowering to my knees. "It was all you," I re-alized. Nothing I had done had been for me. My strings hadn't been untied; their control was simply slipped cunningly into far more masterful hands.

I was his ultimate plan.

Get me here.

Play the game.

Win the key.

Free him.

But not me. I was never free.

"Astraea—"

"Go away, Nyte," I barely whispered, but he obeyed. The gray around me grew darker and darker. I became so hollow when the shattered pieces of my soul settled. "I wish that room had been empty."

54

"Nightsdeath, commander of the vampire army," I drawled.

"What made you come to that conclusion?" Nyte asked, leaning against the far wall.

With my back to him I continued flexing my wrist, regaining my strength and remembering I wasn't helpless anymore. I could hardly recall much of the time that had passed while I'd overcome the worst of my cravings for the Starlight Matter, but though I felt a new will to refuse it, I had to find distraction, otherwise the temptation threatened to creep back in.

"It's how the king has kept them under control all this time," I said, reflecting on what I'd gathered so far now I had a face to attach every sin to. "You've been amassing an army behind your father's back, making him believe it was *his* army. The fae—you capture them and strip them of their memories to switch their enemy from the vampires to the celestials."

"That was my father's demand."

"And you enforced it. Even when you were chained. Why?"

"He would have killed them all instead."

I barely cast him a glance over my shoulder, only to see if his expression matched the note of irritation I heard. It didn't. He remained indifferent.

I hated that that only riled *my* frustration.

"The all-powerful Nightsdeath." I continued to toy with the name.

"You flatter me."

"Your ego is incredible."

"Yet if I deny what I'm capable of I'm a coward."

I turned to him then. He kept enough distance between us that I wouldn't be able to reach him through the bars. Lines of moonlight cut his face, which yielded flickers of *something* at my prodding.

"You don't need to deny anything to be that."

"Is that what you think of me?"

"I think a lot of things of you."

"Anything of endearment?"

"All of them." My fist flexed. "Like how I would love for you to open that damn door so I can stab you."

The bastard smiled. "I shouldn't find that attractive."

I had to take a pause for sanity. "Rainyte." I didn't take pleasure in the wince he tried to disguise with the tilt of his head. "You must have a family name."

"Why do you ask?"

"You said no more secrets."

"That's the exception," he said, showing the first flicker of warning toward me.

Good.

I shook my head, taunting him. "What would it uncover about you?"

"Nothing of interest to you."

"What would you know of my interests?" I purposely recited his words from the night we met. It brought him closer, the tension between us toeing the line between anger and desire.

"You have no idea," he said, low and with a gravel that felt enticing over my skin.

"That doesn't seem fair."

"What are you trying to do, Starlight?"

I leaned my forehead to the cool metal. "Let me out."

"We just want to be sure—"

"Why couldn't I have been in my rooms?" I cut him off. My emotions were so volatile, still tiring me out despite all the time I'd spent asleep. Or pacing the floors. Scratching my nails along the walls just to *feel* something. Talking aloud.

I couldn't stay in here a moment longer.

"For this reason. You would have found an escape, and trust me, you would never have forgiven the person who would have done anything to find more of the same drug I destroyed."

My teeth ground. I knew this. I'd run through so many murderous thoughts, even hallucinated I was living them at some points. "I'm fine now."

"Almost—"

My fist slammed the harsh stone. Warmth tricked down as I caught a jagged edge. Nyte's gaze flashed, and his jaw worked. So I did it again.

"Stop."

And again.

"Astraea."

My next try was halted with a grip around my wrist. I breathed hard in a deadly stare-off with his molten eyes. His fingers laced through mine, slicking both our skin with my blood.

"You are the most stunning, volatile, and fair thing," he said, inciting war within me through a mere look as his other hand cupped my neck and jaw, forcing me to angle my head for him. "And it's about time you showed yourself."

His lips crashed to mine, and I wasn't prepared for how wholly it would consume me when I wanted to *hate* him. It didn't erase that feeling; instead it entangled it with an explosive passion. Being pressed to his warmth and tasting him threw a blanket of insignificance over the world around us.

Just him and me, and this battle that was far from over between us. It almost distracted me completely from what I'd goaded him in here for.

My other hand reached out, feeling as though it had been dipped into a pool of sparkling water with the tingles over my skin. My fist closed tight. I didn't hesitate. I'd spent so long deciding on this moment.

We both gasped, barely breaking apart with the firm but slick pressure of my stormstone dagger lodging in his chest. As we shared breath his hand tightened with pain in mine, his other wrapping around me as we stumbled until his back met the wall.

Then he kissed me *harder*.

I whimpered against his mouth. My blood soared with yearning and resentment—a dangerous release despite his faltering.

Nyte lowered himself slowly and I went with him, my hand still wrapped around the hilt of the blade. I straddled him when he sat, and then he wasn't holding me so firmly anymore. His kiss turned labored; his skin paled. He said nothing. His hand on my nape became limp, and he kissed me one final time before his head lost balance too.

I couldn't believe what I'd done. I held him for a few heartbeats in the aftermath.

His face between my palms . . . he appeared so peaceful I thought the blade was lodged in me for the tearing I didn't want to feel. This was Nyte. Not any other name. And for him I pressed my forehead to his as if to release some of my regret.

Then I remembered everything else that lived and lied beneath his guise. I slipped my hand into his pocket for the cell key and left with my heart slowing its beats until it became stone.

55

"Just so we're clear, a dagger through my chest *will* kill me."

Zathrian must have read the contemplation in my heated glare from across the table. Rose sat on his right, though her reluctance could be felt the moment I'd joined them in this great dining hall. She topped my animosity, refusing to engage with either of us. I had to wonder how she'd been coaxed into her beautiful deep pink gown to be here at all.

"You're a deceitful bastard," I mumbled, spearing another piece of chicken. I was so fucking hungry. The weeks of minimal food were catching up to me all at once.

I'd bathed, changed into a dark, silvery silk gown that had already been laid out, and been guided down to this dining hall unnervingly by one of the Golden Guard.

"Am I really though? I never lied to you, Stray."

"You knew who I was—*what* I was—this whole damn time."

That made Rose's attention flick to me. She'd hardly paid attention to either of us despite my trying. I resisted the urge to cover my arms as she trailed her gaze over my silver markings as though trying to decipher a language in them.

"You never knew at all?" She finally spoke.

I shook my head. "Hektor kept me very closely guarded," I said. Every time I thought of the past five years I wanted to rage. At myself and how his *protection* was so obvious now. "I should have thought something of it sooner."

"He manipulated you," Zath growled.

I wanted to hate him. At least for a while longer. But his tight grip of his fork along with his murderous look pinched in my chest that it had been real, his care for me.

"So did someone else. Someone it turns out we both know." I couldn't cool my resentment at that secret. Not yet.

Zath's face fell. "They're not even close to the same."

"They both lied in the name of *protecting* me. Neither gave me a damn choice. Neither gave me a chance to protect myself."

"That's not even slightly true, and you know it." He finally matched me, pushing back. Good. I was still so hurt and livid that I was trembling inside.

"Of course you would defend him. You've been his messenger dog this whole time."

His jaw worked. "I didn't have to do anything he asked. I did it for you, dammit."

I continued eating, and as I shifted a look to Rose I wondered if I ever wore the same look of wariness toward them with their insufferable bickering.

The thought was stolen by a light pattering of four-legged footsteps. Shifting my gaze to the doorway, I couldn't believe the black cat had found me here too. I was about to set down my fork when a blurred, dark motion around it grew tall, and my silverware clattered from my grip. The table shook as I jolted up—

"Please let me explain!"

Stars above. I still had to be suffering from the effects of the Starlight Matter. I blinked several times, but it settled that I'd unmistakably witnessed Davina transform from a black cat. Not just any . . .

"I'm going to fucking kill him," I muttered, snapping my head to Zath. He seemed just as bewildered as Rose.

Meeting my outrage, he held up his hands. "I had no knowledge of it."

"Neither did Nyte," Davina said, timidly advancing as though *I* would transform. "I only followed you in case you needed some extra help—and you did! I brought your pills . . ."

I huffed as I sat back down, too dizzy to do anything else. "Is there anyone else I should be aware of?" I grumbled.

Zath shrugged. "Not that I know of," he said, reaching for an apple. He was so at ease here, not at all like the cold soldier he had been around Hektor, and no longer stiff with caution like he was when the king was in power. He had Nyte's protection now.

"I'm sorry I didn't tell you sooner. I didn't want to distract you," Davina said timidly.

"Just . . . how?"

It was impossible to be mad at someone so gentle. As Davina took up the seat next to me, her expression dropped.

"I'm fae," she admitted. "And a shapeshifter."

My eyes immediately targeted her rounded ears, exposed from her braided coronet. Until my face relaxed with horror and my heart withered with a memory.

"You cropped your ears," I said vacantly, recalling the tale of Lilith's father.

Davina poured herself some wine as if to avoid meeting anyone's judgment. "It was necessary," she said sadly. "To be here, even before I knew about you. Many fae have done so in an attempt to elude the king and help others to hide and escape. Nyte found me when my parents were taken two centuries ago. He helped me to remain hidden, but that wasn't the existence I wanted. I needed to fight back in whatever way I could. I knew he was Nightsdeath, but he also helped save as many of my kind as he could. He gave us hope."

I reached over for her hand, squeezing, and she finally met my eye. "You're amazing," I said. It wasn't enough. I was in awe but aching with resentment for what she'd been through.

She smiled, accepting but not entirely believing my words. "It doesn't end with the king being overthrown. There are still those who were rising up against him anyway, and if we fall to a vampire reign . . . it could be worse."

I shivered with foreboding.

"I lost my sister and parents to a nightcrawler gang attack two years before I met you," Zath interjected. "If we're exchanging tragic pasts."

Just like that, my resentment dissipated to heartbreak for him. "I didn't know—"

"I lost my job as a trade scout. Became a drunk and barely had any care for my existence. I lived here in the Central, and one night I heard a calling. It was him. I found the same hatch you did because he led me there, and when I found him, trust I was afraid and certain I'd leave that place and never look back. But he was the first company I'd had that didn't look to me like a sorry lost cause. He was patient and truthful of the exact reason he'd coaxed me down there. He told me about the star-maiden, what she meant to him—to the world—and all he wanted me to do was go to you. Find out exactly how you were feeling. He was limited through other minds from so far away. He told me if you were truly happy and safe then he would make sure you never accompanied Cassia. But if there was ever a moment of doubt, I was to help you escape."

I was transfixed by his story, disbelieving of it.

"I only got through the borders to Alisus thanks to him. I joined Hektor's group and worked my way up. As it turns out, I have a talent for picking up things I shouldn't, and I impressed him, becoming his most favored spy. And while I despised him, I gave him my unquestionable loyalty, and that wasn't gained without doing things I will regret for the rest of my days. But you were worth it. The moment I met you, I knew you were worth it."

My lips pinched tightly to keep from the waves of emotion that slammed into me.

"You were so quiet, but only because everything you were was bottled up. The more you eased to me, the more I saw what Nyte had tried to explain. Your passion and spirit, even in small glimpses, because H—" Zath's mouth tried to spill a word. He tried again, but when no sound came and confusion passed for a second . . .

Soon you won't be able to speak his name because it will no longer exist to anyone.

Could Nyte really have done it?

"—that bastard hardly allowed you to express yourself," Zath continued without it. My blood chilled. "I knew almost immediately I was going to be helping you get here, to the Central. That the only way for you to break out was to do so physically. I wasn't thinking about the world or what you could do, only that there was this one chance to help you as a *person,* and I was going to do whatever it took no matter where you wanted to run off to beyond that manor."

"Zath . . ." I had no words, only barrels of sentiment I didn't expect from hearing his truth.

He only smiled, and though we had some mending to do before I could trust him again, maybe I didn't want to resent him anymore. "He's not a hero, Astraea. Not even close. But he has never pretended to be."

"I can't do this," Rose said, standing abruptly.

Zath stood too, but before she could even get a step away a shadowy touch caressed my neck. That of a lover made of sin. The room chilled with it, and everyone's attention landed on the doorway to find Nyte strolling through it.

"Stay, Rosalind," he said. A command that took minimal effort, yet demanded submission.

Both Zath and Rose eased back down, and I followed her powerful glare toward the source of the shadow coming to life in the corners of the room. He strolled in with a confidence that was too natural to be arrogance. Even though the room was an expanse of glittering black marble floors, broken only by white pillars and shards of color from the window scenes, his presence seemed to turn down the surrounding brightness wherever he went, drawing out a soothing but deadly kind of darkness that could ignite desire as quickly as it could kill.

I continued eating, trying not to give him the satisfaction of knowing his being here did anything to me. He came around behind me, leaning in close, but I didn't get a second to react to his bold proximity before a thump speared the table next to my plate.

"You misplaced this," he said, his voice low and twistedly seductive. Nyte sat sideways in the seat I'd deliberately left vacant, one away from the head of the table.

"I placed it perfectly, in fact."

Reaching for my dagger, my breath hitched when his hand curled around it first, and at the same time he reached down for the leg of my chair, turning me out effortlessly to face him.

I hoped he would turn to ash with my glare of ire.

I planted my foot on the seat between his legs, intending to push him away, but he caught my calf. With the electricity that surged through me I wanted to fight him. It raised a sadistic thrill. Because fighting with Nyte would be as exhilarating as it would be devastating.

"We should go—"

"No need." Nyte cut Zath off but didn't break my stare.

Zath and Rose tried to occupy themselves with the food and wine.

"If you'd taken it with you after stabbing me, I would have arrived much sooner," Nyte said. The intensity between us grew as his hand slipped over my knee, exposing my leg through the cut of my gown.

"I figured," I said.

He gave a wicked side-smile, sliding the dagger into the empty sheath at my thigh. "If you'd aimed for the heart, I would have arrived much later." His fingers lingered, and *damn him* for the reaction of heat my body craved with it.

From the clean dagger and his impeccable fresh clothing, I knew he hadn't come straight from waking after my attack. I carried a pinch of guilt with me, but I would be damned if I let him know it.

With a deep breath he let me go, standing to right my chair before sitting beside me again. Nyte helped himself to the spread in front of us. "Dying makes me famished too," he said casually.

I couldn't believe his lax demeanor. I didn't know what I'd expected: for him to have stormed in here with bloodied hands from killing someone else; for him to be outraged over what I'd done; or for him to have commanded the room to bow for him.

Anything but this jarring *normalcy*.

"Why don't you sit at the head of the table?" I ground out.

"Until I replace it to be wide enough to fit two there, I'll remain here."

It took me a moment and catching Zath's nervous look to realize what he meant.

"I will never sit by you."

Nyte chewed his food as he turned to me, bracing a hand on the back of my chair. His eyes sparkled. "What do you call this?"

Rose said, "I'm leaving—"

"Rosalind Kalisahn." Nyte drawled her name, and the look she flashed him while bracing her hands on the table was nothing short of deadly. "I'll admit I didn't expect you to make it this far, but here we are."

Her hazel gaze flashed to me, and something equally threatening shifted in Nyte. "How can you betray her like this?"

Those words struck me, each one a new dagger knowing who she meant.

"Careful," Nyte warned, so chilling I might have shrunk if I could have focused on anything but what Rose implied.

"I haven't—"

"She came here to kill *him*."

"And it is not too late to kill *you*," Nyte said.

That made Zathrian shift in his seat.

"Stop," I said, cutting through the growing tension.

"You want to leave," Nyte went on. "Where will you go? Do you want to tell them, or should I?"

"I'll kill you myself." Rose stood, and Zathrian mirrored her.

I couldn't decipher what the fuck was going on.

"What is he talking about?" I asked her, needing to start with that.

"You've already decided you're taking his side?"

"I have no side," I snapped, stunned by my own assertiveness, but I was *done* being considered a mindless pawn.

Rose yielded a fraction of her volatile anger.

"You're not the only one who was never supposed to be in the Libertatem," Nyte said to me, picking a grape and tossing it into his mouth as he leaned back. He said nothing more, leaving it open for Rose to elaborate, and her jaw worked, her fist shifted, and only then did I see the knife she clutched.

His words registered, and I shook my head in confusion, trying to read the answer Rose guarded.

"It seems there is no one among us without a secret to tell." Nyte filled the weighted silence.

I looked to my other side, where Davina met me with a sheepish look. Then to Zath, who stood braced, shifting his focus between Rose and Nyte as though he would lunge between them. Then down at the devil himself, who was enjoying prodding at Rose's anger.

"Except me," I said. "You all have secrets and games, and I have nothing but fragments of a twisted existence." I wanted to believe I was safe and surrounded by *friends*. More than that for how deeply I'd felt for each of them . . . before I found myself wondering if I truly knew any of them.

"We'll talk of *that* situation later," Nyte said to Rose, then he shifted his command to Zath. "Leave us."

"Don't fucking touch me," Rose snapped before Zath could guide her. Her pink hair bounced as she stormed angrily from the room. Zath cast us one last look, something of a plea for mercy, before following after her.

The scraping of wood against stone made me turn to Davina. She gave a warm, encouraging smile. "You can come to me for anything," she said quietly, flicking a gaze behind me, and I appreciated she was trying to offer the comfort of being able to speak freely with her.

It would take time for me to believe my words could be trusted with anyone. I said nothing, unable to break the hopeful brightness on her face. I simply nodded and matched her smile.

"I would say to keep giving him hell, but lord knows the bastard enjoys it."

I didn't expect the casual tease from Davina, nor the easy smile she cast him that was both warming and confusing to see.

Nyte only smirked at it.

It left Nyte and me in silence. I didn't know what to do or say.

"Will you sit with me?" he asked gently. The tone was a stark contrast to the one he'd arrived here with and had used to provoke Rose. It drew my gaze down to him, and I found it was reflected in his entire demeanor. There were no guards in the room, no other eyes; it was as if the weight of the world had been lifted to reveal someone just as vulnerable as any other person.

But he wasn't.

He was Nightsdeath.

"What do you want from me?" I asked quietly. Now I was physically well I didn't know what would come next. I looked over my own skin, at the silver markings that hadn't changed. Nothing felt different except for my unstable emotions, and something within me hummed like it had when I was close to the veil. "I can't do what you think I can. I have no power even without the Starlight Matter."

His hand grazed mine, and I watched him carefully take it. I sat down, not having anything to lose, whether he used me by force or not.

"The things I want from you are entirely selfish and nothing to do with your power," he said. To my bewilderment, Nyte eased off his chair to kneel before me, not letting go of my hand. "Everything from now on is your choice. Your magick—I think it will take time to resurface, and careful learning so it doesn't overwhelm you. It's not going to be easy. In fact, it's going to be damn hard, but I know you have it in you to embrace it all when you're ready."

"Can I ask you something?"

That seemed to lift something from him. "Anything. Anytime you need me. I would stop the rage of a battlefield just to hear you."

My brow furrowed as I watched our hands, every slight movement of our fingers shy of intertwining. "Did I know you as Rainyte?"

I wanted to take it back with the faint tightening of his hand.

"That's the name I was born with," he said. "But it didn't feel right as it was my mother who named me, and she was not here. You knew of it, but it is not what you called me."

"Did I know you as Nightsdeath?"

"Yes and no. It has always lived within me, and you have seen the worst of it before. I can *use* that side of me—have the strength and power and not let him win—though it takes immense focus and energy. But as for what happened in the throne room . . . I can't tell you how sorry I am. I tried to fight it, but having just been freed from behind the veil and finally confronted by my father, I should have known he would find a way. The threat he made to your life *twice,* it took over faster than I could grasp control."

"I understand," I said, and it was the truth. "In fact, I'm glad I got to see you—all of you."

My mind and heart fought with the vulnerability that spilled across his face. He looked so much younger, softer. My heart cried for him.

He raised my hand slowly to place it on his cheek. "What do you see, Starlight?" he all but whispered. "You didn't know who I was, what I was, yet you reached for me as much as I did for you. What do you *see?*"

The question pounded in my chest. I didn't want to give him a wrong answer. Until I became so sure, so undeniably certain, it was the question that wasn't right.

"When it was just you and me in that void, all you wanted was for the light to be gone. So did I," I confessed. His gold irises held me with soft attention. "I might be made of light and you of dark, but I wanted to meet you there. You haven't always been something I can see, but you've always been something I can feel. It's safe and promising. Despite everything, *seeing* threatens the truth of that. When I couldn't be certain Nightsdeath wouldn't kill me, I wanted to see a monster, and only when light winked out did I feel *you* again."

Nyte's eyes closed as if freedom had become him, his head bowed, and all I wanted was to raise him from his knees and set aside everything I still had to learn about him and the role he was to live out here now.

"I would meet you in the darkness. Every time you called," he said quietly.

"Why does that sound like you're running away?"

"That's not what my leaving is. We tried. I've spent five centuries since I was dragged here as a child trying to figure out if I could make my place here, but it will always be at the cost of something too great." His lips brushed my knuckles. "You."

I shook my head. Denial was all I had. This couldn't end before it had even begun. I wanted the time to forgive him, time to understand, and time to remember.

Nyte stood, and I couldn't stop my impulse to copy him. My heart pounded like a war drum to my mind that battled with letting him go and begging him to stay. Gravity pulled us closer until our bodies touched. My hands met his chest, and in those molten eyes it was like I could see we stood on the same battlefield.

Until we both laid down our surrender and made our stars collide.

Nyte's mouth on mine exploded through my body. I barely heard the clash of plates and silverware as one of his arms hooked around me and the other scattered everything on the table before lifting me onto it. Everywhere he touched I came alive with a searing heat. When my leg slipped free, he found it immediately, the groan from his mouth tightening my core.

"Anyone could come," I panted when his lips traveled along my jaw.

"I can stop." The cadence of those three words vibrated over me to scatter any call for decency.

In answer my hands took his face to bring his lips back to mine. His tongue swept across my lips, and I opened for him. Being claimed by Nyte was more than I could ever imagine. Every time we kissed, we touched upon something new and tangled what was already there tighter and tighter. I didn't think I would be capable of letting him go. My selfishness didn't care to learn the true extent of what had made him so afraid to stay.

The stars were dying, and I didn't want to become one of them if he left.

I wanted to fight it.

Fate. Death. Time.

I kissed Nyte as if we could stand against it all. My fingers fisted into his hair, his hand squeezed my thighs as they tightened around him, and with every movement against my core I didn't care for the wildness of where we were.

"This isn't fair," he groaned against my lips, but he didn't pull away.

"For you or me?"

"Both."

We collided again, continuing to push things to the ground with a resounding clatter, and I almost wondered if he would climb atop the table with me. My skin blazed to desire it, but *stars above,* I couldn't believe my own scandalous desire in such a public place. Where anyone could trespass— could even be lingering right now. And that thought only made my lust surge so much sinfully more.

"I didn't plan to be here when you returned," he said, his delightfully rugged breath casting down my chest. "But, fuck, the past three centuries of misery, despite all I became and all I am to you now, I would suffer all again for this." He fixed his attention on my neck, a new palpable fury emanating from him as he traced his fingers over my scar. "Did he do this to you?" The question was strained with wrath.

I couldn't be certain. I tried to revisit the flash of memory that had become a hazy frustration to decipher. Sometimes I thought I remembered another body, as though I was hoping to find some other narrative to explain Drystan's being there.

"I don't know."

His teeth ground. "I'm going to fucking kill him."

"Don't do anything impulsive."

I was becoming attuned to his looks, and this one definitely said "I think we're past that." Gripping the folds of his coat, I pulled his mouth back to mine. With a low growl he pressed himself into me tighter. More clattering surrounded us as he kept coaxing me back. Then he *did* join me, effortlessly climbing over me on the table as I lay down. It was incredible how insignificant any care for the improper became with my body's demand for him.

"My lord." A deep voice disrupted us.

Nyte pulled out of the kiss with a groan of annoyance while my whole body was torched by awareness as it returned to me.

"This had better be something of deadly urgency," Nyte grumbled.

I pushed myself up with him. Nyte's arm around me lifted me off the table effortlessly, and I was glad for his tall, broad form that shielded me while I righted my gown and combed my fingers through my hair. Though nothing could erase the lingering sensation his hands had branded all over me.

"A letter for you," the guard said eloquently.

Not just anyone.

I didn't know how Nyte sensed I was comfortably *presentable* again when he stepped to the side to reveal the Golden Guard. His features were cut so sharp and beautifully with his dark skin and formally short hair. He was the one who had been assigned to Rose. I didn't expect the small smile he offered to me—the first hint of emotion I'd seen from him to erase my fear.

"This is Elliot," Nyte introduced.

"It's a pleasure to finally get a chance to meet you properly, Astraea." Elliot's voice was so melodic it was easy to forget what he was.

"You knew me the whole time?" I asked. My gaze shifted to Nyte, but he tried to disguise his guilt by preoccupying himself with unfolding the letter.

Elliot nodded. "Our loyalty to Nyte has never changed."

Nyte paced away as he read, seeming to disconnect from the room with it.

"Not the king?"

"I was the first to ever win the Libertatem from Pyxtia—an excellent set of trials, by the way. I only recently found out their true origin, and I'm impressed." He paused to ease a teasing smirk. It was so *normal* I was beginning to harbor guilt for believing everything I'd heard and assuming the worst of him. "If we won, we were promised immortality. As you can see, it was given, but as soon as I knew *how,* I didn't want it. By then it wasn't a choice, and we were no more than his experiment to create a new vampire—one by transition, not birth."

"There are only four of you," I said. I wondered about the consequences of the change he'd gone through.

"There are more."

That inspired something dark and sinister, and I became afraid to discover what other nefarious plans the king had been working toward. I was about to ask when a tug within me turned my attention to Nyte. His face was firm and scarily calculating as he paced back over to us. He crumpled the paper tightly in his fist before I watched with awe as it turned to black smoke that leaked through his fingers.

"I won't waste my time penning a response to that," he rumbled low. With a breath he straightened, slipping back into calm authority. "I want you to go personally. Take Zeik with you, or Kerah. Tell that bastard Auster if he wants to talk, he can very well come out of his cowardly hiding place since he's content to send his dogs this side of the veil."

Elliot gave a faint smile of satisfaction. "It's been some time since we got any order of decent action," he said.

Nyte huffed, and the exchange between them shouldn't have been so surprising, but I warmed with the ease of what I could only discern as friendship from the clear respect they shared.

"It's good to have you back," Elliot said.

Nyte gave a tight nod, and Elliot cast me a warm smile with the dip of his head, which I returned before he left.

My mind backtracked to the name he'd spoken—one I had heard once before. "Who is Auster?"

Nyte's jaw locked with my question, his shoulders squared. "I promised you no more secrets, but will you trust me when I say that isn't an explanation you'll want right now?"

My heart skipped a beat as I concluded, "I knew him?"

He nodded, but it wasn't pleasant. "He's a celestial—the High Celestial of the House of Nova."

"What did he say?" I stored the mention of the celestial house to discover more about it later.

Nyte's fingers tipped my chin. "I have something he wants."

It only took a second for my pulse to still. "Me?"

His firming lips were my answer, and I stepped away, suddenly aware I could be used as a bargaining chip for whatever the celestial wanted. Just like Hektor had tried to sell me.

"You have nothing binding you anymore, Astraea. You are safe and free. You can walk out of this room right now and I will not stop you. Walk out of the kingdom and I may follow, but every path we take is yours to pave."

The first part wasn't true. He wouldn't know it, but I was beginning to learn how to form a mental barrier against my surface thoughts so that he wouldn't hear . . .

It had started off small, a thin string that had wound from him to me the moment he stopped my dance. With time it had been winding tighter, with every touch it had been forming thicker, and if I didn't break it now . . .

I feared I could become forever bound to *him*.

56

I sought the stars to calm me.

Finding the secluded space outside the castle had been too easy. Too eerily easy. My own mind was mocking me, leaking only faint guidance to quell the surprise of meeting new faces and finding new destinations. It was only foreign to one life; the other rejoiced deep inside to be back.

I gazed through the stars, losing myself for an incomprehensible amount of time as I soared among them in spirit. Two lives fought in one body, and I didn't know who I wanted to be. If the past could influence the will of my future . . . maybe I didn't *want* to remember.

Between my palms, the egg I held was heavy, but not in weight. I didn't know why I'd brought it out here with me after finding Rose had left it in my rooms.

"It's a celestial dragon egg." Nyte's voice was no more disturbing than a gentle stroke of the wind.

My eyes fixed themselves on the black-and-silver scales with more fascination. "Is it alive?"

"I wouldn't be hopeful after all this time. Truthfully, I don't know much about them."

I hugged it against the cold as I said, "What if I come with you? When you leave for your *home*."

It didn't frighten me. I had nothing in this realm to call mine. In fact, I felt rejected by it, born in the shadow of something so great I didn't even know if I wanted to be it—the star-maiden.

Nyte's whole demeanor changed to a kind of blank stun, as if he'd been struck with a blade, his heart aching to meet the eyes of betrayal wielding it. He seemed to lose his response with the shock.

I shook my head. "It was a stupid thought."

I wasn't unfamiliar with the feeling of not belonging.

"Astraea." He advanced closer before sitting down beside me. "You have to know I would want that more than anything if it were possible."

"How is it not?"

"It's too much of a risk. I have no guarantee you would make it through with me, and even if you did, we would only be taking the problem from one realm to another."

"You don't know that. It could be different—better able to withstand the *power* you think is too much for this one."

His expression remained solemn, and my gut twisted with it. When his palm cupped my jaw, my brow pinched, and I leaned into it.

"This one is *yours*."

The moon flooded his features, highlighting the midnight-navy of his hair, and his irises turned to a pale gold. With him right here it was hard to imagine never finding them. After all this time, they would never search for me again.

I looked over the tranquil city, glowing as if starlight rained down upon it. Casting my sight across, I homed in far enough on the distance to make out a long streak of silver.

"I need to get past the veil to get to where I need to be," Nyte mumbled at my observation.

"You have never been past it before?"

"I watched a vampire turn to smoke and dust with a cry of agony that haunts me still as he stepped through. It's a masterful allurement of beauty, and you are wrong to think monstrous things are only attracted to the darkness."

"You're not a vampire," I said.

Nyte frowned, contemplative. "I am many things—that wasn't a lie or diversion. I was born fae, but because of my mother's bloodline I was also something more powerful than one should be. When my father passed through the mirror with me, he was guided to this realm, but nothing is ever coincidence. There are always meddling fates, and this one happened to be the God of Death, who made a bargain with my father to enter here. He said he would not give the gift to my father because his ambitions were set. I had none. As just a child, that god bestowed more upon me than any being should ever harbor to give my father the unparalleled advantage he needed. It was never a gift; it has always been a curse."

I wanted to touch him, offer some kind of consolation. Nyte stood, and I was drawn to follow. Slipping a hand into his pocket, he began a slow walk to the edge of the wall with no balcony while I stayed back.

"I didn't know what had changed in me at first, only that I had too much of everything. My emotions were always at war, my cravings and desires amplified. I think the cost of becoming everything was never knowing what I am and always fighting to keep myself from reckless impulses. I gain strength from blood, and I enjoy it. I can feel souls, take them. And I have these."

Nyte stepped right up to the edge. My breath hitched when he turned to me, and horror seized me when he leaned back . . .

And fell from the fatally high ledge.

"NO!"

I lunged forward, my heart threatening to leap after him. Then a beat of air stilled me, and what shot up from the place he'd vanished made me stumble back instead.

My gaze fixed itself to him, unblinking, as my back met the wall, and I clutched the dragon egg tightly.

What in the . . . ?

He was absolutely breathtaking.

Nyte hovered in the air, cloaked by magnificent midnight-blue feathered wings—so dark they would be black without the highlight of the moon. I tracked him as he came closer, my pulse racing with exhilaration when his feet touched the ground in front of me gracefully.

"All this time . . ." I breathed, fighting every blink in case it could awaken me from a dream.

Those beautiful towering wings tucked together behind him.

"I couldn't reach them behind the veil," he explained. "It's still taking some time for my abilities to come back to me after so much time out of use. It wasn't a lie either when I said the past century has also been the most peaceful. Only because my mind had never been so silent. My emotions weren't vulnerable to the power. Nightsdeath didn't exist."

No—he hadn't lied. Never. And all at once I was ashamed for ever thinking so, realizing the difference between keeping secrets and withholding full truths that could do more harm than good if spilled at the wrong moment.

Now he was showing me everything.

"May I?"

He held out his hands, and I didn't question him as I passed him the dragon egg. He made it disappear with shadowy starlight, but I trusted he'd sent it somewhere safe.

"You enjoy heights," he said softly. "Until you figure out how to reach your own wings, do you want to fly with me?"

I blinked at the palm he extended. "My—What?"

His smile twinkled with delight. "Surely you understand what you are by now. Not the title."

My breathing came hard. I swallowed, disbelieving, but it settled like an answer I'd searched endlessly for. "A celestial?"

Nyte's grin erupted in my chest. I slipped my palm against his and walked vacantly with his backward steps.

"The most exquisite, beautiful celestial to have ever lived," he said between strides toward the edge.

My adrenaline pumped fast and my smile broke, though my body protested with nerves that this was absolutely insane.

He paused. "Do you trust me?"

My eyes locked onto his. "What are you—?"

It had barely left my lips when he leaned back, the arm around my waist making me tumble with him. I gasped at the flip of my stomach, circling my arms around his neck and holding onto those golden irises as tresses of midnight whipped around them.

For a beat of time, we were two falling stars.

Nothing more. Nothing less.

I kissed him in our free fall. Once, until his arm hooked under my knees, cradling me to him, and the air whooshed from me when a strong pulse stopped our fall gently.

Then it carried us high.

If there were words to describe this, I didn't know them. Soaring higher than I ever thought possible altered my reality, and I didn't want to ever come down. The air was so much sharper up here, pricking my nose and cheeks, but I gave a breathy, euphoric laugh. Buildings stretched out to no end and stars spilled across them. It became a kaleidoscope of scattered color against a maze of silhouettes.

Nothing could compare to this.

"How high do you want to go, Starlight?" he said across my ear, making my body shiver with the warmth that contrasted the nip of cold.

My hand reached up as though I could touch the moon. "Endlessly."

We flew for not nearly enough time before Nyte lowered us to a high cliff topped with snow. When he set me down, I couldn't break away from him. My eyes trailed over the curve of his wing and my hand was compelled to reach up over his shoulder. Nyte tensed at my palm on his chest as I traced the feathers, so much softer than I'd imagined them to be.

"What does it feel like?" I asked.

"Like any other touch of yours—and I don't think I have the words to tell you how burdens lift with it. Even when you're driving a blade through my chest."

I winced, not regretful when it had served as the cause of this moment, but I hoped not to have another.

"I shouldn't have found it as arousing as I did," he murmured.

I met his eyes, incredulous, but all he gave was a light chuckle when I pushed away. The sound was beautiful. Rare, I realized.

Until it was stolen by a serious firming of his face as I anticipated a question.

"You've been holding onto something, Astraea. I've been wondering how to explain it to you."

Trepidation settled in.

He went on. "You feel it in your chest. Like a second heartbeat not in the right place. It warms when you need it."

Memories of that exact feeling echoed through me, then that same heat pulsed under my ribs, and I gasped, raising my hand to it.

"You should be able to do this yourself, but it might be best if I help you."

"What is it?"

His brow pinched with careful sorrow as he stepped up to me, as though the answer was better explained with a demonstration. "Do you still trust me?"

At the same time as he asked his hand slipped under my cloak, around my back, before trailing along my spine and bringing our bodies flush with a firm press between my shoulder blades. This position flashed something familiar, and my breathing grew labored.

"Yes," I answered, my back curving to his guide as his palm slipped over mine at my chest.

We locked eyes, and I held his desperately with the tingling that grew over my shoulders, vibrating every rib. Then a glow broke between us, and my lips parted. Nyte guided our hands to hover, and I felt like my soul was being pulled from my body.

Fear struck me as I remembered the time Nyte had done this before. The day we met. Or at least, he had shown me he was capable of it. With that recollection came the horror he'd warned me of death should it stray too far from my body.

I strained against his hold, letting the thought pass that this had been a trick.

"Relax, Astraea," he soothed.

I tried, but it was difficult to fight against my basic survival instinct.

My palm heated underneath with a promising warmth I became transfixed by. An orb of white and blue pulsed above it. My eyes pricked, blurring the edges of the magnificent life I held, so pulsing and familiar my tears spilled, and I didn't know how this was possible, only that I didn't ever want to let it go. It echoed with a laugh that perhaps was only in my mind. I sobbed with a smile. It filled me with love and joy and all such carefree wonders.

"How?" I whispered.

"You took her soul at the right moment it was expelled from her body," Nyte said gently.

It was Cassia.

I gave a single laugh through my tears. "She's been with me." *This whole time.*

I thought some part of me knew it. Strength had come to be when I wouldn't have otherwise found it. Courage had pushed me against fear. My heart had opened to try to find *friendship* again.

"You have to let her go."

That surged within me a denial that pulled the orb closer to my chest, but Nyte stopped me.

"I'm not ready!" I cried.

"I'll give you a moment, but you can't hold onto it. It's been draining your own energy. Souls were never meant to be held onto. It's time for her to join the stars."

He eased away carefully as if I would defy him.

I didn't. My heart cracked as I stared at the glow I cupped delicately in my grasp. I felt the resistance, knew it wanted to cast itself away, and realized it was only my own selfishness keeping her soul here.

"I'm so sorry," I said. "I'm so, so sorry you didn't get the life you deserved."

The heat pulsed. Three times.

I laughed, trembling with the gift this moment was, but bleeding from the torn wound within me. "I did it. Can you believe I made it through the games? Of course you would. You would say you never had a damn doubt, because you were always the best kind of liar." I chuckled, lowering to my knees despite the snow seeping through to my skin. "What I don't think you would have believed is what I am. *I* don't believe it. But I'm going to try. For you I have to try." My heart calmed with acceptance. "I'm going to make sure Calix stays alive," I promised her.

My body trembled stiffly. If I cupped my hands she would stay.

She could stay with me.

I looked up and tranquility began to lap at me, the memory of two drunk friends who'd filled their final hours together with promises and wishes. If there was one thing I could give her, it was this.

"You're going to see the world now, Cass."

My tears fell as I let go. As though her soul was attached to a string pulling her toward an opposite gravity, I let her fly.

Then I watched. Her brilliant soul became like a firefly as it soared higher and higher. Nyte was behind me, silent and patient. I didn't tear my eyes from the sky, barely even blinking as she became no more than a speck of glitter among the stars—but I didn't lose her.

Seconds, minutes, hours. I didn't know how much time passed before a gentle flare erupted.

Then there she was.

I stood still. Then waited. My lip wobbled when I saw it.

Three blinks.

Finally, my eyes fell down. My neck ached, and I rubbed it as I turned to Nyte with a new kind of despair.

"If you don't leave, the stars will continue to die," I said, unable to meet his gaze.

"Yes."

"How long will Cassia have?"

"I can't be certain."

There was no other way, and this kind of loss—something so damned by fate alone—was soul-destroying.

"I'm coming with you," I said. Finally I looked at him, and the glittering misery in his eyes cut me. "I'll help you get past the veil, then I want to come with you right until it's time." I wasn't done accepting that this was the only way, but if I didn't grant him my acceptance, I feared he'd try to push me away.

"But first we have to stop the king," I said.

A low rumble resounded. I cast my sight up but found nothing as the source. It grew, vibrating under my feet, until the crack of thunder made me wince, the ground shook, and Nyte held me before my footing could trip me.

I went to cover my ears, but it stopped, easing away like a distant quake.

"We don't have much time," Nyte said, glancing at the stars.

"What was that?"

"It happens every now and again. It will become more frequent, the realm refusing the cosmic power growing on it. I think having your power suppressed has kept the damage low, but as you begin to find it again, it will clash with my energy. The celestials have had three hundred years to regain their strength after the two centuries we existed together that were detrimental for them. The impact this time can be stopped far sooner now I can leave."

I couldn't believe it. "Why did I come back?" I whispered in horror. "They could have taken back what was stolen from them without me. I'm not their savior—I'm their curse."

Nyte's eyes closed as if he couldn't bear to hear it. "I'm the curse, not you." His knuckles brushed my cheek. "Destiny is cruel to bring us together. Because you are the most precious gift I can never have."

"How do I know . . . ? How do *you* know that what you feel for me isn't for a person of the past?"

Instead of matching my drop of uncertainty, Nyte's face brightened like he enjoyed the question. "Your soul is magnetic. There won't exist a time or place where I won't be drawn to it. And, love, you might look the same, you might remember everything we almost had one day, but here and now I'm falling for *you*. I found you with a steel heart in my chest, and for the first time in three centuries it doesn't feel so cold. Not because of what you were, but for everything you are. Do you believe that?"

How could I not when inside I erupted with such an unfamiliar feeling?

This . . . Was it possible to belong not to any place, but with a person? To find home not on land, but in another soul?

I didn't know how to respond. He seemed to know it, pulling me into him, and I rested a cheek to his chest, trying not to let the ache overcome this moment.

The agony that had begun to tear open with the cruel countdown of time we had left together.

57

Nyte landed us on a wide-open flat of the castle roof. I couldn't stop lingering my admiration on his tall, beautiful midnight wings. He set me down and almost eased a small smile before his hand stiffened on my waist.

"What's—?"

"You are safe, Astraea."

His switch of tone coiled my gut, racing my blood with alarm as I tried to find what had caused such a lethal, firm guard on his face.

"There's something I need to do before things get any farther out of my hands than they already are. Please trust me."

Boots shuffling against stone shivered my skin. Nyte pushed me subtly— not enough to shield me entirely, but ready to intercept anything that might reach for me.

The first person I saw emerging from the open stone steps . . .

"Drystan."

He gave no warm reception to my voice, but the tilt of his head to observe me as though I were someone different made Nyte shift.

"You're in over your head, brother," Nyte said with a deadly calm. More bodies emerged, and I almost shrank further behind Nyte at seeing the many sets of red eyes and leathery wings. "Have you brought them here to witness me take over what you pitifully believed you could lead?"

"We thought you were dead." The new voice that eased out from the parting vampires stilled me cold.

Arwan.

"That's not his real name," Nyte muttered at my loose thought. He addressed him. "Tarran."

The redheaded vampire cut a wicked smirk.

"How did you elude the king?" I asked.

"Because of me," Drystan said bitterly. He kept his eyes of hatred on Nyte. "You haven't been here, *brother.* I've been the one leading this army."

"A pup running ahead of the pack is not a leader; it's a damned fool."

Drystan stepped forward with a flash of darkness I'd never seen before. Tarran intercepted while a few others shifted at the tension between them.

Nyte went on. "It took tricking me to try to *prove* something. Yet have you told them how you had the star-maiden right before you all those years ago? And you let her escape."

My throat was tightening, my chest heaving. Why would he say this?

"Is that true?" Tarran asked.

"Of course not," Drystan spat.

Tarran's eyes slipped to me as if I would confess for him. I knew Drystan was lying, yet the decision not to tell this vampire was sealed in my mind. I didn't know what was happening, nor how Nyte intended to get us out of this, but right now I couldn't even feel comfort from him. I wanted away from them all and whatever feud this was that had placed me in its center.

"She won't remember," Nyte said for me.

I wanted to shake myself awake from this nightmare. How cold and distant he was as he spoke of me. How he shielded me not like he cared, but like I was a prize those before us wanted.

"Your brother has promised many things in your absence, Nightsdeath."

Nyte laughed dryly. "He doesn't have the power I do. He doesn't have the star-maiden."

My step shuffled back—only an inch before Nyte's hand reached back to hook itself around my waist and a large, warm wing curved to prevent any retreat.

"Let me go," I breathed, panic shooting through my nerves. I blinked against the memory of being in Hektor's office the day he showed me off to the vultures who wanted to *own* me.

I thought I felt the tightening of Nyte's fingers, maybe a wave trying to calm the storm gathering in me, but I couldn't accept it.

"I will have power to contend with you," Drystan said with a challenge. "Once I am Ascended."

"You swore you never would," Nyte growled.

Drystan only smiled as if he'd won. "Times have long since changed. And I am done being in your shadow."

"No vampire has ever survived their attempt to be Ascended."

I wondered if Drystan could hear the note of concern beneath the rage Nyte emanated with. It didn't look likely as the younger brother only shrugged, enjoying the reaction he'd invoked.

"Like you, I am not just anyone. I might have been born here, but I still have the blood of another realm. I'm willing to take the risk and try."

"What is an Ascended?" I dreaded to ask.

"Many have tried it before," Nyte said to me. "Vampires die trying to reach the Realm of the Death God. Not a place of passing, but his realm of dark blessing."

Where Nyte had been. What lived within him from the Death God's *blessing* I thought he carried more like a curse.

"Drystan is willing to prove himself dedicated to a vampire reign. He is already one of us," Tarran drawled. "Who knows what our god might bestow upon him as he did you?"

"I have given *everything* to your damn cause," Nyte growled.

"Except . . ."—Tarran's eyes slipped to me with deliberate slowness—"her. They say we almost lost everything because of your weakness for her."

Nyte shifted, his anger weighing the winter night air so tangible I could choke on it. "Then you are all fools," he said with a low threat. "If none of you can see that keeping her alive is what gives us the advantage and making her believe she was safe was only to keep her content. The next time someone wants to challenge my methods, they can step forward and face me themselves."

"Nyte," I whispered. This wasn't him. He didn't mean it, yet within me was a voice crying out that I never should have believed him so easily.

"You let the king get away with the key," Tarran diverted. "He may very well become more than either of you if it's true what he hopes to do in summoning the God of Dusk and the Goddess of Dawn. I hear their blessing combined could triumph what Death could give alone."

"We can't have that," Nyte said.

Then he turned to me.

I locked stiff.

"Make you choice here, Tarran. I won't allow another."

"What are you doing?" I breathed, panic shaking my body.

"You too, brother. You have the chance to leave now, and make sure I can never find you, because if I do, I won't be so merciful again."

"Nyte, please," I tried.

He never took his eyes off me, and the skin around them flexed. The building anticipation of what he was about to do threatened to suffocate me.

"Then let me leave with one parting gift," Drystan said as a taunt. Though his eyes locked on me. "Since he's too spineless to tell you himself."

"You'd best leave *now* before you're never able to speak again," Nyte growled.

"You have another Bonded, Astraea, and he'll be coming for you. My advice is that you don't believe a word Nyte tries to spin on you next and take your chance to flee when the time comes."

My world didn't just stop; it caved in on itself. I was so afraid Nyte's reaction would turn me to glass and I wouldn't survive the fall.

It didn't make sense. *Bonded.* The term was so vague it meant nothing to me. I didn't feel anything for it—not like what I did for the one who was about to betray me.

"Summon your key," Nyte said—no, *commanded.*

My body felt it, straining to move, but I didn't know what to do.

Then it clicked with cold horror. "You said the bond was broken."

"I said it would be if you *left,*" he said, his voice low. His eyes flexed. Only for a hint of a second, but it was pained. "Yet you ran right into my arms. Just as I hoped you would."

In my disbelief, I scanned our audience of blood- and soul-thirsty vampires. Nyte was one of them as much as he was fae. As much as he was celestial. They saw him as kin and feasted with cruel smiles on my vulnerability.

I found Drystan, who looked between Nyte and me as if this were unexpected even to him. As if he might intervene.

"Summon your key, maiden," Nyte said again, each word more pressing with his demand.

"I don't know how," I breathed, wincing with pain from the bond being denied.

"Yes, you do. You've done it before. Call it through the Starlight Veil and show them. *Now.*"

My throat dried out with the sting of my eyes.

Steps advanced toward us, and Nyte didn't seem to be the only one losing patience. He sliced them with a deadly look that kept them hesitating to come closer. My fear spiked to slick my skin as I raised a hand.

I locked onto his eyes with a plea, and maybe I caught a faint crack in his steely exterior, but he said nothing.

The bond within me forced me to remember. It felt like touching stars, dipping into water that had been given a fizz, and soon pinpricks shot over my arm. Before me a small void of glittering darkness opened, and I reached, picturing the intricate design of the key, how powerfully it had hummed through me in my possession.

As I retracted my arm the key glowed its mesmerizing purple. Exhilaration from the embrace of merging power comforted me. Just for a moment. Then the veil closed, and I clutched the weapon that was mine.

The one that had the vampires *retreating* now.

It flipped in my hand, transforming it into a featherlight blade, but as I spun toward Nyte with it he caught my wrist.

My fight was stolen away. Not out of fear or anger but stunned heartache as an event unlocked in my mind. The flare of purple emitting between us began to fade. So did the streak from his temple to his cheekbone. Golden irises searched mine; he seemed to see what I remembered. As though we both stood in that very memory. A time where he hadn't been so fast, nor had he anticipated . . .

"I know how you got that scar," I whispered.

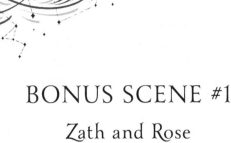

BONUS SCENE #1
Zath and Rose

If I was the thorns, Zathrian was the vine I couldn't pluck myself free from. He'd followed me for all the trials so far, as much as I tried to make that hell for him. I had to give him credit for perseverance though I couldn't figure out why he wouldn't take the damn hint I didn't want him here.

Just one more key piece left.

Then I could win this thing, or Astraea would, and I'd long since come to terms that my life was on borrowed time like Cassia's when I was committed to taking Nightsdeath down.

Midday was breaking as we maneuvered through the growing pedestrian traffic. On the second city level, I couldn't deny being surrounded by pointed ears was unnerving to say the least. I'd seen vampires before. I'd *slain* one. Though I tried not to recall that memory that terrified me still from when I'd only been twelve.

Tracking the ground, I noticed the absence of shadows for some of the passing forms. Blood vampires. I tunneled away on aimless thoughts as I started counting who had a shadow and who didn't. The ratio was in favor of the soul vampires by the time Zath's irritating voice reminded me I wasn't alone.

"Do you even know where you're going?"

He was scrutinizing the riddle I'd gotten from the last trial of greed. I'd already memorized it.

"If you'd stop yapping in my ear, I'm figuring it out," I grumbled.

Where a prize can be seen but never has been found,
Wander in, wander all, into the serpent hall.
Tread carefully here, don't make a sound.
For if you're caught, you might find or you will fall.

"Doesn't sound inviting," Zath commented.

"They can't all be held in a brothel," I said under my breath.

"You never did tell me how that went," he said, edging closer as my marching pace had put a bit of distance between us. "Your trial of lust."

I was glad the afternoon was particularly chilled today when my body flushed with the recollection. I'd been trying expertly for the last week since to bury it so deep it could never claw out.

"There's nothing to tell," I said flatly.

I could practically feel the amusement radiating off him, just priming to taunt the damned life out of me like he always did. It was a miracle I hadn't killed him yet if only by accident with how he'd seemed to have made a game for himself out of provoking me.

"I'm most curious as to what came out in such a test for you."

"I'm sure it was nothing to what you got up to while you waited."

Being in a pleasure hall, I despised my curiosity to know if he'd indulged in the men and women who were enticing us the moment we'd stepped inside. I'd found the room for my trial and ordered Zath to stay outside.

I would never tell him it was because I feared what could come over me in there, and he was the last person I wanted near me if lust was going to cloud my judgment.

Not that the effort to avoid him had succeeded in that trial.

"You could just ask," he said.

"That would imply I care."

"Sounds like you do."

"I don't," I snapped.

We stopped walking at the end of an alley. I pulled out my map, thinking the answer to the location might come to me if I studied it.

Never has been found.

Something lost. A prize no one has been able to find when they got there.

"A labyrinth?" I pondered to myself.

It was like I was gaining a new sense of gravity for Zathrian when I didn't see him move but his presence no longer hummed nearby. Flicking my sight up found him halfway across the street before disappearing into a hat shop.

I was cursing him internally and should have left him to his strange fascinations, but I was already following in after him before I could stop myself.

"What are you doing?" I hissed low with the odd stillness of the interior.

Inside was an explosion of color. I liked pink, but the array of ribbons and bows and hats made the color feel too overbearing and sweet. Perhaps I'd reconsider my hair color when I next needed an enhancement through Starlight Matter. This had lasted the best part of a year.

"Not quite the time for shopping," I murmured to him as he picked up a pink floral sun hat.

He turned to me with a boyish smile. Reaching up, he was too tall for me to snatch it from him before he placed it on my head. His face split to a wide grin.

"You're so easily amused it's concerning," I muttered, taking the ridiculous hat off.

Turning, my intention to step forward was slammed still suddenly with the person standing too close for comfort that I stumbled back instead. Right into Zath who caught me. Between him and the curious blonde woman, I couldn't gain space. Zath's warm body against my back, his hand still on my hip, took the lingering winter chill from outside completely.

She wore a small bowler hat with a sunflower at the back and a long yellow ribbon dangling from it. Her large blue eyes blinked innocently up at me.

"Can I help you?" she asked, her voice a pitch too high to match her age, which I assumed to at least be in her twenties. Her ears were round, and I became really curious about the first human I'd met here.

"We're looking for somewhere," I said.

"There are many somewheres around here," she sang, then walked away. She picked up a deep blue fedora with a peacock feather. "I can help you be whatever you need to be to get there."

She was quite odd in a way that I couldn't be sure what she was thinking at all.

"My name is Erilla, what's yours?" she asked, spinning back to us with her hands clasped behind her back.

"Rosalind," I said warily. Why had Zath come in here? I was going to strangle him.

Erilla's eyes lit up. She bounded back over, taking my hands in her tiny pale ones and the unexpected lack of personal boundary stunned me. She pulled me deeper into the shop, and I couldn't help but cast Zath a look over my shoulder. He merely shrugged, unfazed by Erilla's forwardness.

"You should have told me sooner!" she squealed. "A Libertatem participant, how fascinating."

I could do nothing but root to the spot when we stopped walking and Erilla scrutinized me. Her delicate fingers traced over my sigil of Pyxtia. Then she giggled for no reason and went back to searching through her hats.

"I can tell you where you need to go," Erilla said, her voice traveling around the shop and it was hard to keep up with her in all the mountains of disorganized hats.

She skipped around the stacks, plucking various and tossing them aside. Her shop wasn't the best kept. Though the hats of all shapes and sizes seemed in perfect condition, they were piled high in overwhelming bundles and I wondered how she ever found what she was looking for. Every now and then, she looked between me and the new hat she pulled, as if trying to decide which would suit me best.

I hoped then she didn't find any to be a match.

"Maybe this wasn't the best place to stop and ask," Zath leaned down to my ear to say.

"You think?" I whispered back to him, casting him a disgruntled expression. We were wasting time.

"Aha!" Erilla shouted, but I'd lost her in the mountains of hats.

Several tumbled down as she jumped out and I cursed the fright that leapt my heart up my throat. She came rushing back with a black bowler. It had a pink ribbon around it with red and pink roses climbing one side.

"This is the one," she beams.

"Oh, we're not looking to buy," I said. I'd never been fond of hats.

Her bright face fell. "You want my help, don't you?"

"We're just wondering if you might know where this is?" I held out the riddle to her.

"I do," she said without looking. "But nothing is free. It'll take trading a lock of your hair."

My brow pulled together at the odd request.

"Why?"

Her head merely canted, and the way she looked over me like admiring a statue she was about to buy made me uneasy.

"What are you going to do with it?" I amended my question.

Erilla rolled her eyes with a groan. "So many questions. Do we have a deal or not?"

"It could take days off our search," Zath interjected.

"Then you give your hair," I grumbled.

"She didn't ask for mine or I would."

Zath hooked a lock of my pink hair, already holding a blade to it, but didn't cut until I gave him the word. He knew I'd do it to save us time.

"Fine."

His dagger cut through and I didn't know what I expected. My pulse skipped when the lock in his fingers started to turn brown. I couldn't stop staring at it, not anticipating the lashing of a reminder of its true color.

"I don't know how I forgot humans aren't born with pink hair," Zath mused, examining my natural hair.

Erilla giggled and I gasped as she darted by me, snatching the hair from Zath. She took it over to a bench full of clutter. Tools to make her hats. My adrenaline started to race, daunted by what I'd done. *It's just hair.* She couldn't do anything with it.

I was wrong.

After Erilla tied the hair to the hat she raised a hand to it. My shock parted my mouth at the glow of blue that emitted from her palm.

She's was a mage.

Now I was fucking terrified over what she could do with that piece of me.

Zath edged closer like he was ready to brace with me against a threat. I caught a glance of his hard-lined face targeting Erilla now and it would never fail to make *me* firm and ready when someone as laid-back as Zathrian was on edge.

The hair *moved*. Like it became threads that wove into the ribbon and became undetectable.

When Erilla stood and turned to us, it was like she became a different person. A cunning smile edged her lips and I didn't know why a wash of dread overcame me.

Until she removed her sunflower hat and lifted the new one to her head. When it sat on her blonde hair, that was the first attribute to change. Pale yellow slowly engulfed by deep brown and the waves turned to curls. Her blue eyes flooded with hazel. Then her skin darkened to a golden brown.

She became me.

I almost stepped back until Zath's hand curled my waist. Normally, I would shrug out of his unnecessary subconscious protection, but I was still in horror over what I was seeing.

"This should fetch a generous price as one of our esteemed Selecteds for this Libertatem. Especially if you die." Her laugher was eerie and my blood chilled to it. "There's a new life to resume at the wear of a hat. You should be honored, really, for someone to carry on your name when you're gone."

"I change my mind," I breathed. Oh god, what had I done? The implications could be endless. "We don't need your help."

"Too late," she sang, brushing fingers over her hat and heading to admire herself in the mirror.

Who she looked like was so uncanny to my former life. The brown hair, the stiff lines of the leather uniform with hints of red as Pyxtia's color.

Spinning on my heel, I didn't even care for the answer I needed for giving up the lock of hair. Air was becoming too thick to breathe in here and I needed out.

"The place you're looking for is the Maze of the Mad Serpent," Erilla called at my back. "There is a sleeping creature within, wake it, and the value of my hat will be delicious when you're gone."

I shivered to the final notes of her haughty laugher, like it aged a century and I had been a fool to fall for the trickery.

"Shit, we couldn't have known that would happen," Zath said, catching up to me.

My fear and dread turned to resentment that I targeted him with. "This is your fault!"

He accepted the blame and I even felt a note of guilt as his expression tried to apologize.

"If you would stop following me I would be far better off," I said coldly.

I turned my focus to my map as I picked up my walk again. I knew he wouldn't leave me alone, and what I couldn't bring myself to admit, even internally without unease, was that I would be disappointed if he finally listened and stopped being my company.

"I'm going to get that hat back for you," he promised.

My gut clenched. I wanted to believe him, but somehow I didn't think it would be that easy and could be sold to someone we would never find by the time we could go back and negotiate again.

"Is there a reason you chose pink?" Zath asked after a moment of silence.

No one had ever asked me *why,* and though he only wanted to know the color preference, I wanted to release the reason why I chose to abandon my natural deep brown in the first place.

"When I was orphaned, my uncle took me in. He was the Captain of the Guard at Pyxtia's central keep for the reigning lord. I was to follow in his footsteps, but he didn't treat me like any other of the guards. Because I was a woman to his dismay, he made me train harder, longer. I didn't mind, I was determined to be better than all of them anyway. But what started to get to me was that any time I wore a dress the other guards would mock me. Any time I styled my hair pretty or did anything feminine they would make me feel weak for it. So I started taking Starlight Matter even though it cost most of my earnings in the guard. I made my hair pink as a color I liked to show them I could be feminine and best them. One time, I even put a guard on his ass in dress. They stopped mocking me after that."

Zathrian's silence weighed on me enough that I needed to check for his reaction.

"You sure showed them in winning your Selected trials. I'm proud of you, Thorns," he said, meeting my eye with a smirk of amusement.

I actually smiled with him. I'd never heard that before and I wondered if he really meant it.

I'm proud of you.

Those words were like lighting a candle. Something that always existed the same, but now it was lit, it noticed. Appreciated for what it could do.

It doesn't matter, and recalling the Selected trials . . . my face fell with a past I needed to keep buried.

"Then when you and Astraea win this thing. . . ." he added.

I didn't bother mentioning that it didn't matter if we managed to come out of this together. It would be short-lived the moment I got my chance to confront Nightsdeath. Once this was over, I hoped whatever was in the temple could help me take him down.

We arrived at the maze and didn't hesitate to go inside.

One final key piece.

It was all almost over.

"The beast she mentioned . . ." Zath trailed off with an edge of caution.

"Best keep our wits sharp," I said. "Never thought I'd say this, but I'm glad you're here."

"For comfort?"

"For bait."

"You'd miss me."

I scoffed. "I've been wanting to get to the end of this thing to be rid of you."

During our many long weeks together, he was gone intermittently to check on Astraea, but when I would ask why he didn't trail her side the whole time instead he merely said she had other help.

After descending underground, we stopped in a room with two tall chairs and a fireplace. No windows.

There was a head of dark hair I only caught a glimpse of as they moved, standing. When they turned . . .

My blood ran cold and I didn't think this was real anymore. It couldn't be. My uncle wouldn't have left Pyxtia. Yet he came around the chair and I took in every dauntingly familiar detail. His cropped brown curly hair, his aging dark brown skin, his captain's uniform.

"What are you doing here?" I breathed. My heart was slamming in my chest.

I'm not afraid of him. I'm not afraid of him.

I'd proved myself more than he could ever try to diminish long ago, yet being in his presence would never fail to bring out the ghost of the frightened child in me that didn't believe I could ever live up to his standards.

"I wanted to be here in person to witness your failure," he taunted.

My eyes pricked, and I didn't know why embarrassment washed me to know the belittlement was in the presence of Zathrian. I turned to him, but my spine straightened when I spun right around and didn't find him. It was only me and my uncle in the room and perhaps Zath had gone ahead without me.

"I'm going to win this thing," I said, targeting my uncle with a hateful stare.

"As soon as the king knows what you did to get here, you'll be sent right back to your reigning lord for judgment."

My body broke with a shiver of fear.

"I didn't mean to," I said quietly.

How I ended up in the Libertatem would forever taint my conscience, but I *had* to get here. To liberate Pyxtia and everyone beyond. Something I would have done with Cassia but now I became protective of Astraea *for* Cassia to see it through with her instead.

My uncle drew his sword when I didn't realize I'd freed mine and was clutching it with a tight grip.

"You always underestimated me," I said with a cold calm.

Wrath was taking over me. Anger I'd buried in every corner clawed its way out all at once and I saw nothing but an enemy I had to cut down. Only then would I be free of his shadow.

"You really want to fight me? You will lose," he taunted.

"I figured someone with your ego would block out the time I put you on your ass," I said, angling my blade. "You must have anticipated it though, to have challenged me without any witnesses."

I moved first, ducking down to one knee with my back curving to the horizontal path of his blade. He cried out with the jab of my elbow into the back of his knee before I stood, spinning to clash blades when he collected a stance in the nick of time.

I knew his habits, his weaknesses. When I'd dueled him before I hadn't wanted to kill him. He was the last of my kin—my kind father's brother. But right now an unexplainable rage took over all logical thinking and all my hate for him drove every vicious attack out of me.

The dark underground room expanded and now we were in Pyxtia's central keep. In our elite training facility I'd exhausted many days in for years.

My uncle came at me with a growl of irritation, meeting me strike for strike as we parried through a round of crossing blades. He was the captain for a reason—a highly skilled and respected warrior—and defeating him was no fast or easy task.

Drawing a dagger, I caught him unaware to my triumph, slicing across his arm when we'd switched sides. It distracted him enough that I kicked the back of his knee and this time it felled him. I crouched, angling my blade to his neck from behind, but he grabbed my wrist and I could only brace with a cry of pain when he pulled me hard over his shoulder. My back slammed to the stone. I gritted my teeth, rolling back to hook my foot up. It struck him under his jaw as he leaned over me.

"Rose, stop," he said. His voice didn't sound right. He would never ask me to stop.

I rolled, lunging for him while he was on his back. My knee dug into his chest and he hissed. My arm holding my dagger drew back and so much pain and anger drove my need to plunge it into his chest.

"Why was I never enough?" I cried angrily, clenching my teeth against the pooling in my eyes that threatened my vision. I blinked rapidly, thinking his face changed.

When he didn't answer my arm pulled back farther with a cry of agony, but he caught my wrist before I could end it. His leg hooked around my waist, flipping us.

"Rose, please, stop," he begged.

It wasn't like him to call off a fight. He held my hands by my head, only restraining, not attacking while I thrashed.

"You are more than enough," he said, letting one of my hands go to cup my face, and something was different—warm, and safe, and gentle—about his touch that managed to seep through the cracks of my armor and start to diffuse my wrath. "Fuck, you are the most incredible person I've known."

Then his voice became clearer than ever. The illusion was broken. The trial of wrath ending.

Zathrian straddled me. His forehead leaned to mine and for once . . . I didn't want to be free of the closeness.

A single tear slipped down the corner of my eye and I didn't want him to pull back to see it, but he felt it with his hand still on my face. He was panting as hard as I was and our hearts were close to pounding against each other.

"Zath," I said weakly, still fearing the return of my wicked uncle.

"It's me," he said, breath fanning over my lips. "I've got you."

When he pulled back enough, the fire flickered entrancingly off his blue eyes. They drew me in like the marching flames were an army that would come for me in every danger. Every thought of how beautiful he was that I'd slammed away with denial now rushed to the surface.

"I hope you don't kick my ass for this," he said, voice so thick that my stomach tightened with the anticipation.

Zath's lips crashed to mine and the unexpected eruption in me slipped a moan from my throat. He responded with a low groan, slipping his hand from my face down my side and pressing more of his weight into me. I thought I had impeccable control and resistance but it all unraveled to a single kiss. One that quickly deepened to tangle tongues, teeth, and lips in a heated passion I couldn't have prepared for. My body responded in ways I wasn't consciously in control of anymore. My spine curved into him and somehow he ended up between my legs and my knees hooked around his hips.

Not close enough. Or maybe it was the barrier of clothing that riled a frustration that came out in the grappling of clothing and touches I couldn't keep track of.

This release was something I didn't know I needed and had been burying a craving for. I didn't want to lose my focus in this game and Zathrian was nothing more than an irritating, insufferable distraction. But I realized every time I pushed him away I wanted him to keep coming back. I pushed and pushed, waiting for him to give up like everyone else, but he never did.

Why? I couldn't figure it out. Maybe if he got what he wanted from me then he would stop chasing, and while that thought emitted a dull ache, part of me wanted to give him it if only to prove my tormenting thoughts right.

"You're absolutely stunning," he rasped, trailing his mouth along my jaw.

"Stop talking," I said breathlessly, pushing his chest and flipping our positions.

His hands planted on my hips and the hard feel of him at my core gathered heat I needed friction against.

"Fuck," Zath hissed with the movement of my hips.

I kissed him hard, and what detonated between us was both bliss and torture. I couldn't wait any longer, reaching between us for the ties of his pants, but his hand caught my wrist.

Pulling out of the kiss, we shared breath and I waited for him to take over. To flip us again and take control like I was on edge for.

"What are you doing?" he asked.

Confusion pulled my brow together.

"I think that's rather obvious."

"If you're going to let me fuck you, the first time is most certainly not going to be in a place like this."

My lust was smothered by irritation in an instant.

"The first time?" I challenged, pushing off him.

"I don't desire you for a quick single release simply because your emotions are running high," he snapped back.

"You're nothing more than that to me."

I wanted to take the words back as soon as they slipped from me, but it felt too vulnerable to do so. Watching the flinch of hurt on his face cut into me more than I thought it would.

Zath let the silence linger before he said, "Well, when that changes, I'm not going anywhere."

My brow curved. "When?"

He gave an arrogant side-smile before he reached down, swiping my discarded dagger. I didn't move but my heart picked up as he stalked to me. He was all tall, blond attraction. Built like he could shield from stones but guarding a tender heart that would never belong in hands like mine. He would see that soon.

I let him hold my waist, enjoying the igniting touch when I knew our time was limited. He slipped the blade back into the holster on my thigh.

"When," he repeated, and angled his lips to mine again.

He was too easy to find addicting. I couldn't place what it was about him that made a sample not nearly enough.

Zath pulled away when he'd stolen my willpower to be able to.

This wasn't me. People didn't get close enough to me to find the inevitable cracks in my steel composure.

"Your uncle," Zath murmured, steadying his voice while his forehead hovered over mine so he couldn't see my dropped expression. "Is still alive?"

I didn't know why he cared. He shouldn't.

"Yes."

"Did he . . . hurt you?"

"Not physically. I could just never please him."

"What about when you won your trials to come here?"

I couldn't answer that and I was washed with shame and guilt. This is why he couldn't get close to me. No one could.

It was time for the pretend to be over.

"We could have had that key piece by now," I said, and for once I regretted the coldness in my tone that was a lashing to our peaceful moment of surrender.

I stepped away from him. Zath said nothing, but his hard, searching expression crawled over my skin and I had to get away before I panicked with the thought he could develop some power to pull every lie and sin out of me with that stare alone.

Storming past him, I welcomed the envelop of darkness. The halls smelled damp and tainted with old musk. The only sounds resonating were those of the scuffling loose debris under our boots.

When light broke again at the end of the tunnel, we stepped into a huge arena that had two levels of a square balcony for onlookers. It was empty, and a chilling foreboding shook through me.

"You completed your trial—thanks for not killing me by the way—so where's the key piece?"

My eyes flicked sideward to him with a sense of guilt. I would have killed him, but he brought me back.

You are more than enough.

Those words . . . I'd craved them for a lifetime from my uncle. I never could have expected them to mean so much more coming from Zathrian.

"We don't even get a map for this?" he complained.

It snapped me from my pitiful wandering thoughts. We were surrounded by dark high walls on our ground level. The maze.

I marched forward without direction, desperate to get this over with. We wound through a few passages and my frustration grew.

I glanced up. "One of us should get up there and lead the other through."

"That would be a great idea, but how?"

"Let's try to get to the other side, I guess."

Every now and then my skin pricked, thinking I heard movement and something like gentle hissing. Zath hovered closer than he usually would. We reached one side and my eyes lit up at the gap leading to a staircase at the end.

"You go up," I said.

Zath shook his head. "I'd be terrible with direction, you go."

I wanted to argue, knowing it was a poor excuse for him wanting to *protect* me if there were any creatures lurking in the maze.

"Fine," I said. "I'm not opposed to a great view of watching you getting eaten by monsters."

I headed through the stone.

"You'd miss me, Thorns!" he called at my back.

I was hidden in the darkness of the stairwell to let a full smile bloom confidently. It didn't last long, not when I thought of who caused it, and *why*. I couldn't let Zathrian affect me more than he already had. I couldn't allow myself to want him in any way.

People who got close to me either left, or they died.

BONUS SCENE #2
Nyte

Astraea was angry with me for the measure I included in our blood bond. Furious, in fact. It might have been sadistic that I paced a dark corner of the cave, alive with the thoughts of her rage toward me. Her passion, however it came out, awakened my soul.

Astraea is alive.

She came back to me. So close yet so far that there were times I thought I felt the creeping return of Nightsdeath within me from my tangible temper. The veil was a mockery. It silenced my magick but there's nothing in all the realms that could erase my feelings for Astraea. They were absolute across space. Inevitable across time.

I'd tried to lock them away. Stay cold to them in all the years I had to prepare for her return.

Yet all it took was one second to shatter one hundred years of convincing myself I could be selfless this time.

Astraea was mine. I was hers.

What rattled a dormant thrill in me is that she knew it too. The moment I infiltrated her mind it had been too easy to make myself at home. At first she yearned for someone, anyone, but what made it so easy to return to her time and time again was her longing for it to be me. I believed some part of her remembered. Some thread of her mind reached for me and all that was left was to feel her. Truly feel her in my arms again to obliterate the nightmare of the past three centuries without her.

Astraea was alive.

She came back to me.

It was all I could repeat to settle the clawing demons of my mind. One hundred years down here would drive any person mad and there were times I had hallucinated her appearance in this tragic, lost dwelling with me.

She was becoming too skilled at blocking me from her mind like she did now in her anger with me. So I could only follow her through the unwitting minds of others I knew.

Zathrian, for one. An unexpected but invaluable asset, I had to admit.

Even though he strayed his course in finding intrigue in Rosalind, I could take it from here with keeping eyes on Astraea and giving her my most convincing company even when she claimed she didn't want it. I smiled to myself, her resistance is my absolute pleasure.

I was enjoying a moment of silence while I couldn't see Astraea. She was in her rooms alone, and I hoped she would return to me soon. My peace was broken with a different kind of intrusion.

The chain of my shackles clanged in pursuit of me as I wandered deeper down the dark, winding cave passage. I had two viewpoints out of the darkness; the wide-open expanse of the cave that once homed celestial dragons in legend, and this, a far more stunning but smaller opening at the other end.

A warm pool made up most of the space with a crescent moon landing around it. The water was an inviting turquoise that reflected off the thousands of crystals climbing the walls.

I had company today. Though I often wished my solitude to this cunning water nymph.

Fedora was beautiful with long straight black hair and depthless black eyes that lured sailors to her waters with no endeavor. It was only when she smiled that her trap revealed. Two rows of sharp serrated teeth to tear through the flesh of her victims. Her tail was an iridescent black too—an outcast to her people. I guess we bonded under that mutual understanding when she'd first showed herself here fifty years ago.

"To what do I owe the pleasure," I drawled, slipping my hands into my pockets and leaning against the wall.

"I was bored," she said. Her voice had a lilt to it that drew people in like music. Deceptively inviting. "And I wanted to see how much longer I have to wait for my reward."

I figured as much.

"I'm not in these bonds out of want," I said.

Fedora pouted, leaning her head on her crossed arms over the ledge.

"Does your star know what you gave her all those years ago?"

"She doesn't need to."

"It was kind, though. Don't you wish your kindnesses to be noticed?"

"That's not why I do it."

Fedora sighed, pushing up on braced hands and sitting on the ledge. Her long wet hair clinging to her bare chest, stark against her ghostly pale complexion.

"It's because you love her?"

I didn't need to respond. Fedora was a wicked creature. She liked games, toying with people's emotions. The only way to keep out of her manipulation was to give her nothing.

"Why are you here? It's been many peaceful months," I said lazily.

She angled those dark eyes at me like she was offended by my ask. I didn't believe she'd ever felt that in her long existence.

"I want my prize," she repeated, edging on venomous this time.

Years ago, I asked Fedora to retrieve and deliver Astraea's stormstone dagger that had remained in the bell tower. I hoped it would awaken something in her, perhaps trigger a memory of who she was. It didn't, but I liked to believe it invoked a sense of intrigue and power to have it back in her possession.

The cost of such a favor with a water nymph . . . was far higher than my task.

"You knew it would have to wait until I got out of here."

"And what if you never do."

She scowled, lifting her tail out of the water to splash it back in. Her spirit was rather dramatic. Sometimes her company curbed my boredom for a while, other times the intrusion was a nagging annoyance.

"Then I'm afraid your prize remains my delightful company for the rest of eternity."

Her tail shimmered before turning to human legs. She was fully naked, but my eyes weren't even tempted to wander. It's what she wanted, of course. To lure me like she'd done with so many others with her craft of seduction.

"If you would stop resisting me, I might just be willing to compromise for that," she said, inching closer, and my eyes flexed in warning though I didn't move. She smiled with deceiving shyness.

"You know that won't happen."

"I would give up my pursuit of the trident to have you."

Fedora wanted power over the people who had shunned her—and I bargained I would get the trident for her if she could lure the current owner to me in exchange for taking Astraea the dagger. I couldn't say I didn't resonate with her; understand her motive. She's not a creature that knew love or would ever crave it. She desired lust and power.

"Stop," I said with enough firmness she halted her advance to me with a fake pout.

"You're no fun today," she whined.

My spine pricked with awareness at my back and suddenly my mood became so much fucking better. I kept any reaction from my face.

"I'll be free soon, and I've never gone back on my word," I said to Fedora in farewell.

I headed back through the passage as I heard her splash back into the water. I doubted she would return again until I was out of this hell.

Emerging into the main area of the cave, the sight of Astraea through the opposite gap in the stone sped my adrenaline every time. It was the worst kind of torture having her this close and not being able to reach her fully. When this gods-damned veil shattered, there would be no escape for her then.

She wore a deep frown marching over to me and I found twisted joy in her anger.

My teeth were sharp in my mouth knowing what my Starlight brought me. Astraea stopped close to the veil and wordlessly threw the vial of her blood. Passing through, it gave a high-pitched chime colliding with the magick before I caught it effortlessly.

I had to breathe for composure. Sanity. The rush of primal desire to drink it now was so powerful my teeth clenched tight.

"You did as I asked," I said, needing to find distraction.

"Like I had a damn choice," she hissed.

I gave her a taunting side-smile which pinched around her eyes in reaction. What charged between us was building so strong the world never stood a chance the moment we found each other again. When I got out of here, there was nothing that would tear her from me again even if I had to burn everything to the ground that left just the two of us in the wreckage.

"What do you need it for anyway?" she grumbled, folding her arms.

I pocketed the vial. "Not important right now."

It was a precaution, really. When she found her key and came to shatter the veil I had to make sure I was strong enough to get us the hell away from this cave.

It was so close I was near trembling with the anticipation. I'd been down here countless days that passed without a care to measure time. Now, I was becoming a restless beast in a cage. Starved for Astraea's touch. Whether she wanted to fight me or let me worship her body like she deserved, I was desperate for anything she would unleash upon me.

Astraea turned to leave and my pathetic, yearning side for her clawed out before I could stop it.

"Stay," I said.

She cast me a look back, and her contemplation was enough to soothe the sharpness in me. I wouldn't tell her I only added the measure—that she couldn't deny my orders—for her safety. I knew how she thought, how she was likely to react and put herself in the line of danger. While she was still figuring herself out and what she was capable of, I knew everything but it was fascinating to watch new pieces of her unfold in this life. I was greedy for everything old that made it feel like she'd never left me, and everything new that was like falling slowly for the first time and that was a gift I didn't expect.

I didn't stand a chance against it.

It festered inside me—being unable to tell her. But it would only shatter her focus in these trials and she needed to find her key as the only one who could.

Then I would tell her everything. Every tale of the star-maiden she is, every truth of the captive she made of me to her every call.

"Why would I stay?" she asked.

I kept the amusement from my face. This push and pull with her was addicting.

"Because it's too late to go out in search of your next trial today and you'd only be pacing your room in anticipation. Let me distract you."

"Being in your presence isn't exactly peaceful either."

"But exciting?"

"Infuriating."

"Entertaining."

"Maddening!"

I smiled, taking up a lean on a large rock.

"Tell me something about you," I said, lying back and closing my eyes.

I would never grow tired of hearing her talk, especially about herself. Astraea's voice was the only sound that spoke to parts of me nothing else could.

"You could just take whatever you want."

"I would never do that." I peeled my eyes open with a frown. Her expression relaxed me, she believed that.

"I'm boring and unimportant to you. So I'd rather go."

She had no fucking idea and it was killing me.

"You are the most important thing to me," I said.

"As I hold your freedom."

"In more ways than you know, Starlight."

When I turned my head against the stone, I found her sitting cross-legged on the ground. She was so precious it hurt. I imagined her silver hair in place of the stark black she wore to erase the unique attribute, but she was still the most stunning thing no matter what she changed.

"I'd rather hear about you if you want to gain back my trust," she said flatly.

"Ask away, I have nowhere to be."

"Don't you have anyone looking for you?" Her tone took on a careful sadness. "Someone that's missing you all this time?"

I stared up at the jagged gray stone of the cave roof. I hadn't expected her question, but I wasn't surprised. Astraea always considered others. She felt other people's emotions and could read them so precisely.

"No," I said.

It wasn't a lie. My kin didn't just know where I was, they put me here.

My father, that was unsurprising. All I felt was rage that was sure to end his life when I was free.

My brother . . . I had to admit that was a dagger lodged that had remained in my chest and twisted each time he visited. He didn't often say much, I hardly engaged. But still he came like clockwork and to this day I couldn't decide if it was an old guilty conscience to check I was still sane, or if he was relishing in my torment for all I did to him.

I slipped off the rock and approached the veil, stopping only when my bonds reminded me I couldn't reach her.

She was right. Fucking. There. And I couldn't ease my centuries of emptiness without her when I couldn't touch her truly yet. I couldn't begin to find out if what we had would come back to her and begin to mend the fractures she'd made of my soul when she died. Astraea held me at her mercy, and she was completely oblivious to it all.

Her anger was gone for a moment and sadness filled her eyes. Though they were a far darker blue right now with her Starlight Matter guise to impersonate Cassia Vernhalla, they still touched me the same, spoke to me the same, as they always had.

"Friends?" she asked quietly.

"Do I look like the type to attract friendship?"

"I think you purposefully aim not to. I just can't figure out why."

I shrugged. "They're a liability. In my experience, they only hold a blade crafted of your feelings that can hurt you whether they wield it themselves, or by someone else."

"Betrayal," she whispered. She wanted to ask more, but seemed to realize the weapons she was at risk of having against her by caring about me.

Astraea stood instead, coming closer to the veil until she was little more than an arm's length away. Standing here with her was like knowing I was awake in a dream. That none of it was real. Even though she was here, she was still as good as a ghost.

"What's your favorite color?" she asked

My brow curved at the unimportant question.

"Violet," I answered.

She gave me a look of suspicion. "You're only saying that because it's mine."

I suppressed my smile. Violet wasn't just her favorite, she *was* the color. It was in her magick she was yet to glimpse, in the star-maiden's key she was yet to find. It was a color the streets would adorn with banners for Star-Maiden Day and what was adopted for her constellation sigil.

Astraea would know all of this. Soon. I didn't care what it would take to help her gain back all that she'd lost. It would take time and careful training after all she'd been through and the memories that were taken from her.

"Astraea—" her name slipped from me. I couldn't say it enough. I was insatiable for the small acknowledgment she gave to it that reminded me she was here. Not just an illusion or a dream.

She took another daring step to the veil that hummed with awakening energy to her. I watched her hand rise to it and she marveled over the ripples it caused.

"Would it hurt to touch?" she asked.

"I think so."

It didn't stop one finger from inching out. She gasped when she made contact, and even though the pulse of magic was a warning and I flinched from it, I didn't dare blink. Not when Astraea's silver markings glowed so mesmerizingly and I could have fallen to my knees at the glorious sight of her power. It was gone in a heartbeat. Her metallic tattoos faded back to a static color. I didn't think she even saw their flare in her shock that backed her away from the veil again.

She was the most perfect thing to ever exist. A brilliant star I vowed with my life would never go out again, even if I had to be the purest darkness for her to shine the brightest against.

"Satisfied your curiosity?" I mused.

Astraea was scowling at the invisible veil like she contemplated attacking back for the shockwave.

"What if it shatters if I tried to pass through?"

"I didn't know you cared about me that much to attempt it."

"I wouldn't."

She was a curious, inquisitive thing. It was what made her highly intelligent and often on the path of danger.

"Are you as excited as I am . . . ?" I asked, tracking her every flicker of expression. "To feel what will erupt between us once I'm free? Will you try run again? Because I warn you, it only makes me want you more and that want is already a dangerous force."

She swallowed hard but there was a spark in her eyes. A part of her she wanted to snuff out with denial but she was always. So. Curious.

"I'm not afraid of you."

"You're still protected against me."

"If I can break the veil with the key, maybe I can kill you with it."

"You can't," I said. But didn't add I would be thrilled for her to try.

Call it a rekindled pastime.

"At least not against me waking up to come for you after. By all means, I encourage you."

Her body turned taut to stifle a shiver.

For a moment I was taken back to the lake—how the ice of her body pierced my heart with a terror I hadn't felt in centuries. I'd come close to losing her before I could even get her back, and since then I became so sharp in my desperation to be freed from this prison to protect her fully.

I'd never forget that first touch, even numbed under the panic of getting her to safety. Sometimes I didn't know if it was truly real. I needed so much more of her it was tearing me apart.

"Why me?" she asked quietly.

"There has never been anyone else," I said. It was torture to give her answers with deeper meanings she was oblivious to. But I could be patient. After all this time, I could wait a little longer and she was worth it. Every second of agony.

"There might have to be if I fail."

"I'm not going to let that happen."

"You're hardly in a place to prevent it."

That only fanned the flames of my simmering rage to be reminded.

"I'm limited. But there's laws of magick I will bend to their breaking point if given the right motivation."

"Like on the lake?"

"Exactly."

"Why were you so adamant to save me?"

Now I had to shield the truth. What I wanted to confess was that I'd lost her once and I would never again. Come the fall of every star in the sky to make sure she remained here, I would watch darkness shroud the land with pleasure even if she despised me.

"Good help is hard to come by," I said instead, delighting in the fall of her face to a scowl. I couldn't help but add, "You haven't had the chance to live yet, Astraea. It would have been a tragic waste to have let you go."

And I'm incapable of it.

She would know that someday.

Know how she captured the heart of the realm's most vicious creature and took it with her when she left.

"It's getting late," she said.

Astraea turned from me but hesitated for a second. Then she reached for the clasp of her black cloak. I realized what she was going to do.

"Don't—"

She threw it through the veil before I could protest.

"It's freezing outside," I scolded.

"I'm not going to turn to ice from a walk across the courtyard."

"I told you temperature isn't the same for me here."

Every time Astraea lingered this kind of look on me I wondered if it was some deeper part of her mind remembering me in some small fraction.

Enough to care despite her anger, no matter what I did. It was likely my own pitiful longing. She'd made a fool out of me.

"I know," she said quietly. Then she left, and I captured the last flicker of her before she disappeared through the gap in the wall.

I picked up her cloak, and I became so overwhelmed with the scent of her my fists tightened to pain in the material. I didn't need it for warmth, but what I gained from it was far more precious.

Oh my Starlight, we're going to save the world or destroy it trying, but either way, I'd make sure we stood in either ending together this time.

PRONUNCIATION GUIDE

NAMES
- **Astraea:** ah-stray-ah
- **Nyte/Rainyte:** night/ray-night
- **Drystan:** dry-stan
- **Cassia:** ca-see-ah
- **Calix:** cal-ix
- **Zathrian:** zath-ree-an
- **Rosalind:** rose-ah-lind
- **Hektor:** piece-of-shit (or heck-tor)
- **Lilith:** lil-ith
- **Davina:** da-veen-ah
- **Auster:** au-ster
- **Tarran:** tar-an

PLACES
- **Solanis:** so-lan-is
- **Alisus:** ae-lis-us
- **Vesitire:** ves-eh-tier
- **Althenia:** al-then-ee-a
- **Pyxtia:** pix-tea-ah
- **Arania:** ah-ran-ee-a
- **Fesaris:** fe-sar-is
- **Astrinus:** as-stry-nus

OTHER
- **Crocotta:** crow-cot-ah
- **Hasseria:** has-er-ee-ah

ACKNOWLEDGMENTS

Thank you so much for stepping into this new world of starlight with me. I really hope you enjoyed reading as much as I did writing. These characters became really special to me, and I can't wait to continue their story in *The Night Is Defying*.

To Lyssa, I truly don't know where I'd be without you. Your support through every dark day and joy in every bright day is so valued. Thank you for being in my corner with the biggest pom-poms and loudest megaphone since I first published *An Heir Comes to Rise*.

To my mum, I don't think there will be a book where I can leave you out of this space. Even far or silent, I can't forget to thank the person who made me believe I was capable of anything I wanted to reach for.

To my family, thank you for continuing to believe in me. It means more than I'm usually able to express.

To my dogs, Milo, Bonnie, and Minnie. One day we'll be out of apartment life and have the biggest garden as the palace you deserve, with the duck siblings you never wanted. I am manifesting it in this space.

To my wonderful agent, Jessica. I can't thank you enough for championing me and my stories. Thank you for all the calls and assurances during this wild journey as we sold this first series together. Here's to a very hopeful and lasting future, forever grateful to have you in my corner.

To Monique Patterson, endless thanks to you for believing in this story and taking it on board at Bramble. We couldn't have found a better home and I'm so excited for what's to come.

To Erika Tsang, I'm so thrilled to have you as my editor at Bramble for these books. We're just getting started, and I can't wait to work with you on the next one.

To the entire Bramble publishing team working behind the scenes on this book—thank you!

To Bryony, thank you for your incredible work and dedication to polishing this book when I independently published. You're still stuck with me.

To Lila, what a stunning cover, map, and page designs. You blew us all away with your talents, and thank you for being truly one of the sweetest, most patient people I've had the pleasure of working with. I'm incredibly excited to continue with you.

To Alice, I'm so glad you got to make your mark on this series with me following the incredible covers of *An Heir Comes to Rise*. You floor me with your illustrations every time. Go Team Rocket!

To you, my readers. Whether you've followed me from *An Heir Comes to Rise* and are still riding that roller coaster with me, or this is your first intro to my worlds, WELCOME. I'm so incredibly grateful for each one of you that while words are my craft, they fail me to express just how much I appreciate your support in allowing me to tell these stories. Here's to you.

ABOUT THE AUTHOR

Eva Peñaranda

CHLOE C. PEÑARANDA is the *USA Today* bestselling Scottish author of the Nytefall Trilogy and An Heir Comes to Rise series. A lifelong avid reader and writer, her stories have been spun from years of building on fictional characters and exploring Tolkien-like quests in made-up worlds from her quiet pocket of Scotland with her dogs. During her time at the University of the West of Scotland, Peñaranda immersed herself in writing for short film, producing animations, and spending class time dreaming of far-off lands.

www.ccpenaranda.com
Instagram: @chloecpenaranda